OF NIGHTMARES & FIRE

BLAKE GALLOWS

ISBN: 978-1-968918-00-2

Of Nightmares & Fire is a work of fiction. Names, character identities, places, or incidents are a product of creativity and imagination. Any correlation to actual events, persons, locales, living, dead, or otherwise is purely coincidental. No portion of this work can be reproduced in any form without written consent from the author, except for the use of brief quotations in a book review or other critical articles.

This book has adult and dark themes that may not be suited for all readers. For a full list, see my website.

YOUR MENTAL HEALTH MATTERS

Editing by Justin Marshall

Formatting, cover, & chapter art by: Blake Gallows

Character art by: @art.bymikki & @a.peculiar.artist

Pronunciation Guide   XII

1. Astraea   3

2. Astraea   13

3. Astraea   23

4. Kyros   33

5. Astraea   41

6. Astraea   51

7. Kyros   61

8. Astraea   69

9. Astraea   79

10. Astraea   91

11.	Kyros	101
12.	Astraea	109
13.	Astraea	119
14.	Astraea	129
15.	Kyros	139
16.	Astraea	149
17.	Astraea	159
18.	Astraea	171
19.	Astraea	181
20.	Astraea	193
21.	Astraea	203
22.	Astraea	217
23.	Kyros	227
24.	Astraea	239
25.	Astraea	253
26.	Kyros	267
27.	Kyros	281
28.	Astraea	291
29.	Kyros	301
30.	Astraea	317

31. Kyros   327

32. Astraea   339

33. Astraea   351

34. Kyros   361

35. Astraea   371

36. Kyros   383

37. Astraea   397

38. Kyros   409

39. Astraea   419

40. Kyros   429

41. Astraea   441

42. Astraea   449

43. Kyros   459

44. Kyros   469

45. Astraea   483

46. Kyros   497

47. Astraea   507

48. Kyros   517

49. Kyros   529

50. Astraea   541

51.	Astraea	553
52.	Astraea	565
53.	Kyros	577
54.	Astraea	589
55.	Astraea	603
Also by		621
Acknowledgements		622
About the author		624

FATHIAN
IROWERTH
EYTHORA
THE DUNES
THE DEAD SEA

CRESHIAN FOREST
VADON
DIEMOS
PYRAXIA

Pronunciation Guide

Tsalalerian (SAL-AIR-RE-EN)
Elysia (EL-A-SHA)
Cessarenah (SES-A-REN-AH)
Creshian (KRESH-AN)
Eathian (ETH-EE-AN)
Diemos (DEE-EM-OS)
Pyraxia (PY-RAX-CEE-AH)
Halcyon (AL-CEE-ON)
Eythora (ETH-OR-AH)
Irowerth (I-ER-WORTH)
Vadon (VAY-DON)
Astraea (AH-STRAY-AH)
Kyros (KY-ROWS)
Mavros (MAV-ROWS)
Colette (COL-ET)
Zinya (ZIN-YA)
Phaedra (FAE-DRA)
Casimir (KAS-MERE)
Kellan (KEL-AN)
Beckett (BECK-IT)
Rowan (ROW-AN)
Runerth (ROO-NERTH)
Zameil (ZAH-MEEL)

When the cruel world we live in forces us to be alone with our thoughts and nothing else to keep our minds from wandering—we become our own enemy. The turmoil we bury day-to-day becomes a living entity, and we become the monsters of our nightmares. The fire we once felt in our soul becomes suffocated into submission, nothing but an ember barely burning. It's then that we're faced with a decision: Either defeat the force of our own mind or succumb to the pain that will inevitably destroy us.

This is to those who refuse to let their fire die.

Chapter One

Astraea

The kingdom wasn't meant to be under my father's rule. He took it by force. The payment for a kingdom was steep, but to my father, any payment would have been worth sitting on the throne. The price was my mother's life—not to mention all the other men and women he sacrificed to win his glorified chair.

I was six.

The memory of the night he paraded me through the devastation replays in my nightmares. That and many other horrors. Every night I am reminded that I am the reason so many people lost the ones they loved because my father killed them, and when it's not him, the monsters in the dark seem to seek vengeance on my soul.

"I did this for you, sweet girl. My heart." He crooned as he kissed the top of my head before taking his seat on the throne. His

fingers flexed as he gripped the velvet-cushioned arms, his hands still covered in the filth of war. Instantly ruining the very chair he fought so hard to win.

His words were a lie, though; he had no heart, and his hands never washed clean of the filth he covered them with. They only became more blackened by the blood he continued to spill. I am a princess of ruin, the governess of destruction. I hate him, and I hate myself for not having the courage to do anything about it, even all these years later.

The room is dark already, the sun having set nearly an hour ago, taking the day's warmth with it. My hearth is lit along with many candles; they illuminate the space in a golden glow and cast shadows around, but none of them are as dark as the ones in my heart as I think of what I'm about to endure. My blue eyes show no warmth, staring back at me as I prepare myself for yet another dinner with the devil himself.

"Princess?" Colette's soft voice brings me out of the dark recesses of my mind. Turning to face her, I do the best I can to bring a small smile to my face. Her eyes fall shut in a slow blink before she turns and shuts the heavy wood door behind her. "I thought you might need a hand?" She asks with a sad smile of her own.

"Or a stiff drink." I roll my eyes, looking back at my reflection.

"Well," She wiggles her eyebrows as I look at her over my shoulder in the mirror; a true smile spreads wide on her face. Reaching into her skirt pocket, she pulls out a silver flask and pops the top. I spin around so fast I nearly fall.

"You didn't!" The excitement in my whispered shout is evident. "Oh my gods, Cole, you are quite literally the best!" She laughs and stretches her hand out to me. Women don't get much for strong drinks in the castle. For the princess, especially. The king says it is not good for childbearing age and weakens the woman's already frail body. A frail woman cannot produce a strong male heir, and he never fails to mention how my own mother was a testament to that weakness. I would sooner like to pluck my eyeballs from my head than bear a child that would become a pawn to the likes of him, though. For that reason alone, I have been taking the preventative tonic since I became of age to bleed, unwitting to him.

"I will remind you of that every day for the rest of your life." She winks before I pour the liquid fire down my throat. The burn of the alcohol is welcomed over the dread that has been freezing my gut. The dinner that is ahead isn't even one that I need to be prepared for. It will just be my father and me. He's been entertaining suitors for me all month. With my twenty-first birthday fast approaching, he has made it his mission to marry me off and make a strong alliance in the process. My feelings on the matter be damned. I would never be able to tell him how I truly feel about all of it. *A woman's voice is not to be heard unless it's singing the praises of men.*

I scoff at the thought.

"What the hell is that? It's awful." I gasp, wiping the back of my hand across my lips. She coughs out a laugh after taking a drink of her own. Father would be furious if he knew. He would likely string up Colette at the gallows for the theft alone. Not to mention the fact that the product was given to *me*. His precious gem—who allows his reach to extend farther by marriage.

"Barrett gave it to me." She tips the flask up again and hands it back to me. I let the liquid splash over my tongue and warm me further before I respond.

"He *gave* it to you?" I quirk an eyebrow.

"Well, unknowingly, but he would have given it to me had I not thrived for the thrill of snatching it." She beams before twirling her finger, telling me to turn around once again. She pulls my black hair back and away from my shoulders, separating the strands and folding it into a series of pleats around my head. I prefer my hair down and flowy, but my father would never have it. *"A woman should look polished. Show your neck and shoulders and how you hold them high, Astraea. No man wants a weak woman in his shadow."* He would tell me. Because that is what I was meant to be. The shadow of the man my father chooses as a successor. Nothing more.

While I am his only heir, he could not fathom a woman leading. He did not have a son, so he will choose one. It's probably preferable to him anyway. Another way to control everything around him. Colette finishes my braids and places a white flower into one of the pleats at the back of my head before I turn to face her.

"I don't want to see him." I say solemnly.

"I know." Her lips press together in a thin line as she pulls me into her. "You will be free of him soon enough." What she doesn't say is that I will have a new man ruling over my life. That's what I'm most worried about. While my father is an evil I must live with,

I know what to expect from him. Once he chooses a suitor for me, it will be a new sort of hell I have to learn. Soon my father will pull me into these dinners *with* suitors. It will become a courting affair, and just the thought of it makes my stomach clench.

I inhale a deep, steadying breath and pull my shoulders back. Regardless of my feelings, regardless of the anger and hurt that are stirring in my heart, I will do as my father says because... *what other option is there?*

Colette lifts my necklace to clasp it around my neck, and I smile as she does. The dainty silver chain that was my mother's is the only reminder of the woman I came from. I wish I could ask her about it. The pendant dangles at the valley between my breasts and reflects the light the setting sun allows to filter into my room. The knotted metal design of the oval piece is still a mystery to me. I wonder if it had meaning to her, or if that hope is just a made-up wish from a little girl who craved memories of her mother.

Nonetheless, when I wear it, it makes me feel stronger. More capable of dealing with the harsh feelings my father brings out in me. I never go a day without wearing it. Since my mother's handmaiden, Colette's own mother, gave it to me for my tenth birthday.

Colette and I make our way to the dining room, and each echoing click of my heels makes my chest that much tighter. Before I know it, we are being greeted by the guards who wear the gaudy silver armor my father requires of them, with our family crest brandished on the chest. A horse's head with roses bordering it to honor my mother, or so my father claims. I think it serves as a reminder of what he is capable of. What he is willing to sacrifice to win.

"Ahh! There is my beautiful daughter. Come, sit. We have much to discuss." He bellows from across the ostentatious dining room table suited to seat twenty and not just the two of us. The same can be said for the spread, which is laid out upon it. The scents mingle and engulf me; all sorts of meat, cheese, and breads fill the center. Fruits and steamed vegetables of all varieties. He always makes every meal seem grand and insists that we have it together. *"The only family we have is each other, Astraea."* I internally groan at the memory. From the outside looking in, my father seems loving and compassionate with me; it's when we are alone and he's had a few goblets of wine that his true nature comes out.

I give him the warmest smile I can muster as Colette pulls my chair out and I join him at the table. She places a goblet next to my plate and fills it with lemon water before backing away with a low bow. I nod my head in thanks but say nothing more. We've kept our friendship a secret our whole lives. If my father found out that I had become friends with someone as low as a handmaiden, he would send her away like he did the last one who got too close. *"Friends are for the weak. If the people around you don't serve to elevate your stature, they merely serve."* He has said it time and time again. I couldn't disagree more.

"Court will begin with sunrise tomorrow." His words rip me from my thoughts like a slap across my face. I stare openly, gawking at him with my lips parted. *Tomorrow? My birthday is yet another month away. Surely we do not need to prolong the courting for that long.*

Snapping my mouth shut when he looks at me with a tilted expression. I compose myself by digging my nails into the palms of my hands under the table.

"Why is it to start so early? Is it not normally only two weeks of courting before the decision and ceremony?" I ask before wiping my sweaty palms on my dress and then picking up my fork to feign nonchalance by pushing around my food. I see the heavy swallow and somber look on Colette's face and make it a point not to look at her again so the tears don't come. We both thought I had more time.

"There are many suitors who've petitioned an audience. Things take more time when courting a princess. They will court in groups. The first group is set to arrive tomorrow. All, of course, will be staying in the castle. We will have dinners nightly, with entertainment, and during the day there will be one-on-one—"

"I know how courting works, father." My vexation winning the battle of wills inside me, the words burst from my lips before I can think better of it. His goblet slams to the table, the red liquid sloshing out and staining the light table covering, and everyone in the room flinches. Our eyes collide as malice enters his dark brown gaze, but he says nothing. The chair loudly protests on the wood floor as he stands from his seat, and everyone in the room is frozen.

"Leave us," he says with a terror-inducing even tone, keeping his gaze locked with mine. When no one makes a move, their feet rooted in fear, his voice echoes, bouncing off every surface, "LEAVE US!"

I see Colette behind my father pause, and I hold my breath, hoping that she just does as she's told and leaves us to speak alone. One of the guards notices her hesitation and gives her an eager nudge in the direction of the door, and I make a mental note to thank him personally for saving her life.

When the door clunks shut and we are left alone, he turns his back on me, crossing the room to one of the arched windows along the wall. He stands there a moment, unmoving like a statue carved from solid stone, and I begin to wring my hands in my lap as I wait with trepidation.

"I'm sorry,"

"Ah-ah, Astraea. Apologizing is for *weak* women. *You* will not be weak. Have your lessons not taught you anything?" He asks, his tone patronizing and low as he turns back around to face me. It's then that I finally see what he was doing. The leather band that held the curtains back is resting across his palms. He slowly tracks his eyes up from the strap to my resilient gaze. "Perhaps it's been too long...turn around, sweet daughter, and drop that lovely dress." I swallow the bile trying to rise in my throat and do as he says. Standing, I reach back, unbuttoning the top of my dress. At the same time, I turn away from him and let the fabric fall to my waist, where I hold it with one arm to my chest.

The first crack of the leather always stings the most, causing me to suck in a sharp breath. The second takes my breath away. The third makes me choke on the sob that tries to escape, but I do as he wishes. I stay silent, feigning strength, and as the silent tears fall, I promise myself this will be the last.

Chapter Two

Astraea

Colette dips the white cloth into the bowl on the side table as I lay on my stomach on the settee. I bury my face into the pillow to attempt to hide my cries of pain as she cleans the wounds. They aren't nearly as bad this time as they have been before. As she lays the lavender-scented solution onto my back, I hiss as the cold healing tonic makes contact.

"Shhh, I know it hurts, but you know if he catches us, he will be inclined to serve punishment to you again and likely kill me for spite." I bite down on my silk pillow as she continues to gingerly clean the wounds. She's right; my father was a cruel man and has only become an even more cruel king—the longer he sits on the throne, the worse he becomes. While many see his rule as powerful and ironclad, I see him for what he is. *Scared of losing it all.* That's why he punishes anyone who speaks out of turn, anyone who defies his laws, and most of all, anyone who is deemed to possess any inkling of the magick that used to flourish in this kingdom.

"Thank you for taking care of me." The pillow muffles my words.

"What are you going to do?" Her question takes me by surprise, and I turn my head, removing my face from where it was burrowed into the pillow. I stare at her through swollen eyes.

"What do you mean?" I ask, looking away when I see the concern she is pinning me with.

"I saw the look on your face when you came out of the dining hall. I know you. That look in your eyes was determination. Like the time you were punished for attempting to climb the tree in the courtyard only to make it halfway and be snatched down by a guard." The corner of my mouth tugs up the smallest amount at the memory. "You had the same look in your eyes then, when you were just ten years old. You were determined to climb up that tree because you were told you couldn't. Do you remember what you told me?"

"If I'm going to pay the price, I may as well earn the prize." My smirk now widens to a full smile. "This is why I love you."

"So are you going to tell me?" She persists, and my smile falls. I want to tell her it's something trivial like climbing a tree or staying out past dark, but the truth is, this could affect us both. So I need her to understand that I can't tell her my plans, not in full anyway. I don't want to risk her life. I won't. Tears fill my eyes as I move to a sitting position. Colette helps me, holding one hand, and guides me up so I don't brush my back on anything. When I'm sitting upright, my front covered with a blanket, I meet her pale green eyes.

"You're leaving." It's not a question, not really. She sees the answer without my spoken words. She can see the truth in my eyes, and I hate the heartbreak I see in hers. Tears blot out my vision, and I blink them away before standing and placing a dark slip over my head. Even the softest of fabric, fit for a princess, rubs across the wounds painfully.

"I love you, Colette. You are more than a best friend to me. You have been like a sister."

"Stop." Her tone is firm even though the word is whispered, for our privacy, and I turn around to face her once again. "Don't say anything else. I don't need to know the details. Just know that I am here for you if you ever need me. You know how to call for me. Just as we did as kids. It's better to face your chances out there than it is for you to die slowly here." My mouth curls up in a tight-lipped smile, more grief than happiness in it, causing the tears to spill and mark the gray stone floor.

"Like a moth drawn to a flame," I whisper in her ear as I pull her into a hug. She's careful not to touch my wounded back, but the pain has already begun dissipating from the healing bath she gave it. I place my hand on the back of her head. Her red hair is down, and I bury my nose in it as I hug her tightly. The smell of earth and sweet jasmine fills my nose, and I do everything I can to imprint it into my mind. There is no one I will miss more than Colette.

"We will dance in the heat or burn in the flame, but either way, together we stay." She says in answer. The line we have told each other from the beginning. Only this time, we won't be together. Not physically, anyway.

With one more look into my eyes, her bottom lip wobbles before she slowly leans in and kisses my cheek. She moves to walk away but looks down at her hands, which grip my forearms. Her fingers blanched with how tightly she's holding on. The tears that have been building in her eyes gently cascade down her heavily freckled face before she swipes them away and rushes from the room. Leaving me alone in the dimly lit bedchamber with only the pain of losing one of the only people I have close enough to love.

Leaving me alone to plan either the end or the beginning of my life.

While my father is a smart man, he is also a creature of habit. So I know when I pull the heavy door to my chamber open, it will be Aeron standing guard at night. The older gentleman is already fast asleep in the chair to my left, his head tipped back and jaw slack, and his soft snores fill the empty hallway.

Ever so slowly, I pull the door shut behind me. When it creaks loudly, Aeron's mouth shuts, stopping his snoring and plunging me into silence. My face scrunches up as I wait on bated breath. I blink slowly and release my breath when his mouth falls open once more and the first rumbling snore echoes through the hall.

Holding my boots in one hand and my satchel in the other, I pad down the corridor toward the staff stairwell. I know it's not likely any of them will be up and walking around at this hour, but guards will surely be on the main stairs. The entrance is covered by a tapestry with my mother's image on it; as I pull it back, it almost appears that she is nodding down at me, giving me her approval. I have to think that she would be proud of me for choosing this. Choosing to run away from the man who ruins so many lives. *The man who took hers.* Letting the heavy fabric fall behind me sends me into complete darkness, and I curse under my breath at myself for forgetting a lantern. I can't turn back now.

I continue my descent, quietly and meticulously, with my forearm as my guide. I let it rub along the rough stone wall to lead me to my destination. A flicker of light at the end of the stairs and a shadow moving in the room at the doorway causes my feet to falter, and I miss a step.

"Shit." The word is only a whisper as I catch myself on the wall, but it is loud enough in the quiet room that the person the shadow belongs to darkens the doorway with their body.

"Who's there?" His voice is deep and unrecognizable. I press my back against the stone, holding my breath, hoping that with a moment of silence, he will think it was nothing. Perhaps the wind outside, or an animal causing a ruckus. He steps into the shadow of the stairs. All I can do is listen to the pounding pulse that's rushing in my ears and think about how my first attempt to run away from the life that is meant to be my noose has failed before I even made it outside the castle walls. Then his shadow moves, and the dim light from the small staff kitchen is in view once more.

After a moment of silence, I let my breath out of my cheeks and creep forward. Once I reach the doorway, I peek around the corner to find the room thankfully empty. I used to sneak down to this kitchen when Sienna was on staff. Before my father had her killed. He said she had magick and was plotting against him, but as I got older, the more I understood that it was my friendship that killed her. My father never wanted me to become close to anyone. She wasn't the first nor the last, but she is the one who helped me put a name to what was happening.

Lies.

My father was lying to everyone in the kingdom. Sienna didn't have magick. She was, however, a part of the Neer. A group of people who support the use of magick in healing and good welfare. She told me about it when I had come into the kitchen after a particularly bad punishment from my father. She had brought a woman into the castle, and together they put on salves and said incantations over me for healing. It was the quickest I've ever recovered. Sometimes I wonder if it was that night that caused her death.

Poking around the room, I pull as many items as I feel reasonable from the cupboards and drawers. Pulling the canvas bag I have strapped across my body open, I shove bread, cheeses, and smoked meat in for my journey. I don't know how long it will be until I find somewhere to settle, but I won't be hungry along the way. At the last minute, I see a knife sitting atop the wood block suited for chopping, and wrap it with a cloth before sliding it into my bag too. I know the realm is vicious, especially for those living near the outer rim of the capital. I will be ill-prepared even bearing a knife, with no self-defense training, but it has to be better than nothing.

Deciding I'm ready to continue, I crack the door that leads to a narrow hall. The end of the passage leads to the courtyard. Once outside, that is where my real mission will be. There will be guards at all exits. I won't get out easily, but if I've learned *anything* from my father, it's that anything worth having is worth working for. With that last thought, I step out into the cool night air.

A wide smile spreads across my face at the luck I must have conjured because the guard at the closest exit is fast asleep. His hands are folded across his mound of a belly, and his chair is tipped back, resting against the stone wall at his back, and his cloak hood is draped over his eyes. I laugh inwardly at my father for employing *only the best guards* for the palace. The guards that run the kingdom beyond the palace walls are of the more...questionable variety. Their nobility only extends to how much coin they can trick out of the commoners. I'm dumbfounded at the ease with which I cross the courtyard. Running, I only look back once I have climbed the nearest tree and hopped over the battlement. I slide down the other side, landing with a laugh. I clap my hand over my face in astonishment as I turn around and look up at the tall sandstone wall—*I'm free.*

Pulling the cloak up to cover my face as much as possible, I can't help the smile that takes over my face as I take my first step toward town. The next step to getting away: find a convoy that will be heading to another town or, preferably, another kingdom. I will pay for passage to leave with them. One thing I know for certain: I cannot do this alone; there is no doubt in my mind. If the dunes didn't kill me; the sand pirates would surely do the job. I may not have fighting skills, so the only thing I have to escape is reading. I have learned all I could about the people I never got to see. The land I was surrounded with but never ventured to. I would have to leave with a convoy. There is safety in numbers when out on the dunes.

Chapter Three

Astraea

Eathian is a wealthy kingdom, but the further I venture out into the parts I've not been allowed, the more I begin to see why. The people are as dirty as the ground they walk on. The stench of poverty thickens with each dwelling I pass, and the further my hatred of my father grows. He would not allow me to see these parts because he knew. He knew that my compassionate heart would not be pleased. He knew that the more I saw, the more defiant I might become, and one thing he hates worse than women is a woman with an opinion.

It sickens me to know the luxury I lived in every day of my life since my father took rule here. Although I don't recall much of my childhood before, I know I was never left wanting. These people? They are not just wanting; they are in *need*.

Men and women lay sick in filth on every corner. Children play barefoot with nothing but what most in the castle would see as garbage as toys. My heart breaks at the sight. Too consumed by my surroundings, I trip over a pothole in the unmaintained path, bumping into a woman who sneers at me as she hurls obscenities my way. Why isn't my father taking care of the kingdom as a whole? Are we not only as strong as our weakest?

I turn toward her, offering my apologies as she brushes me off, and because of the distraction, I stumble again. As I turn to right myself in the bustling street, I run right into the back of a man who is pushing a cart mounted with loads of animal skins for trade.

"Watch where you're going, you daft Kru!" He shouts the insult at me as I wrench upright and put my hands out to steady the angry man, who was at risk of tripping as well from my negligence.

"I'm so sorry. I wasn't paying attention to where I was going. Please forgive me." I say as I place my hands on his back and shoulder. He spins, surprising me by grabbing my wrist.

"Not just a Kru, but a pickpocket too, are ya?" He growls, bringing the attention of others who are passing by. That word again. My eyes narrow on the man. "You know what happens to those who steal from me?" The grip with which he holds my wrist is painful, more so when he twists it further. The skin heats and burns under his rough hand.

"You're hurting me. Let me go!" I shriek. I didn't think this through. I'm not cut out for this. I should have paid a guard to take me. I would have been able to set them up for life judging by the state of the kingdom. My thoughts of *what if* consume me as the anger in the man rises.

"Oh, I'll let you go alright. You fu—"

"Think about your next words wisely, Martier. There are children around." A deep voice speaks behind me, cutting off the brute's slur.

"She's a Kru thief!" I've heard of the Krusaders. The remnants of the people who barely survived my father's usurping. The people who were stripped of what little they had left to their names and those who were now forced to beg, steal, and cheat their way through survival. It's ironic he's calling me the derogatory name when my father is the one who made it so.

"What did she steal?" The man asks as he comes to stand at my side. I can't see his face through the shadows of his hood, but the man in front of me seems to be willing to listen to him, so I stay quiet.

"She...she stole..." He pats his pockets down with one hand, looking around nervously. "I caught her before she stole my coin! I saw where her hand was heading!" He yells and narrows his eyes at me; still holding on tightly to my wrist, he shakes me where I stand. His lip curls back in disgust, revealing rotting yellow and brown teeth.

"I assume that would make her a pretty poor thief then? Since you can barely see the latrine to sit on most days?" The people who have crowded us laugh at the skin trader's expense, and the glower he aims at me worsens. He pushes me as he drops my wrist, cursing. I don't think the man who has come to my aid is making anything better, but since they are occupied with each other and I am no longer detained, I attempt to slip away unnoticed.

I make it around the corner of one of the small dwellings, looking over my shoulder, and let out a sigh just as I slam into a hard body. His large hands curl around my upper arms to steady me. "And just where do you think you are off to?" My stomach drops at the sound of the dark timbre of his voice.

"I—I'm so sorry. I'm making it a habit to run into people today." I try to pull away from his grip, but he doesn't let me go, and I swallow my fear as I continue to try to backpedal. "I'm just making my way to the dune ports. I'm not trying to cause anyone any trouble." I say, looking down. I don't want him to see my face. This man holds himself differently than the others I've seen in passing thus far, and there is a good chance that he could be a high-ranking guard or a nobleman in these parts. Neither would be good for my escape.

Using his gloved hand, he pushes to lift my chin with two fingers, and I sidestep. "If you'll excuse me," I say curtly before continuing my trek, face to the ground. To my vexation, he falls into step at my side.

"Are you a handmaiden to the princess?" My feet stop where they are, and my breathing stops altogether.

"No. Why would you ask that?"

"Your finery is—well, much more *fine* than we tend to see in these parts. What are you trying to get away from?" I dare a glance up at his face for the first time. He's removed his hood, and my breath catches in my throat. He is taller than any man I have come in contact with within the castle, with hair in stark contrast to mine. Where my wavy, long hair falls dark, almost raven-black, his hair is light, a bright blonde with messy curls that beg for a woman's fingers. An uncommon sight.

No! Astraea, keep your wits about you. It's just a pretty face—striking blue eyes, full lips, and—nope. I am not doing this. The thoughts alone evoke enough to think I would remember him had I seen him around the castle.

While my father wished me pious, I am no prude when it comes to men. If I were to be given to a man for the rest of my life, *unwillingly*, then, as I saw it, while I was able to decide for myself, I would bed the men of my choosing...

In secret, of course. Only a few lost their lives because of it. They knew the risks. Even if it hurt me, my father only caught word of their indiscretions by their own mouths. No one who knew of my exploits would have betrayed me.

"Yes. I worked in the castle, but my assignment has ended, and now I seek my next adventure." His blue eyes narrow as he tilts his head, surveying me. I tug my hood forward more, making sure that my face is well hidden in the shadows.

"Very well..." He quirks an eyebrow, the question of my name distinct in his tone.

"Sienna," I extend my hand to him, relieved I took any rings I was wearing off, and he lifts it, kissing my knuckles. I send a silent apology to my deceased friend, hoping she can forgive me for using her name in aid of my escape. I don't think she would mind after knowing what my life was like.

The people here in the wallows of the kingdom may be suffering, but wealth and position can't buy happiness. Even those in great positions have demons they battle. That I know from experience. I am the highest matriarch of the kingdom, save the king himself, and happiness is an emotion that I can't say for certain I've felt. At least not since my mother was taken from me. Since I was forced into this position by my father.

"Safe travels then, Sienna." My cheeks heat at the softness of his words, and I say my thanks in return, then urge my feet to quickly get moving toward the dune ports. I can feel his eyes trail my wake, and I don't look back.

With any luck, a convoy will be leaving today, and I will be out of the kingdom by nightfall. I've heard from talk around the castle staff that it's not every day that convoys are safest to leave. Maelstroms of rain from the north threaten to bring back the long-since-dried sea on some days, and sandstorms from the east aim to bury those unlucky enough to find themselves in one alive on others. The best travelers have it down to a science, or so I've heard. With that thought, I look out at the horizon and the clouds that seem to be rolling further in by the minute. I have a feeling my luck is running out, and today is likely not one of the days that they leave.

Wrenching a door open, I step over the threshold sopping wet. My cloak clings to me and drips on the wood floor, causing a circle of puddles to form around me, but no one notices my entrance. It's a welcomed feeling to be unnoticed. Able to enter a room without an audience of people gawking and pining over your every move. It's freeing. Smirking under my hood, I stomp my feet and close the door behind me. Closing myself into the tavern and away from the monsoon that invaded the land only moments before I reached the ports. I won't be traveling today. There are no travelers who will be heading out until the rain stops.

Keeping my head down and hood up, I cross the room to the back where the bar is. The barmaid looks up as I approach, and I place my hand down on the surface, sliding two coins to her.

"I would like a room for the night," I say curtly.

"Very well, but it's a full house tonight. No rooms are being unshared." She says, sliding the coins into her palm and pushing them into the pocket of her dress. Leaving no room for argument, she lifts the bar, stepping through gruffly and shouldering past me. "This way." She says, not waiting for a response, she cuts through the crowd of people blocking the narrow stairway.

I look around nervously, and my lip rolls inward, my teeth chewing on it. I can't go back out into the monsoon, so I will be forced to share a room with a stranger. If they recognize me, all of this will be for nothing. Taking a steadying breath, I pull steel into my spine and take my first step in the direction the barmaid headed, only to collide once again with a hard body.

"Shit," I curse, and the wide smile on the man's face becomes even more prominent, his straight white teeth sparkling in the low light.

"Very becoming language for a lady, princess." My eyes widen, my pulse ramping up by his words. He can't know I am the princess. My hood surely still covers my face. I take a step backward. The urge to flee burning at my heels. I will find somewhere else to wait out the storm. Surely there is another tavern nearby. If I—

"Miss?" The barmaid leans from behind the man, still looking at me. Her words pull me from my internal turmoil. Reflexively, I glance up at the man who is causing my heart to feel as though it is going to jump out of my throat. His expression has changed from jovial to curious, and he tilts his head as he eyes me. "Did you want me to show you to your room?"

"Yes," I cough, stepping around him. "Please excuse me." I nod my apologies and hurry up the stairs. When I reach the top, I can't help but look back down at the man. *It's the wrong thing to do.* From this angle, he surely sees into my hood. The expression on his face changes once again. Whatever he sees causes his dark eyes to round as they meet mine.

The stranger with golden curls from the alleyway steps up to him, clapping him on the back, breaking the trance we were locked in. I turn the corner, letting my eyes fall closed while I try to take a steadying breath before quickly making my way to the door the barmaid impatiently holds open for me.

"Thank you." I rush into the room, not waiting for her response before I shut the door between us and press my back to the wood. Chest heaving, I tip my head back with my eyes trained on the dark bedchamber as my mind races and those dark eyes haunt me.

Chapter Four

Kyros

The task is simple—we just need to get in and get out. My magick is already thrumming in my veins, telling me that we're close. Martier is a pain in the ass on any day, but I know the people of Eathian. While they normally revere mine and Mavros' arrival, they are on edge with the princess coming of age to marry soon. The king is ready to find the suitor that best fits his mold. Everyone around knows that woman did nothing but bruise his ego. I shake my head as I look up at the cloud-heavy sky. It's not a good sign.

Where the hell is Mavros?

We should have headed to the palace this morning, but my stubborn brother wants to play this his way. Every task we are set on, we flip a coin to see who will be in the lead. Luckily for me, he gets to be the one to play dress-up for the king. I just need to sit back quietly and pretend to be his guard while he is the pompous asshole heir of Diemos. It's not entirely a lie. We are both heirs of Diemos by our queen's word. She has chosen us to rule together if her death shall come. It's the part that I am playing as Mavros' guard and the part he will be playing as a suitor wanting the hand of the princess that is the lie.

Zinya couldn't stop laughing when we were en route here, and we tossed the coin to see what role we would each play. While Mavros is charismatic, his exploits are usually sexual and not the attention of the king of a power-hungry kingdom and his prissy little princess. Mavros needs to be serious if he is to truly keep us here long enough to find what we are looking for.

Rounding the corner, I slow down when I see Mavros talking to the same cloaked woman I saved from sudden disfigurement only a moment ago with Martier. It's not often I am surprised by people, especially here in Eathian. The good in the kingdom has mostly been run out or killed by King Connard Casimir. Even now there are bodies hanging from at least a couple of the cantilevers throughout the city; their crimes are unknown, but their punishment is clear enough to say it was plenty to anger the king.

He's taunting her, and even as she tries to conceal her face, I see the blush that colors her neck and climbs to her cheeks. I roll my eyes. *Asshole.* I curse my obnoxious twin. When she takes off, nearly running away from him, I can't hide my amusement as I lean against the clay wall of the shadowed alleyway and cross my arms, waiting for him to turn around.

"The fuck are you smiling about?" Mavros laughs as he turns around, finding me watching him.

"You need to be serious about this, Mav," I scold, even if my smirk still pulls the corner of my lips up a fraction.

"I think you are serious enough for the both of us." He winks, and I shake my head with a scoff and push off the wall. "Where's Zinya? Are you ready to head to the castle yet?" He pats my chest as he walks past me, and I catch his wrist, stopping him in his path.

"I'm serious, Mavros. You can't treat this like a joke. The king will see through your comedy. He is not one to entertain jesters. Look up, brother; those poles are not just for looks. The hooks are meant for men to hang like flags around this city. He kills and hangs his trophies for all to see." I seethe, looking up at the extension on the clay building, prepped and ready to hang a man. A punishment and a warning.

"You know... Since I am to be the serious one, maybe you can do us all a favor and get laid. Maybe you wouldn't be so—" Mavros stops, looking me up and down, and I level him with a glare.

"I don't need to get laid. I need to get the job done." I growl, looking out at the market. Many of the carts are moving now. Eyes keep shooting up at the sky, and sure enough, the clouds I noticed earlier are churning. The tell-tale sign that a storm is coming. Just what we don't have time for.

"What's the difference?" Mavros asks, and I look at him baffled.

"What?" I curl my lip in annoyance.

"You said you needed to get the job done. What's the difference between that and getting laid?" He laughs, and I take a calming breath. I swear we twins couldn't be more different.

"I think since I was born first, you lacked oxygen for too long. Your brain suffered before you even took your first breath." Zinya walks up just as Mavros' jaw falls slack, but she heard what I said. Her head falls back in a gut-deep laugh at Mav's expense. I can't help but smile a little too. "Come on. Looks like our little *quick stop* has cost us. We need shelter from the coming monsoon. We won't make it to the palace before the storm." My eyes lift just as the first of the thunder rolls, and I push my way through both of them and head to the first tavern I see.

Mavros starts drinking as soon as we step up to the bar. I guess if he needs to get something out, now is the time to do it. We will be stuck here for at least a couple of days while this storm rolls over.

"Sorry, big guy, we can't give single rooms; you either bunk up or sleep at the bar for all I care. There are too many people that are going to need a place to lay their heads in this. Those willing to pay." The red-headed bar maiden is brash and confident; I'll give her that. Most men wouldn't even talk to me like that, yet she just says it matter-of-factly, with just a look of annoyance. It makes me like her right away, so I give her a smirk and step in close. She lifts her chin to show me that she has no fear. The man she is trying to bunk with me, though... he has plenty. He stammers about making some kind of excuse about how he actually would rather spend his coin on ale and would just sleep in a booth if he needed it.

"Well, look at that. My room just became a single."

"You'll pay triple." She growls, and I give her my best Mavros wink. Judging by the angry glower she pins me with, it was lacking his undeniable charm, so I shrug. Tripling the cost for a night of peace is fine by me. I pay the haggler and order a whiskey before finding a table in the corner, far from my brother and the rowdy crowd he entertains. We did bring soldiers with us, but most of them steer clear of The Hawk—Harbinger of Death. My reputation as the silent killer doesn't scream drinking buddy.

The rain is really pelting the clay roof now, and as the storm gets louder, so do the tavern's patrons. The only man who might take his job as seriously as me is Viltarin, and even he is smiling while holding a pitcher of ale. I'm about to get a refill of whiskey and take it to my room when the door to the tavern opens, letting the sounds of the storm pull my attention to the smaller hooded figure that walked in. I recognize her immediately. The same woman from the market. The same woman my brother was shot down by, and the same one who is oddly alluring to me...

I sink back into the booth a little longer as I watch her. Her cloak is soaking wet, leaving a path of water trailing behind her as she makes her way to the bar. The way she looks around and keeps her hood up tells me that she has something to hide and causes me to be that much more interested in what she is doing.

When I see her slide a coin across the bar, I notice the barmaid give her the same bullshit about having to bunk up. I can't help but want to get closer. The intrigue of what is pulling me to her is too strong to ignore. I am about to stand beside her and say hello when she looks around. I watch people for a living. Gain information and kill. I'm an assassin and a spy, and everything about this woman screams mystery, and it's one I can't help but be drawn toward solving.

I can only see her lips and chin from where I stand, the firelight around the tavern casting shadows across her face with the way her hood is drawn. She pulls her pink bottom lip between her teeth, and I catch myself mocking the motion. Distracted by this, I don't realize that she was standing before it's too late. She slams face first into my chest as I walk up behind her.

"Shit," the curse coming from her catches me by surprise again, and I can't help the smile that tugs my lips up at the corners.

"Very becoming language for a lady, *princess*." She takes a hesitant step back, her mouth pulled into a frown. My hand twitches; the sudden urge to reach for her, tell her I'm not going to harm her, screams at me, but all I do is stand here. I stare like she is a god's divine mythical creature.

"Miss?" The barmaid, *damn this woman*, interrupts my personal turmoil, and the cloaked woman looks up at me. Never has a woman of few words ever caused me to become this perplexed. Even my magick stills within my veins. Almost as if it were telling me to pay attention. Think about your next action.

"Did you want me to show you to your room?" The wench cuts through my thoughts again.

"Yes," the strange woman coughs, sidestepping around me. Her shoulder brushes just above my elbow as she does. "Please excuse me." She apologizes, but I say nothing as she rushes up the stairs like someone is chasing her. When she reaches the top, her head turns back to look at me over her shoulder. Her eyes, even through the shadowed tavern, shine the brightest blue. They glow like the flowers of scorpion grass that grows back in Diemos, in the shaded areas of the thick forests. When the sun hits them just right, they have an ethereal sort of beauty. I've never met anyone with eyes like hers. As soon as I think about it, I also have to remind myself—those flowers are deadly. This woman could be too. I don't know anything about her. She could be a siren for all I know, with the way I feel drawn to her.

Mavros comes clapping me on the back, and I cough as he knocks the air from my lungs and pulls my attention from her. When I chance a look back, she's gone.

"What's the matter with you? Did you get into the spicy grass again? Looking a little jumpy." He laughs, and I punch him in the stomach, returning the favor of losing my air a moment ago. He laughs harder, curled in on himself.

"Don't fuck with me, asshole." I growl as I head to the bar. Needing that second whiskey more now than ever.

"Noted." He wheezes, Zinya laughing with him now, but I can't think of anything, even as I look into the liquid gold in my cup. All I see is the blue flower in the scorpion grass with a random ray of sunshine finding its petals and lighting it up like magick from within.

Chapter Five

Astraea

M y dress and cloak cling to me uncomfortably as I stand facing the empty room. I pull in a long breath and let it out with a heavy sigh, and as I peel off the cloak, I shiver. The drop in temperature as the night settles over the desert and the rain has worked a chill into my bones. Hanging my cloak on the hook behind the door, I head to the basin that is set up in the corner of the room. I ease out of the heavy, waterlogged material and my undergarments and wrap myself in the threadbare towel provided by the inn.

Great, I get to sleep naked tonight.

I lay my clothes over the back of the chaise, thankful that the tavern at least keeps fires going in their rooms in preparation for guests. Hopefully, my clothes are dry by morning. The lumpy bed slumps when I sink into it, and my brows pinch when I pull the scratchy linens up to my chin and begin thinking—*what do I do now?*

I lay there numbly, watching the water as it drips and sizzles from my dress. Each drop hits the dark, warm stone below it, hissing out a puff of steam.

My mind whirls with everything that has happened since supper yesterday, but I try to focus on anything other than the worry that is threatening to consume me. The rain, despite causing everything to halt, is a welcome reprieve. The sound is so different from when it rains in the castle. The light patter on stone I'm used to is replaced by repeated heavy tinkling on the clay roof, like a rhythmic song that is almost soothing.

Almost.

The sound of rain, even accompanied by the crackling wood of the fire, is not enough to drown out the raucous laughter that is coming from the tavern below me. I'm so wound up that every time I close my eyes, my mind snags on the sound of a chair scraping across the wood floor, the shattering of a dish, women and men making cries of pleasure or pain. Every noise is more distracting than the next.

With a huff, I throw the pillow over my head and squeeze my eyes shut. I don't know how long I lay there thinking over what's next in my journey, but it's long enough that my breathing finally begins to slow. *This monsoon won't last forever.* The words are chanted in my head as I try to force myself into sleep. Every time I think I might be drifting off, something makes me jump. My heart racing like I'm coming out of a nightmare's clutches.

I am no stranger to nightmares. I've lived in one my entire life. A castle full of reminders, and the weight of multiple lives lost because of me. With the skeletons in my closet, my mind refuses to let me seek peace with sleep.

I guess in a way, I traded one nightmare for another. Right now, I'm trapped between the secret horror that was my life as *Princess Astraea, Eathian's key to the Crown,* and the unknown—which is as exhilarating as it is terrifying.

Pulling in a long breath, I lay there with my hearing muffled by the slim pillow over my head. A click sounds next as a door is unlocked, likely to the door beside mine. I throw the pillow out at my side with a groan and slam my fists to my sides. My eyes, trained on the ceiling, widen as the room becomes brightened by the flicker of a flame from the hallway. My head snaps in the direction of the door as a shadowed silhouette of a man steps into the sliver of light before he shuts it and disappears into the darkness.

My voice is trapped in my throat as my mind tries to play catch-up to what is happening. The old floorboards creak as the sound of leather and metal clang and drop to the floor with a loud thud, followed by a man's voice as he stumbles and curses, catching himself on the bedside table.

I'm tucked in tight on the far side of the bed, pressed in against the wall and shrouded in blankets and the darkness of the room. As he steps into the glow of the moon from the window, half-dressed and heavy-lidded, still my voice remains imprisoned with fear. The mattress sinks in tandem with my heart as his heavy body sits on the edge.

My breathing stops altogether when he lies back on the pillow I just discarded. His arms come up under the back of his head as he settles in. His pale hair is like a halo of silver crowning above sharp dark brows and a jawline cut from Tsalalerian steel. He still doesn't know I'm right behind him as his eyes close. Despite the terror, I'm frozen merely inches from his half-naked body, my own body only covered with the blankets that are now stifling. My hand presses across my lips to hold in a whimper of fear.

I'm at an impasse. I could stay here and risk him rolling onto me in his sleep and if not that, I would inevitably be discovered in the morning... Or I could press my diminishing luck and try to sneak around him and flee. My heart rate is matching the thundering gallop of the king's horses' hooves as I sit there trying to do everything I can to steady my breathing while I wait. The smell of liquor wafting from him is heavy, so if I have any luck at all, he is drunk enough that he will pass out hard and not notice me slipping away.

Just as I'm about to shuffle down the wall towards the end of the bed, he moves. One hand comes down, laying across his chiseled chest, and I swallow, watching the slow descent as it travels down the hard planes of his stomach. Slowing further at the deep V below his navel, he tucks his fingers into the low, *very low*, band of his trousers. My dry mouth suddenly becomes flooded with moisture, and I grind my teeth together to try to reel in my sanity.

"Please, stop ogling, or my gentlemanly control *will* snap." His words cause my heart to seize, my mouth falling open in shock. Then my brain catches up with the fact that he's known I was in the bed all along, and I launch from the shadows and rush to the door. The chair that was pushed into the desk topples and falls as I scramble blindly to get there as fast as I possibly can, causing a loud crash in my wake. I trip on his discarded clothing, and I hear him curse as he comes after me.

I pull open the door, and his hand comes crashing down on the wood above my head, slamming it shut. Leaving me to turn around to face him, naked and trembling, covering myself with a blanket that I am now barely holding onto.

"Princess, if you are worried about what I will do to you in here… I suggest you not walk out of here wearing…" His eyes trail down my body. "That," he continues, as his other hand comes up and pinches my chin between his finger and thumb. He turns my head to the side, and I can't help the small cry that comes from my parted lips.

"Please, I'm just waiting out the storm. Just let me go, and I'll ask for another room." I whisper the words with building trepidation. His low chuckle vibrates through my bones as he steps in closer and angles my head so I am looking him in the eyes. The gleaming blue in the nearly extinguished firelight appears ghastly white, so much so that I think for a second that they flash with the stark absence of color. All other words that were building in my mind go blank, and I hold my breath as he lowers his face to hover just inches above mine.

"Don't even think about it." He whispers.

"I'll scream." I rush the words out, but my threat only pulls a malicious grin to his remarkable features, making him that much more dangerous to look at. My eyes shift to see around him, looking for anything I can use for a weapon, but I fail. Regardless of if I were to find anything, it wouldn't matter. Beyond wishing for the best possible blow, I have no idea how to defend myself. I would be as likely to hurt myself as I would be to hurt him.

"You have the look of someone who is smarter than that," he says, lowering his lips to my ear. "What do you think will happen if you scream in here? Who do you think will come to your aid?" He stands fully, causing my eyes to trail up to meet his, and I swallow back any protest I had building on my tongue. He's right.

"Good girl," he growls as he takes a step away. The small amount of distance he's put between us gives me a tiny amount more air to breathe but also makes me tremble more, as I am more clearly on display for him. The door opens behind me, bumping my heels and causing a yelp of surprise to come from me unabated, and I quickly cover my mouth with my hand as I dip under his arm and press my back into the adjoining wall.

"Can I help you?" The man in the room asks whoever stands in the hall with a broad smile. I have seconds to decide. I could cry for help... scream to gain attention, but what if he is right? I know nothing of being outside the castle walls. Nothing from my own experience anyway. Only stories that I've overheard from the gossiping guardsmen or the help who are allowed to roam further out of the royal boundaries. I could very well be even worse off if I call attention to myself. At least in here, there is only one man.

"It sounded like there was trouble..." A man from the other side of the door rumbles angrily. The cocky stranger I share a room with opens the door wider, but the light from the hall doesn't quite reach where I stand pressed against the wall. Surely a deliberate move, since he sweeps his arm out wide toward the seemingly otherwise empty room.

"Well as you can see..." His eyes meet mine in the shadows. "No trouble here."

"The barkeep says there hasn't been a rain like this in months. Said it will likely last a few days. Meet me downstairs for breakfast." The man in the hall says. My jailer gives a coy smile before he starts to shut the door, and a set of fingers wraps around the wood, stopping it before it shuts.

"Stay out of trouble, Mav. You know why we're here." The other man growls. Mav...pats the man's hand with three taps, narrowing his blue eyes on the faceless stranger before smiling devilishly once again.

"I'll be right here... sleeping like royalty." He winks, snapping the door shut without another word. I take a step forward, but he shakes his head. Bringing his finger up, he taps his ear while pointing at the door. His eyes are now narrowed and aimed at me, the smile he once had vanished, and again my heart rate spikes, and I listen to the other man's footsteps fade in the distance.

"You want to tell me why you were laying in my bed naked and waiting? Or should we just get started?" He smirks. His tongue jutting from his mouth to roll over his full bottom lip. My answering PAH! Makes the smirk fall, and he cracks his neck. "Why are you here then, if it's not to get fucked?"

"Why am I here? What about you? Clearly, this has been a mistake. The barmaid—" as I start, I remember what she had said when bringing me to my room. I was too distracted at the time to question it. *"No rooms are being unshared."*

"Well, roomie, looks like we are stuck together. Do you like the inside or outside?" I don't register his question at first as I stare at him blankly.

"What are you asking?"

"What side of the bed do you want, princess?" He laughs and my eyes clear of the haze they were trapped in.

"I am not sleeping with you." I bark out with a laugh of my own.

"Well, suit yourself." He says with a shrug before he strides to the fire, stoking the flames and adding wood to the blaze. The room flares brighter, giving me a clearer view of his heavily tattooed torso and back as he swaggers around the small space like he owns the place. My back presses into the wall as I lean on it for support. My panic over everything is catching up to me, and as my adrenaline wanes, so does my energy. I can hardly stand up on my own.

Once satisfied with the fire and how his things are placed around the room, he lies down on the bed in the same position as before. It's evident that he thinks I am of no concern to him as he closes his eyes, and he falls asleep quickly with my eyes fixed on him and his weapons laying out in plain sight.

Chapter Six

Astraea

THE DOOR SLAMMING SHUT jolts me awake from where I finally fell asleep. The rickety chair in front of the hearth creaks as it wobbles, and I steady myself before falling over. A deep chuckle followed by heavy footsteps has me blinking rapidly to clear the sleep from my dry eyes. When I see the man looking down at me, his head tilts like a predator. My hands automatically clench around the fabric of the blanket that was most certainly not covering me as much as I wanted it to be.

He doesn't say anything, only stares for a moment before walking over to the bedside table and setting down a plate of a steaming assortment of food and a tankard filled to the brim. He kneels, opening a satchel on the floor, and then turns, tossing a ball of fabric in my direction. It hits me in the face, and I shriek out a surprised yelp.

"Figure you might want to cover yourself, since you're a prude who doesn't want to have any fun." He grins as he turns away, and I can't help the obnoxious face I make in his direction before I pull the offered tunic over my head. It's like a short dress on me; the arms way too long, and the hem brushes the tops of my knees.

"Thank you, I—I'm decent now." I stammer as I try to cover even more of myself, unsuccessfully attempting to pull the hem lower than it reaches. When he turns again to face me, he does not feign to notice my skin that is still on show. He whistles low as his eyes rake slowly from my toes, where they press into the rough gray wood, up my legs, and flick across my chest before settling on my face. Which, I am sure, he sees as clearly as I see his now. I swallow, hoping he doesn't see the crimson heat that floods my cheeks at the brazen path his eyes just roamed. Praying to any god that will listen that he doesn't recognize me. That somehow he hasn't been to the castle, and my mission to get away has failed even before it's begun.

Even though the sky is not its usual gold hue of heat and sunshine, it is shining somewhere beyond the curtain of rain washing the world in a gray glow of light. His eyes linger on my face longer than is comfortable before he clears his throat, turning away.

"Too bad," he says under his breath before rustling through the bag more. "I have trousers too, but they will likely be far too large for your frame. I can get you something from one of the women here while you wait for your dress to dry."

My eyes cut to said dress and the water still creating darkened spots on the stone below it, and I forfeit any rebuttal about not needing clothes. If I were going to be able to leave this room, I would need more coverage than this shirt allotted. Instead I resign, sitting back in the chair and placing the blanket over my bare legs and pulling them to my chest.

"Thank you. You're very kind." I say quietly, meeting the stranger's pale gaze.

"Don't let anyone else hear you say that; I don't need my reputation stained." He traps his lip between his teeth as the corners curl. "It was Sienna? Isn't that right?" My heart nearly stops with his question. I didn't think I would see this man again when I gave him that name, and now it looks like I am going to be stuck here with him at the very least until the rain stops. Could be longer if he is a traveler that is also setting out to find a convoy to leave with. I internally groan, but keep my eyes trained on his without any pretense of the frustration over this whole situation I feel.

"Yes," I clear my throat and lift my chin a little higher. Trying to convey confidence I surely don't feel in the moment. "You remember?" He smirks at my question, his hand resting on the lever to open the door.

"Of course, a gentleman never forgets the name of a beautiful stranger who stumbles across his path. Eat the food while it's hot, Sienna... It tastes like garbage if you let it get cold." He regards me for a moment before stepping into the hall and shutting the door between us.

I listen to his footsteps fade away, and after a moment alone, I sigh heavily, watching the rain wash the window bleary and the steam on the food easing where it sits on the table. Heeding the warning from *Mav*, I cross the room, pulling the plate under my nose and wafting the scent of the food toward me. It doesn't smell awful, but there is a sour note that has me making a face at the stew before I take it back to the chair.

Being used to the food in the castle—even hot— this food is worse than garbage. I have to hold my breath so I can finish the meal without losing the entire contents of my stomach. The carrots are like mush, and the unidentifiable green lumps are where the sour smell is coming from. The meat is more chewy fat than actual meat, not to mention the lack of spices. It tastes like it was prepared in a latrine.

Though, as I think it, I cringe and take the last bite. If I am going to make passage anywhere, I need to get used to eating things I may not like. I won't have the luxury of denying food. That much I know from the gathered stories I've heard from the guardsmen. The land was barren and many starved before they made it to any of the surrounding kingdoms. If they didn't starve, they were at risk of madness from thirst.

The thought alone pulls my attention to the tankard Mav left with the food. Placing the now empty plate back on the table, I lift the heavy drink to my mouth and take a large gulp. Regret immediately gathers at the back of my throat, and I spray the golden liquid from my nose and mouth at the same moment the door opens and a man steps in. His eyes close as the malodorous substance showers his face and soaks the sand neck gaiter that is gathered under his chin. His dark hair sticks to his face with the moisture and the heat that blooms over my face is reflected in the red hue painting his, but where mine is embarrassment… the dark shadows that cast over his eyes as he finally opens them tell me his color shift is something else entirely. I slap my hand over my mouth as I force myself to swallow the remaining warm ale in my mouth. My stomach flips instantly, protesting the noxious liquid.

"I'm so sorry!" I choke out, backing away, and my legs bump into the table behind me. A growl unlike any I have heard, even from the monstrous dogs who guard the king's wing of the castle, comes from the man's throat, and I swallow as I watch his jaw tick.

"Where. Is. Mavros?" His voice is like a rumble of thunder far away, but the threat of the coming storm is clear. The man from yesterday at the market stares at me through narrowed eyes as he pulls the gaiter away from his neck and uses it to wipe his face. The gaze was as penetrating as it felt through the shadows of his hood, *but the voice.* Even though I didn't see his face, I remember that voice and the overpowering aura that pressed in on me just as it does now. I know it is him standing before me now. No hood to conceal his form, I can't peel my eyes away from him. His black tunic is loose, partially tucked into his waistband, and open at the neck, revealing several scars that match the one that runs through his furrowed eyebrow and down the side of his face.

Though I thought him kind for intervening on my behalf in the market, the man standing before me now is just as foreboding as the merchant who wanted to take my hand for thievery I didn't commit.

"I don't know." My voice betrays me, coming out only as a whisper. Showing him every ounce of fear he has brought to me. He steps further into the room, leaving the door ajar. He towers over me, the sneer on his face deepening to a full scowl as he lets his gaze travel down my body and behind me to the disheveled bed, blankets and clothing strewed all about the room. It looks like something it's not, but to try and save face, I lift my chin.

"One of the women here had these; I think they will fit you better..." Mav's voice trails off as he enters the room and sees the silent standoff between me and the dark presence who leers over me. Though I hear him curse, I can't peel my eyes away from the mountain of muscle that looks down on me. Even as he blinks, standing straight once again, he wipes his hand down his face and looks over at Mav as he comes to a stop at the center of the space that seems so much smaller with the two of them in it.

"Mavros. A word." He leaves no room for questions as he looks at me one last time and exits the room with silent fury. Mavros takes the bundled fabric that he had in his arms and curses again as he throws it into a pile on the bed unceremoniously.

"Here. Get dressed before you cause any more trouble." He grunts with a roll of his eyes.

"Me? I didn't—" I sputter, trying to think of words to throw back in argument, but as he turns from the room without another thought and the door clicks between us, I spin on my heel with a huff of frustration. *This is not going the way I had hoped. Cole would be laughing her ass off right now at my expense. What the hell is happening?*

The ensemble—*if you could call it that*—that Mav brought me was more fitting than anything I was used to. No skirt to be found, the cotton material of the trousers breathable and light, but tight to my curves and leaving little to the imagination. The top is even more revealing. A sleeveless, boned corset pressed my breasts up to my neck, leaving my arms bare. Leather straps and belts I left lying on the bed because I had no clue how to put them on, and even if I did, I had no use for them. The most concealing part of the whole thing was the shemagh I had wrapped around my neck. Though, even with its coverage, the rest of the outfit made me feel more exposed than any of my dresses back home. Even with some of the more plunging necklines and slits up the skirts. This was not clothing but a uniform for some kind of woman warrior, if there ever was such a thing.

To my astonishment, a knock sounds at the door, and no one bursts through without a word. I stare at it a moment, wondering what I should do, before I take a deep breath, cross the room, and wrench it open. The female on the other side is another surprise. Her eyes meet mine at the same height, her features starkly opposite of mine. As her hazel eyes fall down my body, assessing, I can't help but feel inadequate as the woman in front of me sizes me up. She is strapped with so many weapons I fear even stepping close to her will be harmful. It's a sight I am not used to seeing, and it makes me flounder for words.

"You?" She quirks an incredulous brow. "You're the one causing the two most dangerous men in this tavern, probably in all of Eathian, to spiral out of control?" Her eyes roll as she shakes her head. "Where is your harness?" She says, pushing past me with no regard to my personal space. Her pauldron clipping me in my shoulder hard as she does.

"I don't need a harness, and I didn't do anything to cause any men a reason to do *anything*." I say to her back. Her answering huff is a dismissal as she twists around, harness in hand.

"Turn around. If we are going to keep a pet, it will be harnessed." She snaps her fingers, swirling her finger in the air, demanding me to turn. I glower at her as I turn my back and allow her to help me into the straps of leather.

"I'm no one's pet." I growl under my breath.

"Yea? Well, tell that to the two alpha males downstairs holding the pissing contest."

Chapter Seven

Kyros

I swear Mavros is going to be the death of me. The bastard always needs a reminder to stick to the task at hand. He is too frivolous with life. Always diving in headfirst and thinking to ask how deep the water is only as he is about to breach the surface. Grinding my teeth, I rip my ale-soiled shirt off and throw it to Viltarin. He bundles the fabric into a ball and tosses it to the side with a huge grin on his face. I'm sweating. My frustration is already overheating me.

"Who pissed in your oats this morning, Ky?" Tarin laughs, and I level him with a halfhearted glare. He's not the one who is pissing me off. Though I can't say exactly who is more—the mystery woman or my asshole brother.

"You can be next, Tarin." I bark out as Mavros removes his shirt next and starts hopping around like a hot coal in a fire. We're all bored, and when men such as us get bored, there are only three things that will keep us from killing each other. The three F's: Fucking, fighting, or food. Since there are not a lot of options for the first F, we opt for the second two even if the food here is next to shit. The makeshift sparring circle was approved by the barmaid, who also seems to be the ward of this tavern. So long as we promise to keep the furniture out of the fights.

Mavros and I came out of the womb fighting with each other. Although he doesn't remember, he blocked out much of our childhood. I remember it all. Likely something about our personality traits and how we handle trauma. While Mavros deflects, I let everything in. Keep things contained in little boxes. An arsenal of memories to bring with me to any kind of fight. I use them as fuel to the raging fire that's always within me. Especially here in Eathian.

"Oh, you can definitely count me in to fight the winner." Tarin chuckles, adding, "We all know it's going to be Kyros. Don't we, boys?" He rouses the crowd that is forming around us. All are betting on who will win the match. He smirks as he picks his teeth with the sharp point of a small knife. Goading Mavros this early in the morning is going to make this fight harder for me.

"Alright, brother, let's see what you've got today. I must say I'm a little tired after *caring* for my new roommate." He says with that damned wink as he readies himself in a crouch, ready to attack. I ignore the fact that he is trying to goad me with the woman.

He thinks I have some sort of affection for her after he saw me watching her at the stairs. Something about her just seems familiar, and I can't put my finger on it. But now more than ever I want to figure it out.

I mirror his stance, but where he is bouncing from foot to foot, I am a statue. My game is waiting. Letting the attacks come to me and then pouncing. I watch his feet. Mavros is good. Better than most, even. He is one of the only true competition that I have ever gone up against, but he's cocky. His overconfidence makes him sloppy at times. Give him a little show, and he will always gloat. When that happens—he goes down just as hard as the rest of them.

He goes low for his first move as he aims for my legs. I jump, rolling over his body, my back pressed to his, and I land behind him. As he whirls around, he's ready to block my coming attack. I throw my body down hard, leading with my fist, and he deflects easily enough, just as I knew he would. He smiles, arms wide, gloating. He doesn't see me loading my weight on one leg and then pushing off in a whirling kick. The top of my bare foot jars the side of his face.

"First blood is mine." I growl, then ready myself for a counterattack. Wiping his bloody smile with the back of his hand, he sucks his teeth and tuts at me before he tries to drop low in a sweeping kick to take my feet from me. We aren't fighting with weapons, only our bodies. It's one of the best forms of release. Men often rely on weapons, and while I would use my magick back home, my hands are just as well suited to hurt an opponent as my magick can.

"First blood, maybe, but don't be jealous when I get the first kiss." He taunts.

"What the fuck are you talking about?" I growl as he lunges, and I spin out of his reach at the last moment.

"The girl. I saw the moon eyes you were giving her." His smile is goading, and as I sense her merely enter the room, my anger wins out. Now, it's me who lunges. He doesn't get away. Our bodies collide, and we wrestle to get the other to the ground. His fist lands at my ribs, and with a wheeze I turn, wrapping my arm around his throat from behind.

"You don't know what you're talking about. You need to pay attention to why we are here. Don't let beauty distract you!" I growl fiercely into his ear; no one else can hear what we're talking about. The people surrounding the fight are much too rambunctious for our hushed words to be caught. He chokes and sputters with my bicep and forearm cutting off his airway, and I hold tight, ready to take the win. When he finally concedes with a tap on my arm, the crowd goes wild with cheers and laughter. I push him away from me with a grunt.

"I think maybe you're trying to tell yourself that, brother." He coughs, still laughing. Clenching my teeth, I turn away and head to the bar. Maybe he's right, and I do need to loosen up a little. It's been mission after mission since our father died. Not our biological father, but the man who was in charge of raising us. Maybe I've been trying to bury myself in jobs so I don't have to deal with yet another personal loss. It doesn't matter. It's not hurting anyone except the ones that I'm tasked to hurt.

I tap the bar, and the barmaid sets down a tumbler of whiskey, and I do my best not to look at the woman I know is across the room, but apparently when it comes to her, I lack all self-control just like Mavros says. She stands next to Zinya at the opposite side of the L-shaped bar wearing the fucking leathers that Zinya wears, leaving nothing to the imagination. The two men that Zinya tells to eat shit keep staring just as I do, but she doesn't look at them. She stares right back at me. Those blue eyes nearly drowning me in the desert.

When she looks away, it breaks the spell she has on me, and I shove away from the bar, knock back the rest of my drink, and storm out into the back hallway. I don't know where I'm going, but anywhere has to be better than staring at her like a lost fawn.

In the back hall I see a door that has to lead to the back alley behind the tavern, and I crack it open. Rain so heavy it's like a curtain of water, obscuring all visibility beyond, falls from the dark gray sky. The awning above the door looks as though it's seen better days and is near buckling with the onslaught of water. I grit my teeth and punch the door frame.

"Damn, I'd hate to hear what that frame said to deserve a sucker punch." Mavros' voice scrapes at my eardrums, and I turn in a quick spin and slam him against the wall. He chuckles, licking some of the dried blood on his lip, but says nothing.

"This is the most important job we have ever held, Mavros! What don't you understand about that?" I growl through bared teeth. I want so badly to just beat his ass into submission or force him to return to Diemos. He knows I won't do either, though.

Regardless of how much of a pain in the ass he is, he is my twin brother, and to be separated from him when he is all I have left would be a fate worse than death.

"You keep saying that..." he drawls, his eyes jumping between mine.

"Then why don't you listen?" I say, pushing harder on the arm barring his chest and pinning him to the wall.

"Because it's just another job, Ky. Nothing about this is any different than any others. It's *where* we are that has you all bent out of shape. It's where we're headed and *who* we're going to be face-to-face with. Why don't you just admit that you're afraid that you won't be able to do it?" He says with his lip curled, yet there is no anger coming from him. His eyes are pleading and brows dropped in concern, but no anger. No, that's all mine.

I'm angry with myself, and I'm fucking pissed off that he's right. The storm has served to only allow me to simmer with my hatred. No amount of preparation would be enough for me to walk into that court and look King Connard Casimir in the eye and pretend to want anything to do with his bitch daughter... and now, just when I thought I was ready, the storm has let the vile emotion pool in my gut and fester like a wound.

"Just another job or not, you need to pay attention to it. You need to already be in character, Mavros. You shouldn't be day drinking, flirting, and fucking your way up to the palace steps."

"And what about you, Kyros? That's not water I smell on your breath. And as for flirting and fucking... that's just me, brother; it won't stop when we get to the palace. I'll have that princess folded in half after the first night. Maybe we can share? Split roast her over daddy dearest, while he chokes on his own blood." He smiles wickedly.

"You're sick, you know that?" I respond as I let him go. Standing upright, I tug my tunic on.

"Look, if it makes you feel any better, as soon as the rain lets up, it's back to business. I will get my shit together, and we will head to the palace with no more stops. No more fucking around." He pats me on the chest, and I glare at him. "Until then, though, I plan to have a little fun in our downtime, so fuck off and stay out of my way." He turns on his heel and swaggers back through the door I came.

I grind my teeth and close my eyes, taking several deep breaths to gather myself before I, too, head back into the tavern. With nowhere else to go, I step back into the chaos that it keeps while we wait out the remainder of the storm.

Chapter Eight

Astraea

The stormy daylight filters through the cracks in the shuttered window, casting the hallway in a shadowed blue-gray hue as I follow the woman, who apparently came to *fetch* me. The chill in the air still lingers from the night, where the sun remains hidden behind thick blankets of rain clouds. The bitter chill always sticks around during the desert rains in Eathian.

Though it's morning, by the looks of the tavern, you would never know it. The wooden shutters are pulled tightly closed to keep out the now raging storm. As I descend the stairs, I'm hit with a wall of heat and a plethora of scents. The fire in the center hearth roars alongside the people who are already drinking and rowdy as ever. The air is rancid with the smell of sweat, sizzling meat, and stale ale. I guess there really isn't much else to do while stuck waiting out a monsoon.

My attention is pulled immediately to the far corner of the tavern. A ring of bodies creates a shadow around a halo of light; all the tables and chairs have been moved to form the makeshift fighting circle. It's similar to what I have seen the guards do in the courtyard at the palace—only in much tighter quarters. The men all along the edges are cheering, laughing, and throwing coins at the two shirtless figures in the center.

Both men are covered in dark swirls and swatches of ink. The patterns are so similar but uniquely their own. Their skin gleams in the low light like freshly oiled armor as they round on each other. I recognize them both as the men I have had the *pleasure* of encountering each twice now since running from the palace.

I didn't realize I had stopped. Entranced by their fluid-like movements and the sweat rolling lines down their skin, until the woman who came to fetch me snaps her fingers in front of my nose.

"They are pretty, but pick your jaw up, would you? I'm getting secondhand embarrassment." I blink out of the trance, and she shakes her head with a grimace as she leads me the rest of the way down the narrow stairs. Keeping an eye on me every few steps, her watchful stare causes my insides to swim, and I chew my lip nervously. She claps on the surface of the bar with three loud thumps and a high-pitched whistle, earning an annoyed eye roll from the barmaid. The same stout woman with red hair from last night.

"Keep your whistles for the dogs, or I'll feed your tongue to them!" She calls out as she shakes her head, throwing a dish towel over her shoulder. She serves two tankards to a couple of men whose eyes linger on me and the woman at my side.

"The fuck are you two looking at?" My grumpy new friend barks out, and they quickly avert their gaze into their drinks. "All men are inept at reading a woman." She shakes her head before snapping and pointing at the stool next to her. This snapping at me like *I'm* a dog is going to get old *very* fast. Narrowing my eyes on her, then at the stool, I think about how I want to react. I've never been talked to in this manner. No one would dare risk the king hearing of such disrespect. To do so would be knotting your own noose for the gallows. Taking a calming breath, I sit as she so politely requested with my lips sealed.

"What's your story?" The woman asks as she shifts on her stool while she has me pinned with her eyes. She fiddles with a small knife she pulled from the strap on her chest. The blade is a dark metal, not unlike any other knife, but as she swirls it, I notice the engravings on each side and how the flickering light from the torches catches the blade's serrated edge menacingly. I shift in my seat. Swallowing, I look away from her and back to where the men are sparring.

"I don't have a story." I lie. Almost too easily. I curse internally at the quick response, but I don't think she heard me anyway. She doesn't say anything for a long moment, but then she leans in close to catch my eye, the tip of her knife pointed in my direction.

"Then you better get one." She sheaths the blade back at her breast strap and pats it once for effect. "If you plan on traveling and surviving the kingdom, you need to know your story, and it's best if everyone else knows the story you want told." Something about the way she says it—it's not necessarily a threat, but the caveat is implicated pretty clearly. The barmaid makes her way over to us as the woman makes an order for drinks. The hair on my arms stands on end as I feel a stare burrowing into me from across the room.

I try to feign looking around at all the obnoxious patrons, but I can't look away when my gaze clashes with a man who now sits around the corner at the bar facing me. He swipes the dark tunic in his hand across his brow to wipe away the gathering sweat, and it's only a brief reprieve from his heavy stare and the dark shadows that linger within it.

"What did you do to piss off Kyros?" My attention snaps to the blonde at my side.

"I—What?"

"He's broody on the best of days, but whatever happened this morning has him wound up like a cobra, ready to strike." Her chin juts out toward the other side of the bar, and heat creeps up my neck as my gaze hunts for the man again, but when I look back to the spot he occupied, he's gone. The men who were casting bets on the fight are either sulking as they slap coins and notes into their grinning counterparts' hands or laughing loudly, howling about who will win the next one.

"Maybe he doesn't like the ale much here either." She hitches her pierced eyebrow at my response and looks at me, waiting for me to elaborate, but I am saved from reliving that horror as the barmaid comes over, setting down two tin tumblers. The blonde woman slips a note across the bar, and the woman on the other side huffs with a nod before she turns to walk away.

"Wait!" I call out a little too loudly, immediately curling in on myself. The barmaid lifts a deep red brow at my call as she comes back to where we sit. "Sorry, I was just wondering if there was another room? One I don't have to share?" I look around nervously, leaning forward a hair closer. "I could pay double." I whisper, hoping no one else hears that bit of information.

"Even if you could pay *triple*, I couldn't room you alone, lady. Do you not see this place? It's crawling with souls as stuck as you are. I suggest you either learn to get along or find someone else willing to switch you rooms. Either way, you will have someone bunking with you." I swallow her words down with the bile rising and nod before she dismisses me with a huff.

"Thank you," I rush out to her before she walks away, then lift the rim to my lips and tip it back—*thank the divine it's not that awful ale.* The whiskey burns more than any I have ever had. I guess castle guards have better choices than those this far out in Eathian. My eyes are screwed shut from another sip of the alcohol, as an arm rests across my shoulders and hot breath puffs out on my cheek. I stiffen at the public intimate touch.

"Careful, Princess. That there—will put you on your back if you're not..." His eyes flick over to the blonde. "Thanks for helping out my new friend, Zinny." He winks, and the blonde rolls her eyes.

"How many times have I told you not to call me that?" She grumbles, throwing her head back. She drinks down the rest of what is in the tin before slamming it down on the counter. "I don't know how I'm going to survive being cooped up with all of you. Traveling here was hard enough." Her stool protests loudly as she stands, shaking her head. She storms off and disappears in the now much more crowded tavern, now that more people are waking and coming down for food and to escape the confines of their rooms.

"Don't mind Zinya. She's nicer than she seems." Mav says, nudging me like an old friend would with his elbow. I look down at the contact as my brow furrows. People in the castle never openly touch me so casually, and now Mavros has touched me twice in just minutes. It's an odd feeling and instantly puts me on edge with more worry—the king has killed for less.

Unsure of where to look or what to say, I focus my attention into the bottom of the drink and chew my lip. I can feel Mav looking at me, but I refuse to meet his gaze. I need to blend in... he is loud, and people notice him. Even now I can feel their eyes lingering on us. The talking that Zinya warned about is already starting. My heart runs away with my thoughts, and before I can think better of it, I slam back the gold liquid just like Zinya did. The regret is instant. The burn sears at my sinuses, liquid fire down my throat, and a vat of lava from the pits of Zameil. I have to hold my breath in order to keep in the coughing fit that is slamming its fist at the back of my throat under control.

"Damn, bet that hurt. You don't look like you're one much for drinking, Princess."

"If you don't mind," I bow my head in dismissal and clench my jaw as my voice comes out as a wheeze. Bowing upon leaving was a common occurrence in the castle, but in the bowels of the kingdom, I doubt such reverence was needed. I hope that Mavros doesn't notice. "I'm still feeling very tired. I think I will go rest for a bit." He narrows his eyes on me with a lopsided grin, a loose blonde curl falling over his dark brow, and his nearly silver eyes light with mischief. Already I can tell this man is going to be trouble if I don't get out of his shadow soon.

"You want some company?" He wags his eyebrows as I pin him with a pointed glare, and his laughter follows me as I make my way through the sea of bodies.

"My brother seems curious about you…" I jump at the sound of the gravelly voice that now greets me as I break through the crowd heading for the stairs. Kryros leans against the wooden pillar that frames the stairs' entrance, his wide arms crossed over his equally wide chest. Mavros and Kyros look nothing like siblings. Where Mav has light features and a stealthy, sharp physique, Kyros is the embodiment of darkness, the epitome of brutality, pure and roguish masculinity. His midnight eyes reveal nothing as he stares into me. Penetrating…searching…

"Your brother?" I ask, my gaze swinging to land on the man in question. His eyes are trained on where I stand talking to Kyros.

"He doesn't need a distraction right now." I can't help the face that pulls my lip back.

"Oh, I'm sorry, I didn't realize there was so much to distract from in a tavern waiting out a monsoon. Please don't let me keep you from doing whatever it is that is so prudent." I roll my eyes and stride past him for the stairs. My eyes round as I pass him. The surprise of my own curt tone shocks me. I'm stopped abruptly with large fingers caging around my wrist, and I look down at the contact before looking him in the eyes.

"Who are you?" He asks in a low voice as he pulls me a fraction closer. I can smell the whiskey on his breath, woven with the scents of earth and fire, smoke and honey. My brows dip to match the shadows in his eyes.

"I am no one." I say defiantly, shrugging out of his grip; his hand falls away, and I stomp my way up the narrow stairs. I don't know why his words bothered me so much, but I can't help but look back when I reach the top. Kyros is gone.

I've had time to let the panic fully engulf me. My heart won't slow, the rampant beat making it nearly impossible to lie in bed and sleep. The castle is likely in an uproar, having realized I am not where I am supposed to be. When the rain stops, there will be a new flood. A wave of silver as my father unleashes his battalion.

Staring blankly at the rain-washed desert, my eyes are drawn to the palace that leers over the city on the horizon. I've never seen the castle from this view. From here, even as the heavens open a floodgate while the clouds churn in an angry dance of fury, the flashes of lightning illuminate the pale sandstone walls in stark contrast to the darkened sky; it's a sight to behold. A shiver of dread rolls down my spine as I think of what could be happening within those walls right now—*of Colette.* My leaving undoubtedly has put her in the line of fire from my father's rage.

I force myself away from the window and sit on the mussed up bed. Kicking off my boots, I pull my feet up as I press my back against the low headboard. The heaviness on my mind brings tears to fill my vision as I take in a ragged breath and bite down on my fist to stifle the sob that is trying to escape.

Sinking into the bed, I cover myself with the rumpled blanket and let my tears fall. I let the worry for my only friend chase me into the nightmares I know are waiting once I drift into sleep's embrace. Just like they always do.

Chapter Nine

Astraea

The darkness is eternal... a vast expanse of nothing that swallows me whole. Even though my eyes are peeled wide, I see nothing. It's how they always start. The nightmares that have haunted me for as long as I can remember.

Then, just like every time, the flashes begin.

Bright white light zooms past me at breakneck speed. The blur of motion stretches into one long white streak in my periphery. My body is thrashed at a steady rhythm like the galloping of a horse's hooves. Screams pierce my ears, straight through my brain. Despite digging the heels of my hands against the sides of my head to try and block out the sound, the screeching, pain-filled wail always gets through.

"Stop." My body thrashes more, trying to escape the cries. *"Please stop!"* Heat wraps around me like a vise. A lasso of fire digging into my skin, around my arms, and cuts into my ribs. I can hardly breathe through the tightness. *"Please."* My voice comes out as a wheeze.

The thrashing of my body slows, and just like every other time it does... The shadows consume me again, and the sound of a deep, rumbling laughter follows me into the dark. Nothing else is there, no one but me and the echoing darkness. Its laugh is taunting me with a wicked peal. The tightness that was once wrapped around me, binding me in place—is gone. Replaced by a cold mist against every part of my skin, and as the shivers take over—*I cry.*

"Just go in there and wake her up."

"No way! You know you aren't supposed to wake someone up from a nightmare. You do it." The sound of boots shuffling, a thud, and then the *"OW!"* that follows tells me enough to know I'm no longer in the clutches of the nightmare... I squeeze my eyes tight, trying to pull moisture into them, but even before I force them open, I know there is none to give. *When was the last time I drank water? I groan, rolling to my side.*

"Well, shit, thank the dead divine! She's awake. See, Zinny, all it took was—*OW! Stop hitting me!"* Mavros is in my line of sight now. The huge man, bent at the hip, looks at me with a tilted head, like I am some sort of piece of art he is here to inspect. He's become more lively with each interaction we have, and I have to admit, he makes me feel... something.

"Don't give me a reason to hit you, and I wouldn't have to." Zinya says flatly, her arms crossed over her chest.

"What the fuck did I do?" Mavros whisper-shouts.

"You keep calling me *Zinny*. You know I hate that. Plus, you're just..." Her hand comes out and gestures up and down Mavros' body as he stands and glowers at her. "You..."

"Just me? What does—"

"Uhh, hell. Could you guys please be less loud?" I grumble, having had enough of their raised voices drumming into my brain. Clearing my throat after my sleep-heavy voice cracks, I press my index and middle fingers into the center of my forehead. A futile attempt to stanch the tension building behind my eyes. Another side effect from the dreams... they are especially worse if I am woke early, or if my sleep pattern is off at all. Considering I didn't sleep at all the night before last, last night I slept in an old wooden chair, and now I have fallen asleep during mid-morning... The throbbing that has begun in the center of my skull is likely to only get worse as the day goes on.

"I came in to see if you were alive, and well, you were crying in your sleep." His face twists. "Well, more than crying. You were freaking out. I didn't know what to do. I don't know what to do with all that crying shit. So, I went and got Zin—and that was a mistake because she's even less in tune with her sensitive side than I am, but you're awake now, Princess. You good?" Mav's face is scrunched up like the question hurts him to ask, and I would laugh, but the pain is too much this time. I let my head roll back, eyes straight up to the ceiling.

"I'm alive and awake." Opening my eyes, I'm met with a hand outstretched in front of my face. Mavros has made warming up to him easy. He's not at all the dominant brute I thought at first. Well... dominant and brute, sure, but not together, not with me anyway. So far, I can only consider that to mean luck is at least somewhat on my side.

"Good. It's time for dinner. Turns out we're in luck; musicians were on their way to the castle and stopped here to take cover from the storm too. Dinner comes with a free show."

"Great divine, just what we need," Zinya rolls her eyes and opens the door.

"I've been looking for you two." A deep voice rumbles from the other side of the door, and heat crawls up my neck in response.

"Shit, Ky. Warn a girl before you just pop up out of thin air." Zinya responds, squeezing past him. "We were just making sure the stray eats. Come on, I don't want to eat the bottom of the pot."

"I would really appreciate less animal references..." I say to no one in particular and I am not at all excited about music, with the ache ever growing in my head. Kyros' eyes shift to me, and Mavros pushes his finger onto the tip of my nose.

"Boop, but you are such a cute pet." He smiles devilishly at my glowering response, and I can feel Kyros staring between us. Mavros winks at his brother as he brushes past him, calling for me to follow. Rolling my eyes and letting out a sigh, I too, walk past Kyros. He says nothing, but his brow dips low as my arm brushes his while walking through the doorway.

The whole way down to the tavern, I feel Kyros at my back like a roaring fire licking the walls of a hearth. He surprises me when we do reach where the food is being served and guides me away from the others with a press of his hand to the small of my back.

"This way." He growls, much closer than I thought.

"We can just sit at the bar," I start to refuse, but he urges me forward.

"Mavros and Zinya will bring the food to us here." His arm sweeps out in front of him as we reach the corner of the tavern. Close to the same corner he and Mav were fighting in. The booth he gestured to is tucked into the shadowy corner. High backs on each side close off the table like its own shadowy cave, but two cream candles sit on a silver platter. Both with overflowing wax pools dripping along the sides. They light the booth in its own amber globe.

Hesitantly, I sit down, scooting to the far wall. Kyros stands there for a moment, and after looking over his shoulder, he slips into the booth right next to me. I keep my eyes down, watching the flame of the candles dance even though I can feel his eyes on me.

"My brother is here for a reason. He can't be distracted. Once the rain stops, you have to be on your way." I flinch at his words, and my thigh brushes his as I turn to look up at him. The hope I had held onto that they were traveling and only stopped here because of the storm, the hope that when they resumed travels I could come with them, fully dissolved with the look on his face.

The stern look, casting more shadows over his face, gives no room for argument. I nod.

He stiffens, looking down at the contact of our legs, and I quickly scoot away, wrapping my arms around myself and looking past him to where Mavros and Zinya carry trays with food and drinks toward the table.

"I never meant to be a distraction to anyone. I was forced to share a room with him. The storm—" I shake my head. "Our paths never would have crossed without it. As soon as the rain stops, I'll be leaving Eathian. No one here will ever see me again." Silence follows my declaration, and chills roll over my scalp, causing my stomach to sway. Unease over my future is really beginning to sink in. Before, I was energized by adrenaline from leaving the castle; now, though, I have had time to let the unknown fully engulf me in its heaviness. The thought makes my palms sweat and pulse race.

"It's no feast, but the alcohol will make it taste like a god's divine decadence." Mavros grins and winks as he places the food down. "Well, don't you two look cozy?" He slides into the booth opposite me, and Zinya next to him. She looks between me and Kyros with narrowed eyes and takes a drink from her tumbler with her eyes trained on me. Her attention feels more intimidating than either of the men.

"Thank you for the food." I say, passing a few coins to the center of the table. Every one of their eyes follows the movement.

"You don't have to pay for the food. I've got you, Princess." Mavros says as he wraps his mouth around a huge bite from his spoon.

"Consider it a parting gift." Kyros says under his breath, but the others hear him just fine.

"Why don't I take this upstairs and just eat there? You guys can do whatever it is you do, and I will be out of your hair. The rain can't last much longer." I say, looking toward the shuttered window where the wind whistles through the cracks.

"Don't be ridiculous. The music is just about to start." Mavros points to the center of the tavern, where a band is setting up to play their string and drum instruments. "Plus, we're drinking tonight!" He brings his tankard up to the center of the table, Zinya follows suit, and after a look from her, Kyros lifts his tumbler also.

"Come on, princess, consider this my last who-rah. Once we leave this tavern, I will be on my way to win over a grumpy old goat." A thump sounds, and Mavros jumps with an ow. "What was that for?" He looks at Kyros with a frown, pulling his mouth down at the corners. Kyros pulls his tumbler back, taking a drink before everyone says salute.

"We don't need to discuss what we are here for." Kyros growls, but if he thinks that is a deterrent, he's utterly mistaken. Now I am all the more curious.

"Why *are* you here?" I say, lifting my cup. It clinks with Mavros' and he smiles before pulling in a long drink. I do the same.

"It's not up for discussion." Kyros looks away from me, and I pin him with my eyes. Mavros laughs loudly, and Zinya just tilts her head. I don't like the way she's looking at me. Perhaps she recognizes me.

"Bottoms up, princess. Once the music starts, we're dancing." Mavros says, and my face contorts.

"I am not dancing."

"Oh, you're dancing alright." He argues with a raised brow. I'd have to have a lot more to drink if he thinks I am going to just start dancing in a tavern. The thought sparks an idea, and I smile.

"Why don't we play a drinking game?" It's one that I've played in the past when Colette and I have entertained some of the more *daring* guards in secret. They were literally risking their lives if they were caught. Colette too.

"Ohhh, I like the sounds of this." Zinya laughs, leaning back against the backrest.

"I don't." Kyros growls again.

"What's the game?" Marvos asks, leaning in and pointedly ignoring his brother. Just as he does, the musicians start playing an exciting tune, and everyone in the tavern beyond our booth takes to their feet and cheers for the entertainers.

"I'll start…" I shout, leaning in too so everyone hears me over the chaos. I toss the coin, bouncing it off the table and into Kyros cup that sits in front of him, making the golden liquid splash over the edge and onto the table. His eyes slowly turn to meet mine in a glower. I make a face at him with a dare in my eyes. "If the thrower makes it, everyone else drinks. If the thrower misses, they have to drink and answer a question. After one turn, we switch. If you're ready to play… take a drink. I made the first coin."

"I didn't think you had mettle, but I'll accept when I'm wrong. I'll go get more drinks. I think we are going to need them." Zinya slaps her hand down on the table and takes a quick drink before laughing and disappearing into the crowd of bodies.

Kyros scoffs as Mavros leans over and pulls the cup to the center of the table, fishing out the coin. He winks before he tosses it. The small silver disc bounces off the rim and lands back on the table with a wobble, and he grins up at me mischievously before his eyes dance to meet his brothers.

"Do your worst, Princess," Mavros whispers just as Zinya returns with pitchers of what looks like the raunchy ale. I wrinkle my nose at it but press forward and ask my question.

"What are you in Eathian for?" I'm immediately growled at by the man next to me. Like he is some sort of beast in the night, wild and rabid.

"No." He says, pinning Mavros with a look.

"Oh, come now... Have a little faith, brother..." Mavros responds cockily; he hooks a finger, calling me forward, and I lean in for the secret, but he doesn't whisper. His voice isn't a yell, but it's loud enough that our table hears him clearly.

"We're here to revive magick to what it once was and will kill anyone who gets in the way of stopping us." He wags his eyebrows at me and bites his lip. Another growl rattles out, sending shivers down my spine, and Mavros busts up laughing as Kyros pushes from the table.

"Can you not take anything seriously, ever? Fuck, Mavros!" He turns on his heel and storms away, creating a divide in the bodies as he pushes through the crowd. Zinya doesn't say anything but does lift her eyebrows, looking down into her drink as she takes a long pull and looks at me over the rim as she presses her lips together.

Unfazed by the outburst, Mavros slaps Zinya on the back and slides the coin to her.

"You're up, Zinny." She looks side long at him before rolling her eyes.

"Oh joy," Zinya coughs with a smile on her face, but I tune out of their back and forth as my eyes hunt for the man who seems to hate my very existence.

Chapter Ten

Astraea

I can count the number of times I've been drunk on one hand. I had to be careful living under my father's thumb. The princess could be called on at any moment. He hardly ever left the castle long enough for me to have true reprieve from him. I think it was his cowardice that has kept him cooped up in the palace since he took it. Always afraid that someone else would swoop in and steal it away, just like he did. Tonight, though, I'm pretty sure I am the most inebriated I have *ever* been. The room is beginning to spin, and my eyes don't want to stay open. I have to stare at my tumbler, still half full of the amber liquid, with one eye closed for there to be only one.

Mavros and Zinya invited a couple of other women over to the booth we were sharing and have been otherwise tied up. I've never seen such a display in person before. Though some of the guards were pretty boisterous about their nights in the city when they weren't on duty. Their stories could have never painted the picture I see now, though.

They are like a coil of snakes intertwined around each other's bodies. Mavros is at the center of all the women as their hands seek skin at every opportunity. Heat climbs the back of my neck as I risk a glance and see Zinya shove her tongue down a busty blonde's throat and, at the same time, slip her hand under the waistband of Mavros's trousers.

I moved to the bar pretty quickly after that all started, and I've silently kept drinking my weight in alcohol. The awful ale even tastes better. All the while, I know Kyros has been watching me from the other corner in the tavern. His steady gaze causing more heat to creep into my cheeks. *Did he see me watching them?*

"You look like you might be done for the night." The barmaid surprises me as she reaches for my cup. I quickly recover and plop my hand over the rim and level her with a look that says *I'm not done.* She quirks an eyebrow. "You better not throw chunks on my floors, girl. I'll have you on your hands and knees cleaning it up yourself." Her sharp tongue makes me slap my hand over my lips to keep the drink I just took in my mouth. Once I swallow down the liquid that is now burning my sinuses, I smile, and she shakes her head.

"What's your name? I think I like you." I hiccup.

"Girl, you need to rest. Go get some sleep." She responds and I snort, but she holds me in her gaze waiting...

"There is no rest in sleep—only the monsters we keep hidden while awake." I say, taking the last drink from my tumbler and sliding the empty cup toward her. "Thank you." I clumsily place a coin next to it.

"My name is Ruby," she says with her brows furrowed.

"Did your parents name you that before or after they knew you had all that red hair?" My question makes her smirk then.

"If I ever find out who they are, maybe I'll ask them." She responds. *I want to crawl into a hole.* I stand up and smile sheepishly before muttering *'thanks'* again and turning away.

"Hey, girl?" I turn back to face her as she is wiping the bar down with a wet towel. "Sometimes the demons we keep hidden in the deepest parts of ourselves are the ones who can hurt us most when they finally come to the light, but ever so often, even nightmares aren't all that they seem." She stares at me for a moment, her hazel eyes penetrating, then she nods as though she's satisfied I understand and turns away.

The whole conversation is unsettling, and suddenly, I feel too many eyes on me. Chewing on my lip, I stumble my way through the lingering people still remaining in the tavern and shuffle slowly up the stairs. It's when I reach the top I notice the presence behind me. I speed up, trying to put distance between myself and whoever is behind me, and stop short, just before reaching the door to the room when he speaks up, far closer than I thought.

"I saw you at the bar. You're quite the lonely thing, aren't you?" A man, whom I've never seen before, now leers over me. I press my body against the wall, trying to create space between us without success. He slowly closes the distance, and I turn my face away from him.

"My friend is waiting for me just inside my room." I lie. *Where is Mavros? Would he come if I screamed? It was him, after all, who warned me screams wouldn't get me the help I wanted when it was him leering over me.*

"Oh?" He questions, the scent of stale clothing and ale wafting to me as he leans in closer, "Is that so? Then perhaps we go to *my* room?" He grabs for my hips at the same moment I spin to run down the hall toward the room Mavros and I were sharing, but the man reaches out, grabbing onto the straps of the holster that Zinya insisted I wear. *Damn holster!* He pins my face to the wall with one hand on the back of my head, while the other trails down my body in an eager conquest, all the while my protests are being ignored. I'm too shocked to scream. My voice is lost to panic as he continues to tug and pull at my body and clothes. The pressure at which he pins me to the wall is painful, and a muffled cry comes from my lips. Then suddenly he's yanked from me. My breath catches in my throat as I turn to see Kyros move through the hall like a wraith. He prowls over to where he has thrown the man to his ass.

"She said no. If you touch her again…" His low, gravelly voice trails off, but even without finishing the sentence, it threatens violence; the louring darkness clouds his face in a promise of pain. The man doesn't even take a second look in my direction. He scrambles to his feet, keeping his eyes fixed on Kyros and slowly backing away.

"Understood," he stammers, but before he continues, Kyros grabs him by the front of his tunic, balling the material in his fist, and pulls him close to his face. All the while, I am bent at the waist, trying to catch my breath, simultaneously trying to keep the contents of my stomach from spilling to the floor.

"If I *ever* find that you try to force yourself on her... or anyone again," he breathes the words through clenched teeth, "I will let rats feed between your legs while I hold you down and make you watch yourself become a eunuch." He shoves him away. The man nearly falls down the stairs as he struggles to find purchase on trembling legs. When Kyros turns back to face me, his eyes are like glittering onyx in the dark. Only reflecting glimmers of moonlight coming from cracks in the shuttered window.

"Are you hurt?" He reaches out for me, then makes a face at his hand before pulling it back stiffly. "You need to get yourself to bed. You have a way of running into trouble." He says, standing back to his full height, and I scoff.

"Clearly." I say, tugging at the boned vest I've borrowed. I sway on my feet, but before I fall flat on my face, Kyros' hands catch me, and I steady myself with one hand on his chest. His large hand is like a heated weight on my lower back, and the stark difference between the other man and his touches has a shiver rolling down my spine. "Who's going to save me from you?" The question wasn't meant to be said out loud, but I can't take it back now. His brows thread so tightly I fear what he is going to say in response, but then he surprises me by helping me find my footing. His hands linger on my arm, just above my elbow. He is so close I can feel his breath blowing the fine hairs away from my face. The scent of sweet honey and the bitter tang of fire and smoke engulf me and take my breath from my lungs. *Gods divine, why does this man smell so good?*

"If it were me in his place, *no one*, not even the divine, could save you. But you would not be protesting my touch. You would be *begging* for it..." He growls, and when he takes a step back, letting go of me, I nearly whimper. Not only his words, but also the confusing heat that they created in my core.

He stalks down the hall toward the door that leads to the room Mavros and I have been given but stills as his hand hovers over the lever. A rumble builds in his throat as he turns to face me.

"It seems my brother is entertaining an audience tonight... if you don't wish to join them, you can follow me." He sighs and continues down the hall, not waiting for me to choose. As I near the door he was standing in front of, I hear all sorts of noises I wish I hadn't, and I no longer question sharing a room with the man who just saved me from being defiled.

He opens a door a little further down the hall and waits for me. As I enter, I look around at the neat space and the cold hearth. The chill from the wet desert rain has fully encroached the dark space.

"I'll leave you to get settled after I build a fire," Kyros says, pointedly ignoring me where I stand behind him, and he starts doing just that. He doesn't so much as glance my way as he works. His movements cause me to watch his hands. Long fingers grasp the wood, and he carefully places it into the heart of the hearth before he reaches to the mantle. I watch transfixed as his muscles flex and pull taut by the movements, and I recall the shirtless sparring session between him and Mavros earlier. When he strikes the flint, casting sparks to flit over the kindling, it quickly catches fire, illuminating his face with its amber glow. I'm entranced by his every movement. I don't realize I've moved closer until he stands to his full height. He's very tall, easily a head taller than me, and I have to look up to meet his gaze.

"Thank you," I say, and he nods as our bodies seem to gravitate toward one another. *Or maybe it's just me?* His throat works on a swallow, and I watch the motion with rapt attention. Being this close to a man such as Kyros is like standing too close to a fire. My entire body wants to rear back from the heat, but my curious mind wants to reach out and touch him to see if I'd burn.

"It was nothing, just a fire," he says, and I watch as the flames dance in the reflection of his black eyes. It's mesmerizing. My eyes grow heavier the longer I stand here, and I can't tell if it's the alcohol or the proximity to the man in front of me, but my courage swells.

"Not the fire. You stepped in and saved me from that man's advances. I'm not sure what would have happened if you hadn't been there." My hand comes between us and just as I am about to lay it on the center of his chest; his fingers wrap around my wrist. It's not a painful grip, just tight enough to stop contact over his heart.

"I'm not a man who sets out to save innocent women. Don't look for something like that in me. You won't like what you find." He says, and though his words are a growl, his eyes say something else entirely. He takes a step backward and lets our hands fall between our bodies.

"I'm not just an innocent woman looking to be saved, Kyros. Sometimes people fight silent battles, but that doesn't mean that they are any less of a warrior." He stares at me for a long moment, with the door cracked open and one hand on the lever. Contemplating my words, a frown takes over his face before he tilts his chin down and speaks.

"Get some sleep, Shula." Kyros finally says, dejected. I can't do anything but stare with my lips parted as he walks from the room.

Chapter Eleven

Kyros

As the flimsy wood door clicks shut behind me, my muscles grow even more taut with tension, as does the clench of my jaw. I may not be a man who sets out to save innocent women, but I am a man who prides himself on his control. Control that the woman in that room just nearly took from me without even knowing.

I take a deep, steadying breath, building up the control that I had felt slipping away like water through my fingers, water the color of her ocean blue eyes. The moment she would have touched me, I would have ruined her. Even now, I can't get the image of her face from my head. Closing my eyes, I pull another lung full of air and then blow it out evenly. *I need to get out of this damn tavern.*

I take my time heading back downstairs; I can't be in the bed-chamber with—*her*. I'm frustrated and distracted when Zinya comes down the stairs and sits heavily into the seat in front of me and my half-drunk bottle of whiskey.

"Can't sleep either?" She questions pouring a measure of the alcohol into the tumbler I opted not to use when I asked for the bottle.

"For very different reasons, I'm sure." I say, taking in her pink cheeks and glowing skin. She and Mavros have had a thing for years. They share lovers, but neither will admit that they are ultimately made for each other. They compliment each other on tasks, in battle, and in any given situation. Sometimes it's subtle when the match is lit and the flame catches, but eventually the fire grows and it's impossible to deny. Other times when the fire catches, it threatens to burn the life you know to the ground and take everything you think you know about the world with it...

"Where's the girl?" She questions, and I blink up at her. It's been hours since I left her in the room that was meant to be mine. It has to be the early morning hours now, and while I need to sleep eventually, I can't bring myself to go back in there with her.

"Hopefully sleeping." I say with a grunt and then take a swig from the bottle. "She is trouble, Zinya. You need to keep Mavros away from her."

"I don't *keep* Mav from anything, and you know it. I wouldn't worry too much; she doesn't seem interested in *him*." She quirks her brow at me, wanting a reaction.

"I'm not worried about what she's interested in. I worry about Mavros. This job is important; it's why we have such a large group—the best of the guild. Yet, he's treating it like every other task. He can't be distracted. Not on this one. Distraction in Eathian means death, Zinya. You know that." I tell her, and she rolls her lips and smiles close-lipped into her tumbler, then takes a drink of whiskey with a shrug.

"Even so, you, of all people, need to trust that when it comes down to it, he will do the right thing. He might be full of shit right now... but you know as well as me, once we are in front of King Connard, he will put on the show he is meant to. We all will." Her brows pinch as she continues to stare at me, then she stands and shakes her head. "Try to relax a little while you can, Ky."

"Will you go check on her? The girl?" I don't know why I ask, but I also haven't seen that asshole Leoric in a while either. Hopefully he's passed out in a puddle of his own vomit.

"The distraction? Yeah, Ky. I'll go check on her." Her gaze lingers with mine for a moment, making me question myself more than I ever have, but when she turns away, the only thing that brings me back down is the anger I have for King Connard and how very soon I will be face-to-face with the dickhead.

Leoric passes Zinya as she heads up the stairs, and I grind my teeth as he makes eyes at her suggestively. *Guess he's not dead... yet.* I have no doubt that she can handle the asshole herself, but I still need to deal with what he did in the hallway upstairs. He's drunk; I can see it in his eyes and the way he sways while standing still, but regardless, my men won't behave as he did without punishment.

Zinya scoffs, telling him where to shove it, and saunters up the stairs to check on the woman sleeping in my bed. With any luck, this will be the last night we have to stay in this damn tavern, and we can be on our separate ways, but with a peek out of the shuttered window, I doubt my own thoughts.

Leoric notices me sitting in the shadows of the corner of the room and gives me a wide berth. Little good it will do him, though. I stand up, and he freezes when he notices my trajectory.

"Leoric, I think you can imagine why I am coming to chat with you..." I say, clamping down on his shoulder.

"I—I didn't know," he stammers, looking up at me with round, bloodshot eyes. The brown nearly blends with the deep red in the shadows.

"You didn't know that you were forcing yourself on a woman that just said no to your advance? No, I don't think that's what you're saying at all. Do you wanna know what I think, Leo?" I bend down so I can whisper in his ear. "I think you just didn't know that you'd been caught. You would have taken her right there in the hallway, wouldn't you have?" Each word, I let leak with malice.

He's trembling under my grip, his eyes even rounder than before. I've never liked this asshole. He is an ass kisser and smells like he's bathed in onion soup that's been left out for days in the cruel desert sun. If he wasn't one of the best dune guides, he wouldn't be here at all. That and the fact that I can't rend a portal anywhere in the contested kingdom of Eathian without it bringing unwanted attention. Had I done that, this mission would have ended the moment it began. No magick usage and all that bullshit.

Instead, we had to let this asshole guide us from Diemos through the dunes. His magick is powered by the stars, and whether it is day or night, he would be able to find his way through. Unlucky for him, he isn't the only one that has that ability, and Queen Phaedra won't blink twice when I tell her about his untimely demise.

"You know I wouldn't mess with someone you've claimed. I—" His words are cut off as I pick him up by his throat and slam him against the wall that I have backed us up to.

"Claim or not, you will not mess with someone who is clearly not interested in your vile touch." I hiss through bared teeth. He shakes his head, but I don't release him. *Claimed?* I let his feet scramble to find just the tips of his toes to relieve some of the pressure that is surely building behind his eyes with the lack of oxygen to his brain. My grip is unrelenting as I lean in close to his ear and whisper to him. "There is a special place in Zameil for people like you. The ones that use their power difference to make the world an uglier place. The ones who aim to break what is not yet broken. I have sent many men just like you to burn there. You know what the difference is?" I ask him.

"MmmMMmM," He shakes his head trying to speak, but while his lips turn white and his face a deep mulberry, he isn't able to get any words but a hum out of his mouth.

"Oh, don't worry. I'm going to tell you." I smile, but it's laced with venom. "We usually aren't on the same team when I snap their necks." His eyes bulge, and he thrashes, trying for his life to get away from me, but he and I both know there is no use. Once I have my mind made up on a target, it's only a matter of time before I meet my mark.

I lean back and look into his round eyes; my smile now faded, and shadows are dancing in my eyes. He begins convulsing with the lack of air to his lungs; his chest jumps with need as his body realizes he is on the brink of death, but he won't take another breath. Reaching up with the other hand, I wrench his head to the side with a quick snap. His eyes fix over my shoulder, and his body stops its fight as his soul leaves this plane and moves on to the next.

"Well, fuck, I thought we needed to keep on task?" Mavros says, coming up behind me as I drop Leoric to the ground with a heavy thump.

"I don't need to hear your shit, Mavros. Since you are here, grab his feet." I tell him, jerking my chin out in the direction of the corpse at my feet. He purses his lips as he shakes his head but still bends down to lift Leo by his ankles. I hook my arms under his shoulders, and we take him to the room he was supposed to be sleeping in. His bunk partner must be with someone else tonight because the room is empty. It doesn't surprise me; most of the team we brought will mostly always revert to finding a body to fuck after they have exhausted all the food and fighting... Mav drops his feet a little too early before tossing him on the bed and laughs when his body falls to the floor instead. I give him a sidelong look.

"Stop fucking around. Get him onto the bed so we can get out of here. I don't need anyone asking questions."

"You didn't seem too worried about questions when you killed the fucker in the middle of a damn tavern... Any one of those drunkards could have seen you." Mav says. He has a point, but in the heat of the moment, I only saw his hands where they shouldn't have been.

"They didn't. I'm not fucking stupid, Mavros." I growl, shoving the asshole as I move past him, and he laughs.

"What did he do to cause you to lose your shit?"

"I didn't lose my shit."

"You killed a man who was our guide, in the middle of a tavern in Eathian, on the way to meet the king and court his daughter while on what you call the most important mission we have yet to face... I think it's a pretty fair assessment to say, you lost your fucking shit." He tilts his head as he says it, looking back at the body behind me.

"Don't worry about it. It's taken care of now." I bark in response.

"Sure, whatever you say, brother." He claps me on the back as we step into the hall. Zinya is coming from the room I left the *distraction* in...

"Good, I was just coming to look for you." She says as she sees us. "The girl is having some pretty lucid nightmares." Her eyes catch on mine. "The room almost feels charged..." She looks between Mavros and me, and I grind my teeth. *Great.*

Chapter Twelve

Astraea

Everything that has happened since the moment I decided I'd leave the castle has played on repeat in my head since I laid my head down on Kyros' pillow. The scent of him on the sheets has tried hard to distract me enough to, at the very least, keep the nightmares at bay for a while. But right now, the thought alone is enough to be debilitating. It's not a new feeling, but one I should be used to by now. Every time I'm alone, especially in the dark of night when I lay in bed... as my mind wanders the line between sleep and awake, I know the nightmares are waiting to reveal themselves.

Dark whispers call me toward sleep, an echo of words I don't understand, but the feeling they leave imprinted on me will likely never leave my soul. The shadows envelop me, and the rumbling hoofbeats beneath me begin. The same as they always do. My body is thrashed. Even in my sleep state, I can sense the sweat building on my unconscious body. The white flashing and screaming cut through my mind like razor-sharp teeth, and the pain causes me to try to break free of its clutches, but without fail, I never can.

Thrashing continues as the laughter and wailing chase me. The lasso of pain erupts through my center. Liquid fire pumping through my veins, then I hear something new: a voice far in the distance I cannot make out. My head swivels as I spin, looking for who or what it is coming from. I can't understand the words; they are too muffled. Unclear.

I try to speak, to call back to what I feel is calling to me, but nothing comes from my mouth. My throat feels as though it is filled with the sands of the Dead Sea, both hot and dry like the burned coals of a fire. I want to wake up, but I can't. My heart races with my adrenaline at the feeling of claws wrapping around my arm, just below my shoulder, but I am stuck in a chaotic psychomachy. I need to know what is calling me and compelling me to turn and face the darkness that nearly has its claws sunk into my soul.

My eyes fly open with a gasp filling my lungs as the dark blanches in a flare of light.

"Woah, easy." A large hand presses me down when I try to sit up. It's a gentle press, warm, but my arm aches where it rests. "You're ok. It was just a night terror." *A night terror.* It's what everyone has called them. Well, anyone who has witnessed a glimpse of what is now my nightly routine. Some nights are worse than others, and this was one of the bad ones. Even as I slowly peel my eyes open, I can feel the lingering terror in my bones, crawling across my skin, slithering through my mind.

At first I can't make out the face that the hand belongs to. A dark silhouette is staring down at me, but as my mind comes around to the present, I notice the long hair loose from its tie and the wide shoulders the ends brush. Slowly, his face loses its blur of sleep, and I see the man who resembles a dark god reborn.

"Zinya called for me when your thrashing became worrisome," Kyros says as he removes his hand and stands at the bedside. Zinya comes to his side then and offers me a tankard. My mouth immediately waters as my stomach drops thinking of the alcohol I consumed too much of. Then flashes of what happened when I tried to come to bed. The realization of who stands before me and the embarrassment floods my senses; crimson heat rises from my chest and blooms feverishly in my cheeks.

"Do you always sleep all day, Princess? I'm starting to wonder if you are a princess at all or a creature of the night. A vampire here to suck the life from the kingdom." Mavros laughs, and Kyros levels him with a glare.

"It's just water. You need to drink... heard you were a bit—"

"Wasted." Mavros interrupts Zinya's laughter. The throb between my eyes starts its nagging pulse as it always does after my nightmares, and I squeeze my eyes shut trying to force it away. I know it's futile, but every day, time and time again, I try.

"You two go busy yourselves. I'll be down after I gather some things." Kyros says quietly, and I peek through my lashes to see him still staring at me. As though I am a puzzle he is trying to piece together. I don't like the attention he has had on me. All last night he watched me. I can't have him or anyone else realize who I really am.

"Sienna, just... drink the water, ok?" Zinya says with more kindness than I have heard from her, and it both surprises and hurts me. If she is offering me true friendship, I have already ruined it by giving her the false name. I can't respond yet with words, so I nod. Sitting up, I take the tankard with both hands. Mavros laughs again, strolling from the room, but Zinya pauses at the door, looking between me and Kyros with an indecipherable look crossing her face.

"Go, Zinya. *Leave it.*" Kyros says without looking at her, causing my brows to drop a fraction in confusion. She takes a deep breath in through her nose and blows it out her cheeks.

"If you say so." She returns, glancing between us once more before snapping the door shut, leaving Kyros and me alone. Every concern I have over the man looking down at me, the two people who just left the room, and the impending doom that is the journey that I face in the future comes to an abrupt halt as my ears finally pick up on what is *missing*. My eyes widen at the sudden realization the lack of sound could mean.

"Did the rain—" My voice trails off as I continue to listen for the telltale puttering on the clay roof, the rolling thunder across the sandy terrain outside, and the tumult of inconvenience in the tavern downstairs.

"It stopped nearly an hour ago." Kyros says, watching me with an overly keen eye, and my heart stops. "You know, I don't think I ever asked. Where are you headed?" *Where am I headed? Where am I headed?* The question replays over and over. Without answering, I throw the blanket from my body and rush to the only window in the small room. My head swims at the sudden movement, and my heart sinks further; buried deep, the thump in my chest ceases to exist when my eyes fall on the sight below me.

"Shula?" Kyros says, crossing the room to stand by my side. "It'll be a little while before the sands—" His words stop short when he sees what has me in a stupor.

My father's battalion lines the mud-heavy streets, and the sun crests the horizon as the night settles over the kingdom, but the darkness is lit by a never-ending sea of fire. Torches glint off the silver armor as they move through the city.

"What is *that* about?" Kyros asks under his breath. I risk a glance at him out of the corner of my eye; his brow is dipped low, pulled down by the frown overtaking his face.

"I have to go." I rip myself away from the window and rush to the door. Tripping over my boots, I curse. Snatching them up by the laces, I wrench the door open. Mavros stands in front of the room I need to go into, and I pay him no mind as I dip under his arm and run in to swipe my dress off the chaise.

"Princess?" Mavros says, confused.

"Did he do something?" Zinya asks as she pushes past Mavros to come in. Before she can enter, though, I slam my body into the wood. The door latches between us.

"He didn't do anything. Just—give me a second." I call out. I have to get changed and leave this place. I have to get away before they catch up to me. All of these people here are now at risk because of me. If they catch me with them, they will all just be more skeletons in my closet.

Stripping off the borrowed clothing, I step into the dress, and just as I pull the fabric to cover my shoulder, the door bursts open, and Mavros, Kyros, and Zinya storm in. Their faces are all an array of questions I need to avoid.

"Did I just miss you naked?" Mavros groans, and Zinya hits him with the back of her hand across his chest. "Stop. Hitting. Me." He growls at her with a wicked smile. Kyros is silent, watching me as usual, but now his eyes keep flicking over my shoulder, out the window, and to the damn army that is hunting me down. Their metal clangs loud with each stomp of the feet, the sound alone alerting the people of Eathian that there is hell to pay if anyone is to stand in their way. *Shit. Shit. Shit.*

I ignore Kyros' gaze and Mavros and Zinya's back-and-forth bickering, thanking the divine that my dress is nearly dry. Only the thickest areas across the waist and the bottom of the skirts are still damp. I skirt the other two people in the room and yank the cloak from the hook on the wall, not wasting any time. I throw it over my shoulders and rip open the door, ready to make my run for it.

I don't know where I'm going to go, but anywhere has to be better than in the direct path of my father's men. I don't make it far, though. As I run from the room, I'm caught by the tail of my cloak, falling backward from the momentum of being yanked back. I land on my back, eyes round with shock, and my breath is knocked from my lungs. Kyros stands over me with a furious glint in his dark eyes.

"Do you want to explain why you are running from the king's guard?" He growls, his hands balling at his sides. I cough as I suck air back into my lungs, and he releases my cloak from under his foot with a huff and lets me get up on my own. Mavros and Zinya come barreling out of the door after him. Everything is now happening so fast. If I wasn't already dizzy, I would be now. I meet their eyes and shake my head.

"I'm so sorry," I say before turning around and sprinting. As I round the corner at the top of the stairs, there is a blockade of bodies congesting the only exit. My teeth grind with frustration, and I close my eyes, pulling in a steadying breath. Then I hear Kyros' rumbling voice calling after me and ordering Mavros and Zinya to find me.

"That is not going to happen." I whisper, pushing my body into the mass of people and finding my way to the exit. When I finally push through, it's Ruby I come toe-to-toe with.

"No one can leave, girl. The king's guard has issued a sojourn edict. No one leaves." Her words are pleading, and as I look to the side, I see two men closing in on the exit. Her muscle.

"I *am* leaving, Ruby. Either you let me go…" My words trail off, but she narrows her eyes on me. The threat is easily read with what I'm not saying. She looks behind me and then to the side where her men approach.

"I can't let them all see me just *let* you go. It will be my death, and you know it." She says under her breath, a secret and a plan passing between the two of us. She keeps her eyes flicking around the room. I nod in understanding.

"Then I'm sorry for this." Her eyebrow twitches, but she nods the slightest before I shove her hard enough to make her fall. She curses loudly, and chaos breaks out behind me as I run from the tavern. My boots sink into the waterlogged sand and squelch with every lift of my legs. I will get away. I'll save these people from the deaths that await them if I am caught under their hold, and I will save myself from the wrath of my father.

Chapter Thirteen

Astraea

The streets are no longer hard-packed but instead boggy. Each step I take is difficult, and soon after stepping foot out of the tavern, the bottom of my dress is once again weighed down with moisture. *Maybe I should have left the warrior's clothing on from Zinya. They would be looking for me in a dress, not pants and a leather holster. But with a sojourn edict, I guess it wouldn't matter either way.*

Silence fills the air around me, apart from the sand as it squeaks under my weight. The water pools with each step around my booted feet. I do the best I can to stick to the dry areas that line the structures and under awnings that have stayed through the storm, but no matter how hard I try, I can't keep my lower half from absorbing too much water. The weight of it causes my trek to be that much harder. By the time I reach only a few blocks, I'm not only covered in the rain muck but also have a layer of sweat causing my hair to stick to my neck and face.

I don't know where I'm going, or if I'm even heading in the right direction. I curse myself for not knowing more about my own kingdom outside of the palace walls, but I can't be faulted entirely. My father has made doing so nearly impossible, and by only seeing what I have, I understand why. He would have known my reaction. He would have sensed the headache I would have given him over the state our people were living in, damn the consequences. It is unjust and inhumane to allow people to suffer as they are. There are plenty of jobs that could be given and voyages that could be made in order to allow the land to flourish.

It wouldn't be like this if he would allow magick once again. Before magick was the fruit of the realms. People traveled to and from all sorts of lands, and the monsters that dwell in the crevasses of disrepair didn't seek out the souls of the innocent. The magick fed the land, and the land fed the people and its creatures.

Firelight flashes out of the corner of my eye, and I stop dead in my tracks. I am the only one out on the streets right now, save the soldiers who have been tasked to hunt me. If they catch me now, there will be no leaving the castle ever again. I will be kept prisoner even more than I was before. Trying with everything I have in me to be stealthy, I pray to whatever divine entity that will listen. *Please let me get away. Let me be unseen.*

I run as fast as the sodden sand will allow to the closest shadowy alcove. A pair of brown eyes look out at me from one of the shuttered windows. The boy is small, likely less than ten years old. With slow movements I lift my finger to my lips. A plea for him to keep quiet, and I suck in ragged breaths as I try to think of where to go next. My only option for leaving was with a convoy through the Dead Sea, but now I'm not sure that is an option. The port is probably as abandoned as the streets of Eathian right now.

"Movement!" A man calls out. "Eastern flank, sweep!" *Shit. Shit. Shit.* My mind scrambles as I try to think of what to do next. There is nothing. *You are an animal. Caught prey—the hunter is just waiting for you to come out of the shadows to make the killing blow.* I see guards coming from both directions in the narrow alleyway I'm hiding in. There is a blocked path hidden by a cart where goods are sold right in the center. I'm close to it. If I can be quick, I can get past them and into the next alley, but if there is another guard that way... I grind my teeth and shake my head. *No questioning this.* I sprint. The movement catches the attention of the guard behind me.

"Stop! There is a sojourn edict, and you are in direct violation!" The guard bellows. Each one of their heavy armor-clad stomps squelch in the wet sand, but they are not quick. Their armor only serves to slow them down. Our movements are not the same, despite me being held back by this soggy dress. I am faster and more capable of maneuvering in tight places.

My eyes snag on the small opening under the cart that I can slip through and into the back alleyway without them being able to easily catch up. They will have to move the cart to get to me. This is my only chance. I slide to my knees, landing heavily on the palms of my hands. The sand cuts into the soft flesh like tiny shards of glass on my delicate skin, and I wince, but I cannot afford to slow. I shuffle under the cart, all the while pulling at my heavy dress, now leaden with sand and water.

A wide smile spreads across my face as I make it to the other side. I can't help but feel a little pride as I pull myself upright with a satisfied laugh. The triumphant celebration is cut short, though, as I'm met with the cold bite of metal gauntlets wrapping around my upper arms. I guess the gods are *not* on my side today. A choked gasp comes from my mouth as the guard spins me in his arms and my eyes round.

"Kellan?" My voice trembles with my lip. Maybe he will let me go. He knows the terrors that my father puts me through. He knows...

"Princess Astraea," His eyes bore into me, pleading—sorry even. I realize why when they flick over my head. We are not alone. No matter if he wanted to help me get away, his hands are tied now. He will obey my father's rule. My body sags as the reality of my situation weighs me down, but Kellan holds me steady.

"Princess, are you hurt?" Two guards come from behind me, and all I can do is shake my head where it hangs as I abandon all hope of ever escaping my father. "Get her back to the palace at once!" The other guard bellows as a horse comes plodding up. He takes the reins, and Kellan guides me to where it waits. The giant bronze horse whinnies and huffs as I am pulled into the saddle by another set of gloves. The riding guard does not wear the metal armor that Kellan does. His attire is much more ready for combat in the desert, a multi-hued fulvous linen and iron breastplate with the same unmistakable crest that mocks me.

"Was there anyone found with her?" One of the guards barks out at Kellan, and he lifts his chin.

"No sir, she was alone." The guard with sun-weathered skin narrows his yellowing eyes on me where I am held atop the horse. I recognize him as his ruddy brown eyes meet mine. One of the few guards my father favors, Pravin. His ruthless brutality has marked him as high-ranking among the royal guard. *My father's right hand.* Of course my father would send Pravin. Who better in place of the devil himself but his highest ranking demon?

"Were you alone all three days that you were gone, Little Princess?" He taunts me with a predatory narrowing of his gaze. Even though my defeat is evident, I hold his stare with a blank face. I won't allow him to know how much my failure is wrecking me. "We will tell the king we took care of whoever was aiding her. Burn this block down."

"No! No, Pravin. These people didn't aid me. I hid under the awnings and found an empty covered cart to hide in. No one knew I was here. I heard the guards coming and tried to run. You can't burn this block. All the people here will die. Please, Pravin." I beg for him to walk away from this. "You've claimed your prize in finding me. Please leave these people to live their lives."

"You're right Princess, but I don't think your father will just let the people get away with keeping the princess... You see, if they don't know that there is just a *simple minded girl* hiding among their goods, what's to say that they aren't foolishly unaware of magick users, lawbreakers, usurpers in their ranks... You see, they need to be taught a lesson." His voice is vile, like a snake slithering in my ear. Even at the distance we are apart.

"They didn't do anything!" I shout back at him, and the man I sit with on the horse holds onto me tighter.

"Exactly." He growls. "That one. Choose a male. Bring me his head." He spins on his heel and strides away on a quick gait.

"No." The single word is everything: a demand, a prayer, and an unbelievable declaration. My eyes track to the door that Pravin pointed to and the guards who are making their way to it. The man at my back tightens his grip, as though he can sense where my mind is going. I have to stop this. I can't let anyone die for my selfishness. My need to get away can't come at the cost of an innocent life.

"It's too late, Princess. Let them do what they were ordered. If you fight it, you know that more will come." The man growls in my ear. My nostrils flare as I grind my teeth together, and he steers the horse to begin the trek back to the palace. Tears blur my vision as I see a young man, not much older than myself, pulled from the quaint home. His clothes are ratty and patched in places. He is shoved to his knees, but my eyes are glued to his face as he looks back toward the door with strength. His chin is raised, his chest puffed out, but I see the glimmer of a single tear roll out of the corner of his eye and down his cheek.

"Look away, Astraea. There is no need to watch." My keeper says.

"May the gods guide you in a way that men have not. May you burn in the divine fire and be reborn in the ashes of Runerth." I hoarsely whisper the prayer of the Neer. It's treasonous, but I don't care. These people didn't do anything to deserve this. I can't watch it happen. I close my eyes as the largest of the guards swings the broadsword to end another life on my account. The thump of his head hitting the ground reverberates through my soul like the echoing knell of death bells. I roll my lips to trap the sob that threatens to burst from my throat, and my eyes squeeze together even tighter as I hear the screams of his family coming from the door they pulled him from.

By the time we near the last corner toward the inner gates of the kingdom, I am numb. The iron gates barricading the palace in another ring of protection reach out like the metal claws of the monsters within. My body feels heavy, and though I don't feel the heat, sweat builds on my brow. Not from the temperature of the evening air, but from the despair that has wrapped itself around my bones.

"Hide your eyes once more, Princess. There is no need to suffer more." The man holding me says, but I've already seen what he was trying to warn me of. I can't look away. A series of newly formed gallows hangs from the wall on either side of the gate. Each one illuminated with a torch of firelight on either side and a body hanging from a rope. Their faces are hidden by a canvas sack, but their bodies are already blistering from the Eathian sun, which had barely shown back up today after the monsoon.

There is no holding back the sobs that rack through me.

There is no holding me in place either. I lunge from the horse, falling hard on my hands and knees. My wrist instantly burns with searing pain, but I can't care. I only slightly hear that the man that was holding me is yelling at me to stop. He dismounts the horse behind me and takes chase. I can't hear past the rushing blood in my ears as I shuffle through the drying sand and force my body to move toward the bodies. My thoughts are spiraling in wicked grief. *Please, don't let her be gone. Please don't let Colette be one of them.* The two bodies on the right are women, wearing plain dresses that the staff wear; the other two are soldiers. My legs stop working as I fall to my knees beneath the two women.

"Leave her." The command comes, and slowly I lift my puffy gaze toward the sound of his voice. "After all, they were gifts *for* her." My eyes meet my father's as he stops just on the other side of the gates. He shakes his head. His disappointment in my running away, my reaction to the meaningless lives that hang above me. Killed for no other reason than to show me what happens when I disobey. It has been the same my entire life. When my lessons are not harsh enough to wring fear into me, he knows my compassionate heart will wither and die with the people he takes from this world in my name.

I say nothing as I stand, keeping eye contact with the man who sired me. My father has always wanted me to be a strong flame of perseverance, to stand behind the heir of his choosing as an illuminating light, burning bright in the shadow of a man. A union bringing more than just a strong heir but an unbreakable force of power to our name. If he wishes for me to be a strong woman behind the man, he better hope that whoever he chooses is strong enough to contain the raging fire that he has stoked, because he has ensured one thing with the torment he has put me through—*I will not be tamed.*

Chapter Fourteen

Astraea

My eyes are heavy and swollen from the tears I shed all night, but I can't fathom closing them and allowing my nightmares to make one of the most horrible days of my life—*worse*. Guards have been patrolling the hallway beyond my door relentlessly. Their footsteps like a never-ending fall of the sands in an hourglass.

"The king requires your presence in the dining hall, Princess Astraea." A guard says from behind me. I heard the door open, but my mind and body have not caught up to the outside world. My internal turbulent thoughts are drowning me in a torrent of emotions. I still can't bring myself to turn and face whoever it is that was tasked to fetch me. My eyes are glued to the battlement, where smoke now eddies into the once again scorching mid-morning sun. The stench from their fires blankets the kingdom and announces their deaths.

"Of course," I say absently. Turning from one devastation to another, I follow the guard through the halls of the palace. To keep myself calm on the outside, I focus on counting the wide corbel arches leading to the dining hall. It's a ritual I have performed more times than I can remember. The many times I have made my way to the summonings that my father has called upon me.

Twenty-four.

The number that marks the entrance of the dining hall from my quarters. It's the number that makes my adrenaline spike and my palms sweat. It's—

"Princess Astraea Casimir of Eathian." The court master calls out, catching me off guard. The collective gasp as I enter has me blinking in surprise. I suddenly feel even more overwhelmed by my surroundings. My father sits at his usual spot at the head of the table, and on his right is Pravin, a smug look of satisfaction pulling the corner of his mouth up. My father, on the other hand, is red with fury as he takes in my appearance.

I never changed. I didn't wash the filth from my face or even my hands. The evidence of my distress is written on every inch of my body. The moment my father slams his hands down on the table, shouting as he stands, knocking his chair back with a loud crash. I see this for what it is. The man to his left turns abruptly to see what has my father so flustered.

"Look at what they have done to you!" He comes rounding the table, and the other chairs squeal as they push out from the table as well. His jewels and crisp, cream linen clothing are immaculate, and the gold stitching gleams in the sun-drenched room. "My daughter, I'm so glad that you are home, safe with us." He pretends to shake as he reaches for me, unsure where to touch me. One hand rests lightly on my shoulder as he wraps his arm around me, and the other hand wraps around the crook of my elbow.

Confusion and anger flood my eyes with moisture. The sickening feeling of being helpless to this man yet again as he lies to the kingdom, an inexorable silent fight to keep my tears to myself, but there is nothing that could keep the emotion held within. Not after everything that has happened in the recent days.

"Sweet Astraea, had I known the condition you were in, I would have postponed this meeting." His thumb scores a line through the ever flowing stream of tears, and a choked sob escapes from me. This only adds to his show, and I hate myself for it. He knew of the condition I was in. *He made sure of it.* A throat clears as a man comes into my periphery.

His round, golden-flecked brown eyes are kind as they take in my appearance. A mournful recognition pulls his mouth into a frown. He runs his hand through his long, deep brown curls before taking my hand, still covered in filth; his strong brows dip before lifting it to his full lips. His eyes meet mine as he places a light kiss on my knuckles as he bows.

"Princess, I am so sorry our meeting has come at such a difficult time." His eyes stay trained on me, even though I can feel my father's gaze burrowing into our hands where they are clasped and the place where his lips made contact with my skin. "My name is Cadoceus Natharia, Prince of Iorworth. You can call me Cadoc." I say nothing, but I nod. Accepting his greeting but making it clear I am not here willingly. He stands upright, easily taller than I am, but not quite as tall as Kyros.

Another pang of sorrow crashes into me with the thought of the people from the tavern. Mavros and Zinya may not have been what I am used to, but they were kind to me, and I could have very well caused their deaths. Though, I'm sure that if it came down to a fight, they would probably be ok, judging by what I saw of their sparring.

"Astraea, dear, why don't you head back to your room? I will send help in for you to get you bathed. I will also send in food; I'm sure you are just ravenous. Prince Cadoc and I will start discussing terms of the trials, and you can start your first courting after a full night's rest." My father says matter-of-factly, and the way he adds the pet name to my own makes my sadness turn hateful.

Everything catches up to me. My breathing is coming too fast, and the room begins to tilt. I think I try to say something, but I'm not sure anyone hears my hushed words. I'm not even sure that I said them aloud or if it was merely a thought, as my vision begins to wobble.

"As though a meal and a night's rest will make everything just—*okay*? You wish for me to pretend that you didn't just *kill* at least five people!?" My lip curls back as I round on my father. The room goes breathless. My own breathing is erratic, though, and I know that this crazed behavior is going to come with great punishment, but I cannot get the vision of the bodies hanging from the battlements out of my mind. I can't think past the man's head rolling to the ground at his feet and the ear-piercing scream that was so much like the one I hear in my nightmares.

"You parade me around like a prized goat, bartering my life to the highest bidder—" I growl through clenched teeth. My father is beetroot red, ready to explode at any minute. I can see it in the way his jaw ticks, in the way that his fists clench at his sides, but Cadoc has the decency to look ashamed. His face drains of color as he takes a sidelong glance at the people who are watching my emotional outburst with unabashed curiosity.

It's Kellan who surprises me. He steps forward without being addressed. A gasp echoes through the dining hall as he cuts in with a bow. My father scoffs at the interruption and being addressed by the guard. Confusion crosses Cadoc's face, and my own shock is amplified by whispers from the crowd.

"I'm sorry for interrupting, majesties; perhaps the princess is feeling a bit overwhelmed and needs time to unwind. My squad and I would like the honor of escorting her back to her chambers for, as you said, my king, a meal and rest." He says quietly, his eyes staying low with his voice, so it is less likely that the rest of the dining room hears his words. *The valor and stupidity of this man, calling attention to himself like this!* I look at him with enough hostile fire; I hope it burns him. If it's not my wrath he will receive, it will be that of my father's and likely his death.

Lucky for him, Pravin steps to my father's side, pressing a hand to his arm; he leans down and whispers something in my father's ear. Then my father looks down at Pravin's hand and takes the missive he has there. He unravels the scroll, and his eyes scan the parchment before he rolls it neatly back up, and his spine straightens.

"Very well, take my petulant daughter back to her room. She needs time to think about her actions, and I have a court to run." He turns his vicious tongue on me, "It appears your next suitor has arrived early. I will greet him and make sure he has the accommodations he requires while *you* collect your wits." I open my mouth to show him just how much wit I currently have, but Kellan steps between us as my father turns his back on me.

"Princess, would you please allow me to take you back to your room?" He offers me his arm, and I look at it, then up at him in displeasure.

"Please excuse me. I will see you tomorrow, Astraea." Cadoc says with a nod, and then he, too, turns his back and follows my father from the dining hall. They take the opposite exit that Kellan will take me though. Looking around at all of the eyes that are still lingering on me, I let out a long sigh. A wave of defeat taking over, I place my arm through his.

"Thank you," I say, making sure not to address him by name in public. If what he did doesn't cause a stir, me knowing his name surely would. The guards are not supposed to interact with me, outside of my father's select few. I'm surprised that the man who is usually my keeper is nowhere to be found. Tarkan isn't as bad as Pravin, but he is still one of my father's men.

Kellan guides me from the room quickly, and before I even think about counting the arches, we are standing in front of my door. He looks around, making eye contact with the closest of the guards, and says, "Rhett, keep an eye. If anyone is coming, tap twice." The man, Rhett, nods once before turning away, and Kellan pushes into the room, pulling me along with him unceremoniously. As soon as the door shuts, he closes the distance between us.

"What were you thinking!?" His breath puffs out, and I scrunch up my face. When I open my eyes, his are closed. He is taking a deep breath, filling his lungs; he lets the breath out slowly. I push him back gently out of my personal space.

"I was thinking that I wanted to get away from this place, Kellan. I was thinking, I want to *live*!"

"Astraea," he pleads, reaching out for me, but I spin.

"No, Kellan. And what about you? What was that? You know you can't approach the royals so openly like that. He has killed for less! I don't need another death hanging over my head. I've already caused too much." My lip wobbles as the emotions from earlier come swimming back. I turn away so he can't see the tears as they well in my eyes.

"You were going to hurt yourself with that display. You and I both know it." He steps into me, his armor cold on the back of my arm. "I don't want to see you hurt again. I care about you." He whispers in my ear, and I freeze. He can't care. That was the rule.

We mess around, but we both know that nothing can come of it in the end. I turn to face him.

"Please, don't." I utter, my eyebrows tenting above my nose. My cheeks are likely blotchy and tear-stained. "Don't care about me, Kellan. Find someone you can build a life with. I told you from the start. Nothing can come of us. There can be no *us*." His jaw feathers as he thinks about what to say next. I can see all the words he wants to say flash across his warm eyes, but in the end, he knows I'm right.

"Regardless, I don't want anything to happen to you, Astraea." His hand cups my face, and he moves in closer, hovering over me just inches away. I place my hand over his on my cheek.

"This isn't the end of my battle, Kellan, but the show you just put on display… You got my father's attention with that. He will be watching you now. Please, if you truly care about me. Leave me alone. Don't step in when I say something I shouldn't. Don't offer assistance or guidance. I don't want my father looking too close at what we have. I don't want him to take our friendship." Not just our friendship, but his life. He knows what I mean, though, without me saying the words. He takes a step back as though my words wound him. "I'm sorry," I whisper. "Truly, I am." He shakes his head, refusing my words.

"Don't be. I knew that; I just… I don't know what got into me. I will make sure a platter of food is brought to you. Please, princess, eat, clean yourself up, and get some rest." He turns, pausing a moment with his hand on the lever to leave, and without turning to face me, he asks, "Did you ever feel anything over lust for me,

Astraea?" Silence stretches between us while I think about what he is asking. I know that any answer I give is not going to be enough for him. For what he is looking for.

"You will always mean something to me, Kellan. I would never want to lose your friendship." I say honestly, but I see him flinch. I knew anything I said would hurt him, but I hope that at least knowing that he is dear to me is enough.

"Goodnight, Princess Astraea." He opens the door, and without a backward glance, he closes it between us. As I stare at the tall wooden door, I can't help but feel like I've now lost two of the only friends I had.

Chapter Fifteen

Kyros

The guards demand attention as they storm through the city. Their call for order has me bristling in frustration. Sojourn edict, *sojourn edict*—it's all I hear from every corner, from every mouth all around us. I can't risk running after her, not with a sojourn edict from King Connard placed on the kingdom while he hunts whatever it is he wants down. I knew there was something about her. Something calling to me; something demanding my attention. Yet, I let those ocean eyes tell me something else when I should have listened to the thrum of the magick in my veins. There are only two possible reasons that she reacted the way that she did at the sight of the king's guards: she has magick, or she stole something important from the king.

"Dammit," I say through gritted teeth as I pace the room she slept in for, likely, near the hundredth time. This is the second night since the rain stopped and the girl ran. I went back looking for any trace of the feeling I had with her here, but just as I suspected—it's gone.

Gone with her. I haven't slept, even though night has come and gone and morning shines brightly through the window now.

"Do you think that we were just picking up on the magick in general, or do you think she actually stole the relic?" Zinya comes in and stands in my path, forcing me to stop and acknowledge her. It's not the first time she's asked the question. I just don't know the answer, so I haven't given her anything.

"You're going to have to talk eventually. The guards are just entering the building across from us. They are searching every building in the kingdom. Whatever they are looking for...it's valuable to the king, Kyros," Mavros says from where he is leaning in the doorframe, his arms crossed over his body and his ankles crossed just the same.

"I don't have a fucking answer. I don't know what to say or to do right now. Is that what you want to hear?" I pin my glare on him, and his answering one is just as sharp. "*For once*, I just don't fucking know what to do next. Let me think." I guess that's one thing we have in common. When it comes down to it, both Mavros and I are absolutely lethal when it comes to our anger. Silent fury you don't see coming until we erupt. That look in his eye, I know, matches mine; it's the only thing our twin genes gave us alike.

"We're out of time to think," Zinya says, pulling our attention to the window with a jerk of her head. "They are coming in now." I step up to the window, peering over the ledge, and see the glint of the sun off the shiny metal of the guard's armor. The armor has to be more of a nuisance than it is a protection. All for show. Anyone who knows anything about combat would be able to see that the only thing all that metal does in the cruel Eathian sun is bake the person inside, making them nearly useless in a fight.

"There is only one way to find out if she stole the relic. We need to get into the palace. Let's meet the guards downstairs. Remember the roles." I say, storming past Mavros; he takes a step out of the doorway just in time to miss the clip of my shoulder.

"Here we go," I hear him rubbing his hands together like this is some sort of game, and it takes everything in me not to whirl on him and tell him to keep his fucking head right. The guards tear through the door just as we make it to the bottom of the stairs, and they come in just as I knew they would. Eathian soldiers are always the same. They will run their people into the sand face-first every time. Especially this far away from the palace. The people in this outer rim are dispensable. Useless to the king and mostly consisting of the Neer people. *My people.*

"Sit the fuck down. Remove all hoods and masks. We're to see every face in this shithole!" An older guard yells. His leathery skin and white hair make him look older than he likely is. I glower at him as I look around the room at all the men and women who are a part of my unit. Each one of them looking back to me, awaiting my command. I give it with a simple nod and a tug on my ear, signaling them to listen.

Mavros and I don't comply, but we aren't the only ones. A man I don't recognize puffs his chest and hits his fist to the center, dropping his arm with a grunt. A Neer way of saying 'fuck you.' The guard's lip curls right before he brings the butt of his sword up and connects it to the man's nose. Another guard, with greasy brown hair and sweat-coated bronze skin, brings his steel covered knee to the back of the man's leg, making him instantly buckle. Using a foreign tongue, he curses the men and their misuse of power. It takes everything in me to keep my feet firmly planted where they are. Especially when leather skin reveals a small knife at his hip.

"Magick! Don't curse me with your witchy language, you Kru!" The knife slashes along his throat without questioning. Without caring.

The rest of the room falls into a stunned silence as the one man who stood up to them is cut down. Breathing heavily, the guard turns from the man before his life even leaves him to face us where we stand. We are not like that man, though, and the apprehension is clear in his stance. Our imposing size is that much more noticeable when everyone around has just shrank back by his tyrannical display.

"Do you have a hearing problem, son?" He says, trying to sound formidable, but as my eyes bore into his, we both know who would be left standing if he were to try anything. My magick bristles under my skin and makes me antsy to release it, but now is not the time. This man is not worth the trouble that would cause here.

"Perhaps you consider using a tone more respectful, and I would be more inclined to listen." I say, lifting my chin so I look down my nose at him.

"And just who the hell do you think you are?" His voice cracks as he comes to a stop before me, crossing his arms and looking up to meet my gaze.

"I am Mavros Kahzal of Diemos, here to court the princess of Eathian. This is my brother Kyros. I think that it would be wise for you to stand down before you are put down," Mavros says as he steps up beside me.

"Is that a threat to the king's guard?" The man scoffs.

"It's a promise." I growl as I step forward and cast him in my shadow.

"Well, now, now, boys..." Zinya steps forward, smiling wide and stealing all the guard's attention with her looks. The woman is dangerous in more ways than one, and she knows how to wield her weapons. "I think what they mean to ask is if your men can escort us to the palace? We have been holed up here during the storm, and while Miss Ruby has been more than hospitable, the men are used to different conditions and are just rather on edge. I hope you can excuse their dog-like growling and posturing for dominance." He melts a little more with every movement of her hands, every syllable spoken from her mouth. Like she were a siren of the Dead Sea, her song lures them into a spell. He is nodding before he even comprehends what he is agreeing to. I roll my eyes and strut right past him with Mavros on my heels.

The sun is already blistering. It radiates down on everything, causing the air to be thick and difficult to breathe. I grit my teeth as my eyes adjust to the brightness I step out into. The guards split, giving us a wide berth as we make our way to the stalls down the rundown street where we housed our horses.

Khol chuffs when I walk into the stable, his deep silver fur shining in the dimly lit stall at the end. Beside him, Eidola, Mavros' white mare, shakes out her blonde mane with a whinny when he steps in behind me. The huge dune horses are as much in tune with us as our magick at times, and just like our magick, they have been bristling the moment we stepped foot over the border back into Eathian. Lifting my hand, I run it up the velvety, scarred nose of my steed in hopes of calming him.

"Shhhh, I know." I lay my forehead on the flat between his eyes and continue to rub him down with my hand. "It's hard for me to be back too." Even though I hardly recognize the city, it clearly recognizes me. The energy just being here makes my magick hum, but I push that feeling away and focus solely on the purpose of my coming back here.

"What has gotten into you two?" Zinya comes to a stop with her hands on her hips. "Threatening the king's guard and making me openly use my magick?"

"They didn't know." Mavros rolls his eyes dramatically as he begins saddling Eidola.

"She's right. It can't happen again. We need to focus." I grunt as I pull the billet strap tight around the barrel of Khol's chest. "No more magick. No more games."

"Yea, yea… No more fun. Got it." Mavros says under his breath, and I give him a sidelong look before guiding Khol back into the elements. His long lashes flutter mostly closed to protect from the tiny sand particles on reflex, even though it is right after a rain and the sun hasn't quite dried the granules enough to allow them to become airborne in the light breeze we are granted.

Even on horseback, the short journey to the palace gates is long. The devastation the storm did to the town is nothing compared to the devastation on the faces of the people it affected. Some streets are still not usable because of the heavy water accumulation. *At least they have more fresh water now.* A commodity that they are always low on.

As we approach the gates, which I once thought I might never see again, Mavros stiffens at the same time I smell the stench that permeates the air. It's not the gates or where they lead that has him sitting a little straighter. It's the display that is mounted on either side. The bodies that hung from a noose for all to see now burn where they have fallen. They don't burn in respect for the souls that they carried, but as a means to dispose of the bodies the souls once had.

Rage consumes me inside like a tempest as I do everything I can to remain unfazed by the sight on the outside. My fingers blanch as I squeeze the leather lead in my hand, and it's the only outward display of anger I can allow because just as soon as we breach the gates, we are met with the gaze of King Connard himself. The throne-stealing murderer looks down on us from the interior balcony that overlooks the bailey.

"Come, you can dismount, and you will be shown to your room. Dinner will be served soon. It's best that you hurry along so you can get cleaned up." An older gentleman says as he guides us to the stables along the northern-facing wall. He continues rambling on about how, as luck has it, the princess' beauty is unmatched. Spewing things about the health of the kingdom. All lies, I'm sure. I can't pay attention, though, not when my mind is elsewhere. I begin pushing my magick out to look for the relic, and the first thing it finds is a familiar essence. Blue eyes flash into my mind like lightning, but I push it away. If she didn't steal the relic, she doesn't matter. The only thing that can matter from here on out is that damn relic. If she did steal it, it's only a matter of time before our paths cross again.

Chapter Sixteen

Astraea

Invisible vise-like claws grip my shoulders painfully tight, and a rumbling growl causes my body to tremble. The lasso of fire wraps around my body with a tightness I've only ever felt in my nightmares. The eternal darkness clouds everything. My mind, my eyes, the very air I breathe is heavy with it. I can't help but strain my eyes to try and see through the endless chasm of shadows, searching, and begging them to show me why I am here, but every time is the same...Once the flashing white stops, the shadows take me into their embrace.

The growl changes to a deep, rough laughter, and the echoes of it cause the hairs on the back of my neck to prickle and stand on end. Sweat beads on my forehead and coats my skin with a sheen. I'm on the edge of consciousness, and I can feel my body trying to drag me back to reality.

"Sssssenkaaaaaa," the word is whispered like a wicked secret, and it's the last thing that wraps around my senses before I wake up with a gasp, wrenching upright. My eyes fly open, and my chest is rising and falling rapidly as I try to get my bearings on my surroundings. My door is shut, as are the heavy cream curtains. No light comes into the room other than the small sliver cast through the center of the room, where the moonlight sneaks in.

Exhaustion overtook me when Kellan left. I refused the food brought to me shortly after. The chambermaid left it on the table anyway in hopes I would eat, but the fact that it was her who brought it to me, and not Colette, just made things worse... I couldn't fathom eating with the way my stomach was in knots over everything. I lay on my bed, too tired to even pull back the duvet. I curled into the smallest ball I could, and I cried. Only this time, sleep stole me away from my misery and thrust me into the nightmare.

This was new, though. I've never heard anything like words in these nightmares before. I've never not felt the thrashing of my body, or stood still enough to sense the hairs on the back of my neck prickling... My hand reaches up and wraps around the back of my neck on instinct, and a chill runs over my skin.

Unable to sit still any longer, I shuffle from the bed and head to one of the lofty, arched windows and pull the curtain back. What I thought was moonlight creeping into my room was actually the start of an early morning sun, rising in the east, being filtered through the gossamer layer of fabric. A glint on metal catches my attention, and I watch as a caravan of soldiers approaches the castle. Only the soldiers are not my fathers; they bear no armor that I am used to seeing, but their war scythes look just as deadly as they catch the sun.

Taking a deep breath of the already dry morning air, I let out a heavy sigh. *This is really happening. And now I don't even have Cole here to help me through it.* My room is on the eastern-facing part of the castle that looks out over the city, and the bailey is just below me. I have the perfect view of who comes in through the gates and the single road that leads to those gates. My heart rate spikes as I follow the path where the men are dismounting their horses within the castle grounds, out past the gates, and to the multiple groups that are making their journey this way.

My brows dip as I think about it. My father has prepared me for this, but it was supposed to take weeks. Courting would be formal dinners, as small groups with the royal family, and many trials that must be passed before the choosing ceremony. In the past, the princess had chosen her suitor, but my father, being the controlling bastard he is, will be the one to choose for me. He didn't care about tradition when he stole the kingdom in the first place. His rule is already not traditional. A king not born of royal blood has not ruled before him in a very long time. He has taken to making his own rules, bending the ones he does not like, and adding new ones as they fit his agenda.

A knock at the door pulls me from my encumbered thoughts, and I stride forward, cracking it open and looking out to find one of Kellan's men. The one from yesterday that watched outside my door for him.

"Good morning, Princess," he greets me with a nod of his head.

"Rhett, wasn't it?" I ask, pulling the door open wide as an invitation that he does not take. I walk to the corner cart and pour a measure of water as my head begins to throb behind my eyes. He clears his throat, bowing lower.

"Please, your majesty, my apologies for interrupting; I have a request from the king," he says formally, and I slowly turn to face him.

"Where is Kellan?"

"Kellan? He—he will be fine." I take a step forward, eyeing him speculatively at that response.

"He will be fine? Where is he? What are you not saying?" I demand.

"The king wishes to see you, princess. If you don't mind, I would be honored to escort you." He ignores my question, so I take yet another step closer to him and watch closely as his facial expression flickers with the questions behind his eyes.

"Where. Is. Kellan?" I was worried that something would come of his insubordinate behavior in the dining hall. I should have told him to leave the kingdom. To go find work elsewhere to save him from my father's wrath, but the somber look on Rhett's face tells me that whatever it is, it's not good.

"Where does my father want to see me? I ask.

"He would like you to come to the conservatory," he says, rolling his lips and looking down at his feet. I can't fault him for being worried. He is likely worried for his friend, for himself, and maybe even for me.

I cross the room, looking out over the bailey and all the men arriving. My father wants to parade me in front of them. That's why he's calling on me now and to the conservatory across the grounds. I still have yet to bathe since returning to the castle. If I arrive like this, my father will likely lose his mind. A sudden calmness spreads across my face at the thought. I know I shouldn't provoke him, but he has aimed to ruin everything good in my life; perhaps it's time I show him I have teeth too.

"May as well not keep him waiting," I say, turning toward Rhett once again. He clears his throat and offers me his arm, which I take, and he guides me from my room and through the castle. He doesn't take back halls and side doors as Kellan did; he walks us through the thick of court as the grandeur is unloading all around us. Eyes round as they land on me. Whispers echo through the hall. All of which talk of my disappearance. Not for what it actually was, a failed attempt to run from a life they all wish they could live... but a kidnapping by the people who don't deserve to live, according to my father. Usurpers who aim to take his throne and his only heir.

As we round the corner to cross the courtyard, Rhett's body stiffens at my side.

"Wait, Princess, this was a mistake..." His face is set sternly as he looks straight ahead. "I thought they would be done..." Before I am able to ask what he is talking about, I hear it. The whistle and crack of a whip, and the agony-filled scream of the person on the other end of it. When I turn to face what he is looking at...all the blood in my face drains. My body becomes leaden with terror.

"No." The word puffs past my lips at the same moment my feet propel me forward.

"Princess Astraea, wait!" I hear Rhett call out to me, but it's no use. Nothing will stop me from putting this to an end. The rain did a number on the sandy courtyard. The hard-packed sand is now softer, more malleable. Each step I take while running, my feet threaten to slide out from under me. When I reach about twenty yards from the post, multiple guards have reached me and are holding me back where I am.

My eyes collide with the pale green stare I thought I would never see again. The whites of her eyes stained crimson, and tears stream down her face. Freckles are connected with blood splatter, and her cinnamon hair is wild and sticks to her face and neck with sweat and blood.

"Princess, please. You are making a scene." A guard grunts as I thrash in his arms. Kicking and screaming with wild abandon. My elbow connects with something hard, and a curse comes out over my shoulder. Two other guards now restrain me as the other lets go.

"Kellan, stop! Please, NO!" The words slice my throat raw.

CRACK.

My legs grow weak as I see my best friend's back bow as much as it can, with her hands being tied to the post in front of her. She cries out, begging for me to leave her be. Her muddled face implores me to let this play out. Our sobs fill the mere 20 yards between us, and Kellan's face scrunches before he rears back and lets the whip fly another time.

CRACK.

My knees give out as I watch Colette's head roll back after a blood-curdling scream. Her eyes follow, turning white as she passes out from the pain. Even though her body is limp, her flesh hangs from her back, and her breasts are exposed for the entire courtyard to bear witness to. He pulls his arm back, and before he lets it fly again, his eyes meet mine. His brows pulled together in the center of his forehead, he swallows the emotion away before he closes his eyes and brings the cord down on her listless body.

CRACK.

She doesn't move, even as her blood flies with the impact. Kellan's shoulders slump as he drops the whip at his feet. His eyes don't leave the damage he has inflicted on her pale skin. His face is stark white, and ever so slowly his gaze lifts, meeting mine. His expression is haunted and lingers within mine for what feels like hours but could only be seconds. I see the pain there, nearly a clear reflection of my own. His eyes close in defeat before he turns around and slowly walks away, leaving Colette to bleed and my heart shattered.

"Come, daughter, enough theatrics." My father's voice sounds from behind me, and suddenly my muscles that were once heavy with grief are tense. I forcefully shrug out of the guard's hold, narrowing my eyes on all of them before facing my father.

"What have you done?!" I question through clenched teeth.

"What I must do to keep order in the kingdom, Astraea. It's something you will never understand. Come inside so we can discuss the formalities of what I expect of you starting tonight." He demands, snapping a finger toward Colette, waving in a demand to clear her from the courtyard, and holds his hands behind his back as the guards open the expansive glass doors to the conservatory. Each one is three men tall and at least the same in width. When my father's feet cross the threshold, he finally turns back, and I swallow, lifting my chin.

I was meant to see this display. He wanted me here at this precise moment in time, showing me that he knows about Colette and my friendship. This was a warning for me as much as it was punishment for her. Next time it will be her death, and the fact that he has Kellan carrying out the punishment rather than Pravin tells me that this was his punishment too.

I close the distance between me and my father with much more sure footing than I thought I would, and I come to a stop just feet from him. He looks down his straight nose at me. His brown eyes darken as he senses my intention. There is no turning back from the decision; my hand comes up and makes a loud clap against his clean-shaven face as I strike him. His head cranks to the side with the force of my blow, and slowly he turns it back to face me where I stand with my chest puffed out and my teeth bared. Guards rush toward us to take me away from the king, but he holds up his hand in order for them to stand down.

"I guess you are finding the spine your mother never could. It seems my lessons are paying off after all."

Chapter Seventeen

Astraea

My father's lessons *were* paying off, though I'm not sure what he meant by that... If he wanted me scared and cowering, he wouldn't have said it that way. He always said he wanted me to be strong, but I just assumed that only meant to *appear* that way. Lies of strength, just as he always showed. Every time I actually showed what I would call strength, I would receive another punishment... yet now I have the spine my mother never had because I slapped him? It didn't save me from another punishment, though.

The mirror in the bathing chamber is fogged with steam from my overly warm bath. The hot water was healing all in itself to my aching muscles and bruised skin, but it did nothing to ease my wandering mind. I knew my father was cruel, but I guess all of these years he was holding back. To my friend's misfortune, I found that out the hard way. He punished me first by making me watch them—the torture in Kellan's eyes as he whipped a woman who he knew didn't deserve the punishment, and the raw agony on Colette's face...

I need to talk to Kellan to let him know I don't blame him for what he did. If he had refused, he would be dead. I have no doubts that my father would have him strung up immediately for refusing an order. Looking over the bruises I endured was nothing compared to what they must be feeling. My father's switch has marked my skin many times over; this part was nothing new.

When I made the decision to leave the castle, it was easy, but I didn't think of what would happen to those who were meant to be protecting me. What it would cost, and that will forever be my debt to pay. My reckless decision was the reason at least five people were dead, and two of the closest people I have in my life have been tortured for the connection.

The dress laid out on my bed when I return to my bedchamber is the palest lilac. The evening sun creates a stunning effect on the mixed metal accents of silver and rose gold as I move it about. Its intricate lacing around the high back bodice is likely a deliberate choice to mask the marks that have been brandished on my skin there. Along with wide, bell translucent sleeves to hide where I fell to the ground and split the skin on my elbows. In the center is a panel that is a strike of muted plum and deepens in color at the bottom. It's a beautiful lie to hide the ugly truth. Even though people oftentimes see beyond the mask, to the scars underneath, they still smile and compliment the facade of beauty. It's as though the allure is enough to outweigh the poison living within.

I slip into the dress and pull the front ribbons tight before securing my hair in the coiffed up-do's my father demands of me. I paint on a deep wine lip stain and pinch my cheeks, although with the amount I have been crying, there is no real need. My cheeks are raw and pink from the steady flow of tears anyway.

As I make my way to the door, my eyes snag on the cloak laying over the back of my chaise and the rip in the fabric at the bottom. Likely caused when Kyros snatched it in an attempt to keep me from running. At least there is hope that I saved *them* from my father's wrath. Hopefully now that the rain has stopped and the desert is once again dry and barren, they are well on their way out of the city. After leaving the dune port as quickly as possible, Kyros said whatever they were doing was of utmost importance anyway. They must have left right away.

Rubbing the fabric between my fingers, an idea begins forming, and the longer I look at the worn linen cloak, the more I know I need to act on it. Night has fully settled over Eathian, so it won't look entirely out of place for a woman to be walking around with a cloak on. Though much further into spring, that wouldn't be the case. Right now the night brings a chill that the lingering warmth from the sun can't even chase away. Pulling the cloak over my shoulders, I secure the clasp at my throat, concealing the fancy dress underneath with its bland exterior. Pulling the hood over my head, I peek through into the chambermaids' pathways between the walls, and when I see no one, I slip inside.

Only those with access to the royal chambers can use these passages, but that means men and women who are loyal to my father too. My breath is frozen in my lungs the whole way to the healing quarters. I have to hold onto the hope that Colette was taken to the healers. If she was taken to the dungeons, there is no way I am getting to her.

I'm nearly to the turn I need to enter the wing when someone steps into the passage right in front of me. The man's hand comes out, covering my mouth and pressing me into the wall. My eyes round as my mind turns frantic. Maybe my father does have a point. He has many enemies that would gladly see my head removed for the terrors he has unleashed on the kingdom. A whimper escapes past his hand, but he isn't looking at me. He's looking over his shoulder toward where he just came from. It's too dark to make out any features on him. All I can tell is that he is taller than me, which doesn't mean anything.

"Shhh shhh shh," he says when he finally turns his head back toward me. I can barely make out the profile of his face. "I'm going to remove my hand; be quiet, please." My heart sinks when I recognise his voice.

"Kellan?" His name is a relief on my lips.

"Astraea? What are you doing here? You can't be here." He tries to turn my body around and force me to go in the direction I came, but I plant my feet.

"I have to see her. I have to know she's okay. Kellan, *please*." I feel him flinch behind me.

"She's okay. I was just there checking on her. I'm so sorry. I didn't have any other choice. You have to know that I would have never done it if I had another choice." I turn around to face him, and he stops trying to push me away. Instead, he is pulling me closer. Holding onto me as though I am what is keeping *him* on the ground. I lift my hand and let it run along his jaw.

"Oh, Kellan, I know that. I promise I do."

"He threatened my family for stepping in yesterday. Said my punishment was to dole out punishment to someone with a far worse crime. I had no idea it would have to be Colette when I agreed. Not that I had much of a choice. You know as well as me, if I had refused, we both would have been dead." His voice cracks with the emotion it's holding back. The pained expression on his face is enough to show me his desperation. He's right. It was probably better that Kellan was the one who did the whipping, even if it wrecked him at a soul level... I believe that deep down, he knows he saved more than his family with the act.

"I need to see her before I can face him again." I say imploringly.

"There are other guards. I had to lie to get close to one of the healers in order to slip a jar of salve in their hand. There is no way you won't be noticed. I'm sorry, Princess. You need to turn around." I take a deep breath, accepting his words. He's right. If there are guards, I would surely be spotted right away, and that would only end badly for Cole.

"You brought a healing salve into the palace? Even after everything yesterday?" I ask.

"I had to. I tried to be easy on her, but the amount of lashes he ordered... after a certain point, it doesn't make a difference how easy you are. Skin begins to slough off." His fingers push into the hood of my cloak, just into my hairline behind my ear, and normally, especially in times when my father has been particularly cruel, I would welcome the touch. However, I feel as though in the time since I left the castle, things have changed; I have changed. His hand pauses, and I know he noticed my hesitance.

"You promise she is okay?" I ask him.

"You have my word, Princess Astraea." He takes a step back. "Please return to the royal wing. Forget you saw me here, and please don't come back. She will be released if there is no hold on her outside of her punishment at the post. Otherwise she would have been taken to the dungeons." He's right, and although he likely can't see me, I nod my agreement. "I'm sorry, you know?" He asks, and I pause mid-turn. "For everything. We should have never—"

"Don't speak it," I interrupt. "You know as well as I, it was bound to happen. Perhaps in another life we could have been something other than a few shared moments."

"Maybe," he whispers, and then we both flinch as the click of boots on sandstone approaches quickly from behind Kellan. He pushes me forward. "You can't be seen here, especially not with me. *Go.*" I turn without another word and rush all the way back to my bedchamber. When I exit, I press my back against the narrow wooden door and slide down, sitting with my head hung toward my knees.

My whole life I have been a prisoner in my own home. Every decision I have ever made has inevitably been made for me. I don't know that Kellan and I would have ever come together had I not been his ward. The first people I have met out of my own decision-making were Mavros, Zinya, and Kyros. Even they didn't have much choice but to endure me because of the storm.

A tear tracks down my face. One day I wish to have a choice in my life. One day I would like to be chosen for more than my title, for more than my looks. I want to be *seen*.

If my father wishes me to marry; become a trophy queen for a new king he chooses? Fine. He can think that is what is happening, but he has another thing coming. What he did here today has undoubtedly had the opposite effect on me. Coupled with what I witnessed in the city? I will be his usurper. I will play coy for the show he wishes me to put on for suitors, and while he searches for the new king, I will plan for the new *queen*. If I can't leave this place, I will make it my own.

My father is going all out tonight for dinner with the suitors. When I went missing, the moment the rain stopped, he called for all of them to come at once. He said that my return and the courting would *make for a grand event worthy of celebrating*. Of course he is making the first formal dinner be held in the great hall. It's one of the most ostentatious rooms in all of the castle. Even the breezeway leading there reeked of wealth and power. Two of his favorite things. Its two-story arches reach for the star-studded sky like the knuckles of a giant on a raised fist.

"Don't look so sad, Princess. You are about to meet your future husband after all. The highest point in a woman's life." Pravin says contemptuously. I ignore him just as I always have, but he continues pushing. "It's too bad that your mother couldn't give your father a son... all of this could have been avoided." I pause, looking sidelong at him with disdain coating my tongue.

"Yes, Pravin, it is such a shame that my mother's life was ripped away from her before my father was able to pump her full of his vile seed to create a male spawn he could mold into something more sinister than himself." His brows hitch as he balks. "Pick up your jaw, Pravin. You act like you have never heard a woman use *her* voice before."

I can feel his eyes on me as we walk, but he says no more as I walk ahead of him. I don't like coming to this wing of the castle. This side holds all of the most opulent rooms, one of which I try to avoid altogether—the throne room. Not to mention that I try to keep as much distance as possible between myself and my father. It's been that way my whole life. At first it was his doing. He didn't care to see me, as I have heard most fathers do for their children. He would check in with my caretakers and send Pravin to make sure that I was studying and learning to be a lady fit to be queen. Other than that, it was dinners a couple nights a week and punishments when I needed them. Lessons increased as I got older and my mind started developing thoughts of its own. Colette and her mother have a lot to do with that. That's also when the worst of the nightmares started.

Cole's mother gifted me the necklace—an heirloom from my mother. She said my mother told her a long time ago she would know when the right time was to gift it to me. I almost never take it off. I swear, even though my father hates magick, I feel as though the pendant is imbued with it. When I do take it off, the nightmares seem to be so much worse. *Or maybe it's all in my head...*

Absent-mindedly my fingers roll over the intricate carvings on the pendant before I take a deep breath and let it out in a heavy sigh. Coming to a stop at the closed doors, I take in the massive entry more than I have before. Something about today feels like the end of life as I know it. Maybe it's a good thing that I feel as though I'm dying. If I felt otherwise, what would it say about me? So, like the dying woman I am, I pay attention to the more beautiful things this life has given me, if only for a moment. These doors are some of the last pieces of artwork left from the previous ruler. The carvings in the deep red wood are like a story. Each one melding into the next like the pages of a book.

I wish I knew if they had meaning or if the royals before my father just had the taste for beautiful things. Right at eye level, there are two ravens, one black and one white. They embrace like doves. Lovers. This thought, something that I will never have, causes emotion to build in the back of my throat. I never wished for love, but now that the chance is being taken from me, it seems like I am grieving someone I needed more than the air I breathe. The Neer believe that our souls are like the wick of a candle. Just like a candle needs fire to burn, our life never truly starts until we have met our match. Only then do both souls ignite and the twin flames burn.

I'm looking down at my feet, still deep in thought, when Pravin opens the doors.

"Astraea Casimir, Princess of Eathian." The court master announces loudly, making me jump out of my own head. Lifting my chin, my eyes trail into the room of snakes, each one of them as beautiful as they are deadly. Pravin offers me his hand, and I look down at it, then lift my gaze to meet his before walking past him in open disrespect. The low growl from him is not missed by me; though it was low enough no one else heard, the sound of it brings me a moment of triumph, and my lip curls at the corner in response.

Striding into the room on sure feet, I greet my father, and he embraces me like the prized child I know I never was. Someone who he cares for very deeply, but I smell the stench of lies with every touch and kind word he says. He seats me at the center of the table, and the men there take their seats all around. Though the seating for us is smaller, the room is filled with bodies, and all their eyes rest on me. The table is filled with an abundance of colors and decadent exotic foods. More than enough to feed all of the poor families I saw living in squalor. It makes my stomach recoil.

"Well, they weren't lying when they spoke of her beauty." I hear one of the suitors say. My eyes clash with liquid gold. Beautiful and dangerous, and the corner of his lips quirk up as though he could read the thought as though it were displayed on my face.

"Ruaan, respectfully, shut the fuck up." Benat, one of the only familiar faces I see, says under his breath, but the wicked glint in his eye tells me it was more out of jealousy than anything else. Taking a deep breath, I roll my eyes, blocking out all of the hushed conversations around me.

Still standing, I pick up the delicate wine glass my father is allowing for the celebration. I reluctantly lift it to make the entry toast that is mandatory, but the doors open once again.

"Mavros and Kyros Kazhal appointed Heirs of Diemos." My wine glass slips from my hand. Shattering and spilling wine all over the table in front of me as my eyes clash with the deep umbra of Kyros' stare.

Chapter Eighteen

Astraea

THE HEAVY WOOD DOOR closes, and I feel like fire has caught in my cheeks. Everything is unfolding in slow motion, but at the same time it feels too fast to comprehend. I look down at the spilled wine at the same moment that Cadoc begins guiding me away from the table, one hand on my elbow and the other low on my back.

"Careful, Princess. I don't want you to get hurt." He says, and a low whistle echoes through the great hall. My attention leaves the staff attending to the spill as it's pulled to the man the whistle belongs to. Mavros' eyebrows jump up, looking between me and my father, then to Cadoc.

"What a *royal* mess." His eyes narrow on me knowingly. "I hope you can accept our apologies. We seem to have been given some *misconstrued* information." He continues shifting his eyes from me to my father. Kyros stands at his side, but his gaze never leaves me. I don't think he has yet to blink.

"Why are there two of you from Diemos? Who is the suitor for my daughter's hand?" My father asks blatantly. Kyros doesn't move, but Mavros smiles wide. I only barely register the movement behind them and notice that it's Zinya making her way into the room and through the crowd of people; sitting at one of the tables, she watches.

"I am," Mavros says at the same time that Kyros growls the same words. Mavros' head whips in his brother's direction. His confusion mirroring my own. Kyros continues to stare at me as the tension in the room becomes so thick I feel I may choke on it.

"So you will go through the trials *against* each other then?" My father presses.

"No—" Mavros starts, but Kyros speaks over him.

"Yes." The brothers look at one another then. A silent conversation seems to be had within their gazes before finally Mavros looks back at me.

"I guess it appears, we will..." His chin raises, and the muscle along his jaw feathers. He glances out of the corner of his eye to Kyros, but Kyros ignores him. Instead, he moves across the room and pulls out the one chair left at the royal table. Sitting without another word. Mavros scoffs, shaking his head.

"I don't suppose we can get a place for me to sit? Or would the princess like to *share*?" He grins, and I narrow my eyes on him. His dual meaning is not missed. Some staff rush around the table, putting a place setting out next to Kyros, and the other men all keep a wary eye on each other. As though at any moment, any one of them could turn on the other. All but Kyros. His onyx eyes have not strayed from me save for the moment with his brother. He has yet to even acknowledge the king. I don't know if I should be embarrassed or concerned at this point. Concern wins out because I can feel my father vibrating with anger. They are both pushing him. He is not a man of patience and does not handle disrespect well.

I clear my throat; still standing, I reach for another glass of wine on the table to make the opening announcement. The start of the courting affairs, just as I have been trained, but when my fingers are about to reach the glass, my father whips his hand in front of mine, blocking my attempt.

"Perhaps we keep your mind unmuddled, dear. You have already made quite the mess of things without a sip." My father whispers, not so quietly. A few of the men snicker, but out of the corner of my eye I see Kyros' fist ball on the table, and even Mavros levels a glare in my father's direction. The simple show of abhorrence catches me off guard.

"Surely it would be highly inappropriate for a princess to partake in overindulgence; you never know what kind of *wild* things might happen..." Mavros chides. None of the others pay him any mind, but I see my father's eyes narrow in his direction. Heat floods my cheeks nonetheless, thinking of the things I saw him doing on the night he is referring to, but I need to get my father's attention off Mavros. I may have lied to them, but they were kind to me when I was out of my element. They don't deserve my father to rain down hell on them for the mere fact that they were in my presence when I ran away.

"Of course, father." I recede, sitting back in my chair.

"As all of you know, we are gathered here for the courting of my daughter. Your betrothal would secure a very powerful alliance with Eathian. Which, as you know, has the largest, most skilled horde of soldiers in the realm." My father drawls on, and Mavros covers his scoff with a cough. My eyes flick to his, and he *winks*. *This man is going to get himself killed.*

"When do the trials start?" The man, who I have not yet met, says from the right side of Kyros. His sharp chin lifted high, a mess of shorter, wavy, deep brown hair falls across his hazel eyes, more gold than brown, and his tattooed arm is slung over the back of his chair like he's not in the presence of royalty. He inspects his nails as though he is bored, and many of the men bristle. He must sense my eyes lingering on him, because he looks up through his lashes, and a barely visible smirk lifts the corner of his mouth. *Oh, divine.*

"Don't worry, Prince Ruaan, the first battle is likely the easiest. You won't have to worry about messing up those pretty nails." Benat chides, and the Prince, Ruaan of Pyraxia, if I recall from my studies, levels him with a menacing glare. A throat clears, and I quickly avert my gaze. It's easy to lose interest in the conversation around me. The talk of trials and warriors, of weapons, and time.

Eventually, they all ignore me, and I pretend to eat the food that is on my plate as I watch all of them. Each man here is beautiful in their own right. Every one of them radiates power and authority, and a few of them even kindness. Cadoc is one of the only men who pays me any attention. Sitting to my left, he mentions foods that are delectable—tells me to taste the honey-glazed meat but to pair it with the white cheese. The night is calm yet filled with chaotic conversation, and through it all one thing has remained the same.

Kyros has not let his eyes stray from me.

My father claps as the food is being cleared from the table, and musicians come in, standing at the far back of the room on a raised dais. They set up their instruments and begin playing a soft melody. It's beautiful, and if it weren't for the situation I find myself in, I would almost enjoy it.

A hand extended over my shoulder causes me to jump, and I look up to the man offering it. A glittering obsidian gaze collides with mine, sending a chill down my spine. I was so lost in thought, I didn't even notice him get up.

"Shula," he breathes, "Perhaps since the night is waning, you would give me the honor of a dance?" I blink, taken aback by the gentleness in his voice. My eyes turn toward my father for direction. This was not discussed with him for the first night of events, so I'm not sure what he would want me to do. He looks between me and who he believes to be a stranger and nods a wary acceptance. Swallowing as I place my hand in his, I feel the whole room's gaze on us. Tension is breathing on its own as I stand and he walks me to the center of the room. No one else is dancing. My heart rate accelerates. I have danced in front of people thousands of times, with hundreds of partners, but something about this moment feels *different*.

The hand that is in his feels like a weight, and when his other hand wraps around my body and rests on my low back, pushing me forward to press against his chest... my breath hitches. No—this doesn't just feel different. *It is different.* This is not a dance I am used to; here in Eathian, there is hardly any touching when it comes to dancing with the princess. There is typically not much interaction with me at all. The men who are able to dance with me do so with the image of their own body hanging from my father's noose between us. But not with Kyros. He dominates. Impeding on my personal space with the press of his body.

I can basically feel the whispers of the people in the room. My father's heavy gaze watching every move made. The other suitors stop their conversations to see the silent war that Kyros has just started.

"You're not breathing, Shula," he says quietly, and my eyes flick up to his.

"This is—*inappropriate.*" I murmur. Letting out the breath I didn't realize I was holding.

"Where I'm from, this is perfectly acceptable. But you know what is frowned upon?" I'm lost in the question in his eyes, re-maining quiet for far longer than what his question requires to think of a response. He spins us around in a steady but slow rhythmic motion in tune with the music. Much more rhythmic than you would think an imposing figure such as him would be able to accomplish. When I don't answer, he brings his head down just a fraction. His nose is just inches from mine and I know it must appear even closer to those looking in.

"Lying, *Sienna*," he whispers, and dips me low just as the music comes to an end and my heart plummets into my stomach. Pulling me back upright, I'm breathless as his hands fall from me. He bows low, keeping his eyes locked with mine, and as he lifts my hand, he places a chaste kiss on my knuckles. Even though we are in a room full of people, the gesture alone feels inexplicably intimate.

Before he has turned away, another hand is placed in front of me. An invitation to continue this show of dancing as the next song begins. My eyes linger within the shadows of Kyros' for a moment longer before I place my hand into the next suitor's hand without even seeing who has offered.

I am pulled hard with a yank of my arm; I'm spun into Mavros' chest. A much quicker song begins to play. He smiles wide down at me.

"Eyes on me, Princess." He says it deviantly, his tongue rolling out over his bottom lip. He too presses his body into mine and twirls us all around what is now the dance floor. Many of the people have joined us in dancing as the alcohol has continued to flow. Some of the dances are turning much more provocative. I didn't even realize I was still watching Kyros until Mavros said something about my wandering gaze. My face turns toward him abashedly and heated from within.

"Good girl."

"I didn't agree to dance with you so you could tease me." I roll my eyes and try to push him away, but he only holds tighter.

"Teasing is what I do, but believe me, the follow-through is what's best." He winks, grinning, and then brings his head closer to my ear in a particularly fast spinning motion. "You wanna talk about why you've made a bit of a habit out of running away lately?"

"No, not particularly." I respond solemnly.

"I understand why you lied about your name if you were trying to run away... But, tell me, why would a princess, who has everything they need, want to leave it all behind? What is it that I'm not seeing?" He asks, his blue eyes cutting into me like the jagged, ice-capped mountains of the kingdom of Halcyon do the sky. After a moment of silent steps, I finally break my resolve.

"I'm sick of people demanding things from me. I'm sick and tired of everyone making decisions for me. Maybe I just wanted to be in control." I finally say, unsure why I have decided that now is the time I let my truth be known.

"If it's the control you want, why not just take it? You say you're sick of this?" His chin gestures to the room around us. "Tired of it? Why don't you use the energy you have to dominate the fucking world?" His head falls back as he laughs loudly, calling more attention to us. He may have been joking, but his words resonate with me on a deeper level. Bringing me back to the feeling of when I chose to leave in the first place. Bringing me back to the moment that I decided to slap my father in his smug face. Flashes of Colette's face blaze like a wildfire in my memory, and I stand a little taller.

"Maybe I will." I say with more conviction than I believe Mavros was expecting, but whatever he sees causes him to narrow his eyes on me, and that ruinous grin is back on his face.

"Atta girl. Maybe you will be the warrior we all need to defeat in the end." I don't understand it, but in a matter of minutes Mavros has eased the tension in my shoulders and brought a lightness to my feet. Courting generally would end in the princess making the decision of who won her hand, but I know my father has other plans. Unfortunately for him, those plans ride on the shoulders of an obliging daughter. He may be using me as a tool, but it is I who will sharpen myself into a blade. I choose to no longer be a timid princess. Today I choose me.

Chapter Nineteen

Astraea

The nightmares have become debilitating. Two nights in a row they have had me lurching awake in a puddle of sweat and breathing heavily. I have begged Pravin to leave me because of the agony behind my eyes. My entire body throbs with a reminder of the terror I am so tense with. Today, though, he has demanded that I get out of bed. He informed me that the first event is to take place, and if I didn't get out of my bed, there would be a punishment. I don't think I would be able to take one of my father's punishments right now. The marks across my skin are still ever-present, and I couldn't fathom the pain of that adding to my head. So here I am.

I hate being down here.

To keep out of the vicious onslaught of the sun, many times my father hosts entertainment below the castle. He has created a deep amphitheater within the ground below. The expanse of the oval space is surrounded with tall, burned bronze braziers, all lit and casting the dark space in an ominous orange glow.

This is where warriors come to die.

"Why does it have to be this way?" I ask no one in particular, but Pravin looks over at me with a grin, no doubt searching for an opportunity to push me. I'm sure he is annoyed that I didn't argue about coming, and now he doesn't get to watch me receive the punishment I was promised if I had.

"To weed out the weak, of course. You will have your first solo courting as soon as this is said and done." He crosses his arms over his chest as he looks down on the pit below us. "The winner gets the prize." That's all I am to them. A prize. Rolling my eyes, I look out over where the men have gathered.

We are in the center of the large oval arena, a crow's nest box sitting high above the rest of the spectators. Of course my father has gathered most of Eathian here to witness all of this. They will be invited the whole time. Then when it's over, there will be a ball where the winner is announced and handfasting is completed.

It used to be that magick would seal the handfast, a magickal ceremony where each person entering the betrothal had to sacrifice lifeblood to tether their two souls to one another. Now it's a mere promise to uphold the union. Their word.

My gaze is immediately snagged on two brothers as they enter the arena last. They are the least armored but the most deadly in appearance. Both are shirtless, with only a band of bronzed metal wraps snugly around each bicep, and their harem pants are held in place by a thick leather band around their tapered waists. Kyros has his longer dark hair pulled back and tied messily and low at the back of his head, and Mavros has his longer blonde hair at the top of his head pleated into a mohawk, the sides freshly shaven, showing more of the tattoos above his ears.

Mavros, of course, has a smile brandished on his face, and the opposite is said of Kyros; like night and day. As they walk forward, the other soldiers, all in varying levels of armor, tense. I see a couple even take a step back, and my brow furrows.

"Those two are going to be an issue." I hear Pravin say to my father as he comes to stand at our side. My father lifts his chin and narrows his eyes, and something almost protective rises in my chest as I see him assessing Mavros and Kyros.

"They will make for impressive entertainment. You know as well as I do that most of the magick is gone from the realm. I have no doubts those markings are for show. The kingdom of Deimos is on our side, even if it is reluctant. Queen Phaedra wouldn't risk the repercussions of enlisting those with magick into her inner circle, and she definitely wouldn't send them here if she did." My father says confidently. "Come, daughter, you will give your favor to one of the warriors now." He clips, not waiting for me to follow. He takes the set of stairs to the right of the balcony, leading to a platform set up to the side of the main fighting ring.

Cheers ring out all around as we are spotted by the people of Eathian and probably the neighboring kingdoms too; our presence signifies the start of the games. A fight to first death. I've only read about this in history tomes. The games my father hosts for entertainment have nothing on the sheer amount of people here today. I guess the kingdom wants to know what kind of king they may one day have.

The men line up in the very center of the amphitheater, and my father nods at me to begin. Swallowing my fear, I take the last set of small steps, and when my feet hit the dirt ground in the pit, the crowd roars with excitement. The energy of the massive room is the only thing that propels me forward. I've taken a few hours of each day since meeting the men to get acquainted with their faces and learn a little more about their heritage. Mavros and Kyros are the only ones I have found little on. I can't help but wonder if the alliance that my father has with Queen Phaedra Lazuro is as strong as he outwardly makes it seem.

Every man here is beautiful in their own way. I'm sure many of the women in the stands would be thrilled to be in my place. To seemingly have a choice in what can only be a righteous and bountiful future. The thought makes my stomach sour, though, and apprehension bites at the back of my mind as I reach the first man.

Cadoc beams as he reaches for my hands. My lips curl up on one side into a small, meek, almost sad smile as I accept his touch, and he leans in, allowing me to kiss his cheek.

"Prince Cadoc Natharia of Irowerth, thank you. It honors me that you should wish to fight for the chance of our betrothal. Your courage does not go unseen. If you should fall in the fight, I will pray that your ashes fly free and your soul not carry the burden of burning for eternity in Zameil." I say just as I rehearsed.

"Thank you, Princess. The honor is mine." He nods a bow and takes a step back into line. Moving on, I step forward to greet the next man. Son of Lady Kenina and Lord Ezequiel Caius of Eythora, one of our biggest cities within Eathain. I've met Benat many times, as his father and mine are as close as one could consider friends. They are both horrible men, and they equally love the idea of power and ruling over actually caring for their people.

"Hey beautiful, I told you it would be no time at all and those lips would be on me." He smirks, and I recoil the slightest amount. As I do, I notice movement to the side and make eye contact with Kyros and then Mavros. The latter gripping the former by the wrist.

"Benat." I nod my greeting, letting my gaze fall on him again. He has the look most women love. Straight teeth and nose, fiery passion in his narrowed cinnamon-hued eyes, and the same cinnamon-brown hair to match. I ignore his cocky remark and continue with the blessing. "It honors me that you should wish to fight for the chance of our betrothal. Your courage does not go unseen. If you should fall in the fight, I will pray that your ashes fly free and your soul not carry the burden of burning for eternity in Zameil."

When I finish, I lean in to kiss his cheek just as I did with Cadoc, but instead of accepting, he turns his head, stealing my lips with his. The crowd grows to a frenzy. Stepping back with a gasp, I look down the line. Many of the suitors look angry, but two of them are planted where they stand with barely contained rage. Kyros and

Mavros don't look at me; they vibrate with fury, their gazes locked on Benat.

Clearing my throat, I eye Benat as he laughs and rallies the crowd further by touching his lips and letting his tongue roll out to take my taste into his mouth with a groan. The tension between those on my left and the brothers intensifies with the display.

Faolan Damalis, nephew of Lord Ophir Damalis of Halcyon, one of the outlying cities, looks apologetic as I approach him. His kind brown-hazel eyes flick between mine, and he bows his head before brushing back his shoulder-length dreadlocks from his tattooed face, giving me access to place a kiss on his cheek. I recite the same blessing to him, and he accepts it with a respectful bow, narrowing his eyes at the previous suitor, who was less than courteous.

Mavros is next, and as I approach him, he gives me what I now know is his signature smirk and wink. I roll my eyes as he openly laughs. Taking my hands in his, he tugs me toward him, and I have to roll my lips in to keep myself from laughing at his antics. He has been easy to like; I suppose I am grateful for that.

"Lay it on me, Princess." He turns his head so I have easy access to his cheek. "I knew the *princess* nickname was fitting." He whispers as my lips make contact with his skin, and they bring a flush to my own as I step away from him. Shakily, I say the blessing, and he pins me with a look I don't understand. Then, he just shakes his head and takes a step back.

When I reach for Kyros, he levels me with a glare. The negative energy riveting from him leeches into me, and I have to grit my teeth not to say something about it. He does not take my hands; instead, he just stands there, staring into my eyes like he is searching past what he is seeing and diving into my every thought.

"I don't need a recited blessing written by ancestors long forgotten. Those words mean *nothing* coming from someone who doesn't even want to be here in the first place." He growls under his breath. The crowd is still rowdy from Benat's display, and no one is particularly close enough to hear what he said, but it causes my heart rate to spike regardless. I don't know why, but something about his declaration causes me to pause and look at him in a different light. Perhaps there is more to his standoffish presence. The scar down the side of his face stands out in the low light of the amphitheater, and I find myself curious to know how it happened. He sees me looking and tilts his head, allowing shadows to cover his face as he waits for my response.

"Kyros Kazhal of Diemos, regardless of what you think of me. I do wish you an honorable end, if one must come for you. I will not give you a false blessing, because believe me when I say, I have seen enough of the pain in my own eyes to know when I see the same in the gaze of someone else. I don't give empty promises—and I promise you—those words? They don't mean *nothing*." His jaw feathers, but his anger falters for only a moment as he bends down and I reach up to my tiptoes. I place a hand on his shoulder because he would not give me his hand, and I need the balance. Fluttering wings take flight in my stomach as my hand presses against the warmth of his bare skin and my lips press to his scruffy cheek.

He does not thank me, and he does not bow, but he keeps his narrowed eyes and heavy brows locked on me as I retreat. Even as I make my way to give the *recited* blessing for the others, to both Ruaan, Prince of Pyraxia, and Wrensford, future Lord of Vadon. Both Ruaan and Wrensford accept the blessings without pause and without causing an uproar, unlike Benat. Looking back at my father, he twirls his finger with an impatient face, urging me to get on with it. I look at the line of men, each one of them waiting eagerly for me to choose one of them to have my favor, but there is only one man who stood out to me in this line. Only one man seemed to understand the feelings I have about this *game*. The only man who, instead of looking at me like I am a prize, looks at me like I am a puzzle.

I know who I am *supposed* to choose—who I have been *told* to choose. The decision was made by the discussions of men behind closed doors, sitting in high-back chairs, with a conversation over a table carved of bone. The heightened awareness of his eyes burrowing into me causes my heart to send a surge of anxious energy through my veins at the decision I am choosing to make instead. I step back, toward the center of the line, and reach up, pulling the hairpin free, my long loose, ebony waves falling around my shoulders and down my back. When I step forward, the crowd goes silent. I can feel the heavy press of my father's eyes on the back of my head as I reach for Kyros' hand, lock my eyes with the endless shadows that are his, and place the hairpin in his palm.

"I would like you to not only have my blessing, Kyros Kazhal, but my favor as well." I take a step closer, and before I lose my gall,

I lift my other hand, wrapping it around the back of his neck, and I push my fingers into the hair at the nape and pull his face down to mine. Slowly, I close my eyes and press a chaste kiss to his lips. He freezes. He doesn't even breathe. No words. No response at all other than turning to stone, and for some reason I feel like it was the *right* response, more so than any other he could have given.

I feel everyone's silent stares on me as I return to the royal box in the stands. My father greets me with unbridled aggression as he grabs my arm above the elbow and pulls me in close so he can growl in my face.

"What were you told?" He asks with barely contained rage. "I fucking told you that you would choose Benat for the first round! Stop playing like you have a mind of your own and do what you're fucking told! You just made sure that you are going to go to bed *sorry* tonight, sweetheart." His fingers are bruising where they dig into my arm, and I feel myself losing the confidence I had a moment ago as a feeling of disquiet floods me.

He pushes me back, letting go and causing me to stumble, and it takes everything in me to not reach up and rub my throbbing arm. I turn without looking down at the men below. I have a feeling if I were to see Kyros staring up at me right in this moment, tears would spring free, and that is something I will not let my father see. When I finally take my seat, I focus on my hands in my lap. I am both proud of myself for taking a stand and choosing who actually deserved my favor and also concerned for what will come of it. The decision will likely put more focus on Kyros and Mavros by default, which was not my intention. But as I look up at my father and I see the way he and Pravin have their eyes glued to the brothers, the decision turns sour in my stomach.

The battle drums start their pounding rhythm. The vibrations rattling the ground and echoing off every surface. The fire keepers at each of the braziers toss a handful of powdered aluminum into their flames, causing a theatrical plume to light the space. An ode to the old magick people once had in our kingdom. A mockery of what is no longer allowed, and I grip the edge of my chair to stop myself from shaking my head at the distaste. The amount of people my father has killed because they have shown just sympathy for those who have magick or use any amount.

As soon as the flames level out and the clash of the cymbals strikes, the men begin moving. All but two are running for weapons that line the sphere. Mavors and Kyros stand true without moving a muscle, waiting for the fight to come back to them. And the fight definitely comes.

They are bombarded with attacks at all angles, but they move like a storm. Fluidly working together, back to back, they block each blow, disarming the other men with ease. My father and Pravin are bristling with pent-up rage. Each one has their hands on the railing, their knuckles blanched with how tight they hold on to it, and just noticing them makes me realize that I too have a death grip on my chair.

The disarmed men change their trajectory when they realize that they are not getting past the brothers' defenses and turn on each other. This is a fight that could end in death; it's likely what my father would prefer. I, however, hope that they just tire—

"END HIM! END HIM! END HIM!" The crowd chants, and I can't help but lurch from my seat to the railing to get a better look. All of the suitors are panting, exhausted from the fight. Mavros circles, who I now see is Kyros with his knee pressed into Benat's chest, my hairpin angled under his chin. He says something to Benat, which causes his already reddened face to grow deeper in color, and he spits in the direction of Kyros' face. The crowd makes the ground quake with their stomps. Cheers are bellowed in response to the blood they see spray as Kyros sinks the sharp end through the soft underside of Benat's chin. He rips his weapon free, the motion causing more blood to spray, and it coats him in the red paint of war. He spins it in his hand as he turns to face the stands.

To face me.

Our eyes lock, and a shiver of fear ripples through me at the sight of him and the almost intimate fervency that enters the shadows of his eyes. Crimson drips from his face and coats his bare chest. His tattoos blend together in a wave of shadow and blood, and with the mark of the death bell, the victor has risen.

Chapter Twenty

Astraea

"Do you have any idea what you have done?!" My father screams at me. The power of his voice blows the hair out of my face, and the spittle makes me flinch. "Our closest allies and one of our biggest threats and their heir, whom I may remind you was meant to be the *victor* of that fight, are now sitting in my war room, ready to discuss what I am going to do about this betrayal of yours!" He spins on his heel, tucking his hands behind his back, and paces the short distance in front of me in my bedchamber. Where I have been escorted like a prisoner.

"It wasn't my promise to keep," I say under my breath. His feet stop immediately, and he pivots to face me.

"What did you just say?" His lip is curled back, and his hands drop to his sides, where he continues to clench and unclench his fists. I know I'm making things worse, but something in me is choosing this battle.

"It wasn't *my* promise to keep. Therefore, it was not *my* betrayal." I say with my tone surprisingly even. His eyes nearly bulge out of his head, but I don't stop there. "I followed the tradition that was set by our ancestors. Well, the royal family before *we* became the royal family anyway. They can't argue if they want to claim to be loyal to the realm." I say, looking down at my hands and more blood I feel tainting the skin there. Even if it weren't my hands that made the killing blow. It's never my hands, but nonetheless, now I have Benat's blood there.

I should not have taken my eyes off my father, though. The retractable switch that my father keeps in his chest pocket comes down on my hands like a strike of lightning across the delicate bones. I recoil, pulling them to my chin as I cry out in pain.

"I can't even be the one to deliver the punishment I wish to because I have to deal with the repercussions of your actions!" With those words, Pravin slithers into the room like the snake he is.

"Wait, right now? Before my dinner with Ky—the winner?" I almost slipped by using his name. Marking myself a little *too* familiar with the newcomer. It wouldn't be like using Benat's name, but he is too flustered to notice as he retracts the switch in his hand and turns to face his number one guard dog.

"Keep the marks somewhere that is able to be hidden; I don't want anyone poking their nose where it doesn't belong before the time is right." He says, ignoring my questions, and strides from the room, slamming the heavy door behind him.

"We can do this the easy way or the hard way... what's it going to be, princess?" My gut reaction is to spit. I don't know where it came from or why, but the saliva floods my mouth, and I let it fly into his wretched face. He is stunned silent for a moment as he stares at me wiping the spit from his eye, but after that brief moment, we both start sprinting. He chases after me while I run for my bathing chamber.

"You fucking bitch! You are going to pay for that!" He growls and chases me into the room. I don't know what I was thinking by running to the only spot in my chamber that is a dead end. I turn around to face him, and he laughs. "Not a very smart girl, are you?" He taunts, and my lip trembles with building anger and fear. He's only punished me a handful of times, but for some reason, it always seems worse. Dirty, almost. I look at him and the space he occupies in the large doorway. He's not a huge man... I could force my way back into the bedchamber. I could try...

I run for the small wedge of space, but he is quicker than me. His arm snaps out, barring my exit and wrapping around my middle. He throws me toward the counter, where the basin of water sloshes as my hips ram into the stone. The heavy stone bowl wobbles so much from the impact that it falls, crashing and splitting in two as it hits the ground. His hand comes to the back of my head, his fingers tangling in my hair that is still down from the battle, and he shoves me forward. With his other hand, he rips the buttons of my dress down the back. Ruining it completely.

"Hold still, and this will be over quickly. You know, as well as I do, that it hurts you a lot less if you don't struggle." He says through clenched teeth as he tugs at the material more. The seam in the back splitting over my ass. My eyes fly wide when the skin there meets air. He growls as he slaps my bare ass with the flat of his hand. The sound of the contact competing with the crack of a whip. I cry out in pain, and he groans.

I thrash in his grip, bruising my hips as he pins me harder with one of his legs. My face aches where he presses it to the counter, and with each painful hit, I hiss as my head hits the wall below where the mirror hangs. The hand that holds my hair becomes tighter in its grip. He's ripping strands out at the root. I can't help the tears that bloom in my eyes as I finally give up my fight. My muscles weaken as I give in, and he rips my head back so that I can see my reflection in the mirror.

My eyes are bloodshot from the tears, and my face red from the fight and being pressed into the counter. My hair is a mess of knots, and behind me he stands, chest heaving and his trousers tented. The sick bastard is getting off on this. Just as I think he's done, he leans down, rubbing his arousal on my ass cheek as he does.

"Why don't I punish you a little bit for myself too? That stunt you pulled spitting on me..." The hand that isn't holding me down comes around, and he holds it out in front of my face. "Go on, princess... you want to spit? *Spit*. I'll give you at least that before I punish you the way I really want."

"I hope you burn in Zameil." I ground out with my lip curled back.

"Fine... have it—"

"Princess Astraea?" My heart flops at the voice that comes through the bathing chamber door, and I'm quicker than Pravin this time.

"Be out in a minute!" I call to her. Pravin's grip tightens a little more before he finally pushes me forward and yanks his hand free of my tousled hair. He stands up straight, adjusting himself and slicking his muddy brown hair back in its usual style.

"You pull that shit again, and I will make sure you can't sit on that pretty ass for a week." He walks from the bathing chamber without a backward glance, and when I finally let out the breath I had been holding, it comes out on a broken sob.

It's only a moment later that the door swings open again and I come face-to-face with the jade green eyes I know and love. The emotion from everything floods from me. Tears stream down my face, and snot clogs my nose. She sits on the floor with me, and we start rocking. I'm not sure if it's her or me, but when I can finally see through the moisture in my eyes, I see that she is crying too.

"We tried," she whispers, as her lip trembles, and I nod. "We tried." She says again, and her thumb strikes a line under my eye, wiping away the tears, and I sniff the snot that has worked its way into my breakdown. I lock my gaze to hers.

"If I leave again, you are coming with me." She nods immediately, agreeing with my declaration with a sad smile. We both know there is no way that my father is letting me get away again. It would take a miracle to be so lucky. No. She may not know it yet, but I can feel something shifting within me. I'm getting tired of living my life being told what I have to do. "I'm glad you're here." I finally say.

"They can't get rid of me that easily." She jokes, but her smile still doesn't reach her eyes as she stands. She grits her teeth, but she doesn't complain as she helps me to my feet.

"Are you okay? Your back, I mean. Kellan told me that he brought you *a salve.*" I ask, whispering the last word. She shakes her head.

"Yea, he did. I don't blame him for what happened, you know?" She asks, and I dip my chin. She doesn't have to say who she blames. It's the same man I blame for nearly everything bad that has ever happened in my life, but I also blame myself.

"I know. I'm sorry about Barrett." I say, meeting her gaze.

"Me too. He is the reason I only got a whipping, though. He saved my life. He lied to the king. Said that I never returned to your chamber after preparing your bed while you were at dinner. He was late to his post the morning after you escaped. They are saying that is when you were kidnapped." She says, and I scoff, stepping out of my ruined dress. My backside is pink around the edges, and the center is red and raw where most of the punishment was.

"Things are going to change, Cole." Wrapping a towel around my middle, I level her with my eyes. "I can't live like this anymore, and if I got one thing from my father, it's my stubborn ways." If I can't please him doing what I'm told, I may as well do what I want and damn the consequences.

"I have some more salve. Let me help you." She pulls a small tin from her skirt pocket and holds it out in offering, but I put my hand up in refusal.

"Absolutely not. This is nothing compared to what you endured. What you must still be enduring. You keep it."

"Wherever he got this batch... it's stronger than anything I've ever seen before—I have my back wrapped in bandages, but Astraea... It's not to hide the wounds. It's because *there are no wounds.*" My brows hike up my face, and as though I need to see the proof for myself, I push her to spin around. A knock at the door of the bedchamber stops me, though. "Trust me. They are gone." After I chew my lip for a brief moment, I tip my chin and look down at myself.

"I can't go to the door looking like this. I'm sure they are here to collect me for dinner with—the winner. Would you tell whoever it is that I require a little more time to prepare?" Hurriedly she makes her way to the door, and when she turns around after closing it, her face is ashen.

"What?" I ask as I drop the towel and pick up the tin she placed on my vanity table. As I begin rubbing the cream that's inside over my skin, my senses are hit with a particular, familiar smell. Something that reminds me—of something, but I can't for the life of me figure out *what.* There are other scents too—warm, maybe cinnamon and clove; it's spicy and—*oh, warming on my skin.*

"Astraea?" I look up from my jarring experience with the salve, remembering my friend who just answered the door and is now looking at me the color of sun-bleached sand.

"Who is it?" I ask, straightening my spine. In my experience, not much can get Cole speechless, so seeing her standing there, with her jaw nearly on the floor, has all the hair on my body standing on end.

"Kyros Kahzal of *Deimos*..."

"Why is he here? Doesn't he know that—" I begin, but she interrupts.

"Astreaea!" She whisper-shouts my name, and I stop where I am, pulling a new dress up over my thighs. "Deimos, as in, the last kingdom to relinquish its magick... As in The Mad Queen Phaedra Lazuro... How is he a suitor? I thought the queen didn't have any heirs." She asks, and I keep getting dressed as quickly and quietly as I can. I wrap my hair up in a quick twist and rub some balm over my puffy lips. There is nothing that can be done about my eyes or the redness in my cheeks. I can only hope that the shadows of the firelight throughout the castle can help mask that.

"He was announced as the 'appointed heir'—well, he and his brother actually. I have a lot to tell you, Cole. Will you be here when I return?" I come to a stop in front of her, and our hands immediately gravitate to one another.

"I will be waiting. Please stay safe."

Chapter Twenty-One

Astraea

Stepping out into the dark hallway, Kyros is standing with his back pressed to the opposite wall, his foot propped up behind him. He's dressed now in black, head to toe, just like at the tavern, which casts his figure that much more into the shadows. If I weren't looking for him, I likely wouldn't have even seen him at all.

"I'm surprised you came to fetch me yourself," I say, stopping in the middle of the hall, where he doesn't move, his arms still crossed over his wide chest.

"Why would I send someone else? Aren't you supposed to have dinner with me?" He asks, pushing off the wall. When he offers me his arm, I look down at it with a quirked brow.

"Are we being chivalrous now that you know I'm a princess?"

"I think you're mistaken. I recall being very chivalrous when I saved you from losing your hands in the market," he says, then leans closer and whispers, "And that's when I was led to believe you were just a mere commoner." I snort and anxiously look around, hoping that none of the shadows my father employs heard any of that statement. I start walking in the direction of the dining hall without taking his offer, and he growls as he follows close behind me. *Good, I hope he's annoyed.*

"I was never going to lose my hands. It was all a misunderstanding. I would have gotten out of it myself." I chance a look out of the corner of my eye when Kyros easily catches up to me and takes a slow stride to stay at my side.

"Keep telling yourself that." He almost laughs, and I quicken my steps with a huff, but then his hand reaches out and wraps around my arm at the crook of my elbow. I wince at the placement. The bruises my father left behind scream, and I hope he doesn't notice.

"Wait, look—" He pleads, and I stop abruptly, whirling on him. If we are seen having a heated conversation like this, it will give away the fact that we are familiar with one another to some level, and that *will* get back to my father, which won't be good for either of us. I look around, and Kyros' nostrils flare, and even in the dark I see his pupils, black on black, dilate. His breathing quickens just a fraction.

"What is that smell on you?" He asks, and I screw up my face in vexation.

"Excuse me?" I grind out between my teeth, yanking my arm free of his hold. Shit. Shit. *Shit.* Does he smell the balm? I thought the scent was fairly light, but perhaps it's not. Does he know what it is? If so, wouldn't that mean he is a magick sympathizer? Or could he have magick like Pravin said... What was it about his tattoos?

"Nevermind, but we are going to the terrace off the library. Not the formal dining hall." Kyros announces, dismissing my question. My eyes jump to his.

"We are?" I question, looking around more cautiously. "Why?"

"I requested it. I thought it might give us a little more privacy than the formal dining room could provide. They should be done setting it up now." My brow furrows as I look at him.

"Um, ok..." Turning on my heel, I head for the stairs that lead down to the lower level. The library is located almost directly below my bedchamber. It's one of the many places I would sneak off to through the passages within the walls.

My father almost never came into the library. He says, *'History is where it belongs. In the past.'* Just the thought makes me roll my eyes. If we don't learn from history, we will be stuck making the same mistakes over and over again, but that's one of the many areas we are different. He doesn't, and never has, cared about changing anything. Other than the weight of the coin he owns and the ability to rule over those with less, he has no interest. The only way he knows how to rule is to instill fear into the people he leads. If they fear the world around them or what will happen if they embrace it, he can control them better than by just telling them what to do.

Kyros stays close the entire walk, silently at my side. He is an enigma. Most men in his position would be falling over themselves for my attention...for my favor, but not him. However, I can feel his eyes on me at every chance. Any time I look away, I feel his gaze drift back to me, and it makes me curious, if not annoyed.

"Why are you here?" I ask the same question I did in the tavern, and he huffs out an unimpressed laugh, staying silent, and I roll my eyes. When we reach the doors to the library, there are no guards standing at its entrance. Guarding knowledge is not important to my father, so why would he waste men on its doors?

Kyros opens the door and gestures me inside. The library is dark; not one flick of firelight to see by. It's an enormous space, so the light that does come in doesn't reach much. The previous ruler clearly had a love for books. Sometimes I imagined that *he* was my father and many of the beautiful spaces he created within these castle walls were made for me to enjoy. Building scenarios in my head to make the honesty of my life more bearable. The far wall is tall, with a beautiful stained glass mural of a king in battle with a beast. His sword is dripping in blood, and the manticore's mane is just as blood-coated and matted. It's beautiful and deadly. It makes me think of the man who I've come here with. He too seems lost looking at the beauty of it as the moon lights the panels in a muted multitude of colors.

"You know there are two stories about the battle the king fought with the beast?" He pauses, tilting his head as he thinks for a moment. I can barely see him through the muted colorful light that shines through the colored panels. "One about the king that had to fight the beast. A battle to the death after also winning the first war against the kingdom." He looks down at me, just briefly, before continuing.

"The other story is that the manticore chose to fight alongside him. Helping him win a battle he otherwise wouldn't have. He risked everything by choosing to trust a monster who could have ended everything because he sensed something in the beast that was no different than what was in him." He scoffs; the sound is small and laced with something, but he turns, facing me once more. "Either way, it was the gods proving him worthy of the crown, don't you think?"

I'm not sure what to say to this. I agree, but to say so would be admitting I think that my father is not worthy. I would be admitting that the title of Princess should not be mine. Instead, I say nothing, and he eventually begins walking again. I look back over my shoulder as I follow. At the dance of fury the man and beast seem to be in. I can easily see the way both of those stories align with the art. I can easily see that what I didn't admit is true.

I lose my sure footing in the dark. While I've come here many times, the deep darkness and the moonlight filtered through the heavy drapes along the terrace make it difficult to navigate. The only light comes from the colored tiles of the stained glass. I don't trust myself to not fall on my face, so I slow my pace.

"Would you please just take my arm? I would like to get on with this before the morning." Kyros grumbles at my side, and reluctantly I reach for him. When my fingers find his arm and he covers my hand with his, heat floods my cheeks, and for once I am grateful for the dark.

"How is it you can guide me through this dark library, but I have grown up here and would still end up knocking over a priceless artifact?" I question out loud, and I swear I feel him chuckle, but he says nothing. Before I know it, we are coming to a stop at the archway that leads to the terrace.

"After you," he says, pulling the heavy curtain back. I step through the exit and onto the terrace that I have sat on many times over, but somehow, tonight, it feels bigger, like I am tiny in comparison to this moment in time. The deep indigo sky is dotted with twinkling stars, and the swirls of light trapped between them give the perfect backdrop to the table in the middle of the balcony set for two, with a single candle burning in the center. It's romantic even. My brows furrow. Romance is not something I came to expect from this whole endeavor, but maybe that was because my father only ever treated it as a business transaction, something that I was meant to do regardless of my thoughts. I swallow as Kyros comes to stand next to me, and our arms barely brush. I cross mine over my chest and rub my exposed skin with my hands, feeling a little uncomfortable with my thoughts.

"If it's too much, we don't have to do this." He says quietly, but I shake my head.

"It's—it's not too much. It's just *unexpected*." I manage to say.

"Are we not meant to be courting?" He questions, and I turn to face him.

"I just," my voice gets caught in my throat. His eyes are nearly all black, like the glittering black blade of Tsalalerian Steel, and they seem to see further into my mind than any other man has cared to look. *This* is dangerous. I can't let his stupid pretty face cloud the fact that all of these men are the same. They signed up to be here to marry me—*for power*. Each and every one of them has an ulterior motive. This is likely the first of many courting dinners with winners from the games my father has planned for these men.

"What are you thinking?" I jump at the sound of his voice.

"It's nothing." I excuse myself from his side and sit in one of the chairs without waiting, wincing when my backside meets the chair. Though the balm has definitely aided my healing, it's not instant. When he finally moves, he takes the seat opposite, and only a moment of awkward silence later the staff comes bustling out onto the terrace with a cart of food. I'm immediately engulfed in the scents of glazed meats, potatoes, and vegetables. Fruit pies and creamy desserts. They place a plate before both of us, uncovering it and pouring water into our chalices. Of course my father wouldn't allow wine. I roll my eyes at the staff as they go to stand a distance away, but close enough that they can likely hear anything we talk about.

"Are you always this closely monitored?" He questions, eyeing me with a tilt of his head.

"I mean, yeah, pretty much." I admit, looking at the staff out of the corner of my eye. Kyros keeps his eyes trained on me, only making a humming noise deep in his throat, like he is studying my every movement. Just as he did in the tavern, and I can't help but feel inadequate. "Why?"

"It just seems like you are a bit like a prisoner instead of a princess." He says, and I kick my foot out, whacking him right in the shin. "Ow... Did you just *kick* me?" The look on his face is bemused.

"You can't say stuff like that!" I whisper-shout through clenched teeth. Low enough, I think, that the closest of the staff can't hear. Though there is no way to be sure. My eyes are sideways looking at them when Kyros reaches over the table and guides my face back toward him, his fingers gently pinching my chin in their grip. My eyes round at the thought of the many sets of eyes watching him openly touch me outside of a gentlemanly escort.

"I will say and do whatever I want, Shula." He says, leaning in closer, and I swear the wings that live to torment me in my stomach around him take flight yet again. Clearing my throat, I sit back further, taking my chin out of his reach and looking at him through my lashes. If I didn't know any better, I'd think I almost saw a smirk on his face.

"So, Kyros Kahzal of Diemos, what is the point of these dinners, then? Everyone knows that it's my father who the suitors really aim to impress." I say, and his eyes darken.

"You and I both know by now, I don't aim to impress anyone." I suppose he is right in that. I have only seen him rather grumpy and not very friendly; he can't be aiming to impress anyone with such a personality, but still. He keeps looking over my shoulder, and I want to look back, but I already know it's likely one of the staff getting closer and trying to hear our conversation. We continue to eat, and our conversation lulls as I watch him continually eyeing the bodies around us with a hostile sort of tension, and an idea springs to life in my mind.

"Can we go for a walk?" I stand abruptly, and his brows hike; a smirk transforms his face. The semi-joyous look makes the butterflies flutter once again.

"We can..." He stands too and offers me an arm, which I immediately take before I lose my gall, and because I'm going to need him to listen closely. We begin leisurely walking through the library, which is now lit by the hearth on the wall, and I begin telling him about all the time I have spent here. How it's one of my favorite rooms in the castle, and right before we reach the dark tapestry that covers the narrow passage in the wall, I chance a glance over my shoulder. When I notice the one spy disguised as a staff member looking over his own shoulder, I act.

"This way!" I whisper, pulling Kyros by his hand into the crevice in the wall. I have to bite my lips hard to stop myself from laughing. The passage is very narrow, making our bodies nearly press into one another. One of my hands presses into the firm plane of his chest, and his hand rests lightly at my hip.

"Where did they go?" I hear someone on the other side of the tapestry say, and I can't help the giggle that tries to escape before a warm hand comes up and covers my mouth.

"Careful, Shula, or you will give away your secrets." I swallow under his hand, and then when we hear the footsteps fading as they continue looking for us, I tug his hand from my mouth and toward one of my favorite hidden rooms in the castle. When we break through the other side, I have a huge smile on my face. Not only have I not been in this space for far too long, but giving my father's lackeys the slip just makes everything in me lighter. Easier to feel happiness that is entirely harder to come by. Usually, I have at least hours before he is brought in to help find me, but given what has happened recently, I doubt I will be as lucky.

I stop in the center of the tall circular room, and my eyes land on Kyros, but again, he's not looking at the room at all, but at me. In this lighting, the silver glow of the moon shining brightly through all the windows in the periscope of a room, it appears that he is drinking me in like a man without water at the Dead Sea.

"This is one of my favorite, most secret hideaways in the castle. Not many people know about it, but now I am trusting you with the secret." I smile smaller at him and turn to walk to the window seat at the far center.

"What is this place?" His voice startles me at the proximity, but aside from a sharper influx of breath, I keep my voice steady when I respond.

"I'm not really sure. I like to pretend that the old king used to come here to get lost in his dreams, or perhaps he came here to talk to the stars on nights such as these." I laugh halfheartedly.

"And why do *you* come here, Shula?" He is standing so close to my back I can feel the warmth radiating from his body. The earthy, warm scent of a smoky fire, laced with honey, wraps around me and makes it difficult to swallow.

"I guess I come here for the same reason. A place I can just *be*; no eyes watching or no expectations to be something I'm not." A shiver rolls over my skin, peppering the flesh with goosebumps.

"But you brought me here? Is there still no expectations?" He whispers from where he stands behind me, and his breath caresses the shell of my ear. "No eyes watching," His fingertips hover over the skin of my upper arm and barely touches, gliding down to my elbow and back up again. Taking a deep breath, my head tilts to the side, offering him the column of my neck. I don't know what I'm doing. I brought him here to ask questions. I can tell he and his brother are different. They don't seem inclined to trip on my father's every word or every—*OH.*

Kyros runs his nose along the column of my neck in a slow drag, still barely touching, but the heat from him is scorching. He breathes me in, and a growl builds low in his throat.

"Maybe I brought you here so *you* could be lost in a dream." I press him, unable to contain the lust I feel in the moment. I turn around to face him. His eyelids are just as heavy as mine as he leans over me.

"*You* are very dangerous, Shula." He says, his hands still hovering. They come up to trail the line of my jaw. "But I don't get lost in dreams or hide from my nightmares, and neither should you. If you don't want to be something you're not, choose to be who you are."

"Is that what you do? Do you never hide who you really are?" I ask him.

"Sometimes the choice is opposite; the decision to hide what we really are because maybe it's the realm that is not ready for the truth." His lips are hovering over mine. All I have to do is push up on my tip toes and allow him to claim my mouth, but his words confuse me and cause me to pause.

"ASTRAEA!" My father's bellowing voice echoes through the small space around us, and I flinch. "Come out from wherever it is you're hiding at once!"

"Stay here. When we leave—"

"No." Kyros interrupts, but before I can tell him anything else, he turns around and stalks out from behind the tapestry.

"Fuck!" I grind out under my breath.

Chapter Twenty-Two

Astraea

"Where is she? Have you done something with her?" I hear my father growl in question as I, too, come out from behind the tapestry. "Maybe it was you and your heathen brother who kidnapped her in the first place. Have you come to claim your prize another way?"

"You're really accusing me and my brother of kidnapping? Honestly? Do you often make your guests feel so welcome, or am I just special?" Kyros says flatly, and my feet halt as my jaw nearly hits the floor. I don't mean to eavesdrop, but now my curiosity is thoroughly piqued. My stride turns to a crawl as I slowly come closer to where they are talking, just around the corner of a large bookshelf.

"Don't you speak to me like that, if you—" My father's warning is cut off by Kyros' sharp tongue.

"If I what? Will you have my head like those you, so disgustingly, have spiked along your curtain wall? I will speak to you *precisely*, the way that *you*—-speak to me. If you wish to have my respect, you will *earn it*. Just like any other man or woman would," Kyros interrupts, and I about die then and there. *This man is going to get himself killed,* but he doesn't stop there. "Also, I'll have you not forget, while you're king now, I am in line to be one as well," he says proudly as I chance a peek around the bookshelf and make out the men as they stand face to face. Kyros, standing taller than my father, steps forward into his space, and the guards who always follow my father around put their hands on the weapons at their hips. My father throws out his hand, a motion for them to stand down, and Kyros does not so much as flinch or take a step back. "A kingdom is only strong if it has strong allies; it would be foolish to make an adversary out of *another* strong crown. Your empty threats only serve to piss me off." He says to my father, who remains motionless like a statue.

A rough hand grips me by my arm and pushes me out of hiding, and I can't help the yelp that comes at the sudden pain and shock.

"I found your petulant daughter, Connard. Hiding in the shadows and listening in on the conversations of men." Pravin proclaims with an evil smirk plastered on his face, even as his eyes travel the length of my body and linger a moment too long at my ass. Both my father and Kyros turn to face us. My father's glare is ice cold as he sees me, but Kyros' black eyes hone in on the grip that Pravin has on my arm, and his teeth clench tight. The muscle jumping under the shadow of hair along his jaw.

"Is that how you allow your men to treat your daughter? My potential *wife*? The future of potentially two kingdoms?" He says through his teeth, but my father only lifts his chin. Fire flares through my entire body at Kyros' words, though, and I don't know what to make of it. The heat borders on anger and embarrassment as they all speak of me like I am not in the room.

"She is a troublemaker and needs to learn how to follow orders." My father spits out snidely with a curl of his lip.

"Remove your hands from her. *Now*." Kyros growls; the threat isn't in his words, though, not even the sound of the gravel in his voice, as terrifying as it is. The threat and the cause of real terror is in his eyes. Black as night and filled with the promise of something more than pain. Pravin's grip loosens, but not before squeezing painfully and pushing me forward aggressively.

"I—I'm sorry." I start, but I am interrupted by both men in front of me.

"It's not you who needs to apologize," Kyros says.

"You should be sorry!" My father shouts at the same time, and my eyes flick between them both before settling on the ground between us. I am sorry; I didn't wish for this night to go like this. I fear for Kyros and Mavros, even for Zinya, now. My father is ruthless, and I wouldn't put it past him to slit their throats in their sleep while they stay here in the castle, consequences be damned.

He has never handled disrespect with patience, and well, being out worded by a younger man? A man here for his daughter's hand? A man who is not yet king and not even true royalty but only an appointed heir?

It's probably one of the most disrespectful things he has heard aimed his way in a very long time. Save for his petulant daughter that can't keep her mouth shut, of course. This whole thing is my father's way of securing more power. He can't have power over a man not willing to give it to him. Kyros is the lowest on the list of men who would, considering the show he's put on tonight. Somehow though, my father hasn't cut him down where he stands. Meaning, his kingdom must hold a pretty high power. Something my father *craves*.

I chance another look through my lashes, but I know before I lay eyes on him that Kyros is staring right at me. His nostrils flare as he keeps his eyes trained on my face, and I notice his hands splayed wide then clenching into a fist at his side. Like he is trying to avoid reaching for his weapon. Such a threat would not end well, not surrounded by the king's guard in a dark library filled with nothing but history. My father has no qualms about adding history to the books if it pleases him, but something about Kyros and his kingdom has my father pausing. If this had been anyone else, I know my father wouldn't have thought twice about stringing him up at the gallows. I need to find out more about them and where they come from. Cole seemed to know something.

"This is my fault. I should have known you would be worried," I say to my father before turning my words to Kyros. "Kyros, please understand the worry my father has been under since I went missing just days ago. I should have remembered to keep one of the staff with me while we were together." When I speak, I don't look him in the eyes. I keep my focus on the toes of my slippers, and then I see Kyros' hand reach for me. He gently takes my hand into his, and I let my gaze drift up fully.

"Of course, then the apology is all mine. Connard, perhaps the next time I win alone time with the princess, *I* will be allowed to be the one to keep her safe. After all, you do know who I am... If anyone is able to keep her safe, you know it would be me." He says cryptically and bows low, kissing the back of my hand but never taking his eyes from me.

"Yes, of course. This was all a misunderstanding, but Kyros Kahzal of Diemos, you will have to *win* time with her, just as the other suitors." My father says, but I can hear the controlled frustration in his tone.

"And win I shall. Let me walk you back to your chambers, princess." Kyros says, and my father speaks before I can manage.

"That would be highly inappropriate. Pravin will escort Princess Astraea back to her quarters." My father demands, but Kyros keeps his grip on my hand as he turns round to face my father again.

"No,"

"Stop—" I cut in, squeezing Kyros' hand with my plea. He clearly has a death wish. "I will walk myself to my quarters. I don't need assistance." A throat clears, and we all look toward the entrance. Relief floods my veins.

"Excuse me, my king, perhaps I can take the princess to her room? I have already drawn a bath for her and readied her bed. It is quite late, and we all have a very early morning." Kyros and my father are stuck in a staring contest, but with a heavy sigh, my father surprisingly relents. Maybe he has finally met his match in stubbornness.

"Fine, off to ready for bed, but Astraea?" He says threateningly. "Bathe and bed; do not let me find that you have left your chamber. You will be needed at breakfast in the morning with all of the suitors when I announce the next trial." His eyes track to Kyros. "Make sure you don't miss the announcement, Mister Kazhal."

"Thank you, my king; you are very gracious." Cole says as she bows low before urgently taking me by the arm and guiding me toward the exit. Before we leave the men behind, I can't help but look over my shoulder to see Kyros one last time. His eyes are like endless pools of darkness, his gaze darkened even more by his mood, and as he watches me leave, I can't help but feel like something has changed.

"You wanna tell me what the hell that was about?" Colette asks with her eyes wide as she shuts the door behind her. She wasn't lying about having everything prepared for me in my room. The night is unseasonably warm, so the hearth is not lit, but candles flicker around the room, casting shadows with their dance.

"Honestly, I'm still trying to figure that out for myself." I say, sitting heavily on the edge of my bed. "Something about that man is driving me mad, Cole." She quirks a brow, waiting for me to continue. "He is so intriguing and mysterious..." I fall back with a huff, "But also, frustrating and boorish. I both want to punch him and climb him like a tree." I let out a frustrated groan. "What is wrong with me?"

"Sounds like you've got a crush on a suitor." She laughs, and I shoot back up and give her a face.

"I do not have a crush on him. He's angry and annoying, and he's going to get himself killed with the way he talks to my father! Did you hear everything he said to him, Cole? He's got a death wish!" I say with vexation as I push myself up onto my elbows. She is standing over me with her hands on her hips and head tilted.

"Whatever you say, *Princess*." She smiles with candor, and I roll my eyes as I lift my foot. She removes my slippers one at a time. We move easily into our usual routines, regardless of the rather unusual situation we are currently living through. It's one thing I can always count on Colette for. She will always be there to keep me firmly rooted. My safety. My home.

"Do you think that my father is going to punish him?" I finally ask, standing and turning my back to her so she can help me out of the dress.

"I think, in all the years I have been in this castle, I have never once heard anyone speak to your father the way that he just did and live to tell the tale." She places the bathrobe around my shoulders as I turn to face her. She must see the worry I feel brewing in my stomach all over my face, because her eyes soften and she places a hand on my shoulder. "But I also have never seen your father so honestly disturbed by the words of another either. Whatever Kyros is up to, he seems to know exactly what he is doing."

She is right about that, but it doesn't bring me any reassurance that he, his brother, and Zinya will be kept safe. Plus, my father is likely to take his wrath out on someone undeserving if he can't take it out on Kyros or the others, not that they deserve it either, but I'm sure in his mind they do.

My thoughts whirl through my head as I make my way to my bathing chamber. Standing in the doorway, the reminder of what happened here earlier tonight presses heavily on me. I know what would have happened had Cole not arrived when she did. What Pravin would have done had he been given the time to do it. My jaw clenches tight as unease builds in my chest. He's never gone so far.

"Cole?" I say, turning around as she continues to straighten up the bedchamber.

"Yea?" She pauses.

"Will you stay with me tonight?" I chew my bottom lip as I wait for her response.

"Of course I will." She pauses, looking around the room too. "Don't let him get to you, Astraea. Men like him feed on your fear. Show him the strength you and I both know you have." She says, and I nod before turning around and closing the bathing chamber door between us.

I don't realize how tired I am until the heat of the water and steam in the room seeps into my body and relaxes my sore muscles. The fight with Pravin, the beating he delivered, and then the tension through the dinner with Kyros has bunched up everywhere. My eyes drift closed as I lay my head back on the neck roll, a sinking feeling creeping into my gut with every moment that passes. A feeling that has my heart racing and gooseflesh peppering the skin that is exposed from the water. The feeling of eyes creeping closer, watching, waiting—*calling.*

Chapter Twenty-Three
Kyros

I FELT IT AGAIN. That bristling magick urging me towards her like no other feeling I've ever encountered. It has to be the relic. She has to carry it with her; there is no other reason that I would feel the magick coming from her like I know I have. But the thing that is oddly bothering me more is the scent coming from her skin.

"What are you going to do?" Zinya asks as I strap my body with weapons. "You are supposed to be at breakfast in the morning. They will notice if you are not there."

"I will be there." I grunt, once again brushing her questions off.

"Are you going to tell Mavros?" I know what she is really asking. She really wants to know if this is something she is going to need to keep from him. I avoid answering.

"Where is my brother?" I ask, looking around the room one last time before I leave.

"He's searching for the relic. He said he was going to 'take a walk' to see if he *happened* on the call of it." She responds. "What you should be doing—instead of *this*." She gestures up and down my body with her hands.

"So he's still sulking after I took the spotlight off of him." I say, and she scoffs.

"You did just what you told him not to do. Do you blame him for being upset?" She responds, and again, I don't give her an answer; instead, I level her with my eyes and purse my lips. Zinya is one of my most respected commanders; she will always tell me how it is and will always have mine and Mavros' best in mind. We were brought in by Queen Phaedra around the same time, and we have been inseparable ever since. Living in the conditions we did for as long as we did together created bonds stronger than blood ever could.

"I've never seen you this—*erratic*—you have to understand my concern." She says, coming to stand right in front of me, leaving me no other option but to face her.

"I'm not being erratic." But even as I grumble the words, I know them to be a lie.

"You changed the plan. *Your* plan, on a whim, in front of the king, Kyros. What is *not erratic* about that?" She says with one brow hiked. I close my eyes and crack my neck.

"I will tell you again, as I told Mavros several times since being here. Something about this whole situation feels off. I am going to get to the bottom of it. The princess we thought we were coming here to play with while we searched for the relic is not the vapid doll playing pretty in the tower like I thought she'd be. You and I both know it." My eyes flick between hers, and she finally sighs, taking a step back and waving to the door.

"Just don't get yourself killed. The kingdom needs you."

"This kingdom needs more than a man; it needs a miracle." I say before I make my way through the door and into the dark hall. As much as I want to just rend a portal right here to take me where I want to be, I know that can be the last thing I can do. Instead, I sneak through the darkened halls while everyone else is either sleeping or fucking and head to the stables.

It's not surprising I make it all the way there with little to no interference from the king's guard. King Connard has gotten comfortable in this castle surrounded by people who fear him. His guards are lazy, and his grounds have holes with little defense. If they were attacked today, this kingdom would be taken. I have no doubt. The real shock is that he is considered as powerful as he is. He is nothing more than a pompous prick with a mouth that spews hate and hands that serve death to anyone small willing to create a ripple in the sand. Let's see what happens with someone a little more challenging. Someone who won't make ripples but fucking sandstorms.

I hush Khol as he stirs. When I enter, the stable boy jolts awake, staring wide-eyed at me. He can't be more than twelve years old, sleeping in a bed of hay just like the animals he cares for. He's shivering, and since it's still fairly warm from the day, I know it's fear that makes him tremble.

"You are right to be scared." I take a step forward and reach into myself, calling my magick to my palm. It's not a good idea, but it's the best I have in this situation. If anyone catches me on this outing, it will be my neck they will aim to lasso with rope. It won't end that way, but I would rather avoid the mess.

"I—I didn't," the boy stammers, trying to scramble backward. He tries to create space between us, but it's no use. He is cornered, and I am Hawk, death, a moth in the night. My eyes lock with his, and as they do, he stills. My hand comes out between us, and in my palm a pool of glittering black sand and shadows churns like a beautiful storm. A sound like wings thrumming at the center.

"Sleep," I say, then let the shadowy sand reach for him. As soon as it hits his face, his eyes roll into the back of his head. "And when you wake, remember only the nightmare in my place." I help his body fall gently to the bed of hay. Removing my cloak, I lay it over the boy. Wishing there was more I could do, but this kingdom and the rest are fucked unless I get the relic. And as it seems, I need to gain the trust of a princess in order to do that.

I take a look around the stables to ensure there are no other wandering eyes, and when I'm satisfied it's just me and the horses,

I lean my forehead against Khol's. "Ready, boy? We've got to be quick." His answering chuff is as good as any. I saddle him and guide him out the rear exit. Peering out of the stable door, I check to see that the guards are not around, and just as I thought, it is clear. I've been scouting every chance I get, and the fact that I have searched so much of the castle in so little time being here, it's clear the defense is awful. I know I can get out and back without issue, unless luck is not on my side.

If Mavros knew what I was doing right now, I would never hear the end of it.

Throwing my hand out, the markings that are now exposed on my forearms dance along my skin, and the crackling shadows that flow from my fingertips catch fire. The half-circle portal I render glows bright against the night sky; I don't have to order Khol forward. He and I step through the divide before we are seen, and as soon as we are both on the other side, I close my fist, and it snaps shut in a puff of smoke at our backs.

I came here for one reason. I need to know who supplied the princess with the Creshian balm. I would know that scent from a mile away, and if she had it in Eathian, that means someone in the castle has magick or is in legion with someone who has magick, and I need to find out whichever it is. Luckily, I know one of the only dwellers in the Creshian Forest left who likely created the balm.

Khol and I ride for what feels like hours before we reach the clearing where the moon led me to the dweller. Her cottage is covered in moss and wildflowers. The scent and cool air alone bring a sense of ease to my body. The ever-building tension from my time in the Eathian desert washes away with a deep breath of crisp forest air. The flowers smile at the moon's glow as fireflies dance through the darkness and play with the stars. It reminds me of the time I spent here when I was young. The queen was always sending us on excursions to different areas of Eathian and the surrounding kingdoms to learn from its people. *"Knowledge is what makes you powerful, boys. You will always be the most threatening in a fight if you know more than your opponent."* She meant that in every sense, and we trained as such.

Tying Khol's lead to one of the low-hanging branches of the yew trees that surround the cottage, I pat him between the eyes before making my way through the long grasses and to the door. The door creaks open just as I am about to knock.

"Kyros. What brings you to my door in the middle of the night?" Kaeleith says, her white eyes looking directly past my shoulder. "Are you just going to stand there, or are you going to come in?" I learned a long time ago not to question how she knew if it were me or Mavros, or anyone else for that matter. She can no longer see at all with the centuries of age on her. Never once has she seen our faces, and even now, with nothing more than arriving without a word, she knew it was me.

"Since you know that I am here, I assume that you know why I am here as well?" I ask, my tone not giving any of my frustration away. The forest is imbued with more magickal properties than any place I know of, other than the Dead Sea itself, and Kaeleith is just as old as some of the oldest trees and in many ways imbued with the same elements.

"Aye," She smiles, a devilish smirk, her gaze wandering around the cottage as she guides me to sit in front of a fire where she has a cauldron heating over an open flame. She crouches down lower than her old bones should allow and begins stirring the liquid inside before her head tilts in my direction. "I made the balm, and I make more now. You will take it back with you. Go now, ask your questions."

"Who did you give this balm to recently?" I question, and she smiles into the concoction as she pulls it away from the flame and onto the cooling stone just in front of a small door at the bottom of the wall. She hums thoughtfully as she pulls baubles and bottles from shelves. Pouring mixtures and grinding flowers, herbs, and elixirs together before throwing them into the mix. The boiling liquid fizzes and pops, a flame catching only for a moment, but Kaeleith doesn't flinch. She keeps working. Her knobby hands moving in a rhythm found over time.

"Does it matter who? It clearly went to good use. I smell it on you." She says, smiling again. "It is not all I smell on you, though, Kyros Kahzal. You have finally returned to the palace."

"Not in the sense you may think. I don't have time to play games with you, Kaeleith. You know why I am here; please, just tell me who came. Who did you give the balm to?" She sucks her teeth in a clicking sound before quietly using a ladle to pour the liquid into a small tin. She crumbles the familiar dried orange flower into the mortar and uses the pestle to grind the fire poppy into a dust before sprinkling that too into the tin. She whispers an incantation as she uses her magick to stir the mix with a twirl of her finger.

She does the same thing three times, a different flower for each. When she is done, her gaze drifts in my general direction, and she holds all three tins in the palm of her hand in a stack. She steps forward and pushes them into my chest.

"You will know what they are for when you need them, and you *will* need all three." She nods again at the tins pressed over my heart more firmly, and I finally relent with a sigh and pocket the now cooled balms. "As you know, I am close with the Neer. When they come to my woods, I don't ask them why, just as I don't ask you. The princess, though, I have heard tales of her. The beauty she holds, both inside and out. She's curious and smart. She is not cruel like the king, though everyone has their secrets... Perhaps it's time for you to show her something not many have. If it's trust you wish to gain, it's vulnerability you must pay." Narrowing my eyes on her, I think about what she is saying... I swear at times her magick allows her to look inside my mind.

"You really won't tell me who came for the balm?" I ask one more time as she ushers me to the door. Her white eyes drift to mine, and a breeze blows her gray hair across her face, and she smiles as she takes a step backward.

"Use the balms, Kyros. Don't be the stubborn man you were forced to become. Remember *who* and *where* you come from. Be the man you were meant to be." Without another word or a moment for me to think about what she has said, she snaps the door shut between us.

Use the balms. I shake my head.

The thing about rending a portal back into the castle grounds is I don't know who will be on the other side. I have no way of knowing if where I am rending it will have eyes on it or if I will be safe and unseen. The implication of being caught for anyone else would surely be death. For me, it would be a severely inconvenient headache I would rather not deal with at the moment.

But like leaving to find out about the balms or the person with magick within the castle, I have no choice. I step through the divide and the smoke of it closing behind me and Khol dissipates on a desert breeze, but just like me, he freezes as we hear muffled voices whispering as we approach the stable doors. There is a shuffling before the door opens, and a woman startles as we come face-to-face.

"Divine, you scared me." She says, taking a step back and running into a man's chest with her back. She looks up at him over her shoulder, and his chin lifts as he takes me in.

"You are one of the princesses' suitors." He states, and I stare blankly at both of them. Even though my mind is racing with what I can tell them, I remain silent.

"Kyros," I finally say, clipped, before side-stepping with Khol and heading in past them. A couple of the horses whinny and chuff as I begin securing the stirrups and unfasten the cinches on Khol's saddle. He can tell I am on edge, and it's causing him to get antsy. He becomes more vocal, whining and stomping his massive hooves.

"What are you doing riding in the middle of the night?" The man asks, and I ignore him as I turn my back and continue getting Khol into his stall. It's disrespectful, and I hate that I have to play this role, but it's what they would expect of an heir of another kingdom. I hear them whispering again, and when I slowly turn around, they are frustratingly staring at one another before turning their attention back to me.

"What are you doing out here?" The redheaded woman asks as her brow furrows.

"My horse needed to run. I rode the perimeter only and came right back here, but as you have clearly stated... it's late. I should be getting back to my chamber." As I begin to leave, I cut between both of them, and once outside, I freeze. Turning around, I look at both the man, whom I recognize as one of the castle guards, and the woman. The same woman who took the Princess back to her bedchambers, but it's not who is standing before me that causes me to stop. It's the scent of fire poppies. The balm came from both of them.

"Of course. Goodnight." The woman gives a slight bow; the man does not do the same. Our eyes clash for a moment, and a cloud of fear darkens his eyes.

"Goodnight to you too, miss?" I ask.

"Colette." She smiles more and nudges the guard with the toe of her slipper.

"Rest well, Kyros of Diemos." The man finally says and nods at me, and *something* else flares in his eyes. With that, along with the scent, I know who is responsible for getting the balm for the princess. One question still remains, though: why?

Chapter Twenty-Four

Astraea

There was a time in my life that my sleep wasn't plagued by nightmares. A time so long forgotten, I feel as though it never really was. I know I am in a nightmare now because the flashing in my periphery is always the first sign. I wish I understood the meaning, but the more I try to see, the more pain comes when I wake up.

The galloping thrash of my body matches the pounding rhythm of my heart before the lasso of fiery pain and the staunching darkness evades. Every time is the same, but recently that's not been the case. I'm far more aware these days. A little more in control of my movements. I turn my head this time to face where I know I saw the flashing movement to the side, and what my eyes focus on is both confusing and beautiful.

Thousands of trees, so dense that you cannot see beyond their trunks. The bough is so dense that it blots out all light from above. I've never seen anything like it, other than in books kept in the library. Eathian has nothing of the sort. Our trees are few and far between; the sun here is much too harsh to grow anything beyond craggy, straw-like grasses and cacti that sprout here and there. Even the palace conservatory is limited to what it can grow. The longer I stare, the darker things get. Like night is eating up all of the light around me, there is no sun baking my skin from above.

"Sssssssennnnkaaaaaa," my attention is jarred by the deep hissing voice.. I don't know what it means, but it feels familiar somehow. The deep, bone-aching chill runs up my spine at the sound of it, and far off in the darkness, the rumbling laugh penetrates the air around me. The feeling of being chased makes my heart thunder in my chest both in the dream and where I lay in a paralyzed sort of sleep.

A scream rips from my throat as I physically recoil from the clawing hand that reaches for me through the darkness and sinks its shadowy talons into the flesh at my back. My body arches, tears bursting from my eyes and streaming down my face as I cry out in terror laced with pain.

"Astraea?! Shhh. It's okay. It's okay! It's Cole. I'm here." Wracking sobs shake my shoulders as Colette rocks me like a baby in the center of my bed. The room is still dark, even more so as summer is starting to creep over Eathian, making the nights, especially within the castle, darker and much warmer. There is no more need for a fire lighting the hearth.

"I—I'm okay." I manage to say on broken breaths. Each word is a little hard to push out over my frantic crying, but I continue. "It was d-different this t-time, C-Cole. I f-felt someone; *something* was there with me. I still feel the pain." Cole shuffles on the bed and reaches for my candelabra on the bedside table. She strikes a match and lights the wick, illuminating her face in a halo of golden light.

"Do you want to talk about it this time?" She asks hesitantly as she comes to sit next to me but then gasps. She pulls me urgently at the shoulder so my body twists away from her, and she can see my back. Pain slices through me with the motion. "Great Divine! You're bleeding, Astraea! A lot." Achingly, I try to turn my head to look over my shoulder at what she is seeing, but I don't have to see it to know what she's talking about. I can still feel the pain from the attack in my nightmare.

"I don't understand." I say, as a deep frown pulls down on Colette's delicate features. *This can't be.*

"We need to get you to see a healer." She shakes her head with concern.

"You were here, Cole. No one else was in this room." She stares blankly at me for a moment. Bewilderment builds with the thoughts clearly racing through her mind, and then she understands what I'm saying.

"I didn't do this! You can't possibly think I did?!" She exclaims. I have to scrunch my eyes up as her loud voice slices through my brain. The pain from my back only becomes a nuisance to the pain that is throbbing to life behind my eyes.

"No, I know it wasn't you." I shake my head and try to breathe in a long breath before continuing, "We can't go to a healer. On my vanity. The balm." I manage to choke out the words without breaking them to pieces. She rushes over, knocking down perfumes and tonics I had sitting out for my skin and hair. They go crashing to the ground, some of them shattering on the marble floor. She is just as panicked as I am, but instead of my stunned silence—she is frantic. She finally finds the tin in the back of the hidden drawer between the top of the vanity and the mirror hanging on the wall.

Hurrying across the room to my bathing chamber, she comes back with a bowl and cloth. She doesn't have her normal cleaning solution, so she has settled with water from the basin. It's not warm, but the coolness is welcomed on my inflamed and bleeding skin as she presses it to my back.

"Oh, Astraea, this is bad." She doesn't even try to pacify me into thinking it's better than it seems. "I don't know if the balm—"

"It helped your wounds." I bite out, and she snaps her mouth shut with a nod. She continues cleaning the wounds as best she can. Silently, then with two fingers, she places the balm around the edges of the jagged cuts created by the shadowy nightmare claws. The warming sensation immediately brings a sense of relief. I take a deep breath as she continues to wipe it over the wounds. I don't know what I would do without the aid of this balm. Would my own father string me up for heresy if I showed up with injuries that happened in a nightmare? Or would he blame Colette? I know the answer as soon as I think about it. *He will not know of this.* I won't let any more harm come to her.

"It's working." She says, the relief in her eyes mirroring my own. But it's short-lived as a knock comes on my door. Our eyes snap to each other and then to the mess of bloody cloth and red-tinged bowl of water. She scurries out of the bed and rushes to remove all the evidence as I push myself to stand and grab the bathrobe that is lying over my chaise.

"Princess Astraea?" The knock sounds again just as Colette whips the door open and smiles at the guard on the other side. She opens the door wide enough that he can see me too, and his eyes narrow on both of us. I don't know this man's name, but I know that he must be expendable to be on my guard. My father is just waiting for me to mess up. I'm sure once I do, it will be his head next decorating our gates.

A pang of sorrow drops heavy in my stomach as I think of it. He could be a son, a father, or a husband, and because of me, he could already be a dead man walking. Stepping closer, I look into his yellow hazel eyes. He looks kind. Too kind to be in the king's guard... then my eyes track down, and I notice his armor, or rather, lack thereof.

"Who are you?" I ask, and he coughs, taken aback by my abrupt questioning.

"My name is Viltarin," his head bows low, "of Diemos." He finishes, and my eyes widen as they search the hall for my father's men, who are nowhere to be found. My lips part as I take a step back.

"Why are you here, Viltarin?" I ask warily.

"Your guards," he clears his throat, "excuse my lack of a better term, are—*shit*." He says, shifting on his feet uncomfortably. Out of the corner of my eye, I catch Colette rolling her lips between her teeth to hold in a laugh. She's been saying the same thing for years. With the exception of a few, those are now a head shorter and no longer around, though. "I was tasked to keep an eye on them, and if ever they left you unattended, I was to watch guard. You were never meant to know, but I heard the commotion, and well, I needed to make sure that you were okay." He looks me down and then peers over my shoulder. Cole steps into his view then, and he blinks.

"It was only a nightmare. I'm sorry to blow your cover over something so inconsequential. Please send my regards to whichever brother it was who sent you..." I eye him for a moment longer, and I start to close the door when it's clear he isn't going to tell me which brother it was.

"I'm sorry, Princess. I hope your rest is unbothered for the remainder of the morning." With vexation, I let the door snap closed between us.

"Do you think he saw anything?" Cole asks, and I shake my head. I don't think he did, but something tells me that even if he did, he wouldn't go back to my father with the information.

Morning has come too soon, but regardless of the little sleep I got, my father's show must go on. Colette has been once again tasked to stay at my side. Thankfully, my father restored her as my help without question. She is exhausted too after our eventful early morning. I see it in the dark shadows under her eyes, but she helped me dress and get ready early in the morning, just hours after the nightmare, right as the sun began cresting the horizon.

"Do you know what to expect?" She asks quietly as we both approach the door to the main dining room.

"The worst?" I muse, though the humor is lost with everything that has happened as of late. "Just whatever you do, keep your head down. I don't want any attention brought to you," I tell her.

"You need to heed your own warning." She says, pursing her lips.

"Let me worry about myself. I know how far I can push things. You can't push at all." With that, she relents with a nod and pushes the door open. The court master announces my arrival loudly, making me wince. The aching behind my eyes is still ever present, but the entire room grows silent. All conversation becomes hushed as chairs protest loudly on the stone floor, and everyone stands in unison at my entrance. *Great, I'm late.*

Breakfast is not like the lavish dinners my father hosts. The formal dining room is much smaller in comparison to the great hall. All the back windows along the large room open to a balcony much like the library. The thought makes my eyes search for Kyros automatically. The light champagne dress I wear flutters the same as the white sheer curtains that hang along the long wall of open air. I'm grateful for the cool breeze. It's not every day we are blessed with one, and sometimes the desert air can be scorching without it.

None of the other people from dinner were invited to be guests for breakfast. This is only for me, my father and his trusted, the suitors, and theirs. I catch sight of Zinya standing just beyond the sheer curtains, on the balcony. Her blonde pleats in place as though she is going to war, and the same can be said for her attire. Fully suited, just as she wanted me back at the tavern. I smile just a fraction at her, and she nods just as imperceptibly.

Cole hurries off to help the dining staff after escorting me to my chair. Kyros and Mavros stand in front of their chairs with multiple bodies between them. While Mavros is far off to the side, Kyros stands directly in front of me and my father at my side. I felt his gaze on me as soon as I walked in the room, and it has yet to leave me, even after my father clears his throat with annoyance.

"Thank you all for coming to breakfast today!" He exclaims excitedly. *Like they had a choice...* "Sit now, let us eat!" My eyes wander down the line of guests who fill the table. Most of them are staring past me to my father, but when I reach Mavros, he gives me his wink, causing a blush to heat my cheeks. Shaking my head, I take a deep breath as I look down at my plate and release it as my father places a hand on my shoulder. "As you all know, I will be announcing the next event, but first I would like to celebrate an official first win and private courting with one of the heirs of

Diemos." My father raises a glass in Kyros' direction, and I almost miss the sneer Kyros pins him with before he smiles just as fake as my father and lifts his own glass in return.

"To new beginnings," Kyros says, the smile on his face turning nefarious as he keeps it on my father.

Mavros scoffs into his goblet, "...and fatal ends," he coughs to cover his words.

My eyes flick from Mavros to Kyros and then to the man they both openly taunt before I clear my throat and take a deep breath. *They both have a death wish.*

The staff brings out breakfast, thankfully interrupting whatever pissing contest is happening, and the other men jump right into talking business with my father. Marginally including me in conversation. I don't listen to most of it. My awareness lingers on the man in front of me, and my mind constantly thinks of what happened last night. Had it not been for the balm, I wouldn't have been here this morning. I would have survived, but the cost of my survival would have been high. Definitely higher than I would have been willing to pay.

A nudge of my foot makes my eyes jump forward. Kyros gives nothing away if it was he who touched me. *Maybe it was an accident.* He's not looking at me for once, instead keeping his eyes narrowed on my father as he talks animatedly to Cadoc of Iroworth. Cadoc has leaned forward looking my way several times during the conversation, probably hoping I pay him attention. All of the suitors want my favor for the next challenge, and while I find him kind and funny at times, he also seems very keen to want my father's attention, just as much as mine.

When the nudge happens again, I jerk a little less subtly because it is much higher on my leg this time. Most certainly intentional. Kyros tilts his head, eyeing me, and I can't tell if he is messing with me. I look around nervously as the touch on my leg continues to trail up the outside of it, lifting my dress in its wake. My breathing hitches, my lips parting as I keep my hooded gaze on the one man in the room I have felt drawn to since I ran into him at the market. When Kyros pushes his chair out a fraction and shifts in his seat, exposing the fact that whoever the foot belongs to couldn't be him, my gaze shifts to my left down the line of suitors. None of them are looking at me, but Mavros stares a hole into the side of his brother's head.

Feeling more and more uncomfortable, I push my chair out, calling all attention to myself by default. Lifting my chin, I don't let any distress over whatever was happening show. I smile broadly, thank everyone for coming to the breakfast, and look to my father, hoping that he will get on with the announcement. It's been some time after everyone has finished their meals. Might as well be now. My father stands, easily gathering the attention of the room.

"Thank you, sweet daughter. As Princess Astraea has mentioned, the reason we are here is other than to celebrate the win of Kyros." He tips his chin at the man mentioned, then continues. "I want to also call attention to the next challenge. As the winner of the last challenge, Kyros of Diemos will be sitting out this round, ensuring that the next winner is someone new. You may re-enter the challenges in the next round." He says, and I watch Kyros as his jaw feathers, but he doesn't remove his gaze from my father.

"Additionally, the next challenge will be a bit of a journey and will not take place in the arena as the last one did. The ceremony for the princess' favor will be held at the palace gates, but your next challenge will be in the Dunes of Parreth." My father states calmly, smiling as he looks to the rest of the suitors. Commotion erupts around the table with the announcement. Pravin gleams, standing at the door with his arms crossed over his chest. This was likely his idea. My father doesn't leave the walls of the palace for much. I can't see him willingly putting himself at risk.

A slow screech echoes through the room and causes the melee to fizzle out as all eyes turn to the source of the sound. Kyros holds a dagger about the size of my forearm in his hand, the sharp point digging into the stone table in front of us. It scratches loudly, gaining the attention he clearly wants.

"I will go on this journey and do whatever challenge you ask of the rest of the men here. I will not take to sitting back and playing a waiting game. I came here to win." He growls low, and everyone's eyes widen or brows hike. Everyone but my father and Mavros. No, the opposite is said of them. Their faces are stern with the anger they aim at Kyros.

"*Brother*." Mavros utters through gritted teeth. "You have to play by the king's rules here in Eathian. *Stay here* and keep the princess entertained for me until I get back and claim my win." He says this with that same damn wink in my direction. The brothers lock eyes, and my father tilts his head. Interested in the dynamics of the two, no doubt. I'm sure this is a way to torture Kyros, but as it appears, the two brothers may not be as close as my father probably hoped.

A tension-filled silent moment passes as a seemingly short conversation is had between the two Diemos men through their glares. Everyone in the room is waiting to see what happens. Hoping that one of them will mess up. Hoping that one of them snaps. That they say the wrong thing in the presence of my father and get themselves killed before the challenge begins.

"When does this challenge take place?" Kyros growls.

"We leave at dawn." Pravin announces stepping up to the head of the table with a wide stance and a grin aimed at my father.

"You have the rest of the day and the night to prepare with whatever you see fit. The journey will take two days to get there. The challenge should be relatively quick, then two days of travel back, given that there are no severe injuries. Tonight we will host another formal dinner and entertainment."

"Fine." Kyros growls. "Please, excuse me." He does not wait to be dismissed. He wrenches open the door and storms from the room without another word.

Chapter Twenty-Five

Astraea

I DON'T KNOW HOW to feel about the suitors' challenge not being at the palace and not being there to see the outcome. Something about the way that my father was looking at Kyros... That, the nightmare, and the challenge in the library the night before have me on edge. I don't want any of them to die, obviously, but the Kahzal brothers have become something... I don't know. They have presented a more genuine, maybe not friendship, but connection than many people who I have come in contact with inside these walls. I can't let anything happen to Mavros.

"Astraea?" I look up from where I've wedged myself in the corner of the window seat in my room that overlooks the bailey.

"Are you okay?" Colette asks, crossing the room to look out at what holds my attention.

"It seems they can't get enough fighting in." I say, pulling my knees tighter into my chest and wrapping my arms around my legs. "Do you think anyone will die in the dunes?"

"I think your father wouldn't choose a place like that if it didn't pose the threat of death." She watches in silence with me for a while before she speaks again. "I snuck out of your room last night." My eyes snap to her.

"Last night?"

"I wasn't gone long, but when I returned, that's when I found you crying out in pain. I'm so sorry I wasn't there sooner. Maybe I could have woken you before that happened to you. I—"

"Don't. Cole, whatever is going on with these dreams, nothing about it rides on your shoulders. You could have done nothing to prevent it." My brow furrows as I think about if that is actually a true statement, and as though she can read the look on my face, she shakes her head in denial.

"You don't know that. I—I was just trying to come to terms with what Kellan did. Both what he did for the king and then what he did to help me afterward. I had to thank him, because I know if it had been anyone else to dole out that punishment, I wouldn't be here today, Astraea." Her gaze drifts out the window again. "That's not all I wanted to tell you, though."

"What is it?" I ask, following her gaze where it lingers on the men fighting in the center of a training ring set up in the shaded area of the grounds. Mavros and Kyros are the ones fighting now, and the rest of the men stand with their arms crossed as they silently watch. Their movements are different from the others. More fluid and relaxed.

"When I was meeting Kellan, it was in the stables... Kyros found us there. He was just returning with his horse. He said he was just letting his horse run, but why would he do that in the middle of the night?" Concern furrows her brow as she continues to watch them.

"You think he is lying?" She doesn't answer but does shake her head.

"It makes sense. If his horse is used to running in Diemos, the weather there is much cooler and more wooded than desert. Daytime weather here could be too much for the horse." She gives me a dubious look before turning away from the window. She strides to the wardrobe and pulls a swath of fabric from it and turns, placing a dress out on my lounge.

"I had Calie bring something nice in for you to wear tonight. I thought you would like it, and after everything ugly happening recently, maybe something beautiful would give you even a tiny bit of happiness." Calie is the castle seamstress; it's a miracle that she is still around because you could convince me that she was magick merely because the gowns she makes are like none I have ever seen before. They are like magick themselves. They are always the most beautiful and comfortable that I've ever worn.

"Oh, Cole." I jump from the seat and pick the dress up, holding it up in front of me. The fabric is a beautiful light gray silk with gold detail. It has a plunging neckline, and the higher back will hide my scars. The bell sleeves are airy and light and will be perfect for the cool desert night. "This is beyond beautiful. Thank you, it's perfect." Laying it back down carefully, I let my finger trail the neckline, and a sad smile tugs the corner of my lip up. I wish that a dress could mask the reality that is my life. It really is gorgeous, but I don't know that anything could keep my mind from everything else that has been happening.

"Do you think that even though I am forced to partake in this courting, I could still find love? That there is something truly beautiful waiting for me somehow?" I ask as tears prickle the backs of my eyes and moisture blurs my vision. Colette comes up to my side and takes my hand in hers, lacing our fingers together and looking out at the men below.

"I think that if we didn't believe in finding true love, we never would. The flame would never ignite and would never be the guiding light to find our twin flame." She says, and I can't help the tear that escapes past my lashes. If she notices, I do not know because, as if on cue, my eyes lock with the onyx gaze that I have felt lost in since we met.

"You believe that?" I ask her, unable to look away from him.

"Of course I do."

"What if the shroud of darkness we live in is too thick for the flame to ignite? Are we stuck to an eternity of loneliness?" The question comes out before I can think otherwise. I don't want the answer, though, and regret asking as quickly as it came—I'm scared that the answer will only bring pain. It's a fear I have had to live with all my life.

"Astraea, there is no darkness that can withhold the light of the twin flame. It's the night that evades the flame." Finally, I look at her. She is still looking down at what held my gaze for so long. "He seems different." She says, and I look back down at him.

"I think he is." My voice is a whisper, but I know that she heard me, even though she doesn't say anything. She had already seen what I didn't want to before I was ready. She called me out on my infatuation with the new broody heir of Diemos almost immediately.

No matter, the day drags on, and I am forced to meet with my father to go over who I am to select tomorrow. His decision has been made, and thus, so has mine. He always manages to sour my mood. Colette nearly breaks into a run to catch me as I stomp out of the drawing room that held our conversation.

"Princess, we are meant to go to the dining room for lunch." She says as she hustles to match my furious pace. I look around to ensure we are alone, and I release my breath in a huff of vexation.

"The whole thing is a lie! None of these suitors care about my hand, only the key it holds!" I round the next corner, and I hear her curse. "These challenges are a show of power, and the men only puppets. Toys for my father to flaunt how he can make them dance, Colette. Men! People!"

I stop suddenly and whirl around to face her. Her green eyes are wide, but her brows are pressed together in concern. I look around and notice that in my fit of rage through the castle, we are now not alone and at the archway that leads to the bailey. *I need air.*

"I want—"

"Someone sexy to feed you strawberries while you lounge in the shade?" Mavros comes around the corner, interrupting me with a huge grin on his face, wiping sweat from his body with the tunic balled into his hands. Colette's jaw nearly hits the ground, likely both from what he said to me, the princess, and the sight of him and Kyros as they come to stand in front of us.

"Or is the tall, dark, and grumpy more your type?" He laughs and nudges Kyros with his elbow. He doesn't laugh, but I do, and Cole gawks at me.

"I was actually hoping to go for a walk in the conservatory. I need to get my mind off things." I automatically look at Kyros, and although his lips are pursed as he wipes the sweat from his brow, I notice the curiosity in his eyes. "Would you guys like to come with us?"

"We are supposed to be going to the dining room. You missed lunch already, princess. You must be hungry." Colette interjects.

"Oh goodie, I'm starving. You look like you know where the strawberries are kept. Lead the way, sweetheart." Mavros gives Cole his infamous wink, and I swear she morphs into said strawberry where she stands.

"I'm fine. I lost my appetite after all of that. I'll be fine on my own going to the conservatory, Cole. Go, show them the way to the dining room." I place my hand on her shoulder, and she looks down at it in confusion. I normally wouldn't speak with her like this in front of any other nobles for fear that my father would find out. Something about Kyros and Mavros makes me feel more comfortable, though, and she notices.

"Ok... I will meet you in your chambers after, though, so I can help you get ready for dinner." She says, and I nod in agreement. She looks to Kyros and then Mavros once more. "Ok, follow me."

"I'll escort you." Kyros says, placing his tunic over his head and pulling it down over his tattooed torso. My eyes drag down with the motion of his shirt, and I have to force them back up to his face.

"It's not necessary."

"Yet, I would still like to." He says, and I clear my throat.

"Okay. This way." Before we part ways, Colette catches my eye and wags her brows at me, making it hard not to smirk. I lead Kyros across the bailey, through the sand and the baking sun, and when we step through the high doors that lead to the massive space filled with filigree, trees, and life, he closes his eyes and takes a deep breath.

"It feels like home." He finally says, his eyes opening and landing on me, where I stand staring at him.

"Diemos doesn't have as harsh of a sun, does it?" I ask as I, too, take in the cavernous space. The cathedral-like ceilings are art within themselves, layers of windows forming a flowering peak in the center of the huge dome building. It's one of the most fascinating structures on the palace grounds. It's always much cooler inside than it is anywhere else.

"No, it doesn't, but that's not really what I meant." He walks forward without explaining what it is he did mean. "The king keeps a place such as this but kills for the use of magick daily?" He asks, turning to face me again.

"My father kills for less." I say, and he nods. "This is one of my favorite places in the palace." I say, looking around again, I can't help but smile as I let myself be completely enveloped by my surroundings.

"Like the hidden space in the library?" His voice startles me as his proximity is much closer than before; whereas I am taking in the surroundings, Kyros is taking in me. His eyes dance over my face, standing merely a foot in front of me. "Another place you come with no expectations." I gasp, taking a step back on instinct and losing my balance. Kyros' arm wraps behind my back as he helps me find my feet before I fall on my ass.

"I—" I am lost, fallen into a pool of water so dark and stormy, I can't find my way back to the surface. My breath, stolen from my lungs. "I expect nothing less than magick every time I come to the conservatory." I say, unable to speak anything other than the truth.

"Mmmm, is that so?" He steps closer, leaving his arm behind my back even though I can stand on my own now. "So you do not share the same values as the man who has raised you? You would accept magick?" His body presses into mine as he leans forward, hovering just a hair's breadth over mine. If someone were to come in... this would be the end of him. The end of me. My father would kill him for overstepping. His death would be my eternal punishment, because as I stand here lost in the darkness that is Kyros, I think I can finally see a future that is more—

My eyes are as heavy as my body now feels as I let him support my weight. His hand creates a warmth across my back, only the thin material of my dress separating him from where my scars are.

"Or would you condemn those who speak of magick and all the good it could do for this kingdom just as easily as he would?" His lips brush mine just the faintest, but his words hit me like the kick of the stool at the gallows. Hard and quick. The cloud of lust that surrounded my head clears instantly, and I push his arms away from me.

"Kyros, you can't talk like that here." I look around to see if there is anyone here that would run and tell my father. Of anything that just happened. Whatever that was... "Talking of the acceptance of magick is a death sentence in Eathian. As is touching the princess."

"Yet your father keeps a place like this?" He steps back, gesturing to the room we are standing in. "This room is kept this way by *magick*." I shake my head, not understanding. "And as for touching *you*," he boldly steps forward once again. His thumb and forefinger pinch my chin, and his thumb presses to my bottom lip as he brings my face toward him. "Only you can stop that, but I have a feeling you wouldn't. I think you want it."

"Kyros," his hand drops, and his forehead comes close to pressing against mine. My breathing is as erratic as my heart pounding in my chest. *He's right*. I want to close the space between us. I want his hands on my body, exploring and finding how drenched I am between my legs for him right now, but to allow that... I don't know what it would mean. How it would change everything...

"Think about what I asked, Shula." He turns and strides away without a backward glance, leaving me panting and needy, questioning everything this life has been to me.

Why would my father let tonight be a night of rest for the castle? He couldn't care less that these men should be resting before what could be the journey that leads them to their death. No, my father has been busy discussing the future with the men and their families, gaining promises from all, no doubt. Picking through them like a glutton and making promises on my behalf just as before.

"Sit still, Astraea. You're fidgeting." He growls through a fake smile so people don't see that he is frustrated with me. He sent a red dress up for me to wear. Pravin said that it would be provocative and would get the men even more excited to win a one-on-one audience with me. I took one look at the dress before nearly hurling it into the hearth and setting it on fire. In an act of defiance I instead wore the dress that was given to me by Cole, though my hair is twisted up into a tight twist just as my father likes. I feel the throbbing ache that has not dissipated since the last nightmare. But most importantly, I can't get the conservatory out of my head. I am all nerves waiting to see him.

"They should be resting. It's late. The men have a long journey and a challenge ahead of them—"

"Hush, daughter!" This time his smile is less friendly and more like a rabid animal baring its fangs. "You have already disappointed me once tonight. Do as you have been taught. Shut your mouth, sit there, and be pretty until you are called on to dance. I don't want to hear another word out of you, unless it is agreeing to do as I say.

Do you understand?" His words invoke the fear in me just as they always have, but this time feels different. I feel as though it's not just myself or Cole I need to protect. The tiredness I've felt from my restless nights and emotional days creeps in as the fight leaves me, and just as I have my whole life, I retreat into myself.

"Yes, father," I say, looking down at my hands. I want so badly to pick at the skin along my fingernails. I want to cross and uncross my legs and search for something to latch onto that will keep me from being in the present. But I don't do any of that. If I do, it will only serve to make things worse for me and for them, so I stay still just as my father wants, in hopes that this doesn't last long.

A throat clearing pulls my attention, and as Kyros and Mavros stand before me and my father, only Mavros gives a slight bow. Almost too slight to be considered a bow at all, but Kyros doesn't bow at all. He doesn't even look at my father. It seems as though a scowl is permanently etched onto his face when he is around the king, and I can't help but smile a little at the thought. His eyes flick to mine at the movement, and heat builds in my chest, creeping up my neck and into my cheeks.

"King Connard. Princess. I would be honored if you would give me the first dance of the evening." Mavros states, reaching his hand out in offering.

"Actually," my father says, "Princess Astraea was just about to dance with Prince Cadoc." Pulling my bottom lip into my mouth, I chew the skin nervously. In an effort to please my father and pull attention from the men in front of us, I nod.

"I'm sorry, perhaps the ne—"

"You know, being as I won the last challenge and my night with you was cut short, perhaps the more appropriate choice would be to dance with me first. Don't you think so, Connard?" The use of the informal title in such an open way has me bracing myself for the blast that is about to come from my father, but Kyros does not give my father a moment to respond. He steps between the bodies, taking my hand and pulling me from my chair. I gasp as I fall into his chest, and he twirls us to the middle of the large open space of the formal dining hall.

The musicians' tune slows as Kyros and I reach the center of the room. I can feel my father's eyes on me, and I swallow my nerves as I watch my and Kyros' feet move. His fingers hook under my chin, and he lifts my gaze to meet his.

"Don't let him do that."

"Do what?"

"Dim your light." He says, and the heat that bursts in my chest takes up its space once again. "Right now, you don't have to worry about him. You don't need to worry about anyone else in this room but me. Okay?" I take a deep breath and blink slowly. Keeping my eyes closed for a moment longer than necessary, and when I open them again, I release the breath, and all I see is Kyros. His black eyes boring into mine and blotting out everything else. His warm, spicy, and smoky scent engulfs me as he leans down, whispering in my ear. "That's it, Shula." I feel my body relax as his breath brushes the shell of my ear.

"I don't understand you." I finally say, and he brings his head back so he can see my face clearly.

"Do you want to understand me?" He asks, confusing me further.

"I don't know what I want." The way he is looking at me makes me feel small and more unsure of myself than I have ever felt, and I don't know whether I want to embrace it or hide from it.

"Maybe it's time you figure that out. I know that you have been told to choose someone else, but you and I both know that you want to make your own choices. Like you did with me." Our feet stop moving, and it's the first time that I notice there are others moving about around us, dancing to an upbeat tune. I thought the music to be slow for Kyros and me, but the pounding rhythm instead matches the beat of my rampant heart.

"I—" I whisper, but Kyros' hand trails up my arm and presses into the side of my neck. His thumb pushes the angle of my chin up so my eyes clash with his.

"Choose for yourself, again. Who is most deserving of *your* favor?"

Chapter Twenty-Six

Kyros

She carries the relic with her. I know it. Mavros has sensed it too. Connard has targeted my brother and me from our first meeting. I didn't realize how unwilling I would be to bend for this mission. Every bitter memory flooded back to me the moment I stepped foot over the threshold, and every moment since, my acidic thoughts have only morphed into something heinous. I'm not going to let my brother run off without protection. We have run out of time.

Astraea dances with all of the suitors, as her father wills, but even as she does, her gaze catches mine every time she faces the shadowy arched alcove I stand in. She is everything I'm not, and as I watch her dance with men that aren't me, I think I'm realizing that she is so much more. This mission has had many setbacks already, but *she* is the biggest one. It seems like it is not just me drawn to her. The more I have watched her, the more I have noticed her eyes on me.

"What's the plan?" Mavros says as he comes to stand at my side. He follows my gaze as he crosses his arms over his chest. Astraea finishes her dance with the preppy one, Cadoc. Prince and the one that seems to have the highest favor of the king, now that the other asshole is taken out of the picture... and now Astraea is in an otherwise heated conversation with her father about something. My teeth grind as I watch the interaction. Connard must feel my gaze on him because he turns then, and he and Astraea look right at us. Either they felt our gaze, or it is *us* they are talking about.

"We will talk about it tonight, in my chamber. Give me an hour once I leave, then come meet me." I tell him without taking my eyes off the king and his daughter. It's been a battle to constantly remind myself that's who she is. The vicious murdering king's spawn. She can be nothing else. I will get my hands on the relic tonight. One way or another, it is leaving this kingdom with me, and we have to leave before whatever it is Connard has planned.

"Find out who is on the princess's guard tonight." I growl under my breath. It doesn't honestly matter who it is; I will kill them if I have to, but I am curious. If the benevolent king is *so concerned* over his precious gem's well-being after her so-called kidnapping, why is it that he puts the shittiest guards on her? I have had a secondary patrol on her. Zinya and Viltarin have taken shifts, and only the princess herself has found out. Only because Tarin had to expose himself. It was the right decision.

That's another thing I have questions about. Mavros, Viltarin, and I have all witnessed a surge in magick when she has been sleeping. She has woken every time from a night terror that seems to have a visceral hold over her. To anyone else, it would be just another night terror. A nightmare that felt too real, but to me, to my brother—to those who know the magick we do—we know better.

Mavros doesn't do anything nonchalant. *Of course not, that would be too easy.* No, he walks right up to the royals and their guard. He takes the princess by her hand and pulls her to her feet, whirling her into his arms in the most extravagant way, earning a yelp and smile. The brightness in her eyes distracts me for a moment. I am stuck in them, but the guard that stands nearest to the king reaches his hand for his dagger, and on instinct, my own tightens into a fist. The king's eyes find me instantly. We glower at one another before he calls back his guard dog. I keep my eyes narrowed, blinking away from the king and to the bastard who just threatened my brother. This has been the second time that particular guard has pissed me off.

Of course, this is not what I had in mind when I asked Mavros to listen to what they were talking about, but when I see movement in the shadows behind the curtain leading to the balcony, I realize Zinya and Mavros made a plan of their own.

Zinya is like a ghost in the shadows as she listens to whatever the king and that scumbag right-hand of his discuss. However, the subtle smirk I see on her face gives me hope that she is get-ting good information while Mavros distracts the king from the princess. It's short-lived, though. The night is late, and ap-parently the king has grown tired. He claps, gaining everyone's attention, and Zinya disappears so no one sees she was as close to them as she was.

"Thank you all for enjoying tonight. Let us regroup in the morning for the favor ceremony and before we make our journey to the dunes. Get some sleep; the desert is not kind on the best of days." His eyes hover around the room, pausing on me before a glint of wickedness enters his eye and curls his lip just a fraction into a mocking smile. Anger simmers under my skin as I watch him turn his back on me.

"I think this whole thing is a tactic to get rid of Mavros. They are threatened by our presence here." Zinya whispers as she comes back to my side, but I have not let my eyes trail away from the royals. The princess jerks her arm away from the king's guard, spitting what appears to be venomous words at him before level-ing the king with a vicious glare. Her back is to me, but the king faces me, and I read his lips as he orders his guard to stand down. *'Let her go. She won't leave now.'* What the fuck does that mean?

A dangerous energy swims through the air, wrapping around me, and I act without thinking of the consequences. Spinning on my heel, I aim for one of the servant exits before Mavros hooks my arm with his hand on my bicep.

"Where are you going?" Mavros growls, and I look down at where his fingers tug at the fabric of my clothes.

"Don't fucking worry about it. One hour, Mavros." He drops my arm with only a look, and we both know that something is changing. His brows drop as our eyes tell a story neither of us is ready to speak. He nods, and with that I storm from the ostentatious dining room.

Even though it has been decades since I was last here, I move through the kitchen and tight servant passages like I have made these steps my whole life. Everything, including the scent of the dust stirred up by my feet, brings back memories. Some good—some I wish I could forget.

I spill into the hallway two floors up, right where I know the main hall will lead the princess right to me. I would say luck is on my side that I haven't run into any staff, but as I round the corner, I see a man heading in the same direction as I am. Grinding my teeth, I internally curse for letting my emotions get to my head and make me sloppy. If I had been any quicker, I would have run right into him. I have no choice but to stop my advance and hide in the shadows until the path is clear once again.

My mood fouls more as I realize who it is. He looks both ways through the hall before stepping behind a tapestry I know leads to the hidden passages within the walls that only lead to royal areas of the place. A passage that *he* should not know of.

Soon after, I hear light tapping footsteps heading toward me. The same awareness that is only present around her creeps up my spine and causes my back to straighten. The hall I stand in, which connects to the one she is storming through, is dark. Minimal torch lights have been lit in this part of the castle. Sinking back into the sandstone walls, my shadows react to my increasing agitation. Then I see her.

Her hair is up and wound tight into a crown, held in place by one of those damn hairpins. I've noticed the way she messes with it and rubs at her temples throughout the night. She hates them. I wasn't able to truly appreciate her beauty earlier in the night. With so many other things happening at once, so many eyes on us both. I do now, though, and beautiful is nothing compared to the way she looks. The dress she wears is stunning, and as I look at her, with the moonlight casting shadows over her features, it's like I didn't just watch her all night but am seeing her for the first time. She slows as she comes closer to where I stand, and I almost think she notices me, but then she does something I don't expect.

She stops.

Her hand wraps around the necklace that hangs low between her breasts. I haven't noticed the piece of jewelry before, and my brows drop as she lifts it. She looks at the pendant for a long moment, and tears build in her eyes before she kisses it and holds it against her heart. Taking a deep breath, she takes a few steps toward one of the long arched windows that line the hall, and she stands there frozen. I'm not sure if she is thinking, praying, or waiting for someone to meet her, but regardless of the personal moment she seems to be having—I watch her.

The longer I let myself watch, the more dangerous my thoughts become. *I am erratic*—because of her. I'm not thinking; I'm over-thinking and being completely irrational and nothing like myself. I am losing control—*because of her.*

My heart seizes in my chest when she turns around, having heard the same movement I did, and I sink further back into the shadows. I don't know what I'm doing anymore.

"Astraea?" A man's voice echoes around me. The one I heard in the stables. The way he addresses her makes something possessive stir in my chest, and the scowl I wear only deepens as I watch him come in close and take her hands between his. She flinches back a small amount, and he does not push. "You're crying?" He says, and she doesn't try to hide that is what she is doing. She nods, wiping away a stray tear from her cheek.

"I just know they are going to kill him, Kellan. I don't know what I can do. I'm sick of the blood that is always coating my hands. Is there anything you can do to help? You know I wouldn't ask if I thought there was any other choice." He lifts his chin, but the concern he shows on his face appears genuine. The familiarity between the two is apparent, and I know it shouldn't, but I realize the sensation building behind the wall of my chest is *jealousy*.

"Who?" Kellan asks one of the many questions I'd like the answer to myself.

"Mavros Kahzal of Diemos. Probably Kyros too, but Kellan... I have my ways of getting some information. I know that he has something big up his sleeve for this challenge, and I know who is set to walk away the victor, and it is not Mavros. Mavros... he... I..." She swallows and closes her eyes as she thinks about what to say next. *What is it you want to say, Shula?*

"Astraea," he says again in a whisper, endearingly. My teeth grind in my mouth.

"I cannot let him die. There is something different about the twins. I can feel it, maybe they are what this kingdom has needed all this time. Maybe they are the ones who can relieve me from this purgatory. You know as well as I do, I can never do anything right. I am always blamed for anything that goes wrong. *Punished for it.* You, of all people, have to understand. I have to help him." *Help him? Mavros? She wants to save me and my brother from her father's plans? Did she say she is punished?*

"I brought the healing balm that Colette requested and put it in your bedchamber. I will do everything I can to find out what they are planning, but Princess, I am just a guard... One that is not trusted anymore because of everything that has happened recently." He reaches out again, and this time, she allows him to take her hands in his, and I bristle.

"Thank you, Kellan. You are a good friend. I will remember all the ways you have helped me, and if I am ever in the place to pay you back, I hope you know I will do everything I can to ensure you and your family are well taken care of." Astraea says with a broken voice. It's clear she thinks that she will never have that opportunity. *What the fuck is going on here?*

"Spoken like the queen I know you will be." He bows low, and something sinks in my stomach. When he stands, he offers no more. Astraea watches his form shrink as he walks away. A slight trembling influx of air is the only thing that tells me she is crying again. *Crying for us? Strangers?*

Slowly, she turns back in the direction she was headed before the guard intervened. She should have guards following her, guards who stand at the door to her bed chambers even if she is not in them. The fact that they are not...

She walks slowly, her gaze down toward her feet, so when I step out in front of her, she doesn't take notice until I grab her and pull her into the darkened hallway before her door. Her eyes widen as I press her into the wall with just enough light to show her who has her held here. My hand presses firmly against the warm skin of her lips, and I'm reminded of how they felt pressed against mine.

When she realizes it's me holding her, I feel the relief sag into her body. The longer her eyes train on mine, the more I feel the tension she carries release, even if just a fraction. *I feel it*, and I don't know what to think of it.

"Can you be quiet for me, Shula?" I whisper close to her face. She shakes her head, agreeing to my request. "Mmmmm," I hum and slowly peel my hand away from her face. Her lips part, and as my eyes dance around her face, I see the pain from the way her hair is pulled back so tightly. I reach behind her, and in one swift tug, I pull the pin from her hair. Dark waves fall around her like a waterfall of ink cascading over her shoulder and down her back, and both of us lose our breath. The metal pin clangs on the dark stone floor.

"I think I much prefer this look." My eyes narrow on hers as my hand lingers at the crook of her arm, and she braces herself on mine.

"Kyros? What are you doing here?" She implores. *What am I doing here?* I had a plan before what I just witnessed. My eyes fall to the pendant low on her heaving chest, and I let my fingers find their way lightly down the column of her neck. When I reach her collarbone, I let my gaze meet hers again. She's not protesting; if anything, she is pressing further into me, and as much as I know I shouldn't, I let my hand drop further. My fingers trail the gold stitching of the low neckline of her dress, so low that I feel her breathing stop altogether.

My fingers hover almost touching the pendant, and while I certainly feel magick coming from it, it's not the same as what I'm feeling coming *from* the princess... I have to know. I wrap my hand around the pendant and lift it between us.

"What is this?" I ask, toying with the delicate silver disc with carvings not much different than the tattoos that cover my skin.

"It was my mother's. A gift to me when I turned ten." Ten. The age that magick begins to surface for many of us. I drop the pendant and push my leg between hers. The slit on her dress is open enough that my leg finds her skin, and again, she sucks in a sharp breath.

"You shouldn't be alone..." I finally say.

"I'm not alone." She says, placing her hand on my chest. I look down at her delicate fingers. Keeping my eyes on them far longer than what is natural, but something warm ignites under her touch, and I can't help but stare at the connection, trying to see what has caused the foreign feeling.

"I don't see anyone here to protect you," I tell her, lifting my gaze to hers.

"Does that mean you are here to hurt me?" She whispers, and I stay silent for a moment, watching her reaction to my lack of words. I can see the pulse in her neck thrumming at the same rapid pace as mine. Everything in me is telling me to say, "Fuck it." Pick her up by her ass and carry her into that room with my mouth on hers. Make her beg for anything I am willing to give her. Make her pay for her father's sins, but the other part of me—a part I don't know how to handle—wants to cup her face and tell her I will always protect her.

My hand comes up, the backs of my fingers brush the softness of her face, and just as I am about to possibly say something regrettable, someone clears their throat.

"Princess?" A feminine voice says, and I step back immediately, missing the warmth of her, and a scowl quickly converts whatever weakness my face showed a moment ago.

"Colette." Astraea fixes her dress, and pink blooms in her cheeks. "I was just going back to my room. I will meet you there."

"Of course." The girl from the stables bows and looks in my direction with a cold stare but quickly leaves us. I notice that she does not shut the bedchamber door behind her. *Smart girl.*

"I think it's time I take my leave. I'm sorry." I say, holding her gaze and making a decision. If it's not the necklace that is the relic, it must be in her blood. It wouldn't be unheard of for a blood bond to be tied to a person with magick. Regardless, the princess has secrets, and I plan to find out what they are, but that will come later. Tomorrow we have to save my brother from his imminent death.

"Will I see you in the morning?" She asks, wringing her hands in front of her.

"I wouldn't miss it."

"I wouldn't miss it."

Chapter Twenty-Seven

Kyros

I'm pacing in front of the window when Mavros and Zinya walk into my chambers. Mavros is laughing, but Zinya's smile falls when she sees me. She nudges Mav in the side with her elbow, and when his eyes land on me, he too looks just as somber.

"What is it?" Mavros says, all business for once.

"Did something happen?" Zinya adds.

"We are going to kidnap the princess." Both of their faces pull into a frown before they look from me to each other, then back to me.

"Do you want to elaborate?" Mavros asks with his face quickly turning into an intense glare.

"I went to see her tonight on a hunch. I thought she carried the relic on her. We have all felt magick coming from her to some extent. I thought that maybe I could seduce it out of her." I start explaining, but Mavros' stern look cracks as he grins and interrupts.

"Well, that was your first mistake; you should know by now to leave the charm up to me."

"Be serious for half a second." Zinya quips with an eye roll.

"I caught a glimpse of a necklace; she acted as though it was special, so I tried to get close to her... to get a feel for the necklace." Mavros chuckles and tries to hide it behind his fist, and I glare at him before continuing. "The necklace does have magick, but from what I can tell, it's the princess I felt the most drawn to." Mavros loses his divine mind.

"You don't say?" He says, flopping into the armchair in the sitting area. Zinya groans, dropping her head back dramatically.

"Mavros, do I need to kick your ass?" Zinya punches him in the shoulder, and I growl, spinning away from the two of them and stalking to the window. If they aren't going to help, then I will do it myself. A knock comes at the door, and Zinya looks between Mavros and me before she rolls her eyes again and answers it.

"The challenger must sleep in the soldiers' barracks tonight to ensure there is no cheating planned before the journey." The soldier says from the doorway. I stomp across the room and wrench the door fully open. I recognize the voice. The asshole who has been pissing me off since the first time I laid eyes on him.

"Why does he have to do that now, but we didn't have to before the last challenge?" I growl the question, looking down at the ugly fucker with the shit-eating grin on his face.

"I don't make the rules, Mister Kahzal. I merely follow them, just as you and your brother are required to." He sneers and then has the audacity to snap his fingers at my brother. Mavros attempts to push me back, his hand splayed wide on my chest, but I keep my feet planted and bare my teeth.

"Hey, don't you worry your pretty little head about me, brother. You do what you gotta do here. Spend some time with that princess." He winks before heading out into the hall. With a laugh, he slaps the guard on the cheek with a patronizing tap. "Lead the way, buddy."

"My name is *Pravin*." He growls, jerking his head back and baring his teeth.

"Yea? And?" Mavros laughs as he continues down the hall with a bouncing gait. "Come on, little bird, I'm going to get lost in this big ol' castle on my own."

"Pravin." He growls again with a huff, giving me one last glare before following after my brother.

"Oh, I thought you said Raven... either way, it's a fitting nickname with a beak like that." Mavros is going to get himself in even more trouble if he doesn't quit running his damned mouth.

"Follow them. I will send Tarin too as soon as I relieve him from princess duty." I say to Zinya.

"You're really going to kidnap her? All on your own? And get Mavros out of whatever shit he's in?" She quirks a brow.

"Do you doubt me, Zinya?" I smirk just enough to show confidence, and she narrows her eyes on me.

"If there was ever anyone who I thought could pull something like this off, it would be you." She checks her belt for the knives that she always carries, and without another word, she follows after the asshole guard, *Pravin*, and Mavros on their way to the barracks.

Taking a deep breath, I remind myself why I am here. Connard is a tyrant. He has to be stopped. This is a mission set forth by the queen and her cohorts. I am the muscle, and I'm saving a lot of lives by retrieving the relic that keeps the unjustly usurper King of Eathian in power. It's time that magick flows freely to its people again, and in doing so, we will take what is rightfully ours.

It's been hours since I relieved Tarin from his duty guarding over the princess. Blending into the shadows, I fix my eyes between the door and the tapestry that I know hides the other entrance to the room.

With nothing but time, I'm forced to think about my plans and how I am going to execute them. I'm going to kidnap the princess and somehow get my brother out of fighting in the damn challenge at the dunes. I'm also forced to acknowledge the fact that every time I'm around her recently, she disarms me without even knowing it. It should be interesting trying to kidnap her...

My eyes begin to fall heavy, so instead of standing in place, I begin to walk, pacing between the doors. Astraea stopped making noises about an hour ago; likely fast asleep now. Maybe I should plan to get my brother out and then worry about the princess? Although the princess doesn't have guards, I doubt the same is to be said about my brother. Not if they are worried about him...

A sound from beyond the door causes my feet to halt and my brows to drop as I listen. Is she talking?

The bloodcurdling scream that echoes through the walls next sets me into action without a second thought. First, I try the door but have no success. It's locked from the inside. I run to the tapestry, fling it aside, and tuck into the tight space. The area here used to feel so much bigger and brings back too many memories. Memories I have tried hard to not relive. I grind my teeth together and make my way through the maze within the walls before I finally spill out into the darkened bedchamber.

Astraea's body is bent awkwardly off the bed as she cries out. Her back is bowing toward the ceiling at an unsettling angle. Pain and terror paint her face. Almost as if something is trying to suck her soul right out of her body. I react immediately, and my magick spills out of me like a torrent of glistening black sand and smoke. The storm that lives inside of me cascades from my skin and drenches the room in darkness.

As my magick fills every corner in the room, I drop to my knees and my eyes fall shut. As I do, I am thrust into the space within her mind that is this night terror. An echoing and haunting laughter bounces through my head. When my eyes snap open, I am met by the white bone-covered face. His curved horns bent down as he leers over me. He leans in with his menacing claws stretching toward me like several blades aimed with the intent to skewer me. The tip presses into my chest just above my heart, and I grind my teeth as it pierces the skin.

I growl in pain as I flip my hands palms up and push more magick into the room. Forcing the nightmare to bend to my will, I bare my teeth and push my hand out to wrap around his billowy shadowed wrist. A deep radiating pain shoots through my arm as I make contact with his skin, and I roar with determination as I attempt to cast him out. Squeezing hard at his wrist, I push my magick into the connection.

"Cessarenah!" I growl through my teeth with my face right in his. With a powerful thrust, I rip his shadowy claw from my chest, and at once, the magick I cast into the room is pulled back into me. The swirling shadows that live on my skin vibrate from the immense amount expelled, and I sag in relief as I look to the bed at the same moment that Astraea sucks in a sharp breath and her eyes fly wide.

I am at her side in an instant, crawling, but there nonetheless. Ignoring the painful wound in my chest, I push my arm under her shoulders and help her into a sitting position. Her head whips around the room in confusion.

"K—Kyros?" She says with silent tears streaming down her flushed face. Little wrinkles of worry form between her eyebrows, and her mouth is pulled into a frown. I grunt because as I look at her like this, I worry for what I might say. I gently adjust her position so she isn't pressing against the wound that is burning at my chest. At least it's still dark, so I know she can't see it.

"Shhhh," I breathe into the top of her head as I try to console her, attempting to study her trembling body. I need to know if she is as wounded as I am. "Are you hurt?" I force the question out as the shadows continue to recede back to their rightful place, while also still trying to scan over her body. She begins to pull away, shaking her head as she does. Her fear is so potent it threatens to choke me.

"Wh—why are you here? I—I didn't." Her eyes are wide as she looks between me and the door that never opened.

"Shula, listen. You are ok. I'm not going to hurt you." I say softly, tucking a sweat-soaked strand of hair behind her ear.

"Why do you keep calling me that? What are you doing here? What did you *do*?" She asks all the questions I am not ready to answer. And I don't. I stand with a grunt, pushing my hand to the wound on my chest. Astraea is still on the bed in a panic but awake and seemingly okay, so I cross the room and poke my head out the door. No one. I guess in this situation, it's probably a good thing Connard is so doltish when it comes to keeping the princess safe.

Before returning to her side, I light the lantern that is on her vanity. The soft glow illuminates the room just enough, and I set it on her bedside. Silently, she waits for me to say something.

"You're bleeding." She whispers, adjusting on the bed to cover herself, but I can tell she wants to see the wound for herself.

"It's nothing," I grunt. "Are you hurt?" Her face scrunches up, and she looks down at herself, where she has the blankets pulled up close to her chin, and she shakes her head.

"No. I'm okay. Confused, but okay." Worry clouds her eyes, and for a moment I want nothing more than to brush her sweat-soaked hair away from her face and tell her that there is nothing to worry about, but what just happened... It has even made me concerned about what is going on. She still hasn't calmed. Her chest is rising and falling heavily, and tears still make lines down her cheeks ever so often. I can't take her anywhere looking like I have just assaulted her.

"Stay here." I order, turning and striding away. She calls after me with fear in her voice, but I'm forced to ignore her as I make my way into the connected bathing chamber. Using the hand pump, I let the warm water from the natural spring beneath the castle fill the tub. The water is not hot by any means, heated only by the sun in the reservoir it runs through, but warm enough to relax muscles and calm her frantic mind. I would heat it using my magick,, but it's going to take time to restore what I have used. The thought brings a new surge of worry to my mind. I won't be able to rend a portal out of here with its depletion...

I find tinctures beside her bath and open the first, lifting it to my nose. Lavender and something sweet like vanilla. I pour a measure into the water and also throw a jar of the bath petals into the water as well. The room is filled with a sweet floral aroma as the water, oil, and petals mix, turning the water a milky lilac, and then I take a deep breath and turn to retrieve the princess.

"What are you doing, Kyros?"

289

"What are you doing, Kyros?"

Chapter Twenty-Eight

Astraea

I stand in the doorway to the bathing chamber, looking down at the man I just witnessed use magick unlike any I have ever heard of. I am frozen in shock. Kyros is crouched down next to the bath, where I see he has added oils and petals and filled the tub nearing the edge.

"You need to calm down." He says finally, after what feels like an eternity of us just staring at one another. We both have questions; that much is clear.

"And what about you?" I ask, shakily.

"I am calm."

"You are hurt and bleeding. I—I saw everything." Another stretch of silence fills the space between us as he stands and walks to stand in front of me. His size is imposing, but nothing ever even touches the intensity of his eyes.

"And? What are we to do now, Shula?" I can feel the heat radiating from his body with how close he stands, and all thoughts leave me as I see his blood clouding the fabric of the gray tunic he wears. Before I lose my gall, I toss the blanket to my vanity chair, revealing my sleep dress beneath. His eyes track my silhouette, and I ignore the heat I see entering his gaze as I reach for the jar of healing balm on the tabletop.

"Take your shirt off." I say without turning to face him as I snag the jar.

"And here I thought I was going to be the one getting you naked." He chuckles, and the sound is so foreign that it causes me to pause. I stop, half way done removing the lid to the balm, and I gawk at him. There were no questions about my wanting his shirt removed; he just obliged. I swallow as I take in the sight of him. I've seen him without a shirt from afar and in the Colosseum, but then I was being careful not to let my eyes wander. I was being watched by my father and hundreds, if not thousands, of people. Right now, though? In the privacy of my own bathing chamber, I take my fill.

His body is like a dark god. Crafted of sin and shadows. The tattoos that swirl along his arms, chest, and torso reach over his impressive shoulders and toward his back. And the ones on his stomach dip low beneath the line of his trousers.

"My eyes are up here, Shula." He whispers as his fingers lift my chin to meet his onyx stare. I cough, looking away from him as embarrassment heats my entire body.

"It seems we both have some secrets, but I think I have one that will help you." I turn back around, showing him the jar. "May I?" He says nothing after looking at it but narrows his eyes before responding only with a nod. I hesitantly step around him, and I grab one of the bathing towels from beside the bath.

"Sit." I say, gesturing to the edge of the alcove bathtub. He slowly does as I say and watches me as I dip the cloth into the water. Before I touch it to his skin, I pause, wanting to see his face, but at the same time, I'm also terrified of the truths I might find there.

"You don't have to do this." He breaks the silence and snaps my reluctant eyes to his. There is kindness I didn't expect, and just like last night, a conflict fights for attention on his features.

"It's my fault you're hurt. It was my nightmare." I don't even know what I'm saying. What is he even doing here? If those angry claws had gotten me like they did him, I likely would have been dead. I don't have magick to fight like he did. I look at him through my lashes. "This might hurt a little." I say softly before I press the rag to the wound. He barely flinches.

"Does this happen often?" His eyes track every movement I make with my hands but quickly return to my face between each. The small space feels even smaller with his attention on me like this. I don't think my voice is going to work without breaking, so instead I nod.

He is silent longer than it takes for me to ensure the wound is clean and even so after applying the balm. I've never actually tended to anyone else's wounds. I'd only ever felt Colette doing my back or watched as she did any markings that were made to my arms, and never with a magickal balm, only the cleansing solutions. *This can't be that different, can it?* He doesn't react to its warming or the magick that it's surely imbued with, only watches me.

"Why do you have such a balm?" He finally asks. The question I knew was coming, and as much as I don't want to lie, I also can't face what his reaction might be knowing how weak I am, so I settle on a half-truth.

"It was brought to the castle for Colette."

"Your chambermaid?" He asks, trying to catch my gaze, but I cannot look at him. Not with my father's words bouncing through my head. He must feel the same. A man in such a position that he's in, but the longer I think about it, the more my frustration begins to peek through. As though by looking this closely he can see into the fine cracks in my surface and is trying to whittle away at them, one gaze at a time.

I think about all the interactions I saw of him, with his men, with Mavros and Zinya... He might be an asshole, but I genuinely sense that he cares about people too. Something I can't say at all about my father. I am his daughter, and he whips me and allows his men to abuse me too. My eyes finally meet Kyros'.

"My friend." I tell him, lifting my chin, ready for him to try to cut me down.

"You are a very kind friend to keep such a thing for her in a place like this. When it could mean your life being forfeited just by possession of it." He tilts his head, surveying my response. I can't help the way my mouth pops open in shock. I can't say anything else.

"Have you ever needed to use this?" He's phishing. I can tell by the glint of curiosity I see in his eyes, and even though I have revealed truths to him, I'm not ready to reveal *those* truths.

"You prepared a bath?" I deflect his question, and if he notices, he doesn't say. He stands, stepping away from the edge of the tub, which brings him much closer to me after setting the balm down next to the basin of water in front of the mirror.

"It's for you. I thought it would help you calm down after that experience." My breath catches in my throat, and I flinch just enough that the hand that he had brought up to my cheek pauses before he touches me. My eyes close without thought, tears gathering behind my lashes.

Seconds pass where I know he's watching me, but I'm frozen in place with fear. I don't know if it is the lingering effect of the nightmare or the fact that I was assaulted so recently in this very space, but I couldn't have his touch here. I couldn't accept what he was possibly offering.

"I'll be right outside. I'm not leaving you alone." He whispers, and I nod without opening my eyes.

I don't see him leave the bathing chamber, but I feel his powerful presence dissipate. The warmth from where his hand hovered just above my skin—*gone.* As much as I wanted his touch, I'm also terrified of these feelings he provokes in me. I'm terrified that he will see my scars, the flaws that are proof of my weaknesses; proof that I am just as unworthy of his attention as I am of the crown on my head.

With a heavy sigh, I undress and sink into the bath. The lingering panic from the nightmare is still present, but not like it usually is, and the even more bizarre part is the pounding in my head, or lack thereof. I keep my eyes open as I replay the events of the night and wake up with my room flooded with the most magnificently beautiful magick I couldn't even conjure up in my dreams. I never even read of such magick. If I thought Kyros' eyes were like the glittering black stone that the blades of Tsalalerian Steel were made of, they have nothing on the shadows that bled from his skin.

I curse under my breath as I step from the bath, realizing the only clothes I have in here are those drenched with sweat from the nightmare and left lying crumpled on the floor. Wrapping the bath towel that hangs on the hook around my body, I look at myself in the mirror. My hair is dripping, my cheeks are flushed, and dark circles that seem to always shadow under my eyes these days are ever present. I was calm for a second, but even thinking about walking from this room, knowing that Kyros is on the other side, makes my heart rate spike.

The room is dark when I step into it. Only the slight glow from the lantern I left in the bathing chamber and the moon's light illuminating the space. I expected to see Kyros sitting in one of the seating options in the room, but where I found him was least expected. His feet are planted on the floor, but he is laying on his back in the center of my bed. I can see his chest rising and falling at a slow, even pace. The telltale sign of someone being fast asleep. My heart swells at the sight of him.

I look around, still wary of the monsters that are after me when I sleep, becoming much more real entities. Turning back and grabbing the lantern, I bring it to the vanity and turn the knob on the side to its lowest flame. The armoire door creaks when I open it, earning a wince from me. Kyros must have used a lot of energy expelling his magick and likely saving me from great pain, just like last time. I owe him some restful sleep if nothing else.

I pull a dark-colored nightdress from the interior drawer and duck behind my dressing screen in the corner of the room and slip the lightweight fabric over my head. I check the lock on my door, extinguish the flame on the lantern, and pad over to the bed where Kyros rests.

This may be one of the biggest mistakes of my life, but something is telling me it won't be the last, and for that I am grateful. Bending down, I slowly unlace Kyros' boots. Surprisingly, he doesn't budge, even when I struggle a bit to pull his boots from his feet and lift his heavy legs up onto the bed. When I finally finish getting him into what looks like a *mostly* restful position on my bed, I am panting and have broken a bit of a sweat again.

Looking down at the giant man sleeping in my bed, I laugh lightly at what I just did and everything that has come to light tonight, feeling a bit of the nervous energy return. I don't see how this can't change things between us. We have each other's secrets, both of which could mean our deaths in a kingdom like Eathian under the rule of its vicious king—my father. I stand there staring for what could be a long, embarrassing amount of time before Kyros stirs for the first time.

"Lay down and sleep, Shula. We will face what comes next in the morning." His grunting sentence comes out muffled as I attempt to decipher his words with a frown. Understanding hits when he pulls the blankets back, indicating for me to get into the bed—with him.

"I will sleep on the lounge." I say, turning away toward it, but as I do, his hand scorches where it wraps lightly around my wrist, halting my retreat.

"Now, Shula. Lay. Down." Even though his words are demanding, his grip is loose, and while I stand there hesitating, his thumb scores lines on the inside of my wrist and sends that same heat elsewhere through my body. Swallowing hard, I nod, and he drops my wrist as I move to the other side of the bed and get under the covers.

I lay as stiff as a sword on my back, but he has turned to lay on his side. I feel when he opens his eyes and they train on the side of my face.

"You will need to relax if you ever intend to sleep," he whispers, and the sound of his voice and the proximity of which he lays next to me cause my heart to take up a furious rhythm as it pounds like a drum in my chest.

"I don't think sleep is a good idea after everything." I say just as quietly.

"Are you afraid of the nightmare returning?"

How do I tell him I'm afraid of everything? I'm afraid of the future, the past, the present, and everything that lies between. I fear for the kingdom, its people, and what it will mean if I allow him any further under my skin.

"I am always afraid of what the future holds." I finally admit.

"That's not an answer I would expect to come from the princess of one of the most powerful kingdoms." He says as he too rolls to lay on his back. "Where I come from, we have something that can help with warding off those who seek us in the shadows of sleep." Both of our hands lay at our sides, and as I close my eyes, I feel his little finger brush mine. I don't move. "I won't let you be hurt anymore. Sleep, Shula. Dream of a future you do not fear." And with those words dancing through my mind, I drift into the abyss of sleep.

Chapter Twenty-Nine

Kyros

Exhaustion claws at my mind, even as I try to pry myself from sleep. A weight on my chest gathers my attention there. When I finally am able to crack my eyes open, I realize the weight I feel pressing down on me is a fast-asleep princess with her black waves of hair blanketing me. I take a deep breath, but it's the wrong choice. Her scent, warm and sweet like a drink on a summer night, fills my senses and causes more of my body to wake too.

Think of anything else.

Astraea squirms, and I groan at the movement as she unknowingly rubs her body against mine. The want I feel for her was undeniable from the beginning, but now, as things are beginning to reveal more of her inner workings? I know the careful control I have always had is slipping. She creates a storm inside me I can't seem to control when she is near, and the more time I spend with her, the more I fear that the rest of the world is doomed from the aftershocks.

The muffled, sleep-riddled, yawning groan that comes from her has me holding my breath as it takes every last bit of control I have not to pull her up and devour the sound directly from the source.

"OH—" She says with a gasp as she comes to, realizing how tied up we are with one another. She moves to push off of me, and against my better judgment, I let the arm that was laying around her body brush up her spine and keep her planted firmly on my chest.

"Stay," I say, my voice only a gravelly whisper from sleep, as my eyes meet the churning ocean in hers. I'm losing my mind, in bed with the enemy and completely defenseless. Even if the way she looks at me tells me she has no idea how much I have revealed to her. But, I suppose, she has revealed more than I ever anticipated too. We both lay there stuck in each other's embrace, neither of us moving to untangle.

Her breath flutters from her lips as though she can't catch it, and the warm air brushes my face. The heat that only she has been able to stoke in me threatens to ignite a combustible surge that could burn everything around us. My eyes drop to her mouth, her lips pouting open, and I watch as they tremble before she says my name.

"Kyros," she pauses. "I—I can't do this." Her brows gather between her eyes as she thinks about what she's saying. Her thoughts and fears battle for life across her features.

"I'm not asking you to do anything I think you don't already want to." I barely recognize my own voice. The softness I've brought it to is foreign to even me. Her cheeks are pink as she tries to hide her embarrassment of my suggestive words from me with her downturned face.

"I was talking about the games. The suitors. I don't want this." I stare at her for a long moment, thinking about everything I know about her since our meeting in the market. I know she's telling the truth, but regardless of if I understand why... this works out in my favor.

"I'm sorry," She says, mistaking my silence for something it's not, and I allow it. Despite the tightness in my chest, I make a decision. Her eyes round adorably when my other hand comes up and cups the side of her face. I press my thumb down on her plump bottom lip, trapping it there and blink up to meet her gaze again. My thumb trails the edge of her lip and her already heavy gaze becomes heady.

"Shula?" I whisper, pinching her chin between my fingers I reel her into me. Although the plan has changed many times, the end is always going to be the same. I have to keep telling myself that, because as I stare into her eyes, I'm drawn by an outside force. I fly right into her blaring light and I'm consumed. My lips touch hers tentatively, their feverish heat searing mine. It's a soft question to which she answers with a command.

She pulls herself on top of me, straddling my hips, and sinks her tongue between my lips. My magick churns with my mind, shocked at the zeal of which she moves and how easily I have accepted her touch. Something I don't simply *accept*. I can't help but groan at the feel of her; the taste of her. If her scent was a drink, her taste is the main course. The feel of her body on mine is madness, but yet, nothing has made more sense. Our tongues dance with passion, our lips melding together as one, the same as our breath. It's a building frenzy, but as I recall what I came here for I realize that I could be a nightmare for her too. I came here to kidnap her, but it's her that has stolen my will. I'm buried, the never ending storm she has roused brings a sandstorm of shadows and magick to the core of me.

The thought brings guilt to rise in my chest and I slowly put distance between our lips. Every breath that lives between us makes my vision clear, the plan comes back into sight and I clear my throat. Placing a chaste kiss on her lips, I make her look at me.

"I can help you. I can get you away from Eathian." I say sternly, her face morphs before my eyes, all the emotions playing out in a sequence. "I can tell you're different. You don't enjoy your life here. This place dims the fire you had when I met you in the village. When we were trapped in the tavern, you were *alive*." Her eyes sparkle with tears, but they remain unshed. The squeeze in my chest intensifies, but I pay it no mind. Even if my words are mixed with truths and bent for my benefit. "You want things to be better for the people. Perhaps if you worked with the queen of Diemos. You could change things—for yourself and for the people under the rule of your tyrant father." It's a farce, but one I think that she will take. The queen of Diemos may have taken in many of the orphans of war, given them homes with families who cared for them, even came to show love to some of us. But she did so to create a vengeful army, it was never peace she was seeking when creating such a force. I know that, but I allow the idea to settle over Astraea anyway.

"You would do that for me? For the people of Eathian?" She asks.

"I have a feeling that this is just the beginning of things I realize I am willing to do for you." I say honestly. She is nodding, removing her body from mine. She sits cross legged on the bed next to me, and I prop up on my elbow. "There is one thing though…"

"We need a plan to get Mavros out of the challenge." She takes the words from my mind and I purse my lips nodding. "I have an idea, but Kyros? I have one stipulation." I sit up fully, placing one foot on the floor bracing myself for what her demand is going to be, but her eyes fall to my chest. I never put my shirt back on the night before. The wound that was there is only a darkened area of skin now where my magick dances over the raised skin protectively, as it tries to continue to mend the puncture. I don't shield them, allowing her to see the magick, gaining even more trust for my willingness to be open with her. When she catches me watching her too, she chews her lip and pulls a pillow to her lap, hugging it.

"What is it?" I ask, wondering what it could be that is more important than her getting away like she initially wanted.

"Colette comes too."

"No." I say immediately. We weren't meant to bring another person back to Diemos at all, I can't come back with two.

"Then the plan is moot. I'm not going anywhere without her." She shoves the pillow away, crosses her arms and makes a face while tilting her head. It's both infuriating and also a bit disarming. Both things I have noticed she is remarkably good at. Least with me.

When I stand, she lets out a frustrated huff and I freeze when the pillow she had hits me in the back of the head before landing on the floor behind me. Slowly, I turn my head to look at her over my shoulder. Then even slower, I turn to face her.

"Did you really just throw a pillow at me?" I can't hide the amusement from my voice, but I try as I take a step back toward the bed. I stand over her and she swallows before I see the flicker come back to her eyes.

"Colette will come." She scoots to the edge of the bed, her feet land between mine and she stands. Her eyes flicker as she places her hand over the mark on my chest. "And you will let her." My eyes narrow on the subtle threat she is making.

Threatening me, Shula? Not your best choice.

"Do you have any other demands of me, Shula?" I say, brushing a tousled wave of dark hair away from her face and she shutters under my touch. She shakes her head and tries to look away from me. Doing the same thing I've noticed she does often. Always turning into herself. Always shrinking away from the fire that I know burns within her. Gently, I tilt her head back so she is forced to keep my gaze, giving her a look that says *tell me.*

"I don't want anyone else to die." She says after a long moment staring into my eyes.

"Death will come for everyone at some point." Whether it be natural or because I have delivered it is yet to be seen.

"I can't have any more blood on my hands. My father has ensured that too many people have lost loved ones in my name. I don't want any more." Her father is a vile man who kills innocent people on a whim. The comparison to what I do is maddening, but I can understand her troubled mind.

"I can assure you that there will be death dealt by my hand, but where the blood lands will only be there. My hands, not yours or anyone else's. I don't kill innocent people, Shula," I lean in hovering my lips over hers and growl, "But I will end anyone who aims harm at those I claim as *mine*."

A knock at the door has her flinching but I keep her locked in my grip. Not ready to break away from this moment. Whoever is there can wait. I press my lips to hers and I bask in the warmth of how she melts in my arms despite the intrusion. If only for this moment, I will allow myself to believe that *she* is something I can claim. I will give us both a moment to trust that what comes next won't leave us both battered and broken.

"I need to answer the door before they come in to check on me." She says breathlessly.

"I will allow your friend to come with us, but ensure she knows there is no going back to her old life." I say softly. It's a warning for her friend, but for her too.

"When we leave, everything changes." She says, easily lifting her chin in defiance and the flame that dances in her flares.

With my discarded shirt in hand and my boots unlaced I stand in the hidden passage that leads to Astraea's chamber with my head leaning back against the dusty stone wall. My eyes closed as I try to collect myself.

Nothing is going right.

Every time I feel like we are on the right path, something else happens to change it. *Someone* changes it. My jaw clenches as I shimmy the shirt over my head and into place on my chest covering the last bit of evidence of last night.

"Are you ok? You look flustered." Astraea's handmaid says as she lets her into the room and closes the door. There is no answer from the princess and it brings a smirk to curl my lips. *Did I make you speechless, Shula?*

As much as I want to hear what she has to say to her friend about me and whatever last night was, I don't have time. Astraea told me what she needed from me for her plan and we only have a couple hours to get everything in line for this to pan out. If we can't make it work we will have to follow them into the dunes and that *will* be a problem. Considering I am the only one who can rend in our group, and my magick is not yet fully recovered, there is no way I would be able to transport all of us far.

I have barely made it around the corner, heading toward the main hall, the one that leads to the visitors wing of the castle before I am being halted by none other than the prick, Pravin.

"What are you doing coming from the royal wing of the castle?" He growls in question, his hand lingering on the belt that holds his short sword. My eyes drop to it before I answer him, I crack my neck and widen my stance. The motion makes him eye my untied boots and his eyes narrow.

"I was out for a morning stroll and lost my way... but I'm sure that you would be able to point me in the right direction." The smirk I give him causes his face to redden as another guard comes walking from the same direction I came from.

"The princess has been informed of the change." The guard from last night, Kellan, says, looking me up and down before lifting his gaze to Pravin.

"Good. Then I guess you are the only one left to inform... Is that blood on your tunic?" He questions and I look down at the fabric on my chest pulling it out to inspect it closer.

"Hmm, I guess it is. What changed?" Nonchalance bleeding from my tone.

"Are you injured? That looks like a bit of blood." He asks skeptically. I smile leaving him time to wonder before I finally answer.

"Thank you for your concern, but no. I'm not injured, but there was a bit of blood, you are right." I say, and Kellan clears his throat and brings Pravin's attention back to him.

"Since we have you here, I suppose now is as good a time as any to let you know that the king has changed the timeline in the challenge departure. It seems that there is an approaching sand-storm and they will need to leave within the hour to beat it." His words hit me like the storm he speaks of and I grind my teeth.

"Doesn't it make more sense for them to wait out the storm? Why rush off into the desert when you know the dangers that are headed this way?" As I say the question I realize why. This is another challenge in itself.

"The princess needs to be married by the time she turns twenty-one, we don't have time to wait out a storm. I presume that is not hard for you to comprehend, being that you are an heir to a kingdom too." Pravin cuts in.

"Don't presume anything about the inner workings of my mind, *Pravin*. I assure you, you have no idea what I tend to understand." I begin walking away from them and away from the royal wing of the castle, when I am called after by a voice that is not either men and has me screeching to a halt.

When I turn to face her, her deep shadowy tresses are down flowing along her back and my eyes can't help but follow the cascade of them. She chews her lip at my obvious observation. She's in a cream colored dress, the material light and flowy the hessian fabric that will shield her face from the desert elements hangs loosely around her neck. Everything down to the rose colored tint on her cheeks looks like a desert goddess.

"I would love it if you could escort me to the gates, for the favor ceremony." She smiles then, and Pravin nearly growls in revulsion. Kellan's jaw tightens, but he otherwise looks passive.

"I would love to, Astraea, but I do need to prepare myself." I gesture to my chest, "as you can see, sparring took quite the turn."

"I don't mind at all. I will wait for you." She says happily, without missing a beat. She needs to tone it down even I can see through her charade.

"That is highly inappro—" Pravin starts but Kellan cuts him off.

"I will escort you both." He says, gesturing toward the wing I was headed.

"Great. Then it's settled." Astraea beams, then looks to Pravin with a glare. "Pravin." She strides ahead leaving the three of us watching after her and then Kellan follows. I can't help the smirk that pulls the corners of my mouth up when I look back at the guard on a power trip and the unbridled rage on his face.

"I *presume,* I will see you at the ceremony." I pat him on the chest before I leave him standing there alone and catch up to Kellan and Astraea.

"Kellan is going to help us." She says quietly when I reach her side. Shifting her eyes back at Pravin as she does. This Kellan better be trustworthy or his blood will be the first to dirty my hands since my declaration to Astraea.

We don't have much time to gather anything for the journey, but Kellan assures us he has people working on gathering for the trip. They of course don't know that it's us they are gathering items for, just that a higher ranking soldier has asked for it, so it will be done. I quickly change my clothing and grab any weapons I was keeping in my room before we start heading to the gates for the ceremony.

Through it all, I can't help but notice the many times Astraea and my eyes have clashed as we catch each other stealing glances. Her cheeks pink on multiple occasions and judging by the tension coming from the solicitous guard she has, there are some thoughts churning about the interactions.

"Ready?" Astraea says before we exit the palace. Kellan nods to both of us before exiting first. Astraea moves to follow, but I stop her before she descends the steps. I pull her into an alcove shielded by the sun and I deepen the shadows with my magick. She sucks in a sharp breath as I pull her into my chest.

"Before we do this, I want to make sure you are ready. This is what you want?" It doesn't matter if this is what she wants, but right now, it is easier that she believes she has a choice.

"I've wanted nothing more my whole life than to get away from this nightmare. You are saving my life, Kyros." My stomach sinks at her admission. Though I know that this is a job I am required to do, I can't help but feel a little regret at omitting the truth of why I am helping her leave the kingdom. I grind my teeth and nod, because I can say nothing more that won't be a lie. She has been lied to enough, and because I am a sadist prick, I grab the back of her neck and pull her to me.

Our lips collide and I swear sparks fly out around us. The little magick I have restored trembles around us as we take each other's air until we can no longer breathe. Hiding in the shadows it seems like time has stopped entirely and I finally break the kiss, leaning back to look at my Shula Morana's eyes. That same regret surfacing as I feel like I am drowning in her.

"Ready?" I ask.

"I'm beginning to think I will be ready for anything—with you." She says, taking my breath with her as she steps out of the shadows and catches up to Kellan taking his arm, he guides her where the rest of the suitors have already been lined up.

I don't like this plan, as it takes me so far from her, and my brother... but I can't very well just walk up to the main steps where the ceremony is going to take place. I'm quick to find Zinya. She was the main person I was looking for. I'm confused for a moment when I don't see Tarin. He should be with her. She must sense my confusion because as I reach her she nods in the direction of where the suitors are stationed. Tarin is just behind Mavros. Each suitor has a guard standing at heel strapped with weapons and ready for a journey.

"The king is allowing one guard of their choice to accompany the suitors. No women are allowed." Zinya growls under her breath, with her arms crossed over her chest.

"He would have chosen you, if the king would have allowed it." I tell her, but she knows it's likely not the truth. Mavros would want to protect her if he could, by not allowing her to come. Even if she is one of the most respected fighters in Diemos.

"I want you to know, we have a plan and Mavros will not be fighting in this challenge." Her head snaps in my direction and I look at her out of the corner of my eye. "The princess knows and is coming back to Diemos with us willingly. She is part of the plan to escape." Zinya's head snaps back toward where the king steps from his opulently decorated palanquin. The carved design dipped in golden metal lets off a reflected flash of light as it is lowered for him to take the steps toward where Astraea waits.

"Lovely people of Eathian! It's time for the next challenge to receive my daughter's hand in marriage. Let the favor ceremony begin!" He calls out over the quieting crowd. All eyes are glued on him, but he only finds mine. A smirk playing on his lips. This whole thing is for me. To separate me and my brother. I can't wait to fuck up his plans entirely.

Chapter Thirty

Astraea

My father steps from the palanquin swathed in white linen and blaring gold embellishments. His pompous superiority is on display at every opportunity, and a journey into the desert seems to be the least of his worries. Not when he won't have to lift a single finger. Unease builds in my stomach as he comes closer, announcing that the ceremony is to begin.

I hold my breath as he comes to a stop at my side. *Thank the divine that it didn't take much convincing to get Cole to agree on leaving.* She was already in the moment I told her, no questions asked. My nerves are shot, and I can't help but chew on my lip as I await what is to come.

"Why is your hair not pulled back, Astraea? This look is very unbecoming, especially for a woman who is looking to secure the future king." My father tuts, eyeing me with disgust. His lip curls back as he greets me in front of those who turned out to watch the ceremony. Keeping his features shadowed to the crowd to keep the facade of a doting father. Taking my hands, he bends down, placing a kiss on my forehead, and then whispers the rest of his *praise* of his only child. "If I can't trust that you will be put together like the future queen, perhaps I need to find someone new to help ensure there are no more mishaps like this again." My eyes snap to his muddy brown stare before I fix my silent glare on the crowd. His threat is void anyway. Colette is coming with me, and we will both be gone before nightfall. He takes my silence as yielding and steps away, tilting his head smugly.

My eyes drift across the crowd of people, immediately drawn to the darkness that tends to cloud around Kyros. His dark aura surrounds him and beckons me with its whispered embrace, and for a moment, I get lost in the memory of last night. Everything that happened, everything said... and not said. Kyros is still a mystery, but he showed kindness to me and is clearly loved by his people. I feel myself wanting to trust him. I suppose I do to an extent; otherwise, none of this would be happening.

When our eyes meet, heat prickles up my spine and crawls into my cheeks, but I can't look away. As much as I have tried to convince myself otherwise, after all the deaths my running away caused... I have dug down as far as I can in my gut, searching for any inkling that I am not doing the right thing, but every time, I come up with nothing. I have never felt more sure of a decision in my life.

"Princess, the blessings." Colette whispers into my ear, and I flinch. My eyes flutter as the daze I was in is shattered by the touch of her hand on my elbow and the words breaching my conscious mind. I blink slowly, drawing in a deep breath as I step down on the lower level of the stairway, where the suitors are lined up. Pravin has informed me of my father's decision on who my favor will be going to for this challenge and has assured me that if I disobey this time, he will make good on the promise he last gave. Just the thought makes my stomach churn and bile threaten to burn my throat. *That will not be happening.*

Though it is still morning, the sun is already baking the sand with its radiating heat. The scorching rays will only get worse as the day goes on. Everyone taking this journey looks ill-prepared, save Mavros and his guard. Cadoc, too, seems better equipped than the rest. They dress in the colors of the dunes. I noticed Kyros wearing the same sort of attire today as he blends into the crowd. The shemagh they have wrapped around their necks, the loose cotton fabrics, and light colors are better suited for the harsh elements the desert will undoubtedly provide. Most of the others are dressed in the attire most acceptable for their own lands. Not at all in tune with the arid heat and vicious landscape they are trying to be the next king of.

The rains that flooded the land as most of them arrived in Eathian have dried and will likely not return for some time now. The heat of summer will bring a different type of storm. Storms of the gods fury, winds that blow sand like tiny glass shards that cut through skin. Lightning that will illuminate the land with its radiant light and catch flame to anything able to burn. The heat alone is a slow death if you are not prepared; at least, that's what I've read in journals of travelers. Stories that the unsuspecting guards tell each other when Cole and I are merely shadows around the palace, sneaking through passageways in areas we are not supposed to venture to. I would be lying to myself if I said I wasn't terrified of what this journey will bring, but I'd rather be terrified and doing something than terrified and stuck in the same looping nightmare.

Stepping forward, I move down the line of suitors, each one respectful as ever, not like the last ceremony. This one feels different, though. The energy of the men, their guards, and even just the atmosphere itself feels oppressive as my eyes meet the pleading gazes of those around me. I know that I am not the only one who is feeling the change.

The Lord of Vadon's son, Wrensford Tavares, and then Faolan Damalis of Halcyon each accept the blessing, and when I turn to Cadoc, he gives me a warm and empathetic smile as he accepts the blessing.

"I want you to choose freely who you bless today, princess. Please don't worry about the deal our fathers have placed on our behalf." As I kiss his cheek and look at him out of the corner of my eye, he whispers. "Believe it or not, I would rather your affection be genuine rather than forced."

"Thank you, Cadoc. I'll remember that." From what I know of Cadoc, he would be a fine suitor. Someone I may even be able to see myself with over time. His kindness does seem authentic, but I see the way he is with my father too. He wants to please us both in different ways. I think Cadoc would be too pliable to be under a man like my father. I don't think his kindness is what this kingdom needs. We both would be used by our fathers and be nothing but mere puppets for continuing their reign of terror and unrest. Only we would have *both* kingdoms to tend to.

"Prince Ruaan, it honors me that you should wish to fight for the chance of our betrothal. Your courage does not go unseen. If you should fall in the fight, I will pray that your ashes fly free and your soul not carry the burden of burning for eternity in Zameil." I recite the same blessing crafted by the generations before me, and his lips curl into a close-lipped smile as he holds my hands between us. This time, he rubs the back of my hand with his thumbs. The scoring line of each pass creates tension in my shoulders as I think of the man behind me and not the one before me.

"Thank you, beautiful. Should you wish to give me your favor, I look forward to getting to know you *personally*." His eyes sweep over my shoulder and hold a place there. The exact spot I know Kyros stands, and I can't help but shift on my feet. A strange feeling gathers at the nape of my neck as I hone in on the challenge in Ruaan's liquid gold eyes.

I clear my throat, looking down at my feet. Suddenly feeling anxious about deceiving all these men with the thought that they might get the chance to not only become king but also be able to claim me as theirs too. My gaze shifts back to Cadoc momentarily, and his kindness he exudes. *Perhaps even my heart.* But the more time I spend with them, the more I see a genuine interest in me, and their need for power over the kingdom comes to light too.

Even if the two emotions are twisted together in a mess of root-ed poisonous vines planted by my father. I chew my lip as the thought draws my brows together. All my life I've thought all men to be the same—power-hungry assholes who want nothing more than to dominate, jaded by the man who raised me and those he surrounds himself with—but I'm starting to realize that not everyone starts that way. Some men become hardened by the way that they've been raised, just as I have. But at some point, we have to decide when to break the mold. We have to decide what impression our decisions will leave in the sand.

As I step up to Mavros, he grins, offering me his hands, and it's easy to genuinely smile back at him. Regardless of the way eyes cut over my face from onlookers. The way his energy always seems to brighten my mood when I'm in his presence makes me wonder what his magick is. He tilts his head as he catches me eyeing the shadowy tattoos that swirl around on his skin, just like Kyros has.

"You good, Princess?" He says, watching me curiously. With a small nod, I squeeze his hands, shrinking my smile for the show I am required to put on. When the parchment in my hand meets his, his facial features change just the slightest. The joking brightness that once filled his features becomes serious, and his eyes flit between my eyes in question.

"From Kyros." I whisper against his cheek before I kiss him, giving my blessing for the challenge. When I lean back, he's not looking at me but at his brother in the crowd, and I can't help but feel like an entire conversation is taking place within their eyes as I step back. He finally looks at me, and although others may not see it, I see the narrowing in his silver eyes.

"What has changed?" He asks quietly, keeping a close eye on those around us.

"Everything." I breathe, and with just that one word I know it to be true. I may have decided to run away and make a place for myself in the world, but leaving with the heirs to another kingdom? My father will know that I am leaving on my own accord, but it won't matter. He will blame anyone else. *He will blame everyone else.* I am the key to expanding his reach; without me he doesn't have much else to go on to further the land his vile touch rots. He will bring war to the lands, and if I'm wrong, if Kyros is wrong, we could be the cause for the deaths of thousands.

With the ceremony coming to an end, I turn to look out over the people I am leaving. My wish is that by leaving them today, I will be able to bring them a better life in the long term. I have nothing left of myself here. I will meet with their queen of Diemos, and together we will make a plan to finally rid Eathian of this poisonous bed of snakes. I can only hope that I may be able to find myself somewhere between here and there.

Swallowing, I turn back to face my father.

"Prince Cadoc Natharia of Irowerth, please accept my favor for this challenge." I say with my eyes never leaving the man who sired me. Cadoc steps forward, placing his hand on my lower back, letting me know he is here, and when I turn to face him, his smile is sad as he nods in understanding. The gesture makes my brows drop as my mind whirls on what the plan was... Shit. *What do I do next?*

The deep pound of the drums announces the journey's beginning, and in a hurry to get this over with, I kiss Cadoc on his lips. I feel nothing. A numbness takes over my body, and I wrap his wrist with a delicate gold ribbon. The small smile he gives me causes my heart to ache. I hate deceiving him when he has only shown me nothing but kindness.

Clapping my hand over his, I try to smile back. However, my eyes never reach his as they instead round in panic. In the distance a shadow forms in the otherwise cloudless sky. The trajectory and speed at which the object moves make my brows pull together in the center of my forehead with terror. The massive screech that follows causes everyone's eyes to snap skyward as well.

My father begins barking demands as chaos erupts, but I stand there frozen in place as I look up at what is now clearly a massive beast, feathers the color of deep oiled bronze and a shock of yellow on their underbelly. It drops from the sky like a bolt of lightning that is coming right for me. Its shadow looms over all of our heads, and as I stare into the bright sky, the birdlike creature with taloned hooks at the apex of its wingspan and a dark, viciously sharp beak blacks out the torturous sun in a nosedive for where I stand with the suitors.

I've heard stories of the beasts that dominate the skies, but never here. Not here. Not in Eathian. The Thunderbird opens his shadowy beak and lets out the powerful wave of sky-cracking cries before banking hard to the left, sending sand flying and wind blowing back my hair. Thunder rolls in the distance, and the surrounding air becomes forceful in its whistling and whipping, lifting sand higher as it does.

One moment I am standing on a stage for everyone to see, and the next I am grabbed from behind, tucked under large arms, and a hand covers my mouth as I scream for help.

Chapter Thirty-One

Kyros

"What the fuck!" I grind the words through my teeth as I throw my shadows out around me and Zinya. I can feel her magick pressing against me too, trying to calm the disarray. It helps minimally.

"Why in the pits of Zamiel is a Thunderbird attacking?" Zinya calls out over the shouts and cries of those around us. I would like to know the same. The creature's wings down thrust, generating a powerful wind that makes the loose sand beneath our feet fly into the air. It makes it hard to breathe, much less see. Their cries from the sky echo all around from the people gathered for the ceremony. Thunderbirds are generally not found in these parts, let alone attacking humans. Their sole purpose is to protect, to keep balance within the land, and to steer storms where they are needed most.

I've never seen a thunderbird in person before. The depictions from tomes written by our ancestors, as well as paintings and statues of them, do nothing to serve them as they truly are. The vast expanse of their four, X-like wingspan is incredible. Their dark feathers have an almost luminescent glow even in the bright morning sun, while their yellow underbelly appears as though it has been dipped in gold. Deadly claws reach low, threatening to pluck people from where they are, and many of them do just that. The whole ghastly spectacle is in conflict with the sheer wonderment of the creature itself.

"I don't know. Find Mavros! This wasn't the plan, but we will use it to our advantage. Let's get the fuck out of here." I yell, glancing over my shoulder at her. She nods and runs in the opposite direction that I am heading—toward the last place I saw Astraea. I grunt as I continue to use my magick to conceal me, giving me an advantage as I move through the crowd.

A scream catches my attention just as I see a body fly sideways. I curse, picking up speed, and I slide to my knees, catching Colette as she is cast aside like a discarded match. Her vibrant red hair spilling out around her like a spark from a flame.

"Where is she?" I ask as gently as I can manage, but my heart is racing and my shadows coil around me like black snakes of death...Colette's round eyes track the movement, and confusion and realization battle for dominance across her features. With another demanding grunt, I shake her desperately, asking again. "If you know where she is, you need to tell me. Did you see? Did she run?"

"*Kellan*." She finally says, just as Zinya and Mavros cut through the shadows. Mavros' shadows now join with mine.

"Keep her safe. Do everything you can to meet me at Dune Village just before Creshian." I pass Colette to Mavros as his eyes burrow into mine, and he accepts the shocked handmaiden. Questions and things that will have to be left unsaid for now cross his face, but I shake my head. "The village, Mavros. Get there." Gruelingly, he nods with pursed lips, and I level him with a promise in my eyes before I rend a portal right before everyone. I couldn't say where we were meeting for risk of other people hearing, but he will understand where I meant. I watch them all disappear as Mavros casts his shadows out over everyone to help them get away, and the screaming and disarray only intensifies.

I have to trust my brother to get them all to safety. He has the sense to make sure the rest of the team is accounted for too. As I step through the portal, I unsheathe my sword to prepare for a fight. I know as soon as this portal shuts behind me, I will not have much magick to rely on, as it was never fully restored. I feel my energy depleting already.

The portal snaps shut, and I'm thrust into the darkness of the stables. The horses whinny and shake with my charged presence, but I don't mask my power this time. If the guard Kellan wants to take Astraea for himself, then he will have to go through me.

It's then that I see them. Astraea is wrapped in his arms, and hers are wound around his neck. The pressure in my jaw intensifies as I clench it hard enough to crack the bones. I sheath the sword, and what is left of my shadows leaps from my body without thought. Astraea screams as they pull them apart, and I step between their bodies.

"Wait! Kyros!" She yells as the dark mist lifts the backstabbing guard up by his throat, and I watch with a curious tilt to my head, surveying the emotion in his eyes. Drinking it in when I see the terror fill them as he sees who it is controlling the magick that binds him.

"I should snap your neck for betraying her." The wrath in my voice comes out with an otherworldly rumble as I bring my face nose-to-nose with him. I make sure he feels the promise in my threat as I continue to squeeze him with magick. "You just couldn't stand it, could you?" His face is blotchy red and purple from lack of oxygen, but soon it will be void of all color when I drain him of his life. I barely register Astraea pulling at me through my rage, satisfied enough knowing that she is here and unharmed.

"Kyros, *please.*" She doesn't yell, scream, or hit me. If she had, I don't think I would have heard it at all. But this? This soft whispered plea of my name? Her delicate touch on my arm. It breaks through every hard wall I have. I blink, and my magick falls away when I look at her. Kellan gasps for air as the bastard falls to the ground. On his knees, he claws at his neck as though he can open it further to allow more air into his lungs.

"I told you, I will end anyone who aims harm at those I claim as *mine.* His betrayal was his death sentence, and I'm the executioner." I growl, and I see her lips part with a shaky breath just before I look away from her, back to the man wheezing for breath. I realize what I've just said, but it's too late to take it back now. My brows furrow as I look down on Kellan.

"He didn't betray me. He saw an opportunity to get me away and out of harm's way and took it. You're right, you know? You did say that death would be dealt by your hand, but you also promised me that it would not land on mine. Not only that, but you promised you would not kill innocents. Kellan did not betray us. Spare him, I beg you. If for no other reason but that. Please don't kill him." She says gently, and again, it causes my chest to feel as though it is cracking open, leaving my heart bare for her. It aches, and I want nothing more than to bury the pain. Taking a deep breath, I continue to stare at the man at my feet. His life hangs in the air between my ragged breaths.

"Kyros," she whispers once again. The sound is like a caress to the exposed organ.

"Consider this your warning of what will happen if you so much as breathe a disloyal breath toward her. If you think you've had nightmares before—*you're wrong.*" The guard turns and spits on the ground before wiping his mouth and looking back at me with a look of disdain. I don't care enough to apologize. Something about the bastard just pisses me off.

"Thank you." Astraea stops me as I turn to walk away, and I look down to where her fingers curl along the curve of my bicep. "For not killing him, and for wanting to defend me. I haven't had many people willing to do that in my lifetime." I stare at her for a long moment, more time than we honestly have to spare. The blue in her eyes is like the clearest spring day. Not yet bleached by the summer sun. Crisp and clear, gleaming with a bright radiance.

"Defending you was easy. It was holding myself back when you asked me to spare him; that was the hardest. I am not known for my restraint, Shula." I watch as her fingers tighten on my arm and as an ocean of unshed tears builds in her blue eyes. I stand here planted as though her touch is what roots me in place, and the tears that well in her eyes could very well drown me.

"Get me out of here, Kyros." She whispers, and I nod.

"If he is coming with us, get him up. We don't have much time. We have to make this quick." My chin juts out in the direction of Kellan, where he is pinning me with a sneer and rubbing at his neck where my shadows had him strung up. Before I act on impulse and lift the princess into my arms and claim her fully here and now, I tug out of her grip and stride to the far stall where Khol is being kept. I make quick work of saddling him and Eidola before guiding them through the dark stables.

The mayhem of everything outside the clay walls and wooden doors has the war-trained horses tense and ready for battle, but it's not a fight they will see today. Today we will have to choose stealth. Getting away while the chaos is at its peak. The deafening cry of the Thunderbird echoes through the air as I crack open the back stable door. The Thunderbirds have brought the darkness of cloud cover with them, which will only aid us further.

"There." Kellan points from beside me, and I follow to where his finger aims.

"That's inside the palace walls. We need to get away from the castle." I say while looking for other options.

"The king has been growing more paranoid recently and had more underground passages dug out that are big enough for even carriages to travel through. It's been an ongoing, hushed project for nearly the last year." Kellan says as he adjusts his asinine armor that the king requires his guards to wear. "The only problem is that it leads to the Dead Sea... and it's said that the soldiers that were in charge of locking the gates at the end of the passage were killed by the Scylia."

"Lose the metal. You are dead with it." I say, then turn to the princess. "Do you trust what he is saying?"

"Scylia? Like the pirates of the Dead Sea?" She questions Kellan.

"The passage, Shula. Do you trust that it is what he says? That it will lead us out?" I cut in before Kellan can answer. "I'm not worried about Scylia. I need to know if this passage that you say is there can get us away from the palace and closer to the dunes before Creshian."

"You plan to take her back to Diemos through the Dead Sea, the dunes, and Creshian? This is a death mission." Kellan balks, and my head whips in his direction.

"You are welcome to stay here. The only one with the possibility of death is you. The princess and I will make it Diemos one way or another..." I lean in closer to him and whisper menacingly. "Even if we have to feed you to the manticore that roam the dunes and the eolian caves." He scoffs, and I can't help but smirk when Astraea gives me a pointed look.

"I trust him." She finally says.

"Up on Khol then." I shrug toward my horse, and I see the way she swallows, and fear takes prominence over her features. "Please tell me you know how to ride a horse."

"I... Well, no. I haven't a reas—" Her words are cut off by a shriek as I pick her up by the waist, but she quickly slaps a hand over her mouth as I place her on Khol's back. We don't have time for this.

"We will rectify that. You ride Eidola." I point at Kellan. "If you treat her with anything other than the utmost respect, Mavros will take your balls, feed them to you, and then use your own entrails to string you up as an offering to the Cerkin when we reach the Creshian Forest."

"Kyros! Great divine! Would you stop threatening Kellan? I told you he was helping, and I trust him. He is a friend." Astraea's brows gather between her eyes, and the annoyed look in her eyes causes my lip to tug up at the corner. I've never felt the urge to call someone adorable, but the look on her face right now is just that. It makes me want to frustrate her more... and in better ways.

"No." I respond flatly.

"You're insufferable." She crosses her arms over her chest.

"So I've been told," I laugh under my breath as I move to pull myself up behind her.

"What are you doing?" Her hands frantically look for any-where to hold onto as my weight shifts the saddle.

"I'm riding my horse."

"But I'm riding this one. Choose another one." She argues.

"No." I whisper in her face, and she gapes at me. "Hold on, Shula. You are about to be free of the chains he keeps you in." I don't wait for her to listen, and I don't warn Kellan when I lean down and throw open the wooden stable door. Astraea gasps as the momentum of Khol's takeoff thrusts her back into my lap, and I wrap one arm around her waist, securing her to my body. If Kellan is lying and leading us to a slaughter, it will be his head that rolls first.

The sand under Khol's hooves slows him only the briefest, but after just a few strides he is quickly adapting to the terrain, as is Eidola. Soon after, a branching crack of lightning followed by the deafening call of the Thunderbird breaks overhead. The sounds of battle and terror fade in the distance as we hastily make our way toward our escape. After what feels like too long, we have made it to the passage entrance Kellan said was our exit.

"The guards that are usually stationed here must be trying to calm the people about the Thunderbirds." He calls from behind me, and I gesture for him to lead the way.

"Must be," I say as he passes, still not trusting the bastard guard, my hands reflexively tightening on Astraea's waist. The movement pulls her even closer to my body, and I feel the way she relaxes into me. I clear my throat, take a deep breath, and apologize. "Sorry, I'm just trying to keep you seated." I lie, relishing in the way she feels pressed against me. *Wanting more.*

"Thank you." She says, trying to look back at me, and sways, falling off balance. Her hand shoots to where mine slides along her hip to her stomach, and she holds it fiercely.

"Stop thanking me. I don't deserve thanks." I say, looking down at her, at the color staining her cheeks just before Khol walks us into the shadows of the passage.

"You may not know it, but you are saving me from my death, Kyros Kahzal. You are giving me purpose." She says as her hand loosens on mine; although she tries to pull it away, I instead thread my fingers through hers. I can almost feel the deepening pink of her cheeks through the heat of her body, even if I cannot see her face, but the sinking feeling in my stomach causes my brows to furrow as I feel the weight of her hand in mine and hope that she's right.

Chapter Thirty-Two

Astraea

My heart feels as though it is going to escape from its cage in my chest and run away from me. Its pounding is probably heard by both Kyros at my back and Kellan, where he rides in front of us. As we breach the entrance to the passage, my eyes round. The opening is much larger than I anticipated. Kellan was right when he said a carriage would fit through. It's big enough for a whole platoon. The ground and walls consist of the same firm soil, though loose sand still piles along the edges.

I can't help but lick my lips nervously as I look down the long tunnel, which appears to be leading to nothing. What I can see, though, is every few feet there's a wooden arch acting as a support to the heavy earth, and the further we get from the entrance, the darker it's becoming. The feeling of being eaten whole by the darkness only reminds me of my nightmares and does nothing to help calm my nerves.

We ride in silence for what seems like forever, but no matter how much time has passed, I have yet to get myself to calm. I close my eyes and take a deep breath, trying to get myself to sink back into Kyros. As hard as I try to relax my muscles, it's been futile thus far. My mind continues to spin with everything that has happened. Everything that has yet to happen. My thoughts snag on a detail I had not yet thought of.

With a gasp, I shoot upright, giving everyone, including the horses, a startle.

"Cole! No, no, no. Kyros, we have to go back. We can't leave her!" I nearly jump from the horse's back as I shout the words. He pulls back on the reins, and the horse slows as he curses and holds onto me. The horse Kellan is on whines as it too is pulled to a halt, and sand dust fills the air around us, making it even harder to breathe.

"Shhh, she's ok." Kyros says quietly and continues to pull me back against him.

"Is everything ok? I can't see anything." Kellan calls out.

"Everything is fine. Trust Eidola to guide you through the tunnel." Kyros responds. It's silent for a moment, only my pounding heart taking up cadence in my ears.

"Princess Astraea?" Kellan says my name in question, snapping me back into the present and not taking Kyros' word for truth on my safety.

"I'm ok, Kellan. Just worried about Colette."

"You're sure?" He asks, and a small smile forms at my mouth, even if the concern I feel is ever etched into my forehead. I'm glad to have him as a friend.

"I'm sure." I say, and Kyros untangles his hand from mine, only to splay his fingers wide on my stomach, sliding up and pinning me even closer to him. The caress sends warmth from where he touches and through every nerve ending in my body. When the horses begin walking again, Kyros leans down, brushing my loose hair across my back and over one shoulder.

"You trust me so easily?" His breath tickles the shell of my ear, sending chills all over my skin, even if the air around us is stifling. His fingers dance along the thin fabric at my ribs, and it causes my chest to rise as my back arches, pressing into his touch without thought.

"Should I not?" I ask with a low, shaky voice.

"Mm," Kyros responds before his lips touch the skin just in front of my ear, and he whispers, "I think I like that you do." His grip on me tightens again, this time his hand rising a bit further. His hold is like the tightening coil of a snake around my body, but not constricting in a bad way. More like a brace keeping me steady, an external support for my dwindling inner resilience. If anything, I want more. His thumb scores a line at the underside of my breast, and I lean back into him, resting my head on his shoulder. Even as I want more, my mind still can't seem to ease the worry I carry.

"Promise me. She's ok." I say, turning my head just enough, I know if there were light, I would be able to see his face.

"Mavros has her. He will be meeting us. I assure you there could be no safer place for her." His fingers move lightly back and forth on my ribs, and as relief courses through me with his words, I feel myself also breathing a little heavier. My eyes roll to the back of my head while my forehead rests on the crook of Kyros' neck.

"I can't lose her. I don't have anyone else." I say sleepily, the adrenaline high from the Thunderbird attack and getting away with Kellan, then Kyros, and my worry have my eyes growing heavy as I finally accept where I am and that Cole is safe. Kyros' hand leaves my ribs and instead wraps around my throat, delicately trailing up to the side of my face, pressing my head further into him. On the brink of sleep, he whispers into my hair so quietly I almost believe it to be the start of a dream.

"You have more than you realize. Sleep, Shula."

Stretching my arms out above my head, I arch my back and groan with the tightness of my body. Each muscle riddled with tension, like I slept on a rock. Opening my eyes, everything that has happened comes rushing back, but that's also when I realize I'm no longer resting in Kyros' embrace. Instead, I find myself now sprawled out on the hard floor of what appears to be some sort of desert catacomb. Survival instinct kicking in, I jolt upright.

My gaze is met with a calm set of deep onyx eyes. They rake over my body, and when they trail back to meet mine, my lips part. Something about that look in Kyros' stare. The pained downward pull of his dark arched brows and the subtle purse to his full lips.

"We stopped." I say, obviously.

"We did." He responds with a just as obvious answer. No change in his face. My nervousness augments as he keeps the unrelenting intensity in his eyes. I swallow and try to ignore the heat that gaze sends to my core and try to focus on my surroundings. The deep amber sandstone caves with rippling waves across the surface were formed from hundreds of years, if not more, of windstorms through the area. The dark, man-made tunnel, rigid and purposeful, lacks any beauty. It is within sight, though, to my right. The wooden arch leads to the passage we took from the palace. Like a wound to the splendor of this divinely made cave.

Tipping my head up to look through one of the holes of erosion in the sandstone roof of the cave, I notice the golden glow of the sun. The heat blanketing me and the sheen of sweat coating my skin tells me that it's the end of the day. Nearly sunset.

"How long have we been stopped?" I finally ask.

"It's been only minutes." He responds, and my eyes snap to his. *Only minutes?*

"We have been riding..." Brows furrowing, I look back up to the sun leaking into the cave. "All day? That would make the passage..."

"We are nearly to the Dead Sea already. The horses needed a rest, and we needed to stretch. We will be leaving again as soon as your guard returns." His head tips back, looking to the same spot I was, and I take the moment to watch him. His deep caramel skin and his swirling tattoos seem to be crawling up his neck at this angle. The sand peppers his forearms, presumably from when he laid me down. A bead of sweat rolls down from his forehead into the dusting of hair along his jaw, and I swallow. That same heat growing inside me is making it hard to sit still.

"Shula? You're panting." He says without looking back at me. My jaw drops further, and I gawk at him.

"I am doing no such thing." I stand, brushing sand from my skirt and then from my arms. The grit almost painfully sloughs off the top layer of my skin with each brush. It's enough pain to distract me from the more dirty thoughts I was conjuring up at the sight of him. "Where is Kellan anyway?" I ask aggressively, pulling at the fabric at my midsection and trying to avoid looking at Kyros at all. *Pft. Panting? I most definitely was not panting.*

"I must admit, you are cute when you're flustered." Kyros says, now standing directly behind me. Sucking in a sharp breath, I whirl around to smack him. He catches my wrist, and taking two steps forward, he pushes me to walk. I stumble backward until his body is towering over mine. He pins my hand above my head. My breath catches when his other hand snakes behind me, slowly arching my back so our bodies are flush.

I stare into his black eyes, the pain that was once there re-placed—if only momentarily—by heated lust. For me. My chest rises and falls rapidly, and I stop breathing altogether when he bends down. Dragging his nose along the column of my neck, he breathes me in, only releasing the breath when his mouth hovers over my ear, causing the heat from his lips to cascade over me like liquid fire igniting my blood.

"Are you thirsty, Shula?" He rumbles, his mouth still lingering so his lips brush my earlobe and cause gooseflesh to rise along my skin. I can say nothing. All the moisture in my mouth dried up with the heat of his words. His slight touches have left scorching burns across every nerve in my body. "Breathe." He demands, and I let the air from my lungs out shakily.

"Kellan?" I question moving to look past Kyros, and he removes his hand from my back. Using his large hand to cup my chin, he presses his fingertips into my neck firmly and brings my gaze back to his.

"I never want to hear another man's name on your lips when you are this breathless again." His thumb presses down on my lips, parting them. The gesture is demanding, but the look in his eyes, while definitely fierce, is soft. My eyes begin to flutter closed as I give in, melting into the rough sandstone wall and allowing my body to move against his. "Tell me, do you want me to kiss you?" He's asking? I figured the way I am basically quivering beneath him is enough indication that I want far more than his lips.

"Are we asking now? Ever the chivalrous suitor." I chide, though the humor fades as Kyros pins me with a look that says he is about to devour the petulance from my lips.

"I think it is clear the other suitors never stood a chance." He growls, slowly closing the distance between our lips.

"I don't know, Mavros got pretty close to having a chance... and I think—" I screech as Kyros lifts me where I am, my legs wrapping around his hips and my arms around his neck. He presses my back against the stone wall and steals my breath with his all-consuming kiss. He holds me by the backs of my legs, and his tongue immediately goes searching for mine. I welcome him into my mouth with an unabashed moan. Our neediness blending into an all-out war.

Unintelligible words are groaned from both of us between our intertwined breathing, and Kyros pushes me further against the wall while I writhe and buck my hips, wanting him to sink further. Take more. Never mind that we are in a cave and Kellan could show up at any minute. Right now I am lost in the feeling that is held so precariously between the two of us. I can feel the way he fights his urge just as much as I do, but right now, after everything, we both let go.

His hand works on bunching my skirt, and when the rough pads of his fingers meet the skin of my leg, his touch is like a brand I want marking my flesh always. He breaks the kiss, resting his forehead on mine as he lets me slide down his body so only one foot touches the top of his, the other leg still held by his arm, exposing me to the charged air around us. As my head rocks back, my lips part and my breathing quickens with my racing heart. His fingers trail my thigh and move dangerously close to my core.

"Are you panting now, Shula?"

"Mhmm," My head falls to the side, my back arches further, and I urge him to continue his path to where I want him most. At this moment in time, he is everything I want and everything I never thought I would have. He is *freedom*.

"Don't lose that wicked voice now. Tell me, are you wet for me?" His hand continues its path, and his fingers now teasing as they linger just above my exposed apex.

"I am." I breathe the words.

"You are what?" He asks with a tilt of his head. *Asshole.*

"Panting...and wet for you." His eyes are endless black holes, and I'm lost in them as his fingers brush through my wetness, and he teases my entrance with a groan of his own. His face drops to my shoulder, and he breathes in deep.

"Oh, Shula, you are *drenched* for me." He says, rubbing slow, tight circles right where I want them. The leg that he never put down is hooked over his arm, and he grips onto my hip as he pins me to the wall and works me over with an expert touch.

The moment he sinks two fingers inside me, his lips are devouring my moans as he stretches me. Applying beautiful friction with the heel of his hand. His lips move slowly, making a path down my neck and to my collarbone, where the shemagh has fallen loose.

"I wonder, do you taste as good as your moans? Do you want to help a thirsty man, Shula?" His words are punctuated with his fingers filling me deep, and he circles his thumb on my sensitive bundle of nerves. I shamelessly ride his hand and nod my head, unable to string together sounds to make words. He chuckles, and the sound on my skin nearly sends me over the edge, but just as

I feel the edge of an orgasm; he removes his touch. A whine of protest comes from me as my eyes open when he sets my other leg down, so now both of my feet rest on the toes of his boots. One hand cups my chin, his thumb pulling at my bottom lip slowly until my mouth opens.

He says nothing as he rubs the fingers he had between my legs over my lips. His breathing hitches this time when I lean forward and suck his fingers into my mouth, tasting myself on them. I roll my tongue around both fingers and between them. His jaw feathers as he clenches his teeth and presses his hardness into my stomach with a groan. His fingers drag out of my mouth and down my chin, settling over my throat before he sinks his tongue between my lips next.

"Fuck. I knew you would taste sweet." He says, his nose touching mine, fingers wrapped around my neck, that impossible gaze locked to mine. Someone clears their throat, and heat floods my cheeks as my eyes snap up beyond Kyros' shoulder. Kyros doesn't move. He keeps his eyes trained on mine, and they narrow slightly when my lips begin to form Kellan's name, but then I remember. Bringing my gaze back to him, he narrows his eyes further.

"Kyros," I breathe, and a hint of a smirk plays at one corner of his mouth before he kisses me approvingly, slow and deep. Likely as much for our benefit as it is for marking me in front of Kellan. When he finally releases me, I take a step back off of his boots and use the wall for support. I don't think I would be able to stand on my own. My core is pulsing with need. Kellan stares at me dumbstruck, while Kyros licks his lips with a secret smile, making me want to chase release even more.

"Supplies are here. We should eat before we head out for the night." Kellan says in a clipped tone, and I give him an apologetic look. Even though I know I have nothing to apologize for.

"Good, I'm starved and can't wait to eat." Kyros says, still looking at me with a ravenous look in his eyes and that uncharacteristic smirk on his face. But even with this beautiful distraction, Kellan's words register...

"Wait, we are traveling at night?"

Chapter Thirty-Three

Astraea

Kellan had thought of everything when planning for our travels on a whim, it appears. The horses couldn't be packed beforehand, but Kellan sent some of his most trusted men on the mission of securing us what he thought we might need. Much to Kyros' dismay, Kellan has been an asset to this mission before it had even begun.

"Are you ok?" Kellan asks me again. It has to be probably the tenth time since Kyros began shuffling through the items that Kellan brought back. Kellan went to the location where the supplies were stored on his own, while Kyros watched over me while I continued to sleep. I've surmised that it was longer than minutes, like Kyros had originally said; given how sweat-drenched Kellan was when he returned, the trip couldn't have been quick.

"Yes, Kellan. *I promise.*" I level him with a look that says, 'Don't ask again,' and he blows his breath out of his cheeks, causing a laugh to bubble up out of me. "You worry more than an old lady. Worry about what lies ahead of us instead, would you?" He makes a *pft* sound as he cuts his eyes back to Kyros, where he is now crouched down. Kyros said we would eat and then need to leave. Both he and Kellan agree we don't have much time. The fight has surely stopped, and the search for me and, undoubtedly, the missing suitors and their guards has begun.

"You're sure you trust him? You barely know him." He asks, and I groan dramatically. "Ok, ok. Fine. I will keep my mind open... I guess it's just hard to see you with someone else." He speaks more quietly, and my annoyance fades.

"It's—complicated. I'm not sure there is an *us*. Not entirely anyway..." I say, my brows furrowing as I look at Kyros' back. "But Kellan, you will always have a special place in my heart. You have been a friend when I had no one else. Without you, we wouldn't even be here now."

"I know." He says, and I sense that he wants to say more, but I am worried that if he or I do, it will only cause ill feelings between us. Feelings we don't have time for as fugitives on the run. Well, I guess I am considered *"kidnapped,"* as my father will surely spin to the kingdom.

I place my hand on Kellan's shoulder, and we hold each other's stare for a moment. I give him a sad smile, rubbing under my palm placatingly before I turn and head over to where Kyros is. Kellan doesn't follow; instead, he chooses to check on the horses. I get that he needs his space. It doesn't mean that I like him feeling alienated, though.

"Hey," I smile coyly, sitting across from Kyros. He looks up as he strikes a flint. The stones create sparks that catch embers on the dry desert grass and branches Kellan also collected. He resumes his attention on building the fire. When the flames grow, the fire between us casts its golden glow out in a globe around us, now that night has fully fallen. His eyes flick back to me as I sit, cradling my knees to my chest. He holds my stare for a moment without saying or doing anything. It's honestly embarrassing how just a look from this man gets me all hot and bothered. Cole would be laughing so hard if she saw how much I was blushing under his gaze. He narrows his eyes briefly. It's not a menacing look, more pensive than anything. Like he is trying to figure me out.

"Is the guard bringing the horses around?" He asks, barely gazing over his shoulder as he stands, and in one hand offers me a bundle of fabric, which appears to be holding a slice of bread and some cheese, and in the other hand, a bladder of water. I nod, accepting the rations.

"Kellan." I correct him, and he grunts.

"Good, we need to be on our way. This journey is only going to get harder, Shula, but no matter what we come across, please just trust me. I need you to work with me, especially if we come across any travelers."

"Do you think we will? Come across any travelers, I mean?" I ask between bites.

"Yes."

"Are travelers not kind to one another?" My brows drop as I chew and wait for his response. I don't have to wait long.

"There are many kinds of travelers we might meet along the way, but my hope is that we won't have to be traveling like this for long. Once my magick replenishes... we can get to the dunes before Creshian much faster." He says.

"What do you mean? And how long does your magick take to replenish? Do you have to do something to get it to, like, recharge or something?" I ask, perplexed and unabashedly interested. It's something I have always wondered about: how magick works? I was never able to learn anything about it outside of hearsay because of my father's ban on all things magick. Kyros laughs, and my brows jump as my eyes snap to him. My concentration on the food that sits on my lap breaks entirely at the sound of it. The many questions buzzing around in my head disappear and nothing else matters. My cheeks blaze as hot as the fire in front of us when I take in the smile on his face, and I can't help the way my lips curl in response. He realizes what has me so caught off guard and quickly coughs to cover it. He wipes the smile from his mouth with his hand. My heart flips at the sight of the moment of vulnerability he just gave me, even if he didn't mean to, before it is gone again.

"So many questions." His smile returns slightly, just a curl at the corner of his mouth, and I roll my lips, biting down on the bottom one, hiding my own. "We will have time to answer them, but right now you need to finish eating, and I need to pack this onto the horses. Will you be ok alone?"

"I've been alone most of my life. I think I will survive." I halfheartedly laugh with a shrug. Kyros doesn't look amused, and instead of walking away, he rounds the fire and pulls me up to stand. I scramble to keep the contents of my rations in the fabric as I swallow the food I had just put in my mouth with a cough. "What the hell?"

"You are not alone in that sense. Not anymore." His eyes bore into me as though he wants to dig a hole into my brain and plant the words there so they grow to be true. It's intense and unexpected, but I feel like that is a common factor with Kyros since I've known him. He is all darkness and secrets, knowledge and power. His hand comes up and cups my jaw softly, his eyes flicking down to my lips and back to my eyes. "Not while you're with me." I swallow hard and nod. "Be truthful, Shula. Will you be ok alone?"

"I don't want to be alone." The words tumble from my lips as though he pulled them out by an invisible thread, and before I can even process why I said them, his lips press to mine. The kiss isn't like before. It's soft and over before I can blink. I am completely shocked by the quickness of it, and the way that Kyros then takes the food from my hand, ties the cloth around what is remaining, and tucks it into the small leather bag that now hangs across my body. He doesn't say another word as he gathers up the things that were left around me, then stomps out the fire. Kicking sand over it for good measure.

When he offers me his hand, I look up at his eyes. Reassurance radiates from him. I place my hand in his.

"Then you won't be." He says as he turns away, grabs the leather bags that were at his feet, and guides me to where the horses are waiting. Kellan is looking up at the dark sky, where the first of the stars are starting to flicker into existence. He sits in the sand, his arms resting on his knees and his hands clasped together between them. He looks over when he hears us coming and purses his lips when his eyes drop to where my fingers are laced with Kyros.

"Horses are nearly ready." He clips, standing and brushing the sand from his trousers. He did as Kyros suggested and lost the armor my father requires of his guards. It seems bizarre to see him in anything else. Even when we were alone in the past, he would come in the armor, and when he wasn't wearing it, I didn't do much looking... more feeling. I clear my throat and turn away from him with that thought, placing my hand in the center of the massive horse's nose.

The velvety softness of it makes me smile as I thank the animal for giving us passage through the tough desert. The hairs on the back of my neck prickle, sensing eyes on me, and when I turn, they are none other than the black-as-coal stare of Kyros Kahzal.

"He likes you." Kyros chuffs with the half-smirk I have begun to look for. "Khol doesn't like anyone. Not even me most days." He says, rubbing his large hand down the horse's neck and ending the caress with a pat of endearment.

"Well, it seems Khol has good taste." I tease, nudging Kyros with my elbow, and his smile widens a fraction as he begins adjusting the reins. His eyes shift from me to the horse.

"You likely remind him of his previous rider. She was beautiful, full of fire, and revered by anyone she allowed to get close. Even those who weren't close eventually." Something dark passes over Kyros' eyes, and the air between us feels like more space than I have felt around him since he realized I had lied about who I was. "Anyway... it was a long time ago. It's time we get on with it." He continues gruffly, without looking at me. "Are you ready?" His jaw ticks as he secures the ties on the saddlebag. The sudden shift in his tone and the roughness of his movements have me eyeing him curiously, but I don't pry.

"Yes. I'm ready."

"Good, it looks like your guard is ready to say his goodbyes." He juts his chin out just as Kellan reaches us.

"Are you sure you don't want the other horse? I can make my way on foot." He asks Kyros, and my brow scrunches.

"We have no use for a third horse. We don't even need the second. The princess doesn't know how to ride on her own yet, but Mavros would kill me if I left Eidola behind." Kyros says, gesturing to the blonde mare.

"Wait. You aren't coming with us?" I ask Kellan with panic, and he side-eyes Kyros before taking my hands.

"No, beautiful. You know I have my family I need to think about. You have a plan to save the kingdom, and I will do anything and everything I can from within to aid you. Kyros says he has ways of getting messages to me without anyone knowing. I want you to go." His eyes dance over my face, and a sad smile brackets his mouth, while tears build in my eyes. "You will always be special to me, in more ways than you know, but to this kingdom? You are going to be *so much more* than what your father had planned for you. I know it in my bones." He releases one of my hands and cups my cheek, and as a tear falls, he wipes it away with his thumb. I can feel Kyros trying to give us space, but his eyes have always only ever felt like fire when they were on me, and now is no different as he watches this intimate moment with another man.

"Keep her safe. You may have magick, but I still know how to kill a man." Kellan says sternly, without looking away from me, but we all know his words are for Kyros. "Be careful and tell Colette I will miss her and her constant shenanigans with my men, too." I smile and choke on a laughed sob, but he doesn't let me say anything in return before he turns away from me and begins walking into the night.

"My promise stands true, Kellan! I will always remember everything you've done for me." He doesn't so much as turn his head as my words trail after him, and I can't help but cover my mouth with my hand as a sob tries to break free. Not having many people I can say I rely on in life makes saying goodbye to the ones who matter that much harder. Even though I hope it's not goodbye forever, in this kingdom you never truly know. Especially when he is going back to serve a king like my father.

Chapter Thirty-Four

Kyros

My brows dip as I watch Astraea—the princess born from a man I loathe—break. Not long ago I would have relished the sight. But things have changed. She is not the half-witted princess on a tufted pillow I thought she would be. Though the mission has not changed, my thoughts of her surely have. She wants to get away from the king that I want to decimate more than any daughter should, and it makes me vibrate with anger as I think of the reasons that could be. She won't tell me, and that's fine. We both have our secrets, though I probably have more.

After Kellan disappeared into the dark night and minutes ticked by, the night sky beginning to brighten with stars, I slowly trail my hand down Astraea's arm. My touch makes her jolt in surprise before she stiffly turns to face me. Her face is blotchy; if it were brighter, I have no doubt that it would be mottled with red.

"We need to get going now." I say softly, and she nods. Wiping the tears from her face with the back of her hand, she walks past me, up to Eidola. Reaching for her reins, she steels her spine and puffs her chest while the horse and I both eye her with amusement. She looks from the stirrup to the seat of the saddle and back again, then to her feet. More tension grows in her shoulders while I cross my arms and stand behind her waiting. Curious to see just how tenacious the princess can be.

She kicks her slippered foot up to try to reach the stirrups and grips the reins too tightly, pulling on Eidola's bit. The horse whinnies, lifting a foot and stomping in place. The motion startles Astraea, and she sucks in a breath, stepping backward and then falling on her ass. I can't help but let another unbridled laugh rumble from my chest.

Her head whips in my direction, daggers slicing into me with the sharpness of her glare. The look of pure rage makes me laugh again as I shake my head, uncross my arms, and offer her a hand.

"Are you going to try again?" I ask, and she makes a hmmft sound before snubbing my outstretched hand and standing on her own. I chuckle again, and she whirls around, sending sand spraying out in an arch from her disheveled skirt. I place my hands up in a surrendering gesture, even as a smile is plastered on my face. It feels foreign and light, and the thought fills me with warmth.

"You are just getting a kick out of this, aren't you? Watching me struggle? I've not seen you smile or heard you laugh this much since I have met you." She barks out, frustration leaking from her every pore. What I don't say is that no one has made me feel this way before. While I do joke and play around with the family I have chosen as my own and the brother I didn't... It's not this sort of unrestrained amusement or endearment. Instead, I just shrug with a half-cocked grin on my face.

That grin falls entirely as her eyes well with tears, and she looks away from me with a trembling lip. For a moment I just stare at her. She walks up to Eidola, petting the side of her muscular neck with a gentle touch. She whispers lower than I can hear, and Eidola looks at her with a tilted head. Then the horse's heavy lashes lift toward me, as if to say, 'Console her.' Rolling my shoulders and cracking my neck, I come up behind Astraea and place my hand on her lower back. Gentle not to startle her.

"I—I'm sorry." The apology takes longer to come out than I thought, but I don't often apologize for my actions. "These horses are not like the rest. They are much larger. Anyone of your stature would have a difficult, if not impossible, time getting into the saddle. Let me help you." I say, and she swallows hard before turning to face me.

"It should be me who is sorry." My brows furrow at her words, "I dragged you into my escape, and now you are a criminal. My father is likely announcing to the entire kingdom of your treason." I huff out a breath.

"I am not worried about anything your father has to say against me. And you should not be sorry for anything. I didn't do anything I didn't *want* to do." The double meaning behind my words tastes bitter on my tongue, but they are the truth. "Why don't you ride with me? Just while we get further away from the palace. Once we get with the others... I'll teach you to ride on your own." Her eyes light up, bewilderment casting over her face as she looks at me in a way I have never been looked at before.

"You would do that?" She asks, and again, she pulls a long-forgotten feeling to my features as a warm smile spreads across my face.

"I will." No sooner do the words leave my lips than her arms wrap around my neck as she launches herself at me. I catch her with ease, another chuckle escaping. *Apparently she is making me a laughing fool.* Her feet hang from where I hold her up, and my arms wrap around her like it's the easiest thing I have ever done. When I set her down, I don't automatically release her. My arms linger at her waist, her arms achingly slow to slide away from my neck and down my chest until I'm certain she can feel my thundering heart.

"Thank you." Her cheeks darken, and just like before, if there were more light to see by, I know that they would be flaring with a blush I relish in. She bites her lip, and the action draws my eyes to her mouth. I want nothing more than to bite it myself, but I restrain myself.

"Don't thank me yet, Shula. You will most definitely fall on your ass more." I grin, and her shy smile she gives me before she playfully smacks my chest, pushing away from me, makes my cock want to strain against my breeches. I let her go before this little tryst can turn into anything else. We do need to get going.

"How long until we reach, what did you call it? Creshian?" She asks, running her hand once again over Eidola's neck.

"The Creshian Forest." I confirm. "As long as we don't run into any problems along the way, only a few days."

"Is that how long it takes to replenish your magick?" She asks, looking away from me.

"No, not usually." I answer, and she turns around at that, waiting for me to elaborate. With a sigh, I continue. Though I have never revealed anything like this to anyone—only my brother knows the details of our shared magick. "The power I expelled in your bed chambers the night of the nightmare you had... it drained me more than I am used to. A power expulsion of that magnitude without proper knowledge of what it was I was fighting took more than it should have. Usually, there is no time between my use of power and it being restored because the well is so deep. The magick I used at the ceremony only depleted what had just begun restoring, and then I used Mavros' magick with my own. The shared connection between us allowed me to siphon some power from him. Now, with him so far away, that is not possible." She stands quietly, taking in that information, and slowly nods.

"And what if we are attacked on the journey?" She finally asks, and I merely smirk as I step into her and place my hands on her hips.

"As you have come to learn, Shula, I am a man of *many* talents." I say as I lift her up with a jerk. She squeals, just a small squeak, before throwing her leg over Khol's wide back and into the saddle. I follow, settling in behind her. She fits so perfectly in my lap. I have to focus hard for a moment to make sure she isn't keen on just how much I like the feel of her ass between my legs.

I nudge Khol's flank, and he starts off into the desert. I glance behind us; far in the distance, firelight dances as the city surrounding the palace is likely preparing to turn in for the night. Either that or the king is already gathering his horde of fear-bound soldiers to search for the princess. The latter would not be good for our travels. We have wasted too much time as it is, but I also don't want to shock Astraea, who has barely traveled outside of the palace, much less this far beyond its walls.

I let Khol take up a steady pace, nothing too slow to not give us the distance we need, but also slow enough that the woman riding in front of me can take in the beauty the desert has to offer. It's not always as such, and before long she will likely see just how brutal and unforgiving the desert can be. Hopefully it's not too long, though, and my magick is restored. Then I can rend us a portal to the dunes.

"When I was a little girl, I used to sneak out of the castle. There is a lone tree at the highest point of the grounds. I would climb it as often as I could manage without getting caught. On nights like tonight, as summer is beginning to creep in, I felt like the tree reached for the stars like an outstretched hand. A little closer to the divine." I can almost feel her smiling up at the stars as she speaks, and I follow her line of sight; only a smile isn't what comes to my face. My brows furrow as I think of the tree she speaks of. "I would climb all the way to the top, and I would look out over the city and beyond to the sands of the desert that make up our kingdom, and I would wish for grand adventures, for a life that I could *live*. I would tell myself I would get away. I would survive." That last sentence surprises me, but I wait, enjoying the sound of her voice as she opens her past up to me. When she remains silent, I decide to offer her some truth of my own.

"That tree was planted with magick. It's no wonder you were fond of its branches. I, too, would find solace and fond memories there." My arms wrap around her a little more snugly, and she leans her head back into my chest.

"I feel like tonight, that little girl's dreams are finally coming true. Like I am not just surviving but *living*." She swipes tears away from her eyes, and I feel her swallow hard at least a handful of times. I know she's trying to be strong and not let the emotion flood her. It's always what someone does when they are taught that showing any emotion, especially something so raw as sorrow, is inadequate and weak. I know the feeling all too well.

"You are." I say into the top of her head, looking up to the sky, and the fallen, I hope, are watching over us now. *I hope you know what you are doing.* I tell them through my silent prayers to the stars.

She continues to cry far longer than I anticipated. Silently, I hold her through it a little more securely than necessary. I want her to know she is not alone. As the night yawns and the expanse between the palace and us grows, so does my trepidation for what is inevitably going to come.

Eventually, I come to feel sorry for the sorrow she feels, and using my magick, I let a little bit of shadowy sand pool in my hand and sprinkle it over her as I lean down and whisper in her ear.

"Sleep, Shula. You deserve the peace it will bring." If she finds out that I have used my magick on her more than once now, I'm sure there will be a fight, but I hope that through everything she will understand I only ever have used it for good with her. I know it's not the wisest choice, but when I am trying to regain power, it is something I have to do. For her, and for me. I needed time to think about everything, not having to worry that my thoughts might be too loud as well.

Chapter Thirty-Five

Astraea

The warmth of Kyros at my back and the chill his breath gives as it skitters across the nape of my neck as he leans in and whispers for me to sleep are the last things I remember before enviably submitting to the demand. My eyes flutter closed, and like drifting on a cloud of smoke, I am taken into the space that lives between consciousness.

In this relaxed midnight euphoria, my body drifts on the dark wind. The breeze that carries me through the ocean of darkness is far from cold, though; it's more like the wind of a paradise. Warm, calm, and fluid, until I am drawn to a flicker in the dark. Sitting up, I look at the faraway spark of light with a curious tilt of my head.

That warm feeling I've come to notice around Kyros engulfs me, threatening to cast me alight if I come any closer. My feet touch the ground, and dark earth crumbles beneath my bare toes as the dream state changes and trees begin to come into view.

The light feeling in my heart blows away with the shadows around me when I shake my head, and recognition slaps me in the face. The muscle sinks like a stone into my stomach. I wait for the thundering gallop. The screeching scream. The flashing white trees as I speed down the dirt road... but none of it comes. I'm standing in delirium as I spin in a circle trying to make sense of the scene. The forest that surrounds me is silent as it stares back at me.

"Hello?" I whisper and hesitantly begin walking warily in the direction I've always been chased from. No monster of the dark reaches its shadowy claws for me, but I know I haven't left the place it haunts. My feet pick up pace as I try to see beyond the dense brush, but the canopy is too thick. It shadows what is beneath, other than the bark of the trees that are stark white; a fence of bones in the night.

With each step I take, the rocky dirt road crunches beneath my feet, and the more my heart begins to race. Warmth tracks over my cheek, and I press my fingers there, thinking that tears have escaped. To my surprise, it's dry. Again and again the feeling caresses my cheek softly until I finally close my eyes and lean into the feeling.

"Shula. Come back to me." I hear the deep whisper. Feel it in the breath against my face. The heat tracks through my hair, and I feel it under the base of my skull. "Come back to me." My eyes flutter open. Sunshine is blaringly bright in my bleary eyes. Kyros' face blots out the direct path, though. It highlights around him like a golden halo around the darkest divine. His brows dip deep as he looks down at me. The heat on my nape is still there, cradling my head. Slowly as I regain consciousness, I realize it is his hand and his fingers woven into my hair and holding me snugly to his chest.

"Kyros?" I say groggily, still not entirely sure if I have come out of the dream state.

"Yes, Shula. It's me. Time to wake up." He says, running his thumb along my cheekbone gently. He kneels to my right, urging me to sit up with another hand pressing firmly on my back. Once I'm seated, my eyes widen as I take everything in. Khol and Eidola are happily eating some desert grasses just beyond where Kyros is to my right. Palm leaves are sprawled out beneath me, and the tree they came from is providing the shade we are cast in. Desert shrubs of shades of green and brown line my sight to the left, but it's what is right in front of me that causes my breath to catch. It's like a vision from a dream. An alternate reality. Something I have only seen in books and never imagined I would be able to see with my own two eyes.

"Is—this a mirage?" I ask, rubbing the sleep from my eyes. Pink and white flowers bloom from plants sprouting from the sun-bleached sand in beautiful bouquets. Birds chirp and whistle overhead, from trees and while gliding through the heated air. The beautiful song coming together with the sound of cicadas buzzing in the distance. At the center of the vision, with tall cream-cast sand dunes as a backdrop, an oasis of crystalline water shines brilliantly. It reflects the sun and splendor all around us.

"Welcome to Elysia." Kyros says, looking away from me and to the small city sprinkled around the oasis. My eyes snap to him, my jaw falling open a small amount as I recognize the name.

"The land leading to the realm of the dead?" I whisper, as though the ghosts from the stories I have heard will come for me if I speak too loudly.

"You know of it?" He asks, offering me a hand as he stands.

"I have heard stories." I say, accepting his outstretched hand and then dusting myself off. Grit has settled everywhere from our travels. The blowing sand, sweat, and the balms for protecting us from the sun's harsh rays have me feeling the most dirty I have felt in a very long while, possibly ever. My body aches, and I could probably kill for a drink and a bath.

"Surprising that a princess would be privy to such stories." He chuckles.

"It would be, but I am not a normal princess, and I don't much like being told what to do." I shrug, and that chuckle rumbles from his chest once more.

"You don't say..." He teases, one side of his mouth tilting up at the corner. "Let's go, Shula. We need to get a room, a meal, and a bath. I think we are both—" My mouth falls completely before I snap it shut and cut off his words.

"Don't you dare finish that sentence, Mister Kahzal." His smile flashes briefly before he narrows his eyes on me.

"Mister Kahzal was the man who raised me... You can find something better to call me if you refuse my first name, but I was merely suggesting we are both in need of some humanity after such a long couple days." He wasn't wrong. It's like he dove into my head and stole the thoughts right from it.

"I have to be honest..." I start, and Kyros takes my hand, clicking his tongue at the horses; they follow as he begins leading us toward the sandstone buildings.

"I hope that you are," he says, and the brush over the back of my hand from his thumb causes heat that has nothing to do with the sun to bloom into my cheeks. I pull my hand from his, and he looks back at me with an indiscernible look on his face.

"I didn't think that we would be stopping at a village so soon. If we are close to the palace at all, don't you think this is the first place that my father will look?" I ask.

"No. I don't. Your father is, if anything, predictable." He says, and I snort a laugh, earning another look from him, but I roll my lips. "Do you disagree?"

"No, actually, I agree fully." I tell him, and his eyes narrow in a way that feels like he is trying to piece together a puzzle, and the puzzle is me.

"Anyway, we are currently in the opposite direction of where we are eventually headed. I figured this would be the last place your father would look. Seeing as my brother and I are gone with the coveted princess... he would think we have taken the direct path toward Diemos." I think on that for a moment as we walk, humming my approval of that statement. I know he's right. My father will put two and two together. He already had suspicions raised after the few times Kyros spoke out on my behalf.

The small village is quiet as we stroll right into the center of it. No one pays us much attention as they go about their day, harvesting from their small gardens near the waterfront. They make baskets from dried palm fronds, and others are cooking in outdoor kitchens. The sweet and savory mix of aromas wafting toward us makes my stomach growl in response. Regardless, I close my eyes and take a deep breath of it.

Children are even happily playing in the sand and in the shady areas below the bundles of palms. A small smile is brandished on my face as I take it all in. Such a stark difference to what I experienced in my brief time trekking through the outer rim of the city I called home. Kyros acts as though he has been here a thousand times, taking no notice of any of it. I watch the ruthless man walk through paradise like it is nothing until he chances a glance at me, catching me staring.

"Do you have something to say, Shula?" He asks, that same narrowing of his eyes on me. Never out of anger, but that curious consideration.

"Have you been here before?" I return a question, and he looks away from me as he answers and keeps walking to what I now see is a tavern near a marsh. It extends into the larger body of water just beyond.

"My duty to the queen of Diemos and my training have required me to travel broadly. This oasis is one I have come to many times." He drawls out as though he is bored.

"Why would you need to come here?" I ask incredulously, just as we reach the stairs leading to a wooden wrap-around deck. It's one of the only mostly wood structures as far as the eye can see. One side of the building is wood, halfway over the water and on stilts; the other is made of sandstone, just as the other small dwellings.

The door bangs open just as a woman hobbles out. Frail, white-haired, and keen golden-brown eyes. Her tanned skin is weathered and wrinkled as the most parched leather, but when she slams her cane down, her knobby fingers wrapped around it so tight they blanch, and she curses... It catches me by surprise.

"Fuckin' divine, it's about time ya showed yer face. What were ya hopin' I'd kick the bucket before ya made yer way back? Ya damn well know I'd be one of those ghosts they tell stories of. Comin' to haunt yer ass if ya didn't come finish those jobs I ask'd ya to the last time ya were here." My eyes round as she rips into Kyros with her words and then flash to him to see his reaction. He is unmoved. One eyebrow quirks up, and he looks at her pointedly.

"It's good to see you too, Mortala." The corner of his mouth slides into the hint of a smirk just as the woman's cane comes whistling through the air toward Kyros' head. He catches it in his fist, his lips curling into a full grin. Mortala must notice me rearing back at her caning Kyros and turns her sights on me. My shoulders nearly touch my ears, and my hands are clenched in front of me, wrung tight.

"Who's the girl?" She barks, not addressing me, but asking Kyros instead. Kyros looks at me for a long moment, his brows drawn as a million words cross his eyes. He settles on one.

"Sienna." He finally says, which tells me this woman may not be as close as she seems to my travel guide. It seems to be enough of an answer for the woman, though, and with that she snatches the cane away from Kyros with a grunt and strides back through the door she so hastily exited.

Kyros places a hand on my low back, guiding me to follow Mortala. Walking through the doorway, I am hit with a plethora of scents, ranging from savory to sweet or a pungent, rancid sour, making swallowing noticeably harder with how parched I am. The whole lower level seems to be laid out like a tavern. Although along one of the longest walls, it is an open balcony. Plants in clay pots line the border with green. Vines trail from the covered deck, and flowers hang from baskets in the corners. The colors are richer than those of the only other tavern I had to compare, or maybe it's just the paradise beyond that makes everything just appear more vivid. I don't realize that I have wandered until I reach the railing and lean over to look at the waters below the wooden deck.

"I have to go to one more place before I settle in for some rest." I jump at the sound of Kyros' voice, spinning around to face him. "A little jumpy, Shula?" His eyes flick from my eyes to my mouth and then back. I fold my arms over my chest.

"No."

"Mm." He hums in that way that sets my skin on fire. "Well, while I am gone, Mortala has been instructed to ensure you are fed, hydrated, and shown where you can bathe. I'm not sure when we will be able to stop like this again. Take full advantage of it. I won't be gone long." He says when I open my mouth to say something, the way his eyes drift over his shoulder makes me narrow my eyes on him.

"Am I safe here?" I ask, following where his eyes just swept.

"We won't be safe until we are back in Diemos. Even then, you are a princess from a foreign kingdom. The danger will be there too, but with me, you are safe." He reaches into his belt and pulls a small dagger from a hook, and I look at him confused as he presses the handle into my hand. "Always be prepared to defend yourself."

"I—Kyros, I don't know how to use this." I admit quietly, feeling the heat creep into my cheeks with every word. Verbally acknowledging the fact that I am weak, a burden, causes shame to fill my chest, and I look down at the small knife.

"Cut with the sharp end for now. We will go over more on the road. I won't be gone long, and you are safe enough here." He says, and I nod. "Stay out of trouble." He runs his thumb across the back of my hand that he still holds with the knife. I swallow as I watch him walk away. As soon as he has disappeared, I stick the blade into my pocket. It feels like an anchor weighing me down.

"Sienna, is it?" Mortala says coming from a back room and a swinging door. I nod. "Well then, here's yer food and some water. Never have seen The Hawk bring such a meek girl around." I shrug my shoulders and sit on the stool at the bar where she placed a plate of colorful and steaming food. I have to fight the urge to use my hands and shovel the food into my mouth like a barbaric oaf. I settle on licking the salt from my lips before I take a languid drink of the water.

"Thank you," I say breathlessly as I finally set the water down, trying not to choke as my throat reacts to finally being able to properly swallow.

"Ain't no mind, I'm bein' paid. Eat up and I'll walk ya to tha' bath house." She says before hobbling back through the swinging door and leaving me alone again. *Great, not even a proper bath.*

Chapter Thirty-Six

Kyros

Drabek's caw makes my lips curl up as I reach the far end of the water's edge. His shadow brushes over me like a welcomed hello as he flies overhead. The enormous black bird lands on my shoulder while his low grunts of adoration sound off in my ear. I chuckle back, giving him a piece of raw meat I snagged on the way out here.

"Hello to you too, old friend." I say, and the raven blinks, nearly purring with excitement upon my return. "I need you to carry a message for me." He clicks, his maw opening and closing quickly, urging me on. Drabek was my father's raven, and though my father, *my birth father,* is gone... I feel as though sometimes his lingering magick lives on with Drabek. He found me after we were both displaced by the war. It's as though the Creshian forest's magick sent the creature to watch over me from afar until I was old enough to support the weight of his presence. Not only physically but emotionally too. Drabek serves both myself and Mavros, but we both know he is in service of the older twin. Even if my being born minutes earlier deems me worthy of something more.

Drabek chitters, awaiting the kiss of my magick, and I smile as I run my fingers over his sun-warmed feathers. Closing my eyes only for a moment, I let my magick dance from my fingers. The glimmering shadow swirls along his body before he bristles and absorbs the black tendrils with a shrill cry. It's a joyous sound.

"Give Mavros hell. Find me once the message is delivered." I grin before lifting my arm and watching as his powerful wings splay wide and thrust down, giving him momentum to launch into the sun-drenched sky. He circles overhead, cawing once more before he takes off in the direction of wherever Mavros is.

"The Hawk returns?" My shoulders stiffen as I hear a crackly voice call out behind me. "Didn't think I would see you around here for a while... Not after what you did."

"Karnnen." I say, not turning toward him. It was a risk I knew I was taking coming here, but I needed to rest, and I needed to get a message out to Mavros. This is one of the only areas I felt safe enough doing both. Because that little bit of magick I just gave with sending the message was even too much after everything I had expelled on Astraea's behalf. Karnnen has magick, but it's not much... nothing compared to what lies dormant under my skin. He doesn't know I can't access it right now, though. It's probably the only reason he hasn't taken full advantage of the situation that will likely never happen again.

"You don't even have enough respect to address me while looking at me in the eyes!?" He bellows from behind me, and slowly I turn to face him. He looks different than before. His face is harder. Eyes sharp with rage cutting through them. His once long hair, similar to mine, is now shaved close to the skin. A show of loss to his people. I don't show any emotion as I regard him; even though his brother was not my mark, I killed him nonetheless. I would do it again. Especially now that I have gotten to know the woman he so clearly disrespected. After his hands assaulted what is mine, even before I knew she was.

"His twin flame felt the magick of their bond extinguish like cold water dousing a flame. Do you know the kind of pain that causes? The unimaginable agony?" He walks forward, tilting his head to the side as he leers up at me. "Knowing the only way that has happened is by death?"

"You know that when you are a mercenary, there are risks. Death being high on that list." I finally say, crossing my arms over my chest.

"He was with you! You were supposed to protect him! The infamous Hawk is deadly beyond measure. Loyal to the people he chooses and those who choose to follow him. You let him die." He bellows as my teeth threaten to crumble from the pressure I grind them. I recall his brother's last moments on this plane.

"It's all a lie, isn't it? What the people are saying? Your plans for the—" His words are cut off as my hand takes his breath in a vise-like grip. His brown eyes flashing just like his brother's did in the end. The vision of him in my grip is so eerily the same. His skin darkens with the whites of his eyes, redness crawling into both with his lack of oxygen, and whatever he sees on my face causes more panic to enter his already erratic gaze.

"You know the rules, Karnnen. We do not speak of my plans, that is, unless one wants to lose their tongue. Is that what you want?" He attempts to shake his head. "Leoric was a leech and a menace. He served whatever purpose Queen Phaedra wanted and nothing else. His death was a blessing to the living, and his twin flame is better off with none." I release his throat with a push, and he stumbles backward, falling to his ass and clawing at his throat as though doing so will allow more air into his lungs. He gasps and struggles to do anything, but through it all, his outrage has only deepened the scowl on his face.

"You. Killed. Him." He chokes out, and I crouch down in front of him, lifting his chin so he sees the reflection of his pitiful form in my eyes.

"I did, and I would do it again," I say in a low, guttural growl as I drop his chin and stand. "Keep your distance, Karnnen. If you come at me like that again, you're next," I say as I walk away. I don't wait for him to acknowledge my words or respond. Nothing he can say matters anyway. I keep my eyes on the tavern at the other side of the water and make my way back to where Astraea waits. I don't need this, but I will deal with him the same way I dealt with his brother if I must. I don't need magick to kill a man.

"I SEE IT, HAWK! It's just a flicker, but it burns." He calls out after me, but I can tell that he is still where I left him. I don't give him the satisfaction of knowing his words caused something inside me to stir. It's not the right time to acknowledge what I know is inevitable, and if it's a threat he is trying to send, I would like to see him try.

I crossed the expanse of land to the tavern in much less time than it took me to get out there. The door bangs open as I begin up the stairs, and Mortala steps out.

"The girl ya brought with ya is an ungrateful twat if I ever knew one. Ya best be leaving that one somewhere she can learn some manners." Mortala barks in greeting. "She don't deserve it... should just make'r walk back to'er room naked for that fit she threw." She shakes her head, and I narrow my eyes on the old woman.

"Mortala, what are you rambling about? Where is—Sienna?" I ask, almost calling her by her actual name. The name that would certainly be recognized here even if her face is not. Her father keeping her coddled in the palace actually works in our advantage on these stops because no one really knows what the princess looks like. Sure, she fits the general description, but that could just be coincidence. She huffs, turning around without answering my question and letting the door swing shut behind her. I roll my eyes as I follow.

"Here. Found a old night dress from some of the past hussies. Should fit'er perfect. Yer twit is in the bath house. Made all kinds of demands. Girl needs a lesson, that's what she needs." She continues complaining as she walks away, through the door to the kitchen, and I can hear her still rambling as that door shuts between us too. I shake my head and leave her to stew.

To get to the pool, I take the stairs back outside and head around the tavern, where I know the only entrance is. This time of day there likely won't be anyone around. Most like to bathe at night when the sun's unrelenting blaze has cooled enough to enjoy the heat of the natural bath. I've been here many times, but I've never had any interest in utilizing the communal bathhouse. Mavros, on the other hand, I've found down here too many times to count.

The entrance is like walking into a hole in the ground. The steps leading into the carved-out wide tunnel are rough, natural sandstone, uneven and jagged, with small daylight holes allowing the sun to shine in spotlights along the way. The short tunnel opens up to reveal a shadowed cave, with one side an open window where water falls over the ledge into the round bath, curtained with lush green plants, and a much larger daylight hole above the waterfall, giving the room a peaceful ambiance.

I stop at the bottom of the stairs when I hear her. Soft whimpering cries eaten up by the moving water, so quiet if I had not been listening for her, I likely wouldn't have heard it at all. As I get closer, I finally see her. At the far end, away from the waterfall and hidden in the shadow, Astraea lays her upper body over a boulder, arms crossed and holding her head as she cries into them. Her dark hair twisted up and held in place by the pin she gave me as a favor for the first competition. It's a sight and sound that has everything in me sharpening into a blade for only her to wield. I think of nothing else as I step into the water fully clothed and wade over to her.

She doesn't hear me approaching, too overwhelmed by her own emotions. Whatever it is that has her upset doesn't tell her of the danger lurking over her shoulder. Or perhaps, maybe her soul recognizes mine and knows what I am only coming to realize.

"Shula—" I start, but my words lodge in my throat. She turns, and the low light catches on her radiant skin and the texture that should not be where it is. The unnatural lines crisscrossing, like side-winding tracks from the sand vipers of the desert.

"Kyros? What are you doing here?" She stiffens, covering her body with her arms. The worry on her face tells me it's not her nakedness that she is concerned with covering, but I can't even pay attention to that. My blood is boiling with rage for the marks I see on her, and as much as she tries to drag outrage into her tone, I can feel her relief as though it is my own when she knows it's me. The relief that is quickly transformed into shame. She looks down at my body, realizing I am fully dressed. I don't answer her question as I close the distance between us. She refuses to look at me. Her gaze stuck on the water that laps between us.

I say nothing at first as I stare down at her and the way she seems to cower into herself, her gaze never lifting. It's like a night and day difference from the woman I thought I was beginning to know and understand.

"Look at me." I say, trying my hardest to keep the anger from my tone and failing. She doesn't move. Slowly, I lift my hand from where it's fisted under the water. Drips roll from my arm and splash back into the pool between us, and when my skin meets the softness of her face, her breath hitches. I guide her face toward mine and step in closer, bending down so our noses almost touch. She still refuses to lift her eyes. Her lashes fan out over her cheekbones, and tear droplets collect beneath them and fall down her face in rivulets. "Look at me, Shula."

When she finally lifts her gaze and the storm of oceanic blue crashes into me like a tsunami, my lips part, my breathing growing faster with my turbulent thoughts. Who could hurt someone so perfect? The raw worry drowning her eyes has me shaking my head. I can't help it. I can't help but deny the thought of someone wanting to defile her. Creating scars beyond just skin, I see them on her soul.

"I'm sorry," she says, and I feel my brows pull down tighter than before.

"Who?" I ask simply. We both know what I am referring to. She tries to look away, and I refuse to allow it. I keep her chin in my grip. "Tell. Me. Who hurt you?" My voice vibrates through my chest with each word, and she shivers, her bottom lip trembling.

"My father...*mostly.*" Her voice cracks, and the subsequent fissure breaks through more of my crumbling wall as I swear an oath to the divine. I will send the man responsible to the pits of Zameil if I have to carry his lifeless body over the threshold myself. Once I have reeled in my anger enough to speak again, I roll my thumb over her cheek, wiping away the moisture. She leans into the touch just the smallest amount. Giving me all she can of her limited trust.

"Mostly?" I ask in a whisper. She swallows hard, her blue eyes once again filling with tears and then darkening by the shadows of her past.

"Pravin too." Her chin wobbles before she continues, and my nostrils flare with the building tempest of my fury. "Sometimes my father would instruct him to punish me too. He—" She sobs, and I pull her into my chest, holding onto her tight, as she spills her anguish into my own soul. It's something I never knew I would willingly want to share the burden of, but for her I feel like I want to take it all. "I didn't want you to see this." Her voice cracks.

"They will *never* touch you again. I will make sure of it. No one will ever hurt you like that again." I push her out so she can see the promise in my eyes. "I promise," I say, hoping that she sees the truth. "I don't give empty promises either, Shula." Her eyes flick between mine for a long moment as she thinks, and I wish I could see into that beautiful mind to see what she is thinking of. "What can I do to prove to you I am a man of my word?" Her lip rolls into her mouth and becomes trapped by her teeth as she considers my words.

"You once said that no one could save me from you. That if you were the one pressed to my body, not even the divine could save me. You said that I would be begging for your touch." Her hands slowly fall away from her chest, exposing her breasts to me. I don't look at them, though. I keep my eyes locked with hers, even as I notice the way her chest heaves with her heavier breathing. My own more languid and tangling with hers. "I'm begging you. Make me forget." We both stand there silently, breathing the words she just spoke, letting my own wrap around us and pull us together.

"Every foul touch. Every painful memory. Each scar on your soul... It's mine. I will take the burden of them from you." I gently cup her chin, and I let the pain pull me toward her; just before our lips touch, I make her another promise. "Their deaths are the exception. I will spill every ounce of their blood in your name, but that blood will only stain my hands, and I will wear it proudly in your honor." I seal the promise with a deep kiss, allowing my tongue to explore her mouth.

Her arms wrap around my neck, chest pressing against mine, and I silently curse myself for not taking off any clothing. My cock stains under the wet material as her legs wrap around my hips and she seats herself over the ridge, moaning into my mouth. It takes every ounce of restraint I have not to release myself and bury it between her legs.

Instead I brace her with my hands, each one cupping her bare ass, fingers squeezing as she rolls her hips over me. I can't suppress the groan that builds with the friction of our bodies. She reaches over my shoulders, pulling my tunic up my back and allowing me to shrug out of the constraining fabric. Our bare chests touch just the slightest, and it's the first time I look down at her breasts as I break the kiss. I look between the two hardened peaks, licking my lips, and slowly make my descent to entrap one with my teeth.

She gasps, arching her back beautifully. She pushes her chest further into my mouth as I walk forward and set her on the ledge of the bath. There is a natural underwater seat that she rests her feet on as I release her nipple and give the same attention to the other breast. Growling as something primal seems to take over me, feeling her hand rake through my hair. Her eyes widen at the sound as I pull back and make eye contact with her. I throw one leg over my shoulder. Trailing my hands over her slick legs, I press my thumb over her clit and circle slowly, rhythmically, in time with her breathing. Just as I feel her tensing, I change the motion. I toy with her entrance, her release almost tangible, but not quite there. No, that I want to taste.

"What did I tell you, Shula?" I ask, trailing my tongue between her breasts and dropping to my knees on the step between her legs. When she answers breathlessly, I am hovering my lips above hers.

"I—" My eyes narrow as I drink her in as she lies beneath me. Panting, confused, and needy for my touch. Perfect. "Every touch is yours." I smile into her mouth before claiming it. Between kisses I praise her.

"Good, what else, beautiful?" I ask, moving to her ear and taking the lobe into my mouth. She sucks in a breath as I also dip one finger into her at the same time.

"Every painful memory." She confirms, and I nod, sucking along the skin of the column of her neck.

"Every one of them will be replaced. Pain will now be pleasure." My tongue flicks over her nipple as I make my way lower, loving the way she starts to squeeze her thighs together, needing the friction that I am denying her. "What else?" I ask as I give her some of the movement she wants, pressing another finger into wetness, grinding the heel of my hand over her clit.

"Each scar— Oh divine!" She calls out as I continue the slow torture, and I growl.

"Each what, Shula?"

"Each scar on my soul." She moans, and I drop between her legs, scoring a line between her lips, taking a taste before diving in like the parched man I am. She yells more for the divine, pulling my hair at the root, and I gasp as I come up for air only to dive back between her delicious thighs.

"I'm afraid I won't be sated with just the scars, Shula." I breathe between feasting and fucking her with my fingers. "I'll have you give me everything." I flick my tongue over her clit and curl my fingers as she tightens around them. "Will you give me everything?" My rumbling growl vibrates my lips as I keep them planted, ready to drink down her release.

"Yes! Take it all, Kyros, please! It's all yours!" She exclaims, and I suck her clit into my mouth as she pulses and writhes, pulls and grinds, pants and moans. Her confession, my proclamation—they swirl around like magick, and as she trembles, she drowns me in her come. She melts in the glow of pleasure. I kiss the inside of each thigh where they vibrate with aftershocks.

Letting my hands trail her legs, then her waist, I raise up to meet her eyes, press a gentle kiss to her lips, and then pull her back into the water. I help wash her, silently brushing my fingers over her back. Rinsing away the previous pain and caressing it with a new memory. I pull her into my lap, and she rests her head on my shoulder, not much different than when we were riding. My cheek presses to the top of her head as she lays her back on my chest. I wrap my arm around her middle, and she holds onto it as though it is anchoring her to this realm entirely. And with my other hand

I trail my fingers over her skin in small circles and long lines, each brush saying more than one word could.

Neither of us says anything as we sit there in each other's embrace, but in my chest I know she wasn't the only one giving just now. I know now what he meant, Karnnen... *it's just a flicker, but it burns.*

She gave me her soul, just as I have given mine, and together our twin flames now *burn*.

Chapter Thirty-Seven

Astraea

Time seems to have paused between the bathhouse and now. Everything melding together in a chaotic prism of color. Warmth still surges beneath my skin, painting me with a blush I feel will never end. Kyros' eyes were heavy as he helped me bathe, taking care of me with the most tender touch. A touch I never imagined he could possess. He watched as I exited the bath. I could feel the way his eyes took every inch of me in, the way every rivulet of water rolled down my skin. He watched as though he would later trace the same lines with his wicked tongue.

Once I was wrapped in the towel offered by that cranky old woman, he finally removed his clothes, quickly washing himself too. By the time I was dressed in the scrap of fabric from Mortala, he was out of the water. The same threadbare gray towel I just used was slung low on his hips, and his clothes bunched in one hand at his side. The already wet gray material is doing *absolutely nothing* to hide what is so evidently still rock hard beneath. I have to force myself to swallow, my mouth suddenly flooded with moisture from my overly needy core.

Heat crawls up my neck now just thinking about the look in his eyes when my own finally reaches his. The amusement of watching me basically drool over him standing before me. His black eyes are lit from within, showing the deep gold highlights within, like volcanic veins of fire hidden underneath charred stone.

Now, he breathes heavily as he sleeps. One arm slung up and tucked under his head, the other hand resting on his bare chest. His shadowy tattoos move just the slightest across his bronzed skin, and I watch the magick in fascination. I wouldn't have even noticed had I not been studying him so thoroughly. As much as he tried to insist that he didn't need sleep, it finally won out about an hour ago.

I, however, am not the slightest bit tired. My body feels charged, nearly buzzing with energy. I am more awake than I have felt in a *very* long time. I can't seem to drag my eyes away from him. My heart flips as I recall so many of the words he has said to me. The fluttering feel of wings in my stomach as I replay the way his hands touched me. *His tongue.* I never thought I would ever feel this: A longing for someone still in the same room. The face I see when I close my eyes during the day and the darkness of his eyes I want to get lost in at night. The brutish suitor willing to risk war for me. My brows gather in the center of my forehead. *Why is he willing to risk so much?* A question I will surely be asking him when he is awake.

Judging by the placement of the shadows in the room, I would guess it's almost midday. I slept nearly all night during our ride to the oasis. I still don't know how I managed to do it, and for the first time, also, in a *very* long time, it had been nightmare-free. As though the magick that Kyros threw at it scared it off from returning.

I watch the rise and fall of his chest for a moment longer before deciding that when he wakes, he will need food. I'll go down and speak with that horrible innkeeper Mortala and make sure she has food waiting for him when he wakes up.

As quietly as I can, I slip from the bed. Slowly, I pad over to the armoire in the corner and close my eyes as I try to pry it open without noise, but I am unsuccessful. The hinge creaks, and I scrunch up my nose as I jerk my head toward Kyros. His breathing has quieted, but he is, thankfully, still peacefully sleeping. I let my breath out of my mouth and turn back to the hanging garments. It seems Kellan didn't have many options when it came to women's attire...

I look down at the thin cream sleep dress, lined with lace and nearly see-through, and roll my eyes. It's better than nothing, and it's not as revealing as some I know exist. I'll find Mortala, ask about my clothes she insisted on taking and washing for me, and then get Kyros food. I'm sure there won't be many opportunities to run into many people... The small oasis can't hold many people, or we would have seen more on our way in, I'm sure of it. Truthfully, it can barely be called a village with how small it is.

I creep along the wall and sneak from the room without Kyros waking, and I can't help but smile in victory as I make it to the main tavern without coming into contact with a single person. Though my smile quickly fades as I realize that I also have not even heard anyone. The whole place is empty. Being that it's midday, I find that odd, but I guess maybe they have different schedules than what we carried out in the palace. Deciding it wouldn't be horrible if I just ducked into the kitchen and helped myself to a few things, I make my way through the tavern. I'll make sure that we pay for whatever we use during our stay upon our departure.

Now that I am alone and really able to take in the beauty of the space, I let my eyes wander. It's not like the last tavern I found myself in. Vine plants trail along the wood and clay walls and hang from the ceiling. Large-leaf potted plants fill the corners, and the sun shines brilliantly through all of the open windows, highlighting the lush greens and terracotta coloring of the walls. Truly a paradise. I'm still lost in the vision when I swing the kitchen door open, and a startled Mortala curses me.

"Divine wraith! What are ya doin' back here girl? Tryin' to give an old woman a heart attack? For all who burn in Zamiel!? Are you just going to stare at me?" She squawks, throwing her hands up before shaking her head and angrily returning to her cooking.

"I—I'm sorry for startling you. I was just coming to look for some food." I finally say, and she turns back to me with an irradiated glower, clicking her tongue before she goes right back to chopping whatever the desert fruit is on the counter. "Do you have a platter I can take up to the room—" My words are cut off before I can finish as she whirls around, pointing the sharp end of her knife in my face.

"Hawk can come back here and act like everything is just peachy, but guests comin' in, actin' like they deserve everything served up on a silver fuckin' platter? It don't rub me right." Mortala looks down her nose in an angry sneer aimed at me. *Hawk?* My brows dip as I look down at the sharp object hovering in my face, and I swallow before nodding sternly. My anger building with each bounce of the blade in her hand.

"Is everything not peachy?" I ask pointedly, and she gives a harsh, derisive laugh before slamming the knife down in front of her.

"Ya got gall. I'll give it to ya. Ya make demands... Come stridin' into my kitchen... Who do ya think ya are, huh? The damned princess of Eathain? Get outta here. Go spread your legs for that brute of yours, and then ya both can be gone!" The crazed woman bellows while curling her lip in disgust.

I turn on my heel and stomp from the room before she is even done with her thought. I don't even know what I'm doing. I don't know how to survive in the world outside of what my father kept me in. I'm not used to the way people talk to me as someone who is not royalty. I don't know how to respond to the anger simmering beneath my skin.

Every step feels as heavy as my thoughts, and a dull ache begins behind my eyes as I make my way to sit at one of the tables. I breathe in the heated air slowly through my nose and out the same way as I clench my jaw hard enough to crack teeth. *I can do this.* I slide into the chair at the far table, next to a window. It looks out over the water of the oasis. Birds call, and small creatures frolic through the brush below. My anger quickly ebbs as I try to let the beauty that is not the palace ground me.

Although I am not tired, my soul still seems to carry enough stress to weigh my body down. Resting my head on my arms, I watch nature through watery eyes. Loose sand blows off the tops of the sandy hills in the distance, and I can't help but feel a little like the dunes. Slowly being shaped by the winds steering my life, never truly being the one who carves the path.

"You're new here." A raspy voice startles me from my thoughts, and I turn to face a man with dark hair cropped close to his head and russet eyes narrowed in curiosity. "Just passing through, I assume?"

"Um, yes. I am." I say, shifting in my seat. The look in his eyes as he surveys me causes trepidation to crawl up my spine. I don't give him any more information, but I see how his eyes skitter down over my body and the lack of clothing I forgot I was wearing. Heat blooms in my cheeks.

"I'm Karnnen. Mind if I join you?" He asks, but he sits across from me before I can answer. "Where are you headed?" He continues, and his eyes dart around the room like he's watching for something, or someone. Worry builds as more people enter the dining area and keep their eyes fixed on me too. All the men are dressed similarly to the one in front of me, as though they are about to head out into the desert and not coming in for dinner at the end of a hard day's labor.

"I, um, we are headed—" I stumble over my words. Something about this man feels off, familiar almost, but *dangerous*. His jaw ticks while waiting for my answer that won't come, and the way his eyes keep flicking to the hall where the bedchambers are has my inner warning bells chiming loud in my ears.

"Take the food. Get outta here before ya find even more trouble." Mortala claps her hands in my face, shoving a plate of fruit, cheese, and bread into my hands. Confusion puckers at my mind as I blink out of my panic and at the multiple sets of eyes staring back at me. Whispers hidden behind hands and looks of judgment skating over my body. I look down at my lack of regular clothes, and heat explodes across my skin as my fingers wrap around the edges of the plate. The man in front of me leans back, his arm slung over the back of the chair.

"Aw, come on, Mortala. Can't you see we were getting to know each other? Someone this pretty doesn't need to be traveling alone... I just wanted—"

"I'm not." I cut in. "Thank you for your concern, but I need to get going."

I don't thank the cranky old woman. Nor do I try to make eye contact with anyone else who witnessed any of the conversation with the man or Mortala shooing me out like vermin. With my chin tucked low, I try to hurry from the tavern and make my way back into the room where Kyros sleeps. Before I make it to the hall, though, a hand wraps around my arm, stopping me.

"Careful out there, sweetheart. You don't know what kinds of monsters lie in waiting out in the desert." Karnnen says wickedly, as his eyes trail the length of my body and then linger on my lips. I tug my arm from his grip and pin him with an incredulous look.

"Thank you for your concern, but the monsters I travel with are far more intimidating than anything that could be lurking out there. I can promise you that," I say with vexation bleeding into my tone. He narrows his eyes on me, a silent smirk lifting the corner of his mouth, before I turn on my heel and storm away from him.

I'm not sure if Karnnen says anything else; my pulse is too loud in my ears to hear anything else. I don't know what time it is or how long I was in the dining room, but as I burst through the door of our bedchamber, Kyros hurls himself from the bed. Shadows leaping from his skin and coiling around his arms like whips at the ready.

"What is it?" He says, eyes wild and red. "Are you ok?" I nod but am unable to speak through my nerves. He takes the plate of food, discarding it to the side, and with nothing left in my hands, they tremble as they drop to my sides. I can't steady my rampant heart. His hands press against either side of my face, the warmth matching the fire in my veins. My eyes flick between his and his drawn brow, the stern press of his lips. My hands cover his as I take a deep breath and close my eyes.

"Did something happen?" He asks after a moment of silence.

"I—I don't know." I open my eyes, and his thumbs score lines over my cheeks.

"We need to keep moving. I'm sorry I fell asleep." He looks over to the window and how the sun is beginning its descent in the sky. "We can leave at nightfall."

"You needed rest too. I'm fine, really," I say, pressing my lips together and trying to shrug out from under his intense gaze. He allows it, and I pull open the armoire and take out one of the tunics and breeches. When I turn back toward Kyros, he is still intently studying me; I let out a shaky breath. *"I'm fine."* I say it again, and even I can't tell if I am trying to convince him or myself that it is true.

"Tell me." He doesn't relent.

"It was just a strange conversation," I say, and he closes the distance between us.

"Conversation?" He asks sharply.

"There was a man; he was very interested in who I was and where I was going. He gave me the creeps." I admit, confused as Kyros gets up, shoving things into a canvas bag. He pulls a tunic over his head, tying his long hair back away from his face, and continues to storm around the room. "Kyros." I say his name, and he doesn't even look at me. "I'm sure it was nothing." I finally say, and he stops, slowly turning toward me.

"Why were you so upset?"

"I don't know; he seemed so familiar, but I don't know if it was what he said just as I was leaving that made me feel like he was warning me. I'm sure it was nothing. I'm just on edge, I suppose, plus a little embarrassed." I gesture to the nightdress I'm wearing. Kyros puts his hand out between us, and I place mine in his. Even as I do, the man's voice echoes through my mind. "You don't know what kinds of monsters lie in waiting out in the desert." I repeat the words the man said, and heat fills my body as he pulls me to my feet, wrapping one arm around my back as he pulls me into him.

"You will trust me to keep you safe?" He asks, and I agree as he tucks my hair behind my ear. "As sunset falls, we will be leaving. I'll go get your clothes from Mortala. Don't leave this room." He says firmly. Honestly, even though this place is incredibly beautiful, I am ready to move on. I need to see Cole with my own two eyes, and I need to decide if I will be running away with her or choosing to stay and join Queen Phaedra of Diemos against my father and what would be the end of his tyranny.

"I'll be right back." Kyros growls, his fingers tangling into the back of my hair as he tilts my head back so I am forced to look at him. "Stay. Fucking. Put."

Chapter Thirty-Eight

Kyros

My feet pound the wood planks of the tavern floor as I make my way out, searching for the fucker I know came at Astraea. He will die just as his brother did. I should have killed him earlier for the threat he said to me. But now? It had to have been him. I didn't need to know what the man looked like from her recollection. No one else here would be stupid enough to threaten who they surely know is mine.

"Where is he?" I growl as I burst into the dining room; several heads snap in my direction. Chairs scrape against wood as a few women get up quickly to leave. No one says anything. Mavors is the one with a temper. Mavros is the one who acts before thinking, but with her? I find that every time there is a situation with her, my control leaves me entirely. I pick up a glass pitcher filled with water and hurl it across the room. It hits the wall, the glass shattering into a thousand glittering shards just like my patience, and the water splashes out everywhere, soaking the wall and the floor beyond it.

"Karnnen!" I bellow, but it's not him who responds.

"Hawk! Ya fuckin' heathen!" Mortala comes hurling herself at me with a kitchen knife aimed for my heart. I pluck the senseless weapon from her grip, and she scoffs in frustration before I toss it away and growl.

"Where is he, Mortala? I will level this entire place if you don't tell me."

"Don't you threaten me, ya fuckin' brute. You already made a mess of the place. He left with his dark doers already, so if you wanna kindly fuck off, that would be great. Take that twit with ya too! Probably safe to say keep that one close to ya if ya care about her well bein'... Karnnen had that look about'm." I narrow my eyes on her. "Don't look at me like that. I sent the girl back to you before he could sink his teeth in." She looks at the mess I made. "And look at what that got me. You best never come back here." *Fuck. This is not a problem I need right now.*

I walk over to the bar, slamming down a pouch of coins for Mortala and leveling her with a glare. The crass old hag does well not to say another fucking word. She takes the bag and gives it a jiggle before pocketing it, turning back to the kitchen and returning with a stack of folded clothes I recognize as Astraea's.

"Yer never going to do what ya set out to if you keep that temper. That twin of yers may get away with it… but with a plan like yers…" She trails off, her brow hiked up her face, but the look I pin her with must be enough to stop her words before she finishes.

"We were never here," I say gruffly before turning. The tavern door swings open just as I am facing it, and a guard wearing armor that reflects the glaring sun steps into the room.

"On order of the king, his majesty King Connard Casimir of Eathian, we are here to search the vicinity." He announces, and I use what little magick has resurfaced to allow the shadows to obscure my position.

"Searchin' fer what?" Mortala says, her eyes sliding to where I am easing my way back toward the room Astraea waits in. Just as my hand wraps around the cool metal handle, I hear the response I know is coming.

"The fugitives who ran away from the palace with Princess Astraea Casimir. The bounty for their return to the king is hefty. Any aid in catching the ones responsible alive will be rewarded handsomely." Just as I suspected.

I slip through the door and close it behind me, tossing the bundle of clothing at Astraea as I do. The shock in her rounded eyes is cut off as I place my finger to her lips and tap my ear. I shake my head. We can't risk anyone hearing anything right now, and I grit my teeth as I think about how we are going to have to get out of here. Another setback. Another obstacle getting in the way of us returning to the others and to Diemos.

I make my way around the room gathering everything into canvas totes we have unpacked while here, then turn to find Astraea fully dressed again. Her leg lifted to the bed, and she straps the knife I gave her to the outside of her thigh with a belt. The slippers she once wore are replaced with boots, and the dress is now adorned with a holster, securing two more blades to her chest. Pride and unease fills my chest. The two emotions are warring together, but I shake it off as I reach out to her.

"Trust me." I silently mouth, and her eyes flick from the door back to me before she nods decidedly. At that, I allow my magick to crawl away from me. The energized shadows cracking and popping like hot coals before they ignite in a burst of flame. The arched portal floods the room with the orange glow of firelight, and I look back at Astraea. "Close your eyes, and think only of your trust in me." Even though her worried lip trembles, she nods as she takes my hand. Entwining our fingers in an unbreakable lock, and just as the door behind us bursts open, we step through the rendered portal, and I force it to snap shut before the guards can hurl themselves through, too.

The sky is a blazing inferno of coppered crimson, clashing with the deepest indigo. It's the first thing I see, then our feet land, and I look down as we sink into the glittering black sands of the Dead Sea. Miles of dark dunes like the long-forgotten ocean waves, ready to swallow the sinking sun in the distance. It would be beautiful, but a sound at my back has dread coiling around my spine. The hiss of an unsheathing sword reaches my ears.

"Move, and you're both fucking dead." A calloused voice rings out right behind us, and a cold chill rakes over me as Astraea stiffens at my side. Her hand in mine squeezing a little tighter as fear grips her. "Look what we have here, boys... A render, and he brought a play thing." I can't stand here doing nothing. Not when he's looking at her. Not when I want nothing more than to pluck his fucking eyes from their sockets and rip his tongue from his mouth for speaking about her like that.

I spin, pulling my hand that holds Astraea so that she is shielded behind me, as a possessive snarl rips from my throat. She sucks in a sharp breath but braces herself at my back as what is left of my shadows comes out like a whip in my hand.

"Touch her, and it will be the last thing you do." My voice comes out low and menacing as the sand at my feet begins to vibrate with energy. My eyes flick down at the odd sensation, but I bring them back up within the same second. Not giving the threat in front of us any indication of my wariness.

The men who stand before us are draped in black muslin shemaghs that cover their faces. Leather straps hold an assortment of weapons on every body facing us. Tsalalerian steel swords glittering from nearly all of their hips. I grind my teeth. *Scylia pirates.* Of fucking course, I would have to rend a portal right at their camp. *Fuck.*

An exuberant chuckle comes from behind the one with his sword drawn as the one who it belongs to comes into sight. His shemagh is dropped to a bundle around his neck, his stringy black hair hanging limply to his shoulders, and a smile splits his face as he steps up to the left of the man in the center. The man on his right stands solid, his arms crossed over his chest smugly.

"We don't want trouble." I say, steadily feeling the buzzing sensation building at my feet as I try to focus and count the number of people I may have to kill.

"No? Interesting." The man in the middle continues, his eyes not on me but over my shoulder to where I feel Astraea trying to peer around me. "You see, word has it, you have yourself quite the prize. One with a pretty heavy price on her head." The alarm rings out as the smiley fucker starts his cackle again, rubbing his hands together in front of him.

"I really am grateful now that I've seen her with my own eyes." He takes a step forward, those eyes hungrily looking to devour what is mine, and a surge of energy courses through my skin. My shadows tremble as they come alive, writhing, waiting for me to expel them. "Oh come on, have some fun... aren't you going to ask why, Hawk?" The alarm bells are now fully blaring with the use of the name of my persona. I look again to the stoic one and back to the man in front of me.

"Why?" I bite out. Trying to bide time for the storm I feel building inside of me.

"I'm grateful they just want her to be returned alive... they never said no touching, and fuck, just a brief look at her has my cock standing at attention." He doesn't have to say more. Something in the sand calls to my shadows. They meld together, charging me with more than enough magick. What was once an empty reservoir is filling. I can feel it vibrating through me with my connection to the sand at my feet.

Right as the center man steps forward again, I throw my hands out at my sides, splaying my fingers wide as shadows leap from my body. The shadows dive deep into the sand, and a blast so strong it carries the sand several stories above our heads, swirling around in a cloud. Bodies fly backward in an explosion of power. Embers crackle and spark throughout in a glittering black vortex of smoke and sand. The Scylia begin to rise and scatter out as the sound of thousands of fluttering wings fills the air with a buzzing noise. Multiple pirates unsheathe their swords.

"Stay behind me." I say to Astraea as I square myself for an attack.

The laughing man runs toward me first. His Tsalalerian steel blade gleaming with a reflection of the fiery embers, and his smile now turned into bared teeth as he roars with the blade held high. The cackling joker doesn't even make it to me, though. I wield the sand to take out his feet. He trips, and the sand swallows him whole. The last sound to come from him is a muffled cry as the sand fills his mouth and suffocates him as he disappears into his sandy grave.

"HAWK!" A familiar voice cuts through the chaos and sends anger to pulse through my whole body, especially when I feel Astraea pull at my tunic from behind.

"That's him. From the tavern, he warned me of the dangers in the desert. He—" A deafening roar silences everyone as all eyes turn toward the beast who crests one of the low dunes in the distance. My magick falls; the sand that was being wielded like a weapon falls from the sky like rain, just as the last halo of light from the sun illuminates the ferocity of the monstrous creature. Several Scylia take off on horseback; others begin to run toward the dune caves behind them, telling the remaining to fall back. But one thing I know for certain is if that manticore decides it wants to go after anyone, it *will* succeed in stopping its prey.

There has been only one man I have heard of who fought one of these beasts and lived to tell the tale, and he was the king of Eathian. Not Astraea's father, but *mine*.

Chapter Thirty-Nine

Astraea

The painting from the library in the palace, which I have spent hours at a time daydreaming of over the many years I have spent prisoner of the monotonous life of a kept princess, comes to life right in front of me. I am frozen with fear and awe. My heart runs as wild as the storm of magick that surrounds me, but I hear nothing. Everything slows as the chaotic sounds of wind howling, men shouting, and the shrill sound of blades being unsheathed are muffled, and time slows. I can see Kyros' mouth moving, but I hear nothing as his face strains with his shouts. Something is tugging at me; my body jerks forward from where I stand, but I'm in a state of paralysis, eyes locked with the monster of legend.

Leathery wings bunch and then flare wide as the creature opens its giant maw. Three rows of deadly sharp teeth are glaringly bright in the low light before the stars come out and cast the night aglow. The sound of its roar vibrates my bones, but still I step forward. The urgency in Kyros' eyes changes as he tries to pry my gaze away, pleading for me to face him. Desperate for me to come with him; to hear him. I blink, and with a rushing sound, like water finally coursing through a pump, the chaos comes back into focus. I finally *look* at him. I now see the arched ring of fiery shadows he has behind him, but I shake my head. *I can't leave, not now.*

The creature steps forward with a rattling growl, the curving tail of a scorpion coming into view, as the flames from the portal cast his powerful deep ochre feline form into a casing of red. His fur gleams like ancient copper. He is breathtaking.

"Wait," I hear my own voice, but as I take a step forward, Kyros wraps an arm around me, forcing my body to turn toward him.

"Shula, I need you to hear me. We need to get out of here. If that beast charges... We are both dead. If I run out of power before I can portal us out of here? We may be dead anyway. But please, let me get us out of here." Kyros's eyes flick behind me in worry, and he yanks me toward him, protectively shielding my body with his just before the manticore launches into the sky. It nosedives back toward where I stood only a moment before. He lands with a flare of black sand spraying out around him, but the sound of his jaw closing around flesh and bone is what has me recoiling. A snapping sound claps behind me, and the glow cast from the portal sputters out, plunging us into darkness as the sun finally dips below the horizon.

Five of the Scylia face the beast, weapons drawn and muslin fabric billowing out around them as the wind begins to pick up. They circle him like he isn't the predator but the prey. His strong muscles bunch as he anticipates an attack from one of them. His powerful tail rearing back for a strike with the deadly barbed end. A war cry echoes through the air from one of the men as he charges forward with his blade drawn. The lethal tail comes down faster than anything I have seen. The Scylia pirate's screams are silenced from one breath to the next, as he is pierced through his chest with a sick squelch of flesh and blood and the distinct cracking sound of snapping bones.

Everything blurs—too fast to track, too sudden to stop. The Scylia move in a vicious synchrony after the manticore's attack. Their deadly sharp blades aimed to cut down the magickal being who drew first blood. My heart seems to pause its beating, the moment in time slowing to a standstill. I look at Kyros, my eyes pleading. I cannot see this animal killed. I scream in tandem with the beast's furious roar. The sound ripping from my throat in a savage peal. That lasso of fire I've only ever felt in my nightmares wraps around me, squeezing so tight I feel as though my lungs will burst from the pressure.

"Save him." I scrape out, pressing my hand to the spot just below my heart. His voice is barely audible, but I hear Kyros curse at my side before his magick comes alive, uncoiling from his arms and striking out like snakes at the Scylia. Half of them are flung

backward, while one is torn into by the claws and fangs of the fierce creature of terror. I fall to my knees in the black sand and helplessly watch as Kyros extends his blade out and fights alongside the creature that legends only tell of its brutality. It's fearsome, bloodthirsty savagery. Blood sprays across both man and beast, coating them with the essence of life. But instead of terror, all I can see is art. Specifically, the art in the library in the palace. I stared at it for most of my life. I always had the idea that they were fighting each other. Man versus beast, but here and now, they work together to cut down the evil that wants to bring harm to us both.

When it's just Kyros and the manticore left, they turn in unison, facing each other. Kyros' chest heaves with exertion; the beast's maw hangs wide. Blood drips and sinew strings limply from its teeth. The beast is the one who looks away first, its bright blue eyes almost a mirror of my own, clashing with mine. I don't feel fear when I look at him; instead, something confusing takes over. Something that I realize was there all along. As soon as I laid eyes on him, I had an undeniable urge to go to the beast, as though it was beckoning to me. A glimmer of movement in my periphery has my eyes widening, my heart leaping from my chest. Kyros's blade glints in the low-hanging moonlight, poised to strike.

"No." The word comes out as a whisper, but before his blade comes striking down across the neck of the beast, the manticore does something neither of us expects. It bows its massive head. The hair from its mane falls across its eyes, its deadly paws, lined with blade-like claws, stretched out in front of him. Kyros stalls, turning to look at me at the same moment the manticore's blue eyes flash.

Standing, I push my feet to move through the loose, deep sand kicked up from the fighting. It's a struggle to even get my footing. As I move closer to the two, Kyros growls low in his throat.

"Shula, stay back!" Kyros says through his teeth, panic leaching through his tone.

"He's not going to hurt me. He won't hurt either of us." I say. I don't know why I feel this way. Everything about the creature says otherwise, but the way he seemed to bow, submitting before us instead of turning and attacking us too... Something in his eyes... I slowly reach my hand out in front of me. An offering of peace. Of understanding. Something I have so rarely been shown, I offer the creature a piece of myself.

"Shula!" Kyros hisses in warning, but I don't care. A deep rumble comes from the manticore's throat, but it's not the growl at which it aimed at the Scylia but more of a purr. It extends its neck, and my breath catches as my hand touches the center of its forehead, between the root-like curved horns on its head. A slow smile spreads across my face, but Kyros is a statue of indecision standing to the side, watching this sort of connection I feel forming under my palm.

"Thank you." I say, and when his large head lifts and his eyes come level with mine, he chuffs, looking at Kyros and then back to me before taking a step back and launching into the sky with a powerful downward thrust of his leathery wings. I can't help but watch as he disappears into the night sky with a smile on my face.

"Incredible." Kyros says, pulling me out of my state of awe. I slowly look over to find him only staring at me. Heat rises into my cheeks, and I wring my hands in front of myself.

"Thank you for saving him. For protecting us both." I say, and he plunges his sword into the sand before storming the distance between us and slamming his lips to mine.

"You fucking drive me mad! Why would you put yourself in danger like that?!" He growls into my face, his hands bracketing my face as my own grasp his wrists. "You are insufferable. A constant pain in my ass." His lips are bruising as they claim mine again, not allowing me to respond. "All of this would be easier if you were... not so different." His hands are frantic as they grip my face, keeping me pinned to him. I can't breathe anything but the words he forces on me. Words that are confusing but also making my head spin with a drunken feeling of needing more.

"We need to get out of here." I manage to say through his unrelenting capture of my body. My words seem to fracture the air around us, and he finally leans back but doesn't drop his hands.

"Yes, Shula. We can get out of here." He says while rubbing his thumb across my cheekbone, but the look in his eyes makes my brows drop. What I thought was lust looks more like grief in his eyes.

"You are going to be sorry for this, Hawk!" A voice calls out from behind. Kyros pushes me behind him as he turns to face a Scylia pirate. His face is torn, shredded from scalp to chin. Even in the darkness I can see the deep color that runs down his neck and darkens the already dark fabric that hangs in tatters across his chest. He limps forward, holding one arm at the bicep to his body, likely pulled from the socket. "You will regret every decision you ever made when it comes to returning to Eathian. You and I both know it. It might not be me, but you can see it as well as I can. Death will come for you. *She will be the death of you.* She will be the death of us all." Ice curls in a spiral up my spine, settling over my heart at his words.

"What a fucking way to go it will be." Kyros growls, low and throaty, slowly unsheathing a knife at his thigh. "But Karnnen?" He tilts his head to the side. "*I—will be the death of you.*" The man has no chance to respond before he is cross-eyed, looking at the handle of the knife that is now buried deep in his skull. His lips part as blood seeps from the wound, his nose, and now coats his tongue and lips. He staggers forward, a choking sound coming from him before he tilts forward and lands face down in the sand.

I tightly press my hand across my mouth to cover the scream that wants to break free. I have seen death. I have seen torture and been tortured even, but never anything like that. And what did he mean that I would be the death of Kyros? The death of everyone? I watch frozen as Kyros walks a few feet away, picking up a Tsalalerian steel sword, weighing it in his grip like he didn't just kill multiple people. Didn't just stare down a manticore in the divine dunes of the Dead Sea. When he returns to me, his face is stern, not the wild adoration that I had just witnessed from him. This is the Kyros that I met in the tavern. Detached. Cold. Controlled.

"My magick is restored." He takes my hand and threads his fingers through mine. "Are you ok?" Am I?

"What did he mean?" I swallow, feeling my confusion turning to emotion in my throat.

"Not now." Kyros barks.

"What did you mean?" I ask, the emotion turning bitter, and anger simmers at the surface of my mind as the words 'not now' bounce around my reeling mind.

"Later." He says with a sigh. My jaw clenches tight, but he ignores the way I dig my feet into the sand. Taking his other hand, he releases a pouch at his hip, and he scoops some of the black sand at our feet into it before cinching it back on the hook at his belt. He doesn't say anything else. The conversation is over because he says it is, and even though I feel the fight wanting to break free in me, my father's words crash into me.

Silence, Astraea; that is what we want from you. There is no place for questions from a woman in the affairs of men. Silence Astraea, I will not have another word. Silence, Astraea, or you will get another punishment. I swallow my retort as a numbness settles over me.

Kyros lets his magick pool into his hand before splaying his fingers wide, throwing the darkness into the air. It crackles and pops, catching fire in a wide arch. He looks at me with the same sorrow-filled grieving in his eyes before his thumb strikes a hot line across the back of my hand.

"Trust me?" It's a question I'm meant to answer. It's a question I want to answer yes to, but all the doubt I've ever felt comes crashing into me like a storm as I recall everything that was just said. I nod. "I'm sorry. I promise I will explain; we just—"

"Have to go." I finish for him with all the pain I feel in my words. His jaw ticks.

"Yes."

"It's ok, Kyros, I'm used to being silenced. I trust you. You promised to get me back to Cole. I hope now is when you make right on that promise." I say devoid of all emotion, and his lips purse. His brows drop, and as we step forward into the rendered portal, I think of Cole. Of the one person I know who will never keep things from me. The one person I can trust no matter what. As much as I wanted to trust Kyros, he is clearly still keeping secrets, and if they are big enough for someone to think I am going to be the death of him... of them all? Then it seems that trust is already broken.

Chapter Forty

Kyros

When the portal snaps shut behind us, we are plunged into a sudden silence, the darkness changing to a starlit glow. The words we don't speak linger heavily in the air between us. For a moment we both just stand there, hand in hand. I have so much I wish I could say, but there is still so much I can't. Astraea pulls her hand out of mine, and I ball mine into a fist as I watch her storm away. She kicks up sand in her path toward the glittering of firelights in the distance and, hopefully, the group who will be there waiting for us. *Aithne*. A place I once called home.

"Wait, Shula." I say in a hushed tone as I stride forward too. She doesn't. She doesn't so much as turn her head to throw a stern look in my direction. "Dammit. Just wait." I say through my teeth, taking purposeful strides to close the distance she has given us.

"Why?" She spins abruptly, her hair fanning out around her before settling on her back. Her shoulders are squared, her fists in tight balls at her sides. I can nearly feel the heat radiating from the fire in her.

"You need to stay with me. Even though this place should be safer than the last, you never know where your father has people." I say, lifting my hand to rub the back of my fingers down her arm. She shrugs away from my touch, and I let my hand fall.

"That's not what I'm talking about, Kyros, and you know it. Don't play stupid; it doesn't suit you." She says with her eyes sharp as blades. I know that's not what she meant. I'm aware that she wants to know more about what Karnnen was talking about, but now isn't the time. We are finally about to be with the group, and we have a journey ahead of us. It won't be as simple as rending a portal back to Diemos. Not with the extra bodies we have now. Although the sand in my pocket and the sword at my hip still vibrate with energy and my power seems to thrum with a whole new kind of ferocity... I have my own questions that need answered before I can think about answering hers.

"There is a lot you don't know about the kingdoms. It's not something you need to worry about right now. We are—" Astraea pokes her finger into my chest, surprising me. Slowly, I tilt my chin to look down at her. My own anger, my frustration with myself, and everything I want to say are just sitting at the tip of my tongue, but I can't say any of it. Not when I am *this* close to the goal I have been working toward.

"I'm sick of people telling me what I need or don't need." She says, with anger brimming in her tone, but then she lowers her head, her voice quieting. "For once, I want to be the one to make the decision for myself." I step into her, curling my fingers under her chin and lifting her gaze to mine.

"I'm not trying to take choices away from you, Shula. I gave you my word." She remains quiet, her blue eyes sparkling with the light of the stars as she holds my stare. The pain I see in the press of her brow, the downward tilt to her lips. I want to take it all away, but instead I just stand here. Hoping above everything that she gives me more time to understand myself before I tell her anything.

"HA! I called it. I told you it was him, Zinny!" Mavros' loud laugh breaks the lingering silence between us, and Astraea jerks her chin from my fingers. My hand falls to my side, but my eyes never leave the woman in front of me. "After Drabeck showed up with your message, I knew it was only a matter of time before I would sense your ass again." Mavros scoops Astraea into a hug and spins her around. "Hey, princess! Guess you like us a little, huh? Running away with us and all." My brother has never done well reading the energy of other people. Astraea smiles at him, but it's not at all believable, at least not to me. It falls when her gaze snags where I am watching them, then she turns away as Mavros tucks her under his arm and smiles wide at me with a wink.

"Colette?" I hear her ask as they begin walking away. Astraea looks back at me only briefly before her brows dip and she turns away. Even though I don't want to let her out of my sight, I know at least with Mavros she will be safe.

"She's at training pits, giving Tarin hell, no doubt. That friend of yours is a spitfire." Their easy conversation trails off with the distance they create between us. Zinya steps up to my side silently as I watch them walk into the small village. I let out a long sigh. She is very different from Mavros in sensing energy. Always more intuitive. She eyes me warily, giving Mavors and Astraea plenty of space before saying anything.

"What is it?" She finally asks. I cross my arms over my chest, still staring after my brother and the princess, and after another beat, I finally turn toward her.

"Have you ever felt energy coming from Tsalalerian steel? Or from the sand at the Dead Sea?" A crease forms between her eyes as she thinks about what I'm saying, before one brow quirks up and she narrows her green eyes on me.

"No... Have you?" She asks, searching.

"Not until today." I pull the small bag of sand I collected from the dunes from my pocket and present it to her. She looks at me, unspeaking, before she finally takes the pouch and pulls it open. She dips her finger in, swirling it once before her head jerks up.

"That's not all. There was a manticore. The beast fought *alongside us....*" I tell her.

"Kyros. How?" Her eyes are round with disbelief, and then they fall to the sword at my hip. "And you have a Tsalalerian steel sword? What happened out there?" I turn my head, following the path Astraea just took with my brother.

"I'm not sure, but I intend to find out."

"I was wondering when you would finally show up." The voice sounds from the shadows in the corner of the room.

"You know I can't stay away long." I say flatly in greeting.

"The others arrived much earlier than you. Why?" He says, standing, his eyes bored and lips pursed as he crosses his arms.

"Wanted to keep things interesting, I guess." I say, head tilting, and my mouth lifts at the corner. His mouth splits into a wide grin before he closes the distance between us. Grasping my hand, he pulls me into him, wrapping his other arm around my back with a slap. We both laugh.

"You look like shit, brother." He laughs, pulling me out to an arm's length.

"Yea well, I just had a run-in with some Scylia and a manticore. What's your excuse?" He laughs again, clapping me on the shoulder.

"Come sit. Let's catch up." He says, pouring a measure of whiskey into two glasses and offering one to me. I take it before sitting in one of the leather armchairs that face the largest window in the dark room. With a whisper and a flick of his fingers, he lights the sconces, casting an orange flickering glow around the room. When he finally falls into the armchair across from me, he lets out a sharp whistle.

The far door opens soon after, and three scantily dressed women come striding in on light feet. Their eyes are heavy as they saunter through the room. The golden-haired woman wearing the sheer pink two-piece skirt and top sets up in the corner, her fingers deftly plucking at the strings of a harp in a slow rhythm.

The other two women split, and I watch as Rowan reaches out for the one with the deep auburn hair and a tiny sheer green dress. Her laugh flits from her like bells, and as she straddles his lap, it bares more than just her ass to me. Rowan groans as he grasps her hips and grinds her down on himself.

"You know you are here at a great time." He says before trailing his tongue up the woman's neck. "It's been a while since you have been here for the Shula Morana celebration."

"I suppose it has." I say. Grinding my teeth as I watch him pull the woman's head back with her red hair wrapped around his fist. The movement makes her back arch and her breasts push out toward him. He licks his lips before his other hand comes up, ripping the thin fabric down the middle, and he bites down hard around her pert nipple. Her voice rings out in a shriek, then transforms to a breathy moan. I tense as a small hand runs along the back of my shoulders.

The last of the three women comes around in front of me, her fingertips trailing along my chest until she stops in the center. She stands between my legs, slowly running her long white painted nails down my body. Her hair is dark but lacks luster. Her deep brown eyes lock with mine as she lets the sheer white robe she wears open and fall from her thin body. Slowly, and with a hooded gaze, she begins dropping to her knees. I could use the distraction.

Release some tension that seems to be constant as of late. Maybe Mavros is right. Maybe I just need to get laid.

Just as her knees touch the ground between my feet, my mind flashes to a field. The blue flower in the scorpion grass with a random ray of sunshine finding its petals and lighting it up like magick from within. My hand snaps out, wrapping around her delicate wrist just before she reaches for my belt.

"No." I grunt, and confusion and worry blooms across her face.

"I'm sorry I displease you, sire; perhaps you want pleasure another way?" She asks. Her voice is wrong. Deep and raspy. Her dark eyes and golden skin. She is beautiful in every way but one. *She is not Astraea.*

"Rowan, we need to speak alone." I say tersely. A wet slapping sounds behind the one who is leaving my lap, and when she is out of the way, I see Rowan with his cock shoved down the redhead's throat as she groans around him. Tears running down her face and marking her cheeks with black that runs from the color staining her eyes.

"Oh, of course we can, brother. Just let me..." He tips his head back, the woman on her knees in front of him letting out a strangled choke as he shoves his cock all the way down her throat. He stays there for several seconds, pumping into her before he growls. His body shakes as he lets his release fill her throat. He smiles wide as he lets himself slide out and slaps her. She gasps, looking at him wide-eyed. He wrenches her up by her hair. "Good girl, finishing me like that. Now, take the girls to my chambers. Let me finish this conversation, and I will give you all some attention." She smiles sheepishly, fluttering her lashes at him before all three sway their way out of the room.

"Was all of that necessary?" I say, annoyance coating my deep voice. He only laughs, shooting back the whiskey he has kept held loosely in his fingers.

"Of course it was. You know how I like to start the celebrations. Especially when one of my greatest friends is here to celebrate with us." He says, the leather creaks as he sits back down in the chair with a wide smile.

"Unfortunately, I'm not here for the celebrations."

"Yea well, refusing a beautiful woman willing to open her mouth for you will definitely put a damper on things for you. Your brother didn't have such reservations." He laughs, then finally must see the seriousness in my face, because he straightens, leaning forward. "Ok then, Kyros, what has you all bent out of shape?" At one point in my life, I may have been willing and eager to partake in this sort of senseless fucking, but now even the thought has tension building all wrong, settling on my shoulders. I toss the pouch of sand to him, and he catches it as it hits him in the chest.

He tugs the bag open and looks at me confused. Rowan's magick is unique; not only does he have an elemental affinity to fire, but he can also read magickal signatures. His face transforms as he hovers his hand over the open leather sack.

"What is this?" He asks, all playfulness gone from his tone. His brows now lower, and his lips held in a straight line.

"I was hoping you might be able to tell me..." I say as I unsheathe the sword at my hip. His eyes widen before he cinches the bag closed and tosses it back to me. He shakes his head in denial as he looks from the black blade laying across my lap to the sand in my hand and back to me.

"How?" He asks, and I shake my head.

"The manticore that fought in the dune alongside us didn't leave anyone to ask..." I say, clenching my jaw.

"Manticore?" He asks incredulously, only just now realizing it was not a joke I said earlier. "So you found the relic." He says it simply, and heat floods my veins. Adrenaline courses through me with my raging blood. Many looks cross his face before he finally settles on excitement.

"It's not what you think." I finally say, and his brow twitches with confusion.

"What else could it be?" He asks.

"I don't know for certain, but I don't think that the relic is an object, Rowan. But a person. A woman, and she has no fucking clue." Rowan stares at me for a long moment, and when his face slowly changes into something wicked, the hairs on the back of my neck rise.

"Women can be used just the same, can they not?" His teeth glint in the low light, and a growl builds in my chest.

"No." The single word is menacing, and he quirks a brow.

"Well, well, Kyros. Does this woman...mean something to you?" He asks, with a smile on his lips and a laugh in his tone. I level him with my eyes before standing abruptly.

"What did you read from the sand?" I ask. My back is ramrod straight, and my sword hand fisted around the butt of the one that hangs at my hip. Rowan's eyes narrow at the gesture, and his smile fades before he too stands. He may be an old friend, but I will not risk anything with this.

"Nothing." He says, and the eerie one word whispered in my face makes it feel as though all the blood is draining from my face. Cold sweat prickles my forehead, and I blink slowly. The fact that he can sense the magick but read nothing makes what I think I saw—what I felt coming from Astraea's nightmare—*a very real possibility*. A possibility that I need to know for certain before I bring her to Queen Phaedra.

Chapter Forty-One

Astraea

My heart is pounding in my chest with both anger and adrenaline, deprivation and elation. It's a war of emotion stirring through my blood and making me feel sick. My feet falter, threatening to send me to my knees, but Mavros holds my arm in his firmly.

"Hey, you ok?" He says, concern bracketing his mouth.

"It's been a long journey." I say in response; not sure what I should say or not. The city we enter is similar to the Eathian capital. Smaller in size with no looming palace in the distance. Instead, trees line the horizon. The scent of their wood wafting through the night air like a fresh drink of water on the hottest of days. The dirt on the ground is less sandy here even if dunes lay just beyond the other side of the small village. My feet actually cool walking on the soil, rather than the heat from the sand that holds onto the sun's viscous fire.

An ear-piercing screech pulls my attention away from the new world around me and questions in Mavros' stare, and in the blink of an eye, I am being tackled to the ground by a blaze of fiery red hair and long squeezing arms. The air is knocked from my lungs as we go plummeting to the hard-packed ground, and I hear curses and laughs from all around. Then, all sounds around me are muted by the sobs jolting my body as Cole and I cry. *Finally* together again.

Our cries turn to laughter when she lifts off of me and we see each other's faces. Even in the low firelight of a nearby post, I can see the blotchy red spots all over her face. Her hair is a wild mess and I'm sure I look the same. Pressing up, she gives me her hands and pulls me to my feet but I refuse to let go of her.

My eyebrows hike, eyes widening when I take in what she is wearing. The dark-colored pants do nothing to cover her form; they are skin tight. Her arms are bare, the top nearly as snug as the bottoms. She smiles when she sees the shock on my face.

"Things are different away from the palace. Women don't have to constantly be covered with the same drapes we dress the windows with." She laughs. "And, they are teaching me to fight! I never thought it would be something I loved so much."

"Yea, and I never thought that she would be any good..." The guard I recognize as Viltarin comes up behind her, holding his nose with a bloody rag. Mavros slaps Viltarin on the back, laughing and holding his stomach.

"And *you* are the guard Ky put on princess duty?" He says with a wide smile, pulling a questioning look over at me. Even Mavros, who has always seemed to have a lively personality, seems different here. Happiness radiates from all of them, and I find my own lips trying to pull up at the corners.

"Speaking of princesses. I think she needs a bit of rest. Maybe you can take her and help her get cleaned up? Bring her to the tavern when you're all done, and we will get her some good food. None of that shit we had to have before." Mavros says to Colette and nudges me with his elbow when he speaks of the tavern food.

"Come on, you are staying with me." Cole says, and something seems to flicker in my chest. I look back the way we came, toward the area where we left Kyros and Zinya. I can't see past the darkness. If they are still in the same spot, I have no way of knowing. As much as I want to talk to Kyros, to demand answers... I also don't want to see him right now. I can't be around him knowing that he is keeping things from me. He asked me to trust him. Told me that he doesn't go back on his promises, but how can I believe anything he says? *He brought you back to Cole.*

Colette hooks her arm in mine and steers me away from the two men as Mavros makes more fun of Viltarin. She rubs my arm, and when I look at her, I feel better just being in her presence, like everything might just be ok. As though I didn't just stare down a manticore and watch as Kyros used terrifying and beautiful magick to wreak havoc on a clan of Scylia pirates. *Is this what my life is going to be like away from the castle? Battles and blood? Magick and malice?*

"Where is the suitor?" Cole wiggles her brows, and I blink confused at her.

"Who?" I ask. The grin she had on her face falls, and she looks at me like she is seeing me for the first time.

"Are you ok?" Cole asks, and I nod. She doesn't ask again, and she doesn't say anything else. Instead, she looks over her shoulder, in the direction of the desert we just walked in from. Toward the shadows that hold Kyros and his secrets. She stays silent even when I still don't answer, just points to a narrow set of stairs on the side of a two-story wood cottage. The stairs creak as we climb. I can't help but look up, toward the blackened sky and the sparkling stars that litter the sky like diamonds. When we reach the top, Cole fumbles with the door, and I close my eyes with my face skyward. Is this who I am meant to be? Am I running from one problem to the next? An endless cycle of pain? An endless cycle of wondering if I am making the right choice?

"Thank you, Cole. I know this is a huge change for you, and you did it for me." I say, tears welling in my eyes as I look at the worn wooden door.

"Hey, you know I'm doing it for me too. Palace living isn't all it's cracked up to be...doting on a princess all the time..." She makes a groaning ugh noise and then smiles when I look at her. She bumps her shoulder into mine. "I wouldn't have it any other way. I'm just glad that Kyros got you here safely. I could tell the others were getting worried. Divine knows I was."

The mention of Kyros has my body heating with anger and longing. I don't want to think about him right now because every time I do, I remember the words I don't understand and the searing heat his touch causes. *She will be the death of you. She will be the death of us all.* And even though I know he is keeping things from me, I crave being in his presence.

Colette pushes the door open and holds it for me as she steps inside. The room is darker than outside, and I blink as my eyes try to adjust. She makes some noise moving around the shadowy space, but I am frozen just inside the door. Frozen with my thoughts, and after some more noise, Cole finally turns around with a lantern in her hands.

"This place doesn't have warm water like we are used to in your chambers, but I do have a basin of clean water. I already prepared some clothes for you. You can clean up, and if you want to sleep or..." Her words trail off as she sees the tear roll down my cheek. "Oh, Astraea. What's wrong?"

"It's nothing." I try to smile and wipe away the tears. I'm tired of feeling this way. I want the anger to just take over. I want to be strong and know my place in the world, but sometimes I feel as though I am not enough and the kingdom is just too big. She narrows her eyes on me. "I'm just feeling emotional. I'm glad to see you." I say, leaving out how I'm feeling about the rest.

"I'm glad to see you too." She looks at me with a sad smile, then sets the lantern down and goes around lighting a couple more. The room is more visible now, and I see that it's a cozy space. One semi-large bed in the corner with a window at its side. Surely, looking out into the trees beyond the village border. It's too dark to see for certain. The bed is covered in fluffy linens and pillows in different shades of tan. There is a chair in the far corner facing the center of the room, and the walls are adorned with framed art in a style I have not seen before.

Cole pulls open a chest at the end of the bed. The hinges squeak, and then it makes a loud clap as she closes it. She lays a small bundle of clothing on the bed and looks at me mischievously.

"What?" I ask, looking at the clothing and realizing it's pretty much the same as what she is wearing. Similar to what Zinya wears, save the leather armor. "Cole! I can't."

"But you can! I know you. You love climbing trees, getting yourself into things that are not easy to get out of. I thought it was strange at first too, to wear breeches like men, but it's—*freeing.*" She smiles, looking down at my chest and the holster I have crossed there. The blades that are strapped to me are visible, and her smile widens. "You are already halfway there. It's just another step to freedom." She taps the sheathed blade. My gaze drops to leather, and I nod, realizing that she is right. I unclasp the holster, removing it first, then pull my skirt up to reveal the belt that holds the blade at my thigh. A laugh bursts from her, loud and hearty.

"Don't laugh." I pin her with a look, and she rolls her lips between her teeth before shaking her head. Rolling my eyes, I continue to undress. She shows me to the basin and allows me to wash up. Reluctantly, I slide into the unfamiliar feel of the leggings. They are tight, but not constricting. The tunic is at least a little less fitting than Colette's. It's cream-colored, the style similar to the one Kyros wears, and it has a leather tie between my breasts. I gather the weapons once again, strapping them to my body, and then stand in front of the long mirror that is leaning against the wall on the far side of the room.

Cole comes up behind me with a brush and begins working out the knots that have found their way into my dark hair. When she starts braiding the lengths to twine my hair up the way my father always wanted, I place my hand on hers.

"No." I say softly. The memory of Kyros telling me he likes my hair better down flashes through my mind. The way he hummed in my ear. The way his breath puffed out over my face. The night that I wasn't just a princess, but for the first time I felt as though I was—*seen*. "I want it down." Warmth fills her gaze as she nods in understanding and continues to brush out my hair.

My eyes lock with those of my reflection. I used to look at my own blue irises and see a lack of warmth, a hollow frozen sea of nothing. The pale blue is only a whisper of color in my monochrome world. Now, it's like they are alive with energy—a flash of lightning caught within my gaze. I reach down, strapping the last blade on my thigh, and when I rise, so does my chin. I left the palace to be my own person; live my own life. It's about time I start claiming it for myself.

Chapter Forty-Two

Astraea

MAVROS GREETS US WITH his arms outstretched and a wide smile as we enter the tavern. He wraps me in a tight hug before leaving, his arm slung over my shoulders as he guides us through the place. It is alive with energy, and it seems the whole town has gathered here tonight. Even though it must be late, children of all ages run around tables, laughing and playing. The joyous atmosphere catches me by surprise. I don't realize I'm scowling until Zinya is standing in front of us.

"What did he do?" Zinya asks. The way she's looking at me is curious and probing, as though she is looking at everything I don't say, causing my scowl to deepen with my confusion.

"What?" I ask, looking at her, then to Mavros and Colette.

"You look pissed off. I only assume Kyros did something to cause it. He has a way with being a bit of a hardass. He seemed to be in a similar mood earlier. Do you want me to give him shit?" She laughs, and my gaze jumps around the room looking for said man. I shake my head.

"I haven't seen him, actually, since we arrived." I say, shaking my head, and Colette looks at me with a keen eye. Likely picking up on my subtle tells; the way I chew on my lip or wring my hands. She's always been akin to understanding what I'm feeling. Sometimes even before I do. "I guess I'm just perplexed at the energy in the room. Is this a celebration of something?" Zinya blinks as though she's surprised that I don't know. Then she tilts her head back and nods.

"Oh, well, I forget you don't know the culture of the people outside of the palace." She says, and I flinch, frowning at her words.

"It's not for lack of wanting to know. I was not *allowed* such liberties. I was only the means of securing an heir for the throne. Not actually sitting on the gaudy chair with all the power. My father felt I had no reason to know much of anything that went on outside of the castle." I respond derisively, feeling a little defensive. I would love to know about the people in the kingdom. Especially those who are under our rule. I tried. It's one of the reasons the library was one of my favorite places. The history of our land fascinated me, even though I know I only had some of it. I always listened to what I could through guards passing or palace help gossiping, but not everything was clear.

"Sorry, I didn't mean to offend you." Zinya responds, and I can see the truth behind her eyes. I didn't mean to get offended. "While the palace celebrates the victory of taking the throne all those years ago and, if I understand correctly, your birthday." She clears her throat. "The Neer, or *'The Kru,'* as some of the crown loyalists call them, celebrate in remembrance." I thought the Neer and the Kru were two different types of people. Apparently that was a misinterpretation of gossip. I wonder how much I don't actually know.

"A celebration of life." Mavros cuts in. A stern look on his face. "In memory of all that was lost." My throat is tight, like I have started swallowing my own tongue. All of their eyes land heavy on me. While I know what they are saying doesn't really land on my shoulders, I feel as though it does as an extension from my father. Even though I never had a say in any of what he did.

"Not everyone in the palace celebrates a victory." Colette says softly as she threads her arm back through mine, and I look at her with a small frown.

"I don't know if I should be here. It feels wrong to be who I am and interfere with such a meaningful celebration when it's my father who caused the loss in the first place." I whisper, hoping that my voice is small enough that no one else within earshot can hear.

"On the contrary, princess, I think you being here now is good. You can see firsthand who the people are that your father kills." Another flinch shakes my body at Mavros' words. I can tell that these people mean a great deal to him, and my brows drop. Zinya elbows him in the stomach with a stern face, and he huffs out a breath.

"Do they celebrate this way in Diemos too?" I ask. Zinya, Mavros, and now Viltarin all share a look. A conversation seemingly passing between their eyes. I always feel like I am on the outside of a long story when they are all together. This seems to have Mavros more serious than I have ever seen him, and when he rakes his hand through his white-blonde hair, Zinya answers my question.

"Mavros, Kyros, and I are not originally from Diemos. We are native to Eathian. We all lost our families in the Great War. Queen Phaedra took in many orphans after the carnage left us without anywhere to go. Gave the refugees families and purpose. So, I guess, to answer your question... yes. In a way much of Diemos does, because Queen Phaedra has extended her hand over us when the true royals fell." Zinya says, and even if she didn't intend it, I feel as though I have been punched in the stomach. All the air now knocked from my lungs.

"I'm sorry. I—" My heart races so quickly that I fear it may burst as I think about everything. I knew what my father did was horrible. It was for me too, but I was a child when it happened. I guess I didn't think so much about what happened to those who lost everything they ever knew too. *I can't swallow.*

"Breathe." Cole steps in front of me, blocking out my view of everyone else. My blue eyes latch to her green ones, and when she takes a deep breath, so do I. I mimic her breathing, the way she closes her eyes, and as we grip each other's arms, I feel the panic in me lowering. Slowly, it eases from my limbs, and my grip loosens before I finally open my eyes.

"Thank you," I tell her with a small smile.

"Hey, regardless of all of that. I think it shows who you are to be here right now. Freely choosing to do what you're doing." Mavros says, his charm back in place and a sad sort of gleam in his eye. Zinya looks at me pained before nodding and chewing on her lip as though something else is bothering her. "Enough of all this heavy shit. Let's drink. It is a celebration after all. Your birthday too? What better reason to get wasted." He slings his arm around my shoulders and starts steering me toward the bar.

"I don't know if that's such a good idea," I say, laughing a little nervously.

"Psh, all my ideas are better than good; they're great." He pulls out a stool and gestures at it. "Sit, princess. Let's get you fed and fucked up." He says before he tips his head back with a cackle, slapping the bar to get the attention of the man behind it. "Duscan, let me have your best tonight. This one is with us." He says, and the man, Duscan, drops his mismatched eyes to me.

"Great divine, how did you manage to attract such a beauty to this rundown village?" Duscan asks as his oddly colored eyes travel every inch of my face and then lower. He appears to be older, close to the same age as the twins, perhaps a little older even, but he looks as though he hasn't always been a barkeep. The scars on his face and arms show that he has seen a battle or two that couldn't be from just some drunk bar fights. He runs a hand through his chestnut hair as a roguish smile lifts the corners of his mouth, then quickly falls from his face. A sudden warmness blankets me from behind, and the way Duscan's eyes jump over my shoulder at the same moment his smile falters, I know who must be standing behind me. He tilts his head respectfully in greeting.

"Duscan." Kyros' deep voice vibrates through my body, curling my toes, but I grit my teeth in defiance. I'm upset with him.

"Lord Kyros, I was just admiring the new beauty your brother has just introduced me to. She is something special, isn't she?" He says, and I feel Kyros get closer to me. His warmth presses against my back as one hand comes out to rest on the outside of my arm. Cole watches where his hand rests and then looks back and forth between me and Kyros.

"More than she realizes." He says, and I turn my head, finally looking at his hand. I let my eyes follow the corded muscle wrapping the length of his arm until I meet his gaze. The shadows seem to cloud there, and Duscan finally clears his throat, breaking the spell I was entrapped by, gaining my attention once again.

"My apologies, Lord Kyros, I didn't realize she was spoken for." He says with his voice low.

"She is not spoken for, but she is right here and can speak for herself!" I bark out, vexation heavy in my tone at once again being talked about as though I am not right in front of them hearing the entire conversation. All my life it has been the same, but I won't be that demure princess that my father always wanted me to be. The fire in me was stifled as a child, but I am no child anymore. I am a woman, and I feel the ember wanting to blaze. I shrug off Kyros' touch, and when Duscan places a tankard of ale in front of

Mavros, I don't think twice before snatching it. I bring it to my lips and let the cool liquid fill my mouth. Over and over I gulp down the sweet yet bitter drink. I don't leave a drop left when I slam the metal cup down by its handle with a loud bang.

Cole's eyes are wide, but I see the smile she is trying to hide with her lips rolled between her teeth. Mavros isn't holding back anything. He is gleaming, not looking at me, but at Kyros. Zinya, too, watches the man at my back to see what his response will be.

"As I recall, you were very animated when you said just the opposite. I believe your exact words were, *It's all yours—*" Kyros says, bent down so that his breath puffs out at my ear, but loud enough that those around us hear every word. I spin around so quickly that the stool I sit on goes falling to the floor, and everyone takes a step back. I rear back, my body twisting to give my hit power, but before I am able to land the strike across his face, he grips me by the wrist. Holding it between us, he steps in closer. His eyes narrow, then drop to my lips.

"Well, I can see why you are so enamored by her." A man says, stepping into view. He crosses his arms, looking between Kyros and me with a wide smile. He is tall, nearly as tall as Kyros and Mavros, but where they have stacked muscle, he is lean. His eyes are green, bright, and wild with something I can't interpret. Kyros stiffens as the man extends his hand out to me. "My name is Rowan. It's a pleasure to meet you."

"Astraea," I say, as I jerk my hand from Kyros' grip, meaning to place it in his, but Kyros lets out a near-animalistic growl, taking my hand back aggressively before he threads our fingers together, dropping them to our sides as he faces the stranger. Rowan smiles with all of his teeth before narrowing his eyes mischievously at Kyros and lifting his arms, palms out, in submission.

"Very well, my friend." He winks at me, much like Mavros has in the past, and Kyros' hand tightens around mine.

"I need another drink," I mutter under my breath, yanking my hand free from the possessive ass at my side. *What the hell is happening?* Colette looks at me with her brows raised as she straightens the stool I knocked over. I shake my head. I don't even know what to tell her at this point.

"Seems like it." She says, offering me hers. I take it. Though it's not ale. The liquid in the tin cup stings my nose as I lift it to smell. The noxious liquid makes my eyes water, and I squeeze them shut, shaking my head before knocking it back with one large gulp.

"Well, shit. I guess you are ready to get fucked up after all." Mavros laughs as I cough from my burning throat. Kyros takes the tin from my hand, and I look up at him. He keeps my gaze as he reaches behind me, placing the tin on the bar.

"Another, Duscan." I can't help but swallow hard as his chest brushes mine. He tilts his head so his lips brush the shell of my ear. "You want to let loose tonight, Shula? Fine, but I made a promise to you, and I keep them. Fight it, if that's what you think you have to do, but we both know it's not what you want." I place my hand on his chest; heat radiates from him and through the connection of our bodies. As his breath blows out over my ear, that heat surges and instantly pools at my core. I placed my hand here to push him away, but even as I think about it, my fingers curl in the fabric of his tunic, and I pull him closer. His black eyes ensnare me, and he looks as trapped as I feel, but then I remember. I remember how he is still keeping secrets and has yet to tell me what the man from the desert was talking about. I let him go.

"Kindly, fuck off, *Lord* Kyros." I sneer as I pick up the tin cup that was just refilled and saunter off, hooking my other arm in Zinya's. She scoffs a laugh as a smile as wide as her eyes takes over her face, and she looks at Kyros and strides away with me. Mavros is right; it's time I let loose. I've spent a lifetime under tyranny, and I'm finally free. The people who I'm surrounded with now have suffered, and though they don't know it, I have hurt just as much as they have from the touch my father has placed on this kingdom. I was a prisoner, stuck in an hourglass, but the sands have run out, and I can finally break free.

Chapter Forty-Three

Kyros

My shadows coil around my arms like anxious snakes as I watch her interact with my people. People she didn't know only hours ago, but who have accepted her as she has them. I take comfort in the dark corner; even though my open display of magick would be welcomed here in this village, it is a habit to keep it hidden. Right now, though, I'm watching Astraea and thinking of everything that lies ahead of us and the way that the Tsalalerian steel at my hip makes my magick charge and writhe beneath the surface and all around my skin. My anxious energy needs somewhere to go.

"Are you going to be brooding and hiding all night?" Mavros says as he sits at the table with me. He eyes the shadows we share and how they dance along my exposed forearms, where I've pushed the sleeves of my tunic up.

"I'm not hiding." I scoff, taking another drink of ale. It's warm, and I look into the tankard and suck my teeth before setting it back in front of me.

"Glad you can admit you are brooding, though…You want to tell me what has our magick so fucking wild tonight?" He asks, and I finally look at him. I haven't had a chance to bring him up to speed with everything that has happened yet, but I assumed Zinya has told him something. His eyes drop to my belt and the sword that hangs from it. Instead of answering with words, I slide the bag of sand across the table. When he opens it and looks inside, his expression appears confused for a split second.

"Does this mean what I think it does?" He implores, his eyes lifting to the same woman I have been watching all night. She has no clue. No idea whatsoever that she has the power to change everything, and for the life of me I can't figure out why.

"Yes," I finally answer when he turns his head to face me. I keep my eyes on her, and as she dances in the center of the crowded room, I see only her. Just like in the palace before I had any idea.

"Fuck. What do you think that means for Queen Phaedra?" Mavros asks, and the muscle in my jaw feathers. I've been asking myself that same question since I realized for sure that it is she who holds the key to restore magick to the kingdom. The relic we thought we were searching for isn't what we expected. I don't know what it means for Queen Phaedra, and it's why I wish we had more time. I think we have even less than we thought, too.

"For now, the plan doesn't change." I say.

"Are you sure about that?" He laughs, setting his tankard down and leaning closer as his eyes follow my gaze and land on her, his tone becoming more serious. "Because I think ever since she stumbled upon our path, she has changed everything..." My fingers curl into a fist where my arms rest on the table. I push off the table, standing, and I face him.

"For now, the plan doesn't change. We have a mission, and we don't fail our missions. We will keep our word to both the queen and the princess by bringing them to one another. What happens next, we will deal with." I growl, and he lets out a long breath with a shrug.

"Yea, whatever you say," Mavros responds, and I stand to leave.

"Where are you going?" Astraea's small finger pokes me in the chest with every word, surprising me. I look down at it just as I did the last time she did this. She sways on her feet before a hiccup escapes her, and she covers her mouth with her hand. "Oh—Divine!" She laughs, and my hand whips out automatically to keep her from falling. Shit. I didn't realize she was so drunk.

"I think you're drunk, princess." I say quietly, and she leans on me.

"Princess?" Her face twists up as she looks at me. "That's not what you call me. That's what everyone calls me—*what Mavros calls me.*" She exaggeratedly winks at my brother behind me, and he laughs.

"I think you need to get some sleep," I whisper, looking at Zinya with pursed lips. She should know better than to allow her to get this messed up with such an important journey ahead of us.

"Whaaat is that name... the one you call me?" She looks up, her ear pressed to my chest and her eyes narrowed as she grips my forearm to keep from swaying. "Shhhh—" She looks to the sky as though the word is painted on the ceiling.

"Where is Colette? I will walk both of you back to her chambers." I say, and she shushes again, swatting her hand out as though my words are a pest she is trying to make fly away.

"Shhhooma?" She says, and Mavros tilts his head, looking between the two of us.

"Bed. Astraea." I say, and she blinks, pushing off of me but keeping her hands on my arms.

"Don't tell me what to do! You go to bed. You are grumpy and no fun. You could dance with me again like you did in the palace." She attempts to twirl in my arms but ends up almost crashing into the table beside us, but I manage to steady her.

"*Shula,*" I growl quietly in her ear as I wrap her in my arms. She pushes back again.

"Shula! That's right!" She announces loudly, and I watch Mavros' face morph. The joyous, amused smile fading into something serious and lined with shock. Silently, I stare at him. Hoping that my eyes portray the seriousness and plea for him not to say anything, and thankfully he doesn't, but he does look at Astraea again. As though he is seeing her differently for the first time. His lips purse as he shakes his head, and his eyes slowly drag back to me.

"Don't say it," I tell him through my teeth. Astraea is laughing again, oblivious to the silent conversation between brothers, as Zinya comes back over with Colette in tow.

"Zinny says I'm drunk and need to go to sleep." She laughs again as Zinya pins her and then Mavros with a look sharp as daggers. "Did you know they celebrate for *three dayssss?* And the last day is your birthday!" Colette squeals, and Astraea giggles, pulling me close by burying her hands into my tunic.

"I should have been married off to one of the *suitors* on my birthday." Astraea says, slurring the word suitors with emphasis. "My father would have never chosen you." She whispers loudly as she leans in closer. "Do you know why?" She asks me, nose-to-nose now.

"I could guess a few reasons." I respond stiffly, and she shakes her head.

"Because I would have." My eyes lock with hers, and my pulse thunders in my ears. Even though she is wasted off whiskey and ale, she is breathtaking. My hands grip her hips, and I bring her in even closer as my brow furrows. Again, she steals all of my careful control. She pushes up on her tiptoes at the same time as she pulls hard on the fabric balled in her grip. *She kisses me.* The world around us disappears. My hands come up to cup both sides of her face as I kiss her back. The taste of alcohol is so strong I am brought back to the present quickly, but it doesn't stop me from stealing this moment. Relishing in her words even if they are laced with delusion in her inebriated state.

"Let's get you to bed." I say quietly, my lips still lingering close to hers, and she nods lazily before resting her head on my chest again. "There you go, Shula, you're ok." I whisper in her ear as I bend down and lift her into my arms. "Mav, keep an eye on Zinya." I say, turning around only to be met with Mavros being straddled by Zinya and their tongues and hands battling for attention with each other. I jerk my chin at Tarin in silent command to follow.

"I told her not to drink so much." Colette laughs, twirling a strand of Astraea's hair around her finger as it hangs loosely over my shoulder. "She didn't listen."

"I know." I say, "Follow me, I'll get you guys back to your chambers, and you can sleep it off." Colette may be drunk too, but she nods, seeming a little more sensible than the woman in my arms.

"You know—" She says, kicking a rock as we leave the tavern and begin walking through the street. "She's never been like this." She continues but doesn't elaborate.

"Drunk?" I ask.

"Oh, no, she has been drunk. I mean, she has never been like this... with a man..." She lets out a dry laugh. "She's never kissed a man in front of anyone before. Not even me, but it's more than that. I see the way she looks at you." My lips purse again as I look down at Astraea asleep in my arms. We walk up the stairs to the chambers that Astraea and Colette will share tonight.

Colette stumbles through the room lighting lanterns, and I lay Astraea down on the bed. It's a little difficult, but I maneuver her so I can get the holster from her shoulders and unbuckle the dagger strapped to her thigh before placing them quietly on the bedside table. She groans about the cold before I cover her with a blanket and remove her boots. Her hand reaches out for me, and I let her lace our fingers together.

"Stay. I don't want to be alone..." She blinks slowly before her breaths even out, and I know she is once again asleep. My brows pinch as I look at our hands. Threaded together, like our lives.

"You're not alone, not anymore. Colette is here with you tonight. I'll be back in the morning, Shula." I bend down, kissing her on the forehead. "Stay with her." I say, standing, my eyes landing on Colette while she regards me carefully. "She is not safe like this. Viltarin will be standing guard at the bottom of the stairs until morning." I say, and she scoffs before covering her mouth. Obviously not intending to let the laugh out.

"I'm more protection than he is. I can pin him in the training ring." She beams, and I can't help but laugh a little as well. Seeing as he is a decorated fighter who gives me and Mavros a run for our money, I'm sure that pinning him was only done because he wanted it. I won't tell her that, though.

"Then you should protect her just fine, but he will be there in case you need anything." My shadows leap from my skin when I snap the door shut behind me, a portal rendered just as Viltarin comes to his post.

"Boss." He says, and I nod.

"If anything happens to either of them, you better hope they don't leave you alive." I growl, and he squares his chin.

"No one will bother them. You have my word." He declares.

"Good." I respond, turning and stepping through the portal.

Chapter Forty-Four

Kyros

The portal snaps shut behind me, and the sound of it echoes through the wooded clearing I stand in. Overhead, the moon flickers through the lazy passing clouds and illuminates the forest through dancing shards of silver light. Deep green, black, and gray swim around me, and the darkness in me stirs. I was going to send Drabek with a scroll, but I needed the reminder of who I am. I needed the reminder of what the mission is.

I hear the croaking call before I see him. Drabek drops from one of the tall trees and lands on my shoulder. He chuffs, fluffing up his feathers before settling as I begin walking the hollowed path through the forest. Every step through the thick vines and twisted branches brings me closer to the reality that has been mine for the last fifteen years. Reaching into my pocket, I pull out a piece of dried meat that I keep just for him and offer it. His beak clicks as he swallows the small treat down, and his chest vibrates with happiness like a purr.

"Make yourself scarce for a bit. Things could go awry after this conversation." I tell the bird, keeping my eyes on the tunnel of trees that begins opening up in front of us. When we reach the opening, the castle spires reach toward the night-lit, star-streaked sky like thorns on a poisonous plant. Windows all along this side are lit with the light from roaring hearths that warm the cold castle. At night, its presence is ominous and foreboding, like the moon revealing the wickedness within. Even if, when the sun rises and the sky is painted with the bright colors of day, the castle is an enchanting masterpiece. An apparition of beauty, just like the queen inside. Drabek caws mournfully before launching into the sky toward the castle.

It doesn't take long to reach the village below the castle carved into the mountain. All the doors are closed, the shutters pulled tight. Not a soul to be seen. Even if Diemos is not my true home, the people here are just as much mine as I am theirs. A part of me misses being here. I take one of the tunnels that lead to the lower entrance to the castle. One that not many know about, and even fewer dare to use. Magick pulses around me as I step over a boundary line. As soon as I do, a mage light flashes brightly in the narrow underground breezeway. Two men stand sentinel with their polearms erected.

"Stand aside." I demand without slowing my gait, and both of their eyes widen as I emerge from the shadows.

"Lord Kyros, apologies, we weren't expecting you." One says opening a side of the heavy gate leading to the lower levels beneath the castle. The other scrambles to wrench open his side too, and I don't respond or even look at them as I stride inside. Another man is sitting when I enter; he jumps to his feet, brushing crumbs from his rounded belly and wiping his hand down his beard. He coughs, choking on the bread that he was shoving in his face.

"Lord—Kyros." His eyes fall to the ground.

"Announce me to the queen." My voice reverberates through the passage and makes the flames of the firelight flicker and dance. When his eyes finally raise, they are wide and terrified. My reputation here, within these walls, is much different than beyond. One of the many versions of myself I must maintain, as I've been taught.

"Of course, my lord." He scrambles ahead of me, and I follow on with a clipped stride. He takes the wide stairway that leads to the main castle and clears his throat as he pulls the door open. "Lord Kyros Kazahl," he calls out. I don't wait for permission to enter, and he blanches before pulling the door shut with a resounding slam.

Her back is to me; her long golden hair brushes the top of her hips, and the thin rose silk robe she has herself wrapped in reveals the apple-like shape of her ass. It dusts the floor, making her already long legs appear endless. She feeds the white Creshian raven kept in a large gilded cage in front of the two-panel corner window. She titters and chides, talking to Zuri. The magickal creature snaps her opal-like beak, not careful to avoid her slender fingers.

"I think she is finally warming to me." Her ethereal voice carries over the space between us easily through the pristine room. Zuri has not warmed to anyone since we came to Diemos, least of all the queen. The female raven is wrathful in her misery. She lets out a cry when Drabek lands on the perch the queen had placed on the other side of the thick window. The two are mates, and though Queen Phaedra knows this, she refuses to allow them together until Zuri accepts her. Zuri will only ever accept the queen of my choosing as the rightful king of the land she was born to.

Queen Phaedra turns finally, bored with the bird's heartache and petulance. Her blue eyes are dark as midnight. The fire in the hearth on the opposite wall reflects like stars when she looks at me. Her rosy pink lips curl slowly into a smile as she surveys me.

"My dark prince," She breathes, stepping forward so the glow of the fire fully illuminates her face. "I assume since you are here alone, you have news of the relic for me?" She says, toying with the nearly open front of her robe. Her smile widens when she notices that my gaze is drawn to the movement of her fingers.

"The king kept the relic in the castle all these years, just as we suspected." I reply, letting my eyes lazily trail up her thin figure. She loves being adored. Though half of her body is covered in scars, she holds herself in the highest regard. The scars are not a burden to her in the least bit, but rather an adornment she wears with pride. It seems the sentiment toward them is one of strength, but those who know the woman for who she really is know that what is grotesque isn't the marred skin on her body; it is the blackened heart within.

She glides across the white marble floor silently, circling me where I stand. My shadows still, coiled tight, ready to leap from my skin at any moment; I urge them to freeze instead. Her light pink painted nails brush along my chest and from my shoulder down my arm, hesitating before hovering above the Tsalalerian steel sword.

"You seem *tense*." She tuts, tilting her head and letting her hand continue its trailing as she walks behind me. The sharp point of her nails sends a chill down my spine as she slides them across my shoulders and then rests her hand flat over my heart after she is done with her circle. I take even breaths, showing nothing when I answer.

"You would be too, in the presence of the false king." I say. The idea pleases her. She pats my chest before spinning away with a clap.

"Yes, I suppose you are right. Is he as dreadful as they say?" She asks as she lounges on the chaise in front of the fire. "And the daughter? Did Mavros break her spirit and her virtue?" She smiles wickedly while biting into a plump strawberry she plucked from the stand at her side.

"Actually, that is what I've come to warn you about." I say, taking a step forward. "The relic isn't an object, as we had thought. I have reason to believe that the daughter holds the magick we thought would be imbued into a relic." Her fingers rap musically on the arm of the chaise lounge while her gaze is far away in thought. Slowly, her eyes trail up to mine.

"And the daughter?" She asks pensively. She leaves the question open-ended purposefully, wanting me to fill her in on anything I see fit. I shrug.

"Seems she is unaware." I say, leaving out that she is already out of the palace and we are on our way here.

"Interesting." She steeples her fingers in front of her mouth while she keeps her eyes trained on me. "You know, Kyros, I sense something different about you. The tenseness in your shoulders... It feels almost as though you are holding something back..." Her eyes narrow. She is one I wish wasn't so adept at reading emotions.

"I have been holding back since the moment I stepped foot back in Eathian." I answer honestly. Though Queen Phaedra was kind to us as children and while growing up in her presence, I know that she can be cruel too. I didn't want to show up with Astraea in tow and have the fury of a vengeful mad queen come at her for her father's wrongdoings. I had to come here to let her onto the idea easy. "I think the daughter could be of use." I finally say, and her lips purse. She is silent for a long moment as she considers my words.

"You can get her out of the castle?" She whispers, "*Bring her to me*." Cruelness leaches into her tone, and it curls around my spine.

"I believe that she is innocent in all of this." It's a risk to say, but I can't bring Astraea here if she is in harm's way. I won't. "She is as innocent as I was." I continue.

"And you believe that her father would spare you if he knew who you were?" She scolds, and my jaw feathers as I fight a retort. "No, he would make a mockery of you." She answers her own question.

"He could try," I grind between my teeth.

"He *would* try." She agrees.

"The daughter, she is different. I believe that she will work with you. She is not high in Connard's regard. He treats her as an object." My hand wraps around the hilt of the sword at my hip, and her eyes watch keenly. Gritting my teeth, I stop talking. I've said too much. I've shown too much.

"Very well, my dark prince. Bring the girl here. Together we will take down her father and restore magick to what it was. We will rid her of her burden." She polishes her fingernails with her robe. "When will you arrive with my long-awaited prize?"

"Two days after the Shula Morana." I answer.

"Good. Four days' time. I will be ready to accept my new guest." She says, her voice carrying a new lithe to her tone, and I nod. I turn to leave, but she calls out, halting my exit. "Kyros?" When I turn around, she is gliding across the expanse of the room, and she stops just in front of me. Her hand slides up my chest and cups my cheek, guiding me to bend toward her.

"My queen?" I ask, my breath puffing out between us.

"Do be ready to take your rightful place as King." She says with a saccharine smile on her lips. A warning and a reminder. The scent of roses lingers in the air as she turns away, silently sashaying back toward the chase. My jaw clenches tight, and I shut the door with a quick snap.

The portal disappears behind me with a crackle, leaving the edge of the mountain in silence. The tarn below is like a black mirror of the dark, starless sky. It's the one place I know I can come and not worry about anything or worry about everything. The clouds seem as heavy as my thoughts. Everything about the conversation with Queen Phaedra has dread wrapping around my spine. She said it best: *something feels different about you.*

I am different.

I feel it too.

I can't go back to Aithne right now. I don't want to face what I know is there waiting for me. I need to have a conversation with my brother, and I need to make a backup plan in case the original plan needs to change. Seeing the queen of Diemos' reaction was less than settling. She has been looking for the relic for this long. I thought knowing the magick was imbued into a person rather than an object would make her think twice about using it, but I saw the flash in her eyes. The way that she lit up knowing that perhaps this is better than she imagined. She will not only get the key that makes her the holder of magick, but she will also have something to hold over Connard. Even so, I'm not sure it's his daughter's well-being that he will care about.

Something about all of this feels off. Why would the magick be tied to a person... What I saw in Astraea's nightmare... I need to know for sure. There is so much unknown that is ahead of us, but one thing I know for certain. Astraea is meant to be mine. The moment I saw her, I think I knew who she was. It's only taken this long to accept it. I just wonder if she ever will, especially if she ever knows all that I have hidden from her—everything I still hide.

Sitting with my back pressed against the mountain, I look up just as the clouds give me a peek at the sliver of the silver moon. I turn my hand over in my lap, conjuring a small plume of sandy shadow magick. It whirls and writhes like a storm confined to the space in my hand. I've never done this before, but I need to know what I am up against. I need to know who else is after her. It's late, and she was drunk when I left. Surely she is fast asleep. If I'm right, I will be able to step into her dreams. Even if I am not with her.

I tilt my head back, letting it rest on the rocky surface behind me. I allow my every thought to be consumed by Astraea. The deep umbra of her hair, the scorpion grass flower coloring of her eyes, and her warm and sweet scent—then I unleash the magick in my palm. Urging it for the first time to take *me* into sleep's embrace.

I feel my body slump as soon as the magick rolls over me. A heaviness weighs me down only for a moment before I am weightless. I am floating through nothingness, my soul flying through an endless chasm of darkness, but like a moth to the flame, I sense her. Her fire burns bright like a beacon, drawing me into the consuming heat. I don't know how I ever denied it before.

The feeling of slipping through her subconscious is the same as if I were sitting in the same room with her. I let myself in through the light that encapsulates her essence.

Her mind is dark, and as I enter with my shadows, the darkness only deepens. When the darkness becomes heated, I hear a thundering beat. Perhaps her pulse is rising with the oncoming nightmare. It evolves when bright flashes fill the dark. Then the vision becomes clearer. I am watching as an outsider looking in. A girl who couldn't be much older than five is held tightly in a saddle. The man who holds her is draped in black that flows out behind him like webs of spider silk, and the white flashes are not flashes at all but white bark trees that line the dark gravel road.

The dream morphs, and Astraea takes the place of the little girl. The man who held her no longer there. She rides frantically, the pounding hoofbeats matching an erratic heart. I narrow my eyes and try to send a calmness to her through our connection. After a moment she seems to float with relief. She turns her head, looking right at me. For a moment, I believe she sees me the way I do her. Everything around us dissipates, and I wait to see what she does.

Come on, Shula. See me.

Her brows drop as she stares into the shadows, but the sound that slices through the darkness between us has her eyes wide with fear. The word hissed and echoing around us.

"Seennnnkkaaa!" My blood freezes, and along with it, my shadows. I am powerless as I watch the dark claws reach out to her. They curl around her arm. The same sharp claws that reached for me, piercing my chest with their deadly point. Her eyes close tightly as she fights off the fear of what grips her while I internally scream for her. *See me. Release me!*

I close my eyes and pull my magick as hard as I can into me. I let it create a sandstorm within my body's confines. I let it pulse and writhe before I push it forward. Astraea accepts it instantly. Her shoulders roll back as she is filled with more strength.

"What do you want?" She asks. Her voice echoes through the dreamscape like smoke on the wind. The answering hiss makes my hackles rise. I grit my teeth waiting for the strike. If she is attacked, I can only hope that the magick I shared will be enough to protect her, because I'm not sure I will be able to like this. I've never cast myself into someone's nightmares, and I have no idea what the limitations are.

Feel me. I'm here with you. You have protection. You have strength.

Fight!

Her eyes snap open just as a shred of the moon peers beyond clouds of darkness. I swallow, feeling the threat of my teeth cracking as I fight whatever power is holding me hostage in the shadows. Perhaps this is something that Astraea has to face on her own. She looks into the face of her nightmare, and while I see fear in her eyes, her spine straightens.

My muscles tense and pulse as I continue my fight to reach her without fail. It's seconds, minutes, and hours of torment while time seems to stop as they stare into each other's eyes. When he lifts his blade-like hand to wrap those sharp claws around her throat, I soundlessly scream for her.

Heat.

Fire.

It engulfs me, burning like a raging inferno. It connects me to her. I feel no pain.

"Seeeennnnkkkkaaaa." The voice fades and echoes in the distance, and as soon as he is gone, my shadows erupt. They wrap Astraea and pull her to me. I pull so hard we go hurling back, and when we hit the ground, the fire burns white hot. A lightning bolt through our souls.

My eyes jerk open. I am alone in Diemos, looking out over the tarn I have come to so many times before. Everything is the same, but what just happened... Changes everything.

Chapter Forty-Five

Astraea

Pounding hoofbeats sound beneath me, but where before I felt jostled, now I am weightless. The flashing white that usually comes is slow. I can see into the trees, to the darkness that lies between.

It looks back at me.

Waiting.

"Seennnnkkaaa!" The word is hissed sharp like a blade cutting through the mist around me. The cold, blade-like claws curl around my arm, pulling at me, wanting me to turn. I squeeze my eyes shut, but the lasso of heat that sears at my ribs starts, and the rumbling laugh follows. It echoes and tingles across my skin.

When I open my eyes, I know what I will see. The reaper evading my dreams; the sovereign haunting my nightmares. The difference from every other time he has come is that I know he can harm me just as he did Kyros. I feel it in the way that his claws scrape across my skin, leaving gooseflesh in their wake.

What happens if I seek him out? What happens when I open my eyes and come face-to-face with the monster that hunts me? With my eyes still firmly closed, I grit my teeth before I call back to him.

"What do you want?" My voice doesn't sound like my own but a reflection of the sound. Far away and lost to the void. He hisses in response like a snake. Nothing but my pounding heart fills the silence, and when I can't take it any longer, my eyes fly open.

I stand face-to-face with the cause of torment every time I close my eyes. The white light from the moon reflects off cracked bone as shadowy tendrils crawl from him like darkened smoke. They reach for me from horns, and his long sharp fangs glint wickedly as he comes impossibly closer. The moonlight casts his long, claw-like fingers eerily in a glow of silver light as they reach between us.

I am frozen in my fear.

I have always sensed him. Seen glimpses of the fast-moving terror, but this slow, harrowing movement brings a sense of consternation that I have never experienced.

One long, blade-like finger at a time, he wraps his large claws around my throat. I feel the probing of his eyes in the darkened sockets of the skull staring down at the column of my neck. The drumming pulse reveals every shred of fear I try to contain. My chest rises on an influx of air as his grip tightens and he begins to lift me. My hands reach out for his arm, and even though he appears to be an apparition, his forearm is solid and burns under my touch. My feet dangle precariously as I try to point my toes in an attempt to reach the ground. I cannot breathe. The lasso of fire at my ribs seems to burn hotter.

It's everywhere.

The fire consumes me, burns through me—*from me.*

"Seeeennnnkkkkaaaa," he says again, his voice like a fading call in the wind, and then I fall. I fall into the shadows, then the light, the burn, the fire; everything falls with me until I hit the ground like a blast of lightning. It shatters everything.

I suck in a gasping breath at the same time I wrench up from bed. My body is soaked with sweat, and a cold chill sends ice to wrap around me, and dread coils around my spine. I feel like I can't get enough breath into my lungs with how raggedly I am trying to pull air in. My throat burns, and when I brush my fingers along the skin on my neck, I wince. The pounding grows louder, and I cover my ears trying to calm myself, drown out the throbbing pain, or stop everything.

A loud crash makes me scramble backward toward the headboard, and a scream rips from my throat so loud I fear I may have ripped something.

"Great divine, did you have to—" Colette freezes when she sees me. I must be a sight because her eyes are wide and her lips part on a silent inhale. "*Astraea?*" She questions, her hands quickly coming up to cover her mouth.

"Fuck. What happened?!" Viltarin whisper-shouts, raking his hand through his sandy hair; his hazel eyes are wide as they jump around the room and then from my face to my neck, then to my body. "*Fuck*. Kyros is going to kill me." He says resolutely and balls his hands into fists as he walks around Cole, who is statue-still in the center of the room. The door I now see is broken and creaks as it barely hangs from the hinge behind them.

"You're bleeding. I wasn't here *again*." Colette says softly, still unmoving and clearly unsettled.

"Cole, it's ok. I need the balm. Do you have any?" She is shaking her head before I finish the question. My brows furrow as I try to think of what to do.

"Healing balm?" Viltarin asks, looking back at Colette and then to me. "I can get some from Mavros—"

"No!" I say too loudly, and my throat aches from the damage done when I screamed. "I don't want to alert Kyros of this." Viltarin looks like he is going to be sick.

"Sorry, Princess, Kyros will know. There will be no hiding that injury when he returns." He argues. *Returns?*

"He left?" My voice croaks, but only I know it's from the hurt I feel rather than my throat. They both look at me and then to each other. I don't like feeling like an outsider when it comes to Cole. She has always been the one I can count on to have silent conversations, and seeing her do that with someone who is essentially a stranger to me feels an awful lot like hurt. Something she has never done to me. Colette finally breaks the trance she is in and comes to sit on the bed in front of me.

"He will be back, but right now, all I care about is making sure you are ok. Can I look at it?" She asks attentively. I wasn't aware I was holding my throat. When I drop my hand, it comes back dripping with blood, and a wave of lightheadedness rolls through me. I thought there was bruising. I didn't realize I had been bleeding. I look down, and I suck in a breath of shock. The tunic I was wearing is shredded down the front, and my skin beneath is stained crimson.

"I hate to say it, Princess, but if we don't get that healed, Kyros will be the last of your worries." My eyes lift to Cole as she pleads with me.

"Please, let him go get help." She takes my bloody hands in hers, and I finally relent. I guess they are right. I will deal with Kyros.

"Fine, but first, can I have water?" I croak, swallowing hard with my raw throat.

"Oh, Divine! Yes." Cole jumps up and runs across the room, coming back to hand me a metal cup. The cup is cool as she puts it in my hands, and slowly I let the water soothe the ache in my throat.

"I'll be right back." Viltarin says before glancing at the door and then back to us. "I will only be a minute." Cole nods and then starts fussing over me. She took the basin from the corner of the room and moved it to the bedside table and is now wringing strips of cloth in the water. Who knows where she found the cloth? She avoids my eyes as she stays busy.

"Colette?" I quietly call for her attention, and she finally meets my gaze. As soon as she does, I realize why she has avoided it. "Why are you crying?"

"I should have been here. I was not here when you needed me again. Kyros told me not to leave you, and I was just in the hall for a short while. I was right outside your door, and look what happened!" The tears spill over her lashes and run down her cheek.

"There is nothing you could have done to stop this." I whisper, reaching for her hand and twining our fingers together. She looks down at my blood-soaked chest, and I watch as her jaw clenches and she nods. "This isn't the first time, and I have a feeling it won't be the last."

"We have to do something. Maybe there is someone here who can help. They have magick here. They use it openly. Things are not as your father makes the kingdom believe. The people with magick are not the monsters. I mean, I knew that before, but finally seeing it with my own two eyes. It's different." I can't help but smile at her as she stops rambling. "I'm talking fast." She says, smiling too.

"I love you, Cole." I say, tears now beginning to well in my own eyes.

"I love you, too, Astraea. Always." She takes the fabric strips from the bowl and begins cleaning the wounds on my neck as Viltarin comes striding back into the room, and behind him, Mavros. He looks a bit disheveled and holds a tin jar I recognize as the healing balm.

"Shit." Mavros curses, the sleepy look on his face vanishing. "You said she got hurt in her sleep. I thought she fucking fell off the bed and got hurt somehow. You look like you were attacked by a fucking animal. What happened?" He asks, taking Cole's place as she stands and backs away. The room was already small, and now with the three of them hovering over me, it feels even smaller. Colette seems to notice and places her hand on Viltarn's arm where it is folded over his chest.

"We will be right outside. Mavros, yell for us if you need us." She says, dismissing herself and Viltarin without a backward glance. Mavros keeps his eyes on the wound at my neck. He pushes his sleeves up and shakes his head.

"He's going to be fucking feral." Mavros says seriously. I'm taken aback by his tone. It's so unlike the Mavros I've come to know. I don't have to ask who he means. Kyros has been more than possessive lately.

"Is it ok if I touch you to apply the balm?" He asks as he opens the tin; his pale hair isn't braided back like it normally is and falls into his eyes as he looks at me, waiting for my response. The spicy scent of the healing balm immediately fills the room, and I'm taken back to a time when I was a child. The memory I couldn't pinpoint when I first smelled it floods my memory. My brow cinches together as I recall the image of my mother rubbing the same sort of balm over a cut on my elbow. She had pressed her finger to her lips. The corners curved up into a secret smile. *"Our little secret, my bright star."*

"Mavros?" I say, and he stops with a scoop of balm on his fingers. "This balm... Can it be prepared by just anyone? Like the ingredients, are they easily accessible?" I ask, and his brows drop.

"I mean, I suppose the balm itself, yea, but the healing properties have to be imbued by a dweller to truly be a Creshian healing balm." He gestures to my neck, and I lift my chin, allowing him to rub the balm on the wounds there. I know that this is the same smell from when I was a child. Did my mother seek out a dweller, or was she a part of the Neer people? A magick sympathizer?

"Hold still, let me get every mark. Maybe we can get the worst parts healing before Kyros comes back and loses his shit." He says, blowing air out his cheeks. "Fuck, I don't see how he's not going to."

"I don't see why, though? There is nothing that could have been done. If he wants to be upset, then he can be upset with himself. The nightmares haven't been happening when he is around. I think it's afraid of the magick Kyros pushed back at it." I say, glaring past Mavros and to the broken door to the room, as though the man we are speaking of may storm through at any moment.

"Kyros pushed magick back? *At your nightmare?*" He asks warily, dipping his fingers back into the balm and slowly applying more to the wounds. "Like he was *seeing* your nightmare?" He finishes. His face is stern, rigid with concern, and it's confusing to me. I thought that Kyros would have told his brother about this.

"The nightmare creature stabbed him. He—fought him off—with magick. This is the first time the nightmare has returned since." I say. He is quiet for a moment as he wipes his hands on a cloth and secures the lid back over the jar. "And you saw all of this happen?" He asks, and I hesitate. Of course I saw it. What does he mean? "It's just usually, the dreamer can't really see us in their dream state, meaning there is a reason you can... or you were awake and your nightmare crossed the threshold of realms."

Pounding footsteps sound in the hall, and Mavros' lips purse looking at the wound on my neck like it makes him angry. What he has just said doesn't make sense to me, but I know nearly nothing about magick or its workings. Kyros using magick around me is the only time I have seen it. Other than stories from drunken men in hushed tones, I wouldn't know the first thing about details like that.

Mavros' face is stern as he looks up to the doorway, and I know it's Kyros who approaches. I can feel his presence.

"Shula?" Kyros skids into the doorway; the broken door, pushed further out of the way in his haste to get into the room, falls with a loud bang. I flinch. "Are you—" His words are stopped with a rope of shadow whipping out and twisting around his neck. My eyes go wide as Mavros holds his brother still in the center of the room.

"Mavros?" I say warily, eyes locked to the way Kyros' coloring deepens from lack of oxygen.

"You failed to mention this whole little nightmare situation, brother. Seems you are keeping secrets from everyone lately... Which one should we delve into first?" Mavros sneers with his lip curled back. His shadows whirl and twist along his skin like churning clouds in a storm. The look of them against Mavro's pale eyes and hair gives a whole new appearance to the shadow magick. Kyros lifts his hand, fingers splayed wide, and hell in his eyes. When he closes his fist, the shadows all fall away. Mavros' eyes narrow before he hurls himself at Kyros. The brothers crash to the floor so hard that dust from the wooden floorboards plumes into the air.

"What the fuck?" Viltarin comes to the doorway, Colette right behind him, wide-eyed.

"Stop them!" I call out between their grunts from savage punches and kicks to each other's bodies. Viltarin shakes his head.

"No way. They will stop when they have worked out whatever is going on..." He says with his eyebrows high. "It's been a while since I've seen them fight like this." *This is ridiculous.* They are fighting, rolling around on the floor like children. I stand up from the bed. My feet are still bare, but at least the pain has subsided in my throat. I stomp over to where Kyros holds Mavros in a headlock, and I put my hands on my hips, staring at him. He looks up, and the man has the audacity to smirk.

"Unhand him!" I demand. Kyros eyes me for a moment longer before he drops his hold on Mavros and pushes him away. Mavros rolls onto his back, flat on the floor.

"Thanks, Princess." He smiles, letting his head flop to the side, and grins wide at his brother, his white teeth coated with the red gleam of blood. "Fuck you." Mavros says to him, and Kyros just shakes his head. His eyes are still dark and lingering on me. On my neck. It's my turn to shake my head.

"The more time I spend with you, the more I see that you are both *ridiculous.* You know that?" I say as I spin on my heel and pick up the boots from the end of the bed. "Viltarin, can you take me somewhere to wash up? And will someone find me something else to wear?" A deep growl emanates from Kyros. I look down at him in a sidelong look. Shaking my head, I step over the brothers where they still remain on the ground. Kyros' hand whips out and wraps around my wrist.

"Wait." He says, and I look down at where his hand holds me in place, then up to meet his eyes. "I need to speak with you. Let me help you clean up, and we can talk. Please." He pleads. Mavros pulls himself up to stand, then plops down on the edge of the bed with a scoff.

"I'd go with him if I were you. It seems you have a lot to *learn*." Mavros says condescendingly, and Kyros gives his brother a dirty look before releasing my wrist and rising to his full height.

"Come with me or don't. It's up to you." Kyros grunts, looking at his brother again with indignation. "The sun will be rising soon, and with it so does the city. We will be leaving here after the celebrations end. You should be ready, and make sure that the rest of those traveling with us are ready too." Kyros growls at his brother, but the order was as much for him as it was for Viltarin, who gives a nodding bow as he storms past him. Kyros looks over his shoulder once he passes Colette. "I'm sorry that you had to witness that." Who he says it to is unclear, but the way he looks between the two of us, it seems his apology is to both Cole and me.

He disappears from my vision, and all three of them, left behind, look at me. Waiting for my decision. I roll my eyes and huff out my breath, looking around the room.

"If we are going to be here two more nights, I think we are going to need a new place to sleep." I say, and Mavros lets out a deep-bellied laugh as I step over the door now lying on the ground. Colette rolls her lips together to hide her smile. "You both are ridiculous." I say again, this time to Mavros and Colette. I stomp down the stairs in the same direction Kyros left.

Chapter Forty-Six

Kyros

I LOOK DOWN AT my hands as I flex them out in front of me and squeeze them into tight fists, trying to release the tension still in my arms. After the fight with Mavros, I stormed off, pushing my sleeves up and away from my overheated skin. The shadows that live there twist and curl around, seething on the surface. They have always been harder to still when my emotions are high, and seeing Astraea bleeding and bruised has them just as agitated as I feel. Mavros didn't make anything better. Threatening me, using our magick against me? He doesn't understand, but I haven't allowed him to, and I know that is my own doing.

I get to the border of town and take a quick glance over my shoulder. Astraea isn't far behind me; I felt her presence as soon as she started following. She stomps after me with her arms crossed and anger radiating from her in rippling waves. As furious as I was to walk into that room and see her bleeding and bruised, the vision of her walking toward me coated in blood and provoked causes my pulse to tick up for a whole other reason.

Two days until the Shula Morana. Four until we are back in Diemos, and a whole new challenge awaits. It's kind of ironic that this could be the last Shula Morana, and the princess of the cruel king—*my Shula*—is here planning to celebrate the day too. Not only that, but the day of her birth and the day that her father was supposed to be sealing her fate with a chosen suitor. *How the winds have changed.*

My boots crunch through the fallen leaves and twigs left over by the last fall as I reach the woodline. I glance back at where Astraea is still following; I can't help but smirk at the look on her face. I pick up my pace as soon as I pass the first tree, using my shadows and the darkness of the early morning to conceal me between their trunks. Once she is in the woods, too, I find a large tree and prop myself against its rough bark. The sun starts to cast a glow on the sky, but here, under the cover of the thick boughs above us, it's very much still dark. Add my shadows, and it's nearly dark as pitch the closer she gets to me.

I watch her like I have many of my targets, silently waiting as she gets closer. Her arms have dropped from where she crossed them over her chest, and the anger that she once had painted onto her face is turned to something else. Something unexpected. My brows drop, and I tilt my head as I watch her. I thought I would see fear of where I am leading her, of the darkness beneath the trees, or even of the potential of danger from creatures of the night. Especially after the nightmare she just had. Instead, she is the picture of wonder. Her eyes are brighter than the moon itself. The ground beneath my feet seems to come alive, trembling and threatening to crumble and swallow me whole. A warm sensation pulses through me as she continues to walk toward me. Curious, I urge my dark magick to cloud the space between us, ensuring that she can't see where I watch her. The same pulsing magick I felt at the Dead Sea fills my veins and vibrates from the sand in my pocket and the blade at my hip.

Using my shadows, I push them to unwind from my arm; they slither around my wrist and my fingers and trail through the deadwood of the forest floor. The wind blows a gust of warm air through the trees, causing a whistle to echo through the branches. Astraea stills at the sound. Does *fear fail to evade you now, Shula?* My lip quirks up at the corner. She pulls her hair over one shoulder, listening to the whispering darkness. Where she has stopped has created the perfect opportunity for my attack. The shadows crawl through the air behind her, tickling the skin on the back of her neck. When she shutters, my smirk turns to a full grin, because of course, yet again, it is not fear that is on her face. She closes her eyes and tilts her head, urging the dark tendrils to explore. Every part that they come into contact with on her skin sends shockwaves of craving to twist around my spine.

"I know it's you," she says breathlessly, and I narrow my eyes on her. I can see the pulse in her neck hammering with how close she is now, and I wonder if she is finally scared. I let my shadows slowly curl loosely around her delicate neck, and she takes in a deep shuddering breath, closing her eyes again. I say nothing as I push from the tree and slowly walk around her. My nostrils flare. I'm pissed at Mavros, worried about Queen Phaedra, and troubled by the nightmares that seem to only be getting worse. The kingdom that is plagued with misery at the hands of a monster of a king. The more I think about how much this mission has gone to shit, the more my anger roils in me. The one thing that has been at the center of everything that has gone wrong stands here vulnerable, right in front of me. She provokes me, calls me out, and demands my every attention. I am powerless to the vital force that she wields against me without having a clue.

She stiffens as I inch closer behind her. I let my fingers hover just above her shoulders and down her arms and lean in close, letting my breath trail a line over the exposed flesh on her neck. The way she shivers seems to bleed right into me, and I feel the gooseflesh peppering my skin.

"Do you have any idea what you do to me?" I whisper into the shell of her ear. Her breath hitches as I complete the circle, slowly walking around her. I replace the shadows wrapping her throat with my hand, feeling the thunderous adrenaline coursing in the high speed of her pulse causes my breaths to come quicker—*deeper*.

"Not everything is about you." She responds with attitude, and I tighten my grip on her neck, still gentle enough not to restrict her breathing, but enough pressure to cause her already rampant heart to pound harder. I let the shadows blow away like mist, and her eyes snap to mine, just inches from her. My gaze falls to the way her lips part as she sucks in another breath. After everything—the king, the pirates, a manticore, and now Queen Phaedra—she continues to make the wall I have built containing everything vulnerable in me crumble.

"No, Shula, not since you." Her body leans into mine; I can see the way her eyes heavily linger on my lips. I want nothing else but to kiss her. Give her what she so clearly wants. Claim her mouth and pull her flush to me. Rip the bloodied clothing from her body and claim every inch of her skin with my mouth, but instead my eyes find a stray hair that is stuck to her face, and my other hand comes up, fingers brushing it away and tucking it behind her ear. "Since you—the world seems to have slowed. You threaten everything I know and everything I don't, but still I find myself ensnared." She swallows, and I lean in, hovering my lips above her. I look into her eyes. "Burning."

"What happens if we are both consumed by the fire?" She asks in a whisper.

"We burn the world—" I press my lips to hers in a chaste kiss, "*together.*" I whisper the word into her lips. She tangles her hands into my tunic and tries to pull me closer, but I hold fast where I am. As much as I want to let go and let her in fully, there is still so much between us. I cup her face with my hand and smile softly. "Maybe you would like to clean up before we start." She looks down, as though she is only just now remembering that she is coated in her own blood. "I was hoping to train you to wield the weapons you carry. I want you to be more prepared than you are in case we run into any issues on the way to Diemos. Are you too hurt?" I ask, letting my fingers loosen around her neck and trail down the column of her throat. The marks are nearly gone from the balm that Mavros applied to her. One of the three that Kaeleith gave me. She swallows, and my gaze lifts to hers.

"No, I'm ok." She steps back, and my brows drop as the urge to pull her back overwhelms me. I felt my wall crumbling before, and I felt hers coming down with it, but every step she takes away from me, creating space between us... I feel the foundations trying to rebuild. A lifetime of protections coming to brace everything that has broken.

"You're sure?" I ask, and she smiles. There is sadness that doesn't reach her eyes, and I feel the dip of my brows deepen. She bites her bottom lip, and something like determination flashes in her eyes before she gives a curt nod.

"I like the idea of getting some lessons to protect myself. When can we start?" She crosses her arms over her chest. "I don't need to clean up just to get sweaty again. I've seen the way you guys train." The corner of my mouth quirks up at the snap of attitude even after just facing a nightmare. Every time I am around her, she proves she is not what I thought she would be. I put my hand out, palm up.

"Let's go." I say, and she looks at my hand.

"Where are we going?" She looks around the dense wood and the purple and pink glow of the rising sun just beyond the border, trepidation building in her blue eyes.

"To train." I say, and whether it be the smirk I can't seem to remove from my face or the flash of mischief in my eyes that sets her on guard, she takes a step back. But she is far too close, and I am far too fast. With one lunge I am wrapping my arm around her low back and pulling her flush with me. She lets out a gasp, while I simultaneously whip out a lasso of magick that snaps and crackles like burning wood. The glittering sand catches aflame as soon as I'm ready to transport us. As quickly as I took the step forward, I let my body fall backward into the rendered portal and through space and time with her held tight in my arms. Astraea screeches like a bird of prey, and as she seals her eyes closed tight, I grin and whisper in her ear. "Hold your breath, Shula."

When I learned to use my magick to rend portals, Mavros was furious that he couldn't. We were young. Somewhere around thirteen. I had a temper around that age. My adolescent years were hard for me. Coming of age to be a man, but not quite there yet. I was angry about my parents, the kingdom, and what had become of my life.

The Neer people knew who my brother and I were the moment we arrived at the small village at the border between kingdoms. Diemos was a lush green wilderness I was enchanted by, and Eathian was a scorching desert I was ready to burn the way it did me. The stark differences only became more apparent as I grew older.

Especially with the new king and his tyrannical way of treating the people he was claiming to be his.

It was Queen Phaedra who helped me work through my emotions. She started me in training with her military; it was fairly quick for the higher-level generals to realize that Mavros and I were different. Mavros joined just to have something to do, but it was something that gave me purpose. I needed to feel useful in some way. Before my parents perished, my entire life was mapped out for me. I knew what to expect in the long term and how I was going to get there. When they died, all of that changed. The life as I knew it died with them.

Meeting Astraea feels the same. The moment she came into my life, I no longer knew what my purpose was. I am once again an angry adolescent needing purpose and trying to find my way.

The portal drops us unceremoniously into the Damalis Tarn. Its deep murky water lets no light penetrate its surface, and when we are engulfed with the cool mountain water, it's like we are being devoured by shadows. I keep a tight hold on Astraea even as she panics in my arms, and I kick my feet hard to start back up. When we breach the surface, she gasps for air, and I too suck in a gulping breath before bellowing an uncharacteristic laugh.

"Are you seriously laughing?!" She yells, wiping her hair from her face and the water from her eyes. I fling the hair that has come loose from the tie at the back of my head away from my face too, spraying her with droplets, and she squeals. "Kyros!"

"You should see your face, Shula." I trap my lip in my teeth trying to bite back a smile as I keep one arm wrapped around her waist. I brush my thumb along her lips. Wiping away the water droplets that collected there. We are both breathing hard, wading in the center of the tarn. The mountain casting us in its shadow as the sun makes its way to crown its peak.

She groans, pushing me in the chest, and says nothing before she spins in my arms. She's about to swim away, but then her breath catches and her head tips back, finally taking in the view of the mountain. My lips curl as I pull her back to me, leaving my arm wrapped around her waist, I whisper into her ear.

"Welcome to Diemos, Shula."

Chapter Forty-Seven

Astraea

My breath gets caught in my throat. All of my agitation over being dumped into the tarn is forgotten when I spin around to swim away and I see where we are. The mountain takes up my vision. It stands tall, like a jagged tooth in a monster's mouth. Behind it, rows and rows of sharp points reach into the sky like a beast's maw open in a mighty roar. Lush greens, reds, oranges, and purples paint the trees that crowd the water's edge, and not far off, a thin dark waterfall feeds the small body of water we wade in.

"Welcome to Diemos." Kyros' breath puffs out at my ear, and the heat of his body presses into my back as he slinks his arm around my waist, pulling me flush with him. I'm at a loss for words, so I say nothing at all. I lean into his embrace and let him hold my weight as I rest the back of my head on his chest and fully take in the vision of it all. Never did I imagine I would see such a sight. Its beauty is breathtaking. It feels like we wade in the center of the rounded pool of water for hours, but I know it could only be minutes. Kyros says nothing and leaves me to bask in it. Only when he begins tracing small circles on my stomach where my shirt has risen do I come back into my body.

"Why did you bring me here?" I finally ask. I know it's where we are heading with the others, but something about this place feels almost sacred. I lift my chin so I can see his face. He does not look at me but instead looks out over the water, too. The sun is now fully crowning the mountain, and its shadow is beginning to shift, exposing more of the water. I thought the water was dark because of the shadows, but even now as the rays from the sun shine down on it, they don't penetrate the surface. The water is black as onyx, and the ripples created by our wading and the trickle of water coming from the nearby waterfall cause it to glitter in the sunshine.

"I could tell you needed a little escape," he says, bringing his gaze to meet mine. The black waters reflect in his nearly black eyes and are just as breathtaking as the scenery. His words bring heat to every inch of my skin, and he seems to notice. "Do you want to see my favorite spot?" He asks, and I give him a coy smile.

"I think I would love that." I tell him, and he nods before starting to push us closer to the shoreline. As we get further away from the center of the tarn, I notice more details of the land. Early morning birdsong fills the air, and small animals frolic through the bushes and patches of tall grass. The wooded area is similar to where we were before Kyros rendered a portal, but the air here is thinner. Cooler. Sun filters through the multi-hued leaves, lighting them like a prism of color, and their shadows dance across the deadwood of the forest floor.

When we reach the area where I can touch the tarn's rocky floor, Kyros lets me out of his hold. His hand stays steady, pressed to my low back. I know he said that he brought me here because I needed to escape, but as I watch him out of the corner of my eye, I can see the tension that holds his shoulders tight too.

"Is everything ok?" I can't help but ask him. He takes a deep breath before responding.

"Just thinking." His voice is deep and low, and the crease between his eyes flattens as he gives me a small smile. It doesn't reach his eyes and falls away as quickly as it came.

We are a sopping wet mess when we emerge on land. My blood-drenched clothing is washed pink where it was stained crimson, and it clings to me like a second skin. Kyros pulls his tunic off as I am wringing the bottom of mine out. I feel the blush crawl over my skin as he looks over his shoulder, and I quickly avert my gaze. Heat blazes in my cheeks, and he smirks.

Turning to face the woods that seem alive with their own kind of magick, he keeps his back to me. He is silent for minutes just watching nature. Something about him feels different, like he's lost in his own mind. I leave him to think. I know how it is to have so many thoughts stirring through your mind; you feel as though you are lost navigating the endless static. Sometimes it's best to be left alone to find your way through it.

If I am going to have any semblance of dry clothes when we return, I suppose I too need to hang things to dry. Peeling the fabric from my body, I wring the borrowed tunic out further and then hang it on a low branch. The tree's leaves are like paper gold. A breeze rustles the leaves, and they nearly glisten just as the precious metal would in the sun. A chill rolls over my exposed skin, causing gooseflesh to pepper my arms and stomach as I turn back to face Kyros, with only a band of fabric covering my breasts and the already exposing breeches Cole put me in.

"I was twelve the first time I came to this forest. A year after I lost my parents." Kyros doesn't turn to face me as he begins talking, but I keep my eyes on his back where he stands close to the treeline. The muscles of his shoulders flex in time with his fists at his sides, like the words themselves have caused him pain. I stay silent, letting him continue in his own time. After a few moments, he reaches up, plucking a deep green leaf with orange around its edges, making it look as though it is on fire. He brings it in front of his face, his fingers pinching the stem, and rolls it between them. The leaf spins back and forth, blurring and appearing like he is holding a black flame at his fingertips. It's as beautiful as it is magickal. "Mavros and I lived in Aithne and explored the border but were forbidden to go too far into Diemos. The forest held magick and creatures that we were not yet old enough to protect ourselves against." He drops the leaf, and it flutters to the ground at his feet.

After another moment he turns to face me. His lips part as he sees that I have shed my tunic too. I realized a while ago that Kyros makes me feel seen, but right now, I feel like more than just my skin is exposed to him. I feel like he sees everything—right down to my battered soul—and he is giving me a glimpse through the window at his.

"But you found this place?" I ask, sinking my teeth into my bottom lip as his eyes skate down my body and land back on my eyes.

"It seems like I am destined to find happiness in things that are forbidden." He says solemnly, taking a step toward me. There are feet between us, but it feels like we have never felt closer. I swallow hard. "This way." He offers me his hand, and I place mine in his. Warmth spreads through me as he threads our fingers together and guides me away from the water's edge and further through the trees.

The ground is mostly flat, but as we continue to walk, it does seem to slope upward. The sun filters through the leaves and illuminates the dust particles we stir in our trek. While I watch the glittering specks dance around in my vision, swirling only when my body or Kyros cuts in, I can't help but smile. This whole journey is opening my eyes to so many things I didn't know beyond the castle walls. The world that I always felt was small is now more vast than time and space itself.

"It was the first time I learned I was a render." Kyros' voice startles me out of my reverie, and I stumble over my own feet. He looks back. The hand that he has securely threaded with mine doesn't allow me to fall, and I smile sheepishly as he looks down at my feet. He doesn't comment on my clumsiness. "Mavros and I have always been different. Twins, but polar opposites in everything but the genes we share. We had an argument, and being young near-adolescent men, anger was our outlet. We came to blows. It was the first time we made each other bleed. I caused him to fall down a sharp embankment, and he broke his arm." He stops, seemingly lost in the memory.

"Anyway, after that, seeing him in the infirmary and remembering he was the only family I had left... I felt like something inside me needed to know what it truly felt like to be alone. I needed a reminder not to take advantage of being blessed enough by the divine that my brother and I escaped what was meant to be our fates.

I walked further into the forest than I was ever allowed. Mavros and I just recently learned of our magick. The elders in town were worried about the attention that our markings would bring." As he says it, I look at the black shadows that vibrate along his skin—tattoos when he wants them to be.

"The magick was charged by my heightened emotions, and when I reared back to punch a tree, I unknowingly let the shadows uncoil. When my fist was meant to hit the bark, the shadows whipped out, and my first portal was rendered right there.

I knew of renders, having learned about the magick before my parents passing. It was magick that was said to run in my family, as were the black shadows that mark my skin. It had been generations since all the elements of our magickal line passed to one person. It seems I was the one destined to carry it all." He swallows and looks down at me.

"Mavros doesn't have the same magick? I thought you both had the shadows?" I ask.

"We do. Mostly the same. Much to Mavros' dismay, he is unable to rend portals." He smirks when he catches my lips curling.

"I'm sure he was hell to be around after that. I can't see him taking the news well." I say.

"His ego was big even back then; it could take the hit." He chides, swapping our hands and placing a hand on my low back. He helps me climb as the path we take becomes steeper. "When I rendered the portal there, right in the middle of the woods, I knew that things were about to change. I felt a shift in the air. Almost like I knew my purpose was about to find me. I stepped through the dark arch I had created, not knowing where I was going to come out."

I didn't realize how far up we had climbed until we reached a particularly steep edge, where Kyros had to lift me before he followed behind. My breath catches as I turn around to face him, and I am instead left wide-eyed at the scene beyond where he pulls himself over the ledge. He comes to a stop at my side and slides his arm around my waist. He pulls me in front of him, his arms draped around my body like they were always meant to be there, and leans in so his breath brushes the shell of my ear as he continues his story.

"This is where I stepped through that portal. All this time, I thought that was the moment that the divine deemed me worthy of something greater." I lift my gaze at the same moment that he spins me in his arms. Our gazes collide, and that familiar warmth bursts in time with the fluttering wings in my chest. Like wind making a flame on a candle flutter and crackle, my soul seems to do the same dance. My skin is on fire as the sun crests overhead. The sun showers us with golden light and makes Kyros look like one of the gods given form. "I was wrong." He says, lifting his hand to cup my face, he brings his mouth to hover over mine. My breath stalls in my lungs, waiting for his next words, his next move. I cannot breathe as my thoughts twist and turn into one another, every thought losing meaning. I can only see him.

"The moment you crossed my path in the streets of Eathian, I felt the fault line of my reality shift. Not just the air around me, but the very ground I stood on shook, and every moment since then I have been trying to catch my footing. Trying to get back to where I thought I was meant to be. I don't think I can do that anymore. Watching you with my people, my brother, Zinya? I realized." His thumb brushes strokes along my heated skin, sending prickles of energy through my entire body. I close my eyes. A coward, unable to see his face as he says what I think he is going to say.

"*Don't,*" I say quietly. All my life has been mapped out and ruled by men. He can't be just another. I can't be feeling the same way that he is, just as I have found my freedom.

"Look at me, Shula." I clench my teeth, my brow pulled down taut, and feel tears prickling at the back of my eyes. While I don't want to do as he says, my heart seems to be peering out of the cage it's kept in. The wings that buzz with it are about to burst open the bars to my heart.

I swallow, taking a deep breath, and I do as he says.

When my eyes flutter open and they collide with his. The scent of sweet honey and the bite of fire and smoke fill my senses. He consumes my every breath. He rules my vision. Blocking out even the masterpiece painted by the divine that makes up the scene behind him. He is all that I see, smell, *feel*. The look on his face is like I have stepped right through the divine fire and into the embrace of Runerth. "I am a falling man, and it's only you that I want to be there when I finally hit the ground."

Chapter Forty-Eight

Kyros

THERE IS NO GOING back for me. She may not know every-thing, but this confession gives her *something*. My eyes are lost to the endless moon in her gaze. Her lips part, and the bottom trembles with unsaid words. She doesn't have to acknowledge what I've said. I just want her to be here with me. Everything else will come on its own time.

"I—Kyros," she says with her voice shaking. Everything in me softens around her. Every sharp edge dulls. I give her a sad smile. After everything that I have been through in my life, it's only fitting that I would fall for someone who is meant to be my enemy. Someone whose whole purpose was to take everything I ever cherished away. And now?

She is all-consuming.

The one thing that I don't want to escape. I'm not ready to hear her words. I'm not willing to accept that she doesn't feel the same. How could she?

Cupping her face I press two fingers to her lips, silencing whatever it is she was going to say. Right now I just need her to be here—I'm selfish, but I don't care. I lean in. Slowly dragging my fingers away, I replace them with my lips. Surprising me, she opens herself up, sinking her tongue into my mouth, inviting mine to dance with hers. Her taste floods my senses and lights my blood on fire. My fingers sink into her hair, tilting her head back and giving me more of her.

The moan that releases from her throat has me lifting her from the ground. Her arms wrap around my neck and her legs around my waist while the sun heats my back. She digs her hands further into my hair, pulling it from the tie at the back of my head and letting the strands fall loose. I press her into the flat rock of the mountainside, unable to suppress the groan building in my throat as I grind my hard cock into the center. Thin fabric is the only thing that separates us. She whimpers, and I feel it everywhere.

Our skin sears where it touches. Our bodies seem to meld into one, with hands wandering, gripping, and pulling. I want nothing more than to rip away the little clothing we have covering our bodies and sink into her, but I pause when I feel her hesitate. Her fingers at the tie of my breeches, but she breaks the kiss.

"Kyros," she says breathlessly, and after a moment of deep breaths, I nod. I know what she is saying even without her voice. We need to talk about more than she even realizes, but we are running out of time.

"I know you have questions, and I want to give you all the answers. I do, but Shula, we are running out of time. We have days until we leave. Days of traveling before we have an audience with the Queen of Diemos."

"Are you going to tell me what the man, Karnnen, meant?" The question comes out like a blade. The passion of the fire grows between flashes of the anger and hurt in her eyes. "I will be the death of you? The death of everyone?" She asks, locking her eyes to mine. My jaw clenches hard enough to crack bone, and I take a deep breath.

"I wasn't meant to be a suitor for your father's games." I say, loosening my grip around her and allowing her feet to settle back on the ground. She keeps her hands against my bare chest, and I know she can feel the same pounding beat of my heart as I tell her some truths. "Mavros was meant to be the only one playing his games. I was there to be support." Her blue eyes brighten a little as the sun casts its glow over both of us.

"Something changed?" She asks, the venom in her tone gone, and my lips curl at the corner in a half smirk. *Softening for me, too, Shula? It seems we are both doomed.*

"Everything changed," I say, and pink rushes her cheeks. "The moment I stopped that cranky old skin dealer, Martier..." I can't help but smile at the memory. "When you clearly *did not* need my help." She rolls those bright eyes, and my smile widens before I'm serious again. "I may not have known right away, but there was something. Something I couldn't place. Then again, when we ran into you at the tavern... Something I have never felt before rose in my chest every time I saw you. Every time your wicked mouth bit back at anything I said. You were a wildfire. Reckless and deadly, but like a moth to a flame, I was drawn to you.

I tried to stay away; tried to get Mavros to stay away from you too. I think I knew you weren't who you said you were, but I never imagined you were—well, who you are..."

"The Princess of Eathian. The one your brother was meant to court?" She asks, and I give her a wry smile. My eyes then narrow on hers.

"Something like that." I say, tilting my head as I look at her. A gust of wind blows over the water and crashes into the mountain where we stand. Both our hair are blown across our faces. I shake it from my eyes before I tuck the unruly strands behind her ears. "Truth is, I lost all control when I walked into the palace and saw you at King Connard's side." I say.

"You didn't look like you lost control. It was me who made a fool of myself." The pink blush deepens as she recalls the memory of her shattering the goblet of wine. "I didn't want to lie to anyone. You know that, right? I needed to. I was running from a life I never wanted." My thumb scores a line across her rosy cheek.

"I do. I see that now." Had our pasts been kinder to us both, maybe our future wouldn't be so bleak. I don't tell her that, though. Instead, I kiss her forehead and pull her into me. My eyes shut as she melts into my arms, fitting perfectly in my hold. I swallow hard.

"We have time to talk more on the journey to Diemos. I promise we will talk, but while we are in Aithne preparing for the celebration and your birthday, you will train. Focus on learning what you can. The Creshian Forest can be a dangerous place, and I think it's time we talk to the others about what we are facing with your nightmares." I say resolutely. Astraea chews on her lip. A caw sounds from a distance. I smirk, quickly throwing a glance over my shoulder and then looking back at the wide-eyed look on Astraea's face as she sees Drabek narrowing the distance between us.

She shuffles out of my arms with a screech as the large, Creshian raven lands deftly on my shoulder. I clench my jaw tight as his claws dig into my bare flesh. Drabek doesn't seem to notice my lack of clothes, though, and preens his feathers as he looks her in the eye and tilts his head. Blinking, he surveys the woman I deemed worthy of bringing to this place he knows I frequent alone. Astraea covers her mouth with her hand; her eyes widen as if this feathered creature is more fearsome than the manticore she faced in the dunes. A chuckle rumbles through me, and Drabek leans forward, lifting a lock of her hair with his large beak. He clicks with it several times, hanging the hair loosely in his mouth before dropping it and chittering in approval. As though this was his way of greeting. A gentlemanly kiss to the hand.

"Shula, meet Drabek." My grin widens as her face morphs to fascination. "He likes you."

"He is beautiful." Tentatively, she reaches her hand out just as she did to the beast in the dunes, and usually I would warn someone else not to, but I know without a doubt that Drabek will be accepting of Astraea. Her fingers glide through his feathers, and he fluffs them as soon as her hand retreats. He shakes his large head with a caw. Astraea's face lights up, and she laughs. A truly loud, beautifully joyous laugh, and my stomach tightens. I want to learn all the sounds that can come from her lips. Her gaze finds mine as I watch her, and she blinks, looking at me through her lashes.

"There are depictions of ravens in the palace, I'm sure you saw; they are carved into the great hall doors." She says, and it takes everything in me not to react.

"Yes, I recall the art of them." I say with a shrug, feigning nonchalance.

"I've always loved that art. It's one of the only pieces my father didn't destroy." She says as her eyes catch back on Drabek, who shifts his head back and forth between us. His curious eyes blink a few times at me. I sigh before I run my fingers through his feathers, allowing my shadows to dance and tickle along their lengths.

"It's a blessing from the divine that he didn't destroy it as he did everything else." I say through my teeth so quietly I think she may not have heard me at all, but the words were more for me than for her to hear. There is no way she would understand anyway—not yet. "Drabek, we will be back at the castle in four days' time. Until then I want you to stay close. Keep an eye on things that I cannot." He rubs his head against my offered hand, and Astraea smiles at both of us. "Go." I command, and with a shrill cry, he launches into the sunlit sky and disappears beyond the clouds.

We both watch the clouds for a moment, though I am the first to look away. My eyes are drawn to the woman in front of me. I watch her as I have since the moment she stepped into my life. Still, I don't understand it. The way that fates twist our worlds so impossibly, causing loss, heartache, and destruction only to bring two people together in a way that seems so unimaginable.

Her chin drops, and she is smiling. She could steal every last breath from my lungs with that smile, and I would die a happy man. I lift my hand between us in offering, and she doesn't hesitate.

"Ready?" I ask, and she nods, placing her hand in mine. We walk in silence for a while, back down to the water's edge, but after a bit we fill the silence with plans for the coming days. The trees protect us from the sun and the random gusts of wind that seem to always beat this mountainside. Astraea seems excited to learn to defend herself. We may not have much time to teach her everything, but there is time to teach her some of the basics that could mean life or death, at the very least.

It will bring me peace of mind to know she has the means to protect herself a small amount within the castle walls, too. Once we get to Diemos, I worry about what is going to happen more than I feel concern over the forest, though. Something about the way the Queen reacted to the knowledge of what we found in Eathian doesn't sit right with me. The issue of her nightmares is another concern entirely.

When we reach the tarn, I help Astraea with her tunic, and she leans against a large sun-bleached tree near the water's edge. It lies on its side, hollowed and without bark. The elements of nature have smoothed its surface with time. It's the most at ease I have seen her. Even when she was drinking spirits with the others, I could see the tension she carried. This place seemed to have the same effect on me; it's why I have come here so often over the years.

The pebbles under my feet crunch as I make my way to stand behind her, and she looks up as I place my hand on her shoulder. My finger touches the delicate chain of the necklace she always wears, and my brows pull down.

"Does this necklace mean something to you?" I ask curiously, and her fingers instantly wrap around the pendant that hangs low on her chest.

"It was given to me as a child. The pendant, anyway. I have gone through several chains." She snorts a laugh. "I wasn't the most well-behaved child. Much to my father's displeasure, I tended to get myself into a bit of trouble doing things I was told a princess should not. I found fun in adventure, even when the cost was high. Sometimes I'd do it without thought, and other times... I wanted the punishment. When I made him angry, I would also tend to see him less." Something dark flickers over her eyes then, as though she is recalling one of those instances.

"Where did it come from?" I ask, urging her to tell me about the pendant that continues to cause me to wonder.

"My mother. Well, not directly. My mother passed away when I was just a girl, in the Great War." Emotion seems to clog her throat, and I move around her to sit at her side; she clears it. "Colette's mother was my mother's handmaiden. She was mine for a short time too, but when my mother died and we moved into the palace, he replaced her with another woman. Sienna." She says, her cheeks heating. The name she gave us when she was trying to run. I nod.

"Sienna raised me for the most part, but she was more of a friend as I got older. She never treated me like I was a job. Never treated me like I was anything less than a friend. She taught me about the Neer." She gives me a rueful smile before continuing. "Not until I was older and she knew I wouldn't go running around spewing all the secrets." She sighs before returning her gaze out over the water. Sadness fills her eyes as she recalls this woman who cared for her. I can't help but think of my own mother. "My father killed her." She says, her lips flattening into a line.

"It's not your fault." I find myself saying. It's both me convincing her and confirming to myself it is the case. Nothing about what has happened over the years comes back to the girl who was told she was a princess, even if the crown was dipped in the blood of those she loved.

"Sometimes I'm not so sure." She says, her fingers still wrapped tightly around the pendant. "She protected me. Gave me healing baths that helped with the punishments I would get."

"The scars on your back?" I ask softly, and she nods.

"After one particularly bad punishment, she had brought a woman into the castle, and together they put salves on my back and said incantations over me for healing. After breakfast the next morning my father came to make sure my teachings had been enough..." Her words trail off as she relives the memory.

"It was a healing balm?" I ask, though I can already sense the answer.

"It was the quickest I had ever healed; only now do I realize it must have been magick. I thought there was something in the scent of the balm Mavros gave me, the same balm that Kellan got for Cole's wounds." She swallows hard before continuing. "That breakfast was the last time I saw her alive. By lunch she was hanging in the courtyard, the very place that Cole was whipped. Just like then, I was paraded out to the conservatory, ensuring I would see what I had caused." I reach my hand out and encase hers, pulling it into my lap. I cradle it in mine. She smiles, but it's small and sad. "She said that this would protect me from nightmares... It did for a while. All but one. There was no one who could protect me from my father."

"Protect you from the nightmares? Have you had nightmares since you were young?" I ask now, even more curious as to why this necklace would protect her from the nightmare.

"They weren't much at first, just a feeling of unsettling darkness. Eyes watching through mist. I would wake up anxious, my heart racing. They started after my father took the throne." My brows drop at her confession. If this is who I thought it was and all of this started when her father took the throne... "They were reoccurring. The same nearly every night by the time I turned ten. Sienna was trying everything she knew, but then she recalled the necklace that my mother had left me. She brought it to me, and finally I was able to get to sleep. For years, I would only have the nightmares maybe once a month. They were the same every time, but since I left the palace..." Her brows furrow before her eyes flit to me. "Since I met you, they have changed. They have become more. Fevered. Alive. Urgent."

I can feel my heart racing in my ears, the pulsing causing my vision to dim as my shadows come alive on my skin. I knew Connard was a sorry piece of shit, but everything about the nightmare, the creature I fought off, the way it seems to hunt her. I recall the bruising and claw marks on her neck. It was the necklace. He was trying to remove the necklace.

"Shula, I think your father sold a soul he had no right to barter with. The nightmare—the creature who haunts your sleep? There is only one man who it could be. He is no demon in the pits of Zamiel, but I sure as hell will send him there." I say the declaration through gritted teeth. There is no realm where I will not reach him. The soul he wants to keep for his own already belongs to me.

Chapter Forty-Nine

Kyros

I can tell Astraea is tired, but she said she wanted to start right away with training. I have Mavros running over the basics with her while I do some digging. I need to speak with a few people here in Aithne before we leave. First of all, I need to speak with Rowan. If my suspicion about the nightmare is true, what Karnnen warned me about could explain the urgency Astraea feels from the recent nightmares.

I said I was leaving a while ago, but I can't seem to tear myself away. Instead, I stand in the shadows, just out of sight, under an overhang of one of the buildings lining the courtyard—and I watch. Just as I have since our very first encounter. I grind my teeth as Mavros touches her, angling her body so she knows how to move. He grabs her hips on both sides and makes her pivot away from me. The bastard looks over her shoulder, right where I'm lurking, with a knowing grin. He brings her hands up in front of her and shows her some basic blocking maneuvers, and she catches on quickly. Moving her feet in time with her hands, just as she was instructed. She has surprisingly good reflexes for someone who has never had any training.

"Why aren't you the one training her?" Zinya asks as she casually leans against the wall at my side. People nod their heads in greeting as they pass by. Their eyes also gravitate to the beautiful stranger sparring in the center of the courtyard.

"I have other things to do before leaving." I shrug, and I feel her eyes burrowing into me. I take the bait and drag my gaze away from Astraea. "What?" I ask as she quirks a brow and crosses her arms over her chest, a smug grin on her face.

"Looks like you are doing *so many things,*" she muses. My ignoring her is response enough as I turn my gaze back to the sparring. Mavros stands back with his arms crossed, nodding in approval as Astraea and Colette begin their workout together. Colette surprises me too. It seems she is a natural at hand-to-hand combat. She is quick, her style looking very similar to what Zinya has made her own.

Colette moves fast, throwing a fist out at Astraea. The first time she did this, the hit struck, but this time, Astraea swings her body back in an arch. She creates space between their bodies and quickly earns a hit to Colette's side that would have been deadly had she been wielding a knife. Colette's eyes widen as she is hit in the kidney, and Astraea's grin mirrors my own as I watch.

"You're different with her." Zinya says, and I grunt in response before flattening my lips and pushing away from the wall. Zinya follows suit and keeps stride with me. Before we round the corner, I look over my shoulder, casting one more glance at Astraea, and our eyes collide. She gives me a lopsided smirk, wiping away sweat that has gathered on her brow. I give her a quick nod of approval before continuing my path away.

"Drop it, Zinya." I growl, quickening my stride as I see her about to say more. Her mouth snaps shut, but her lips roll up at the corners nonetheless. She and Mavros have been spending too much time together.

The market is a happening place in Aithne for the Shula Morana. Vendors line the space between buildings. Canvas-covered awnings keep the sun at bay, and people fill the streets selling or buying goods, trinkets, and foods of all sorts. They fill carts and tables hanging from the awnings and even the walls lined with weapons and art.

The Neer people have made this day that was filled with heartache and sorrow into a day to celebrate the lives we lost. We honor those who still live to fight another day with gifts, and we send our prayers and blessings to those who walked through the fire before us. Many of them write their loved ones on parchment folded into little figures and send them through the fire, in hopes they find comfort in knowing we are still here honoring their sacrifice. We are still here, hoping for better days ahead for our people.

Whether or not it is true, it gives people hope. And hope will always keep the ember burning. All it will take is the perfect shift in wind, and that ember is all that's needed to create a blaze of undying fire.

"It's her birthday tomorrow," she says, staring at the side of my head, and when I don't respond, she continues her pestering. "Will you get her a gift?" I stop, giving her a sidelong look before looking at the table setup that holds dried meat. I point to a few selections and buy rations from the dealer manning the cart in near silence, then sling the bag over my shoulder and make my way to the next.

"Shouldn't you be doing something useful?" I ask her with every ounce of annoyance in my tone before walking away again. She grabs my forearm, pulling me to stop and face her. With a flat look, my eyes flick from where she grips me and back to her eyes. It's unlike her to pester. It's unlike her to push me when I have made myself clear I don't wish to talk about it.

"It was a mission to receive an object. That mission changed the moment we realized it was not; don't forget that she is a person. Don't let your stubbornness get in the way of you doing what is right. Change is not always bad, Kyros. Sometimes we have to become something we never thought we would be in order to be the difference the world needs." She gives my arm a slight squeeze, and a small smile brackets her mouth.

"Thank you." I say, covering her hand with mine. That's all I can give her right now. Too many truths and lies are staring at me. Burrowing a hole into my soul. I can't look at all of them at the same time, or I will risk losing myself to it all. "Find Rowan. Let him know I want to have a private conversation before the feast. Just us, him, and Mavros. Make it clear I don't want *any* others privy to the information discussed. I want Tarin to be with Colette and Astraea the entire time. No excuses. It will be a quick discussion, then we all will be able to enjoy ourselves before the journey." She nods, rolling her lips into a flat line.

"Of course. Just think about what I said." She turns away, glancing back over her shoulder one last time, giving me a pity-filled look. The thing is, I don't need to think about what she's said because my decision has already been made.

I watch as she is devoured by the crowd. Her blonde braids and the hilt of the sword at her back are the last things I see of her before I turn back the way I was heading. Slowly, I walk from table to table, soaking in the energy of the people—*my people*. I don't get to enjoy this much. Truthfully, I've never really allowed myself to. I have kept myself busy every Shula Morana since they began, only arriving at the bonfire when everyone else is buried too deep into their own gluttony to notice my presence. I do, however, send my blessings through the flames. It's a tradition I have found comfort in.

The last booth on the street is tucked behind another, its table more scattered than the others. Baubles and gadgets litter a table in an unceremonious way. Dried plants and flowers hang upside down from string in an array of colors and sizes. The sun glints off of a mirror in the corner, its rays reflecting just so on a collection of knives. A robust woman steps in my line of sight, her raspy breathing eating up the space between us.

"What brings a soldier to a table of pretty things?" She croaks, covering her mouth with a rag as she coughs. I recognize most of the vendors here. Maybe not from the market but from the fire lighting and feast that follows. They are nearly all local, some returning yearly just for the festivities, but this one I don't recall ever seeing. Not her nor a table like hers. "Do you have someone you'd like to impress? Perhaps a pretty necklace or ring for a lady to be?" Her knobby fingers run through a section of precious metal chains that hang near the corner of her booth. Each one, a delicate pendant, glints in the sun. None of which catch my eye like the blades on the table just behind her. I shake my head.

"Just passing by." I say, and just as I'm about to turn away, something moving catches my eye. A little boy, probably about five, peeks from below the table's skirt. Yellow snot runs from his nose, and he wipes it on his sleeve. His eyes are red and round, and when the woman coughs again, the wheeze that follows causes me to pause. "I've not seen you here in Aithne for the Shula Morana before; what village do you come here from?" I ask.

The woman swallows, looking around, and then with a heavy sigh, she grabs a rickety old chair and sits. She's quiet for a long moment as she pulls in uneven breaths. She grabs twine and begins braiding a rope around a bushel of dried flowers that are as pink as her cheeks.

"I hail from the cruel city. The outer rim of Eathian. We have traveled some way, stopping only in hopes to refuel ourselves and pay our respects to the royal family who perished in the Great War. I took my life for granted before. Didn't realize that without a fierce leader such as King Kratos and someone as caring as Queen Evren at his side, the kingdom would crumble, taking our lives with it. Every day since has been a struggle, and I fear for my grandson. He is the last of our line when I am gone." She coughs again into her rag. I notice then the deep color caused by use; it is stained red with blood from a deep, ragged cough. It's jarring to hear the fallen kings and queens' names spoken aloud. Not many mutter their names other than in prayer quietly, under breath, or behind steepled hands in fear of what King Connard would do if he heard, but I guess a dying woman doesn't have much else to lose.

"The King and Queen would be honored that you've come to pay your respects. I hope that you join us tonight at the feast. There will be plenty for both you and your grandson." Her gray eyes brighten as I offer her the invitation before her brows crinkle as she looks at me a little closer than I usually like to allow.

"You look like him. You carry the same weight on your shoulders, the same fierce darkness in your eyes. I wished that I might see the day when Eathian was a great kingdom again, but it seems my time is running out. I only hope to get my grandson to the dwellers before the same fate is set on him." I bristle but only acknowledge half of her words.

"The sickness you have, has it spread to him too?" I ask, and she nods just once. Her eyes flicking to the skirt of the table where I had seen the little boy. "I will make you a trade. It will help you with the symptoms until you reach the dwellers in the Creshian

Forest." I pull one of the tins from the pouch at my hip. Her eyes widen, then she blinks fast as she looks up at me tears well in her eyes. "The blades that are behind you. I would like both." Then I take out a few coins and add them to my palm. "If you have a holster for them, I would like that too." The tears that she blinks away roll down her rounded, sunburned cheeks before she coughs, quickly standing and pocketing the bloodied rag. She dips her hands into a saucer of water and dries them on her skirt before turning, revealing the blades that seemed to be calling to me.

"They say that long ago, the material used to forge Tsalalerian steel was imbued with the magick of the divine that killed the sea." She lifts the black glittering blade. Its handle is the same steel but rounded in swirling arches. She places a thick swath of dark fabric on her knees before laying one blade down across it. "The god was angry with the people who sailed his seas. They ravaged the lands they sailed between and caused chaos in their wake. He thought that by drying the sea he would force them to stop... He only slowed them down."

She lifts the second blade, spinning it in a way that shows its beauty from all angles. The sun catches on the clear oval stone at the center of the cross guard, and I couldn't have stopped my lips from parting if I tried. There, cast in resin and forged with time and magick, a small blue flower radiantly lit from within. The flower of the scorpion grass, the same blue as Astraea's eyes.

"He gave a piece of his magick that day—to the land that was drowned in darkness and blood. Legend says the black sands of the Dead Sea became as deadly as the men who once sailed its waters. The glittering shards lingering in its dark surface are the only reminder that the stars are still watching even when they are cast away by the sun. The magick, born of darkness and the heat of the sun, lies dormant until touched by the heat of a flame. There in the fire, where it's forged, is where the magick awakens and becomes a honed weapon, a knife such as these. The divine fire was lost to him when he dried out the sea." She smiles, though there is no light that reaches her eyes. "A legend—a fallacy—a wish that the divine fire would once again be cast on the land and forge a blade strong enough to carve a new path for magick and men."

"Legends have some ounce of truth, though, do they not?" I ask, and at that her gray eyes glitter with that same hope.

"Yes. Yes, I suppose you are right." She says, covering the blades with the thick cloth. She binds it with a string of leather and then reaches into a chest, pulling out a black leather holster with beautiful filigree etched into its surface. It's the perfect addition to hold the beautiful blades.

"Thank you." I tell her as I place both the blades and holster into my bag. "I hope to see you at the celebrations."

"You are kind. Caring. So much like both of them." She tilts her head in reverence, and I incline mine in kind before turning away and heading back through the crowd. Making my way to the stables, I am only stopped a few times by people wanting to sell me baubles or goods. Wanting to offer blessings or support. Though even with minimal stops, it takes nearly an hour to reach them. Finally, I'm greeted with the scent of musty air and hay and the sounds of horses chuffing and neighing.

One of the stall gates slams shut, and a man strides toward me with a muck bucket in one hand and a shovel in the other. His form is backlit by the sun shining in through the other side of the open barn doors; at first glance, I think it's my father walking toward me. It can't be, though. He passed through the divine fire a few years ago now, and my mother soon followed from a broken heart. He was one of the wealthiest men in this village, but you would never know it, judging by the calluses on his hands. Oftentimes this is where I would find him. Khol and Eidola loved him.

"HA! I thought that was you!" Beckett shakes his head, the mop of chestnut curls bouncing with the motion, and a smile like a horned moon stretched out over big white teeth. The corner of my mouth quirks too. It's been a long time.

"It's good to see you." I say, and he wraps his arms around me in a tight hug. The bucket and shovel clattering behind my back. "If you get horse shit on me, I'm going to show you what it's like to muck a stall with your face." I say, and he laughs, letting me go and placing the bucket and shovel at a reasonable distance away. Ignoring my threats, like they mean nothing. He's probably one of the only people in the realm that could. He takes his gloves off and throws them into another bucket that hangs from a hook on the wall.

"You're here earlier than usual. Is everything ok?" He looks around at all the stalls. "Where is Khol? Mav said that you were bringing him and Eidola."

"That was the plan. Things changed a bit on the way. That's actually what I came here for. I wanted to talk to you about supplying some horses for our trip back to Diemos, and I was hoping you had some men who could go retrieve Khol and Eidola from Elysia? I'd feel better with them being cared for here while I handle some important things." I say, lifting a bag of coins between us.

"Your money's no good here. You know that. Father would roll over in his grave if I took money from you or Mavros. Will you be here for the feast then?" He asks with a hopeful glint in his eye. I haven't been to one of the feasts in at least five years. Not since I decided to go down the path I had chosen with the Diemos queen.

"I will be. There is someone I want you to meet." He grins, and I bump him in the shoulder. He's tall, but not nearly as tall as Mavros and me. "Talk to Mav tonight at the feast; we need the horses ready to go the morning after the Shula Morana."

"I'll make it happen." He says with a nod.

"I know you will." I say, taking a deep breath and letting it out as a sigh. One more tense conversation, then we will enjoy the party before we head to Diemos. Where everything will change...

CHAPTER FIFTY

Astraea

I KNOW THAT WE are being kept busy while they discuss the journey to Diemos... Even though I feel annoyed not being a part of the conversation, I can't help but be a little excited for the night. Zinya brought dresses for Colette and me to wear. I've never seen Cole with such a wide smile about a dress that wasn't mine. She stares into the mirror like she is questioning every life choice that has led her here. I can tell her thoughts reflect the same ones I wrestle with as I too stare into a version of myself I barely recognize. *I wish my mother could see me now. I wish she could give me a small smile, words of encouragement—a hug.*

Her hands brush over the smooth linen fabric. It is a design that is much more suited for the cooler climate here on the edge of the kingdom. Not quite the desert heat, but not quite the misty cool mountain air either. The color matches the deep green of leaves in the summer and makes her already green eyes stand out vividly with her red hair. The neckline is heart-shaped, and the back plunges low, nearly all the way to her waist, and thanks to the magickal balm Kellan saved her with, it's unblemished from scars. She looks like a princess.

My eyes flick from her, and for the first time I really look at *me*. She might look like a princess, but I think this is the first time in my life I have ever looked at my reflection and believed I could even resemble a queen. I knew that it was my responsibility to one day become queen, but I always hated the idea. I didn't even dream there could be beauty in it. It was a prison. A punishment for being my father's only heir, but this dress? The feeling of change in the air? I guess it has me seeing things a little bit differently. Perhaps the hope over what is to come is growing.

The dress is thin velvet and a deep, endless black. The neckline is a wide V and low enough to show cleavage but not dangerously so. It leaves my shoulders slightly exposed with only sheer black swaths of fabric capping them. There is embroidered silver-blue stitching along the entire neckline, and it drops down my back like a waterfall. The front panel is solid black but with a slit up both sides, revealing my thighs as I shift or walk.

My waist-length hair falls in loose curls, and Zinya braided the top half in pleats that mimic her usual warrior-like style. My mother's necklace that I usually keep tucked away hangs low between my breasts, accenting the stitching perfectly.

flickering dance toward the stairs, my heart rate increases. I pull my arm out of Mavros' and stop where I stand. He and Cole both look at me over their shoulders.

"Princess?" Mavros quirks a brow.

"I—I just need a second. You guys go ahead; I'm right behind you." I swallow. I can feel him. *I can feel him?* Sweat beads on my forehead, but to my relief Mavros nods. Cole says nothing, but I can see the question in her eyes. "I'm okay. *Promise.*" I nod, whispering to Cole. She gives me a flat-lipped smile before letting Mavros guide her to the staircase, and they descend toward the dining room.

Like a snake coiling around my spine, the hissing call echoes around me. I stiffen. My breaths come as a broken influx of air and an exhale of warm mist.

"SSssseennnkaaaaa...."

"No--" The word barely escapes my throat. A half word, half croak of fear. Squeezing my eyes shut, I press my back against the cool wall. Tilting my head back, I pray to the divine that this is not real. I am fully awake. There is no way that my nightmare has come to life, but I hear that hissing call. Something touches my collarbone, and my eyes snap open. I stifle a scream with my hand covering my mouth. Tears well at the border of my lashes, and the eerie stare of the creature in front of me penetrates through everything.

His long dark claws reach for me in the space between our bodies. The other hand, with sharp, blade-like bones, pins me to the wall. I'm trembling as a tear slides down my cheek. The long point of his finger trails my collarbone slowly, almost sensually, but in its wake a trail of blood paints my skin in beads of crimson. That fire—the lasso of heat that usually wraps around my center—fills my chest, and I take a deep, steadying breath. Bringing my hand to a fist at my side, I grind my teeth and let my lip curl before I hiss back.

"What do you want from me? Who are you?" I demand through my teeth, and he angles his bone-covered face; his menacing, unchanging stare turns, tilting like a predator. Anger rises in me, drowning out the fear as the fire burns behind my ribs. "Leave. Me. Alone." I stand taller, and it brings me closer to his face.

"Senkaaaa," his form dissolves like mist, his one word blown away in an unnatural wind.

"Fuck." I curse in a whisper, bending at the hip, and I hold my stomach as I try to steady my spinning head. Filling my lungs and grinding my teeth, I stand tall, wipe my eyes, and try to reassure myself that I am ok. This will not break me. I am free of my tyrant father. I am working on a better future for myself and my people. *This isn't real.* But just as the thought comes into my mind, I feel a tickle on my chest just above the swell of my breast. Several drops of blood trickle down my skin. My chin quivers, anger causing tears to once again rise. I shake my head, wiping away the crimson stain and then using my dress to hide the evidence. I'm grateful for the dark colored fabric at this moment. I will figure this out too.

Kyros seems to know more than he is letting on. I need to talk to him about everything. I'm done hiding in the dark. Done hiding from my nightmares. I spin on my heel, strength renewed through anger of unanswered questions, and I stomp to the stairs, lifting the skirt of my dress. I get halfway down the stairs before I feel an entirely new presence slam into me.

My eyes snap up and lock with his. He's wearing all black. The collared jacket is much sharper than anything I have seen him in before. His hair is neat and pulled back away from his face, but the unruly waves that usually fall free have already begun to do so. The look he pins me with is so similar to that first night in the tavern, but then, where his face was hard and the shadows lined with questions... Now, his features soften as they take me in.

Kyros doesn't let himself lose control often, but there, in the split second he sees me descending the stairs that he's just starting to climb, he falters. Words linger at his lips as they part, but his eyes drop from mine. They trail my body, and my steps seem to slow to a crawl under his gaze. Such warring emotions stir in me.

The coiling fear the nightmare caused only a moment ago, even while I was wide awake, ceases to exist. Anger of once again being controlled by other people is gone too. Replaced by the rush of fluttering wings and searing heat. Kyros' eyes scale my body like I am the only thing in this world he wishes to conquer. I've always fought through everything. Even silently battling my own will, but with Kyros? He is the only person I have ever felt like I wanted to break for.

His eyes still, the air around us seems to shiver, and shadows peek from the collar, writhing at his throat. I follow his gaze with my own and look down at my chest, where blood continues to bead from the scratch inflicted by claws. The chain of my necklace brushes over the mottled skin, letting the crimson drip down its length in a slow roll. I look up just as he reaches me. One hand holds my arm, opening me up to him, while the other presses firmly into my low back. He holds me still. The muscle in his jaw feathering, he finally finds my eyes again.

"Shula?" He says, his voice low and nearly animalistic. "Why are you bleeding?" I can feel my pulse hammering in my throat, and his eyes fall again to the scratch. I would usually lie. Tell him or anyone else who asked what was wrong that it was nothing, but how can I demand answers from him and keep things in turn?

"It was a nightmare. It just happened for the first time while I was wide awake." My voice shakes, and I swallow. "He said something... It's not the first time I have heard him call out this word... or a name? I'm not sure. I don't know what it means."

"What was it?" He asks, cupping my jaw with the hand that was on my arm. The other one fully wrapped around me now and pulls our bodies flush.

"Senka?" I say with my eyes flicking between his. Trying to read any emotion from this word. His brows drop. Shadows crawl over his face as he presses his lips together. "Do you know what it means?"

"It's a language that is not widely spoken. It means shadowed. The question I have is what it means by that. I spoke with the others, and we think it's best that you are not left alone for sleep anymore... and in light of recent events..." He wipes a trickle of blood away from my collarbone before looking back into my eyes. "I think you shouldn't be alone at all right now. At least until we figure out what he wants." *What he wants?* The question is on the tip of my tongue, and I am about to ask, but Kyros leans down, and my breath seizes.

"You're not going to be hurt again. I won't allow it." He says, his voice is low, and his breath brushes over my lips.

"You've said that before." My thoughts slip past my lips. He narrows his eyes.

"You're right. I failed to see a threat that I should have." He brushes back a loose strand of hair that has fallen in my eyes, and the muscle in his jaw flexes. "I won't fail a second time." He growls through his teeth. My heart rate spikes, his eyes drop to my lips, and mine fall to his. The heat in his gaze brings the kindling in my chest to rise to an inferno, and when his lips finally capture mine, I feel like I am going to combust. My hand lifts to his chest. His pounding heart matches my own.

Even though the kiss was chaste and the moment fleeting, I can't help but linger in the warmth of it. As he lifts his head and looks over my face, a ton of unsaid words cross between us. Colette's words crash into me. *'Happiness looks good on you,'* and at this moment I want nothing more than to allow myself even a glimpse of happiness, undiluted and real.

"Can we do something?" I ask. Kyros has not backed away; his arm still holds me close.

"Of course." He answers immediately. "What do you have in mind?"

"For tonight and tomorrow, until the sun rises on the day we leave... let's forget. Forget who we are, the responsibilities we carry, and who or what we are up against. Let's just be—*happy*." The corner of his lip curls up in a lopsided smile.

"With you? I think that is something I can manage, Shula. Tonight and tomorrow."

Chapter Fifty-One

Astraea

Kyros leads me down the stairs and through the dark halls on our way to the dining room. This house isn't a palace, but it's on a grander scale. Fit for a lord and his lady, most likely. Although there is no art decorating the walls, the quality of the finishes are superior. Carved wood panels create half mandalas every few strides. There are similar wood etchings in rooms in the palace, which makes me wonder if the artist who designed them is the same.

"This place is beautiful," I say as we turn a corner and stand in front of two double doors. It feels strange that there is no one manning the entry. There usually is in the palace, but I have to remind myself of where I am. I can hear the feast has not waited for our arrival. Boisterous celebrating is already taking place within; the energy seems to leak from the cracks of the door along with the light. As soon as we are close to it, I look up and smile at Kyros.

"Thank you," he says, surprising me. My brows drop and my smile falters. *Thank you?* I am about to ask what he means when a man walks up behind him. His hand clamps down on Kyros' shoulder.

"There you are! I've been looking all over for you. No one believes me that you are—oh, this must be her, huh?" The man is young, likely just a little younger than me; nineteen, maybe twenty. The hair on his chin is patchy, and he smells like ale, hay, and black pepper. Kyros smirks, wrapping his arm around the young man's shoulders.

"Princess Astraea, I'd like you to meet my brother, Beckett. He is the one throwing the feast tonight. Beckett, this is Princess Astraea Casimir of Eathian." Kyros says with an uncharacteristic smile. Oh. Brother? I guess now the thank you makes more sense... This is Kyros' childhood home. I look between the two of them, a polite smile pulling my lips up at the corners as I try to see the resemblance. Marvros and Kyros may look similar in features, while starkly different in many other ways. This younger man looks nothing like either. His skin is reddened by the sun, not bronzed like theirs, and his red-brown hair is a curly mop on top of his head. Kyros' smile widens as he realizes the puzzle I am trying to piece together.

"He is our adoptive brother; Beckett was conceived just a few years prior to our parents taking us in. He was just barely beginning to talk then; now he barely shuts up." Beckett makes a face at Kyros' words, and my smile grows.

"Do you have to say it like that? Conceived?" He makes a puking sound in the back of his throat, and Kyros shakes his head with a look of brief annoyance. Though, it's the least threatening reaction that I've seen on his face since I've known him.

"It's very nice to meet you, Beckett," I say just before loud cheering breaks out within the dining room, startling me. It sounds like there are hundreds of people inside, and it distracts me enough that I jump a little again when Beckett takes my hand.

"The pleasure is all mine." He says, before he kisses the top of my knuckles. He looks up and winks just like Mavros, and I can't help but laugh. "Damn, a laugh like that will make your di—Oof!" Kyros throws his fist into Beckett's stomach, and he drops my hand. The boy is laughing, though, doubled over even, holding his middle and wheezing for air, but clearly not in too much pain.

"Watch it, Beckett." Kyros says with a smirk, coming to stand at my side. His hand slides right to the small of my back as though it was always made to fit perfectly there.

"It's fine." I press my hand to his stomach, and all of our eyes drop to the movement. Kyros meets my gaze again, and I hear Beckett let out a low whistle.

"Well, that's something I've never seen." Beckett laughs, pulling my attention back to him. "I never thought I would see the day that someone shut you up, touched you, and they kept their hands."

Kyros lets out a sigh, shakes his head, and wrenches open the door to the dining room. The noise floods the mostly quiet hallway, and Beckett is the first one to walk through, completely ignoring the glare pinned to the back of his head.

"He's—" I start to smile and look at Kyros.

"A pain in the ass." Kyros finishes for me as he pulls my arm through his.

"I was going to say sweet, and a bit amusing." I roll my lips in, a poor attempt at hiding just how amused I am. Kyros shakes his head, takes a deep breath, and blows it out his cheeks.

"In an annoying way... I suppose..." His lips curl up as he looks down at me, and the low light of the room reflects within his irises. For the first time I notice the deep spice coloring of his eyes. Not black, but a bottomless rust, like an ember just barely kept alive by a motionless wind. The deepest amber. He clears his throat, looking away when he catches me staring, and my gaze drops with heat rising to my cheeks.

Kyros doesn't comment on my embarrassment if he notices but guides me through the room of rowdy people. Most of which have had far more to drink than they should, judging by the clear disarray around us. Despite the chaos, everyone still smiles. It's such a strange sight to be at a dinner party that is filled with this much true happiness rather than stiff conversations and forced friendship.

Nothing about the room is like any of the dinners my father hosts. The room is broken into bubbles of tables and people. Each round table is surrounded by chairs, and a feast lies in the center.

People pile dishes high with an assortment of colorful dishes. Their plates are steaming, and the multitude of scents waft from them with every passing. Kyros guides me through the room to a darker corner. He sits in the chair next to me and gestures to the plethora in front of us, and while I load my plate, I feel his eyes on me.

We eat without much talking as we watch the Neer people enjoy the night. There are so many people; I know it can't be just those that live here. Yet, I still have not seen anyone I know. I am about to ask Kyros where the others are when I hear Mavros laugh from behind me.

"Well, fuck me sideways and—"

"Another word, I'll rip out your tongue." Kyros interrupts Mavros. The latter just smiles wide between us before settling on me.

"Well, Princess, you sure look beautiful." He extends his hand, and I turn and take it. His grin turns devious before he gives a playful wink at Kyros. He then pulls me from my seat, spinning me into his arms just as he did at the palace. "I think you need to dance."

"Mavros!" I gasp, scolding him, as I nearly fall, but it's half-hearted and ineffective through my laughing.

"Careful, princess, it almost sounds like you're having fun." Mavros whispers in my ear, and it makes my brows drop. Just as I think that he's right and maybe I *shouldn't* be feeling this way, my eyes snag on Kyros. He's watching us as he talks to Zinya, Colette, and Viltarin. It's the uncharacteristic smile on his face that makes me think of the promise we made each other to forget everything we have to face when we leave here. It's like I feel a heaviness lift from my chest, and for the first time in my life, I truly breathe.

That small reminder was enough. I let Mavros pull me further into the celebrating bodies. Every one of them dancing with a smile on their faces. Even though they lost so much, many of them *everything,* they can still celebrate that very day. Before long, I find that my worries have taken less space in my mind, and I am laughing at the jokes that Mavros whispers in my ear with each twirl or dip.

Time means nothing.

Mavros is a good dancer. He keeps my feet moving for what could have been hours. I'm out of breath, could use some wine, and probably a moment to relieve myself. My face hurts with how much I have been laughing as he spins me off from person to person. A new dance partner every few minutes before being spun back to him.

"Having fun, Princess?" He laughs, and I nod my head. I am for once. "Looks like your escort is getting anxious to get you back." He says with a tilt of his head. I follow his line of sight, and sure enough, Kyros stands close, just at the edge of where people have made this the dance floor. The music slows, and with one last spin, Mavros sends me twirling right to his brother.

"Mavros!" I gasp as I slam into Kyros' chest. He wraps his arms around my waist and keeps me flush to him so I don't fall. I look up to meet his eyes. "Hi," I squeak like a caught mouse.

"What did I tell you about another man's name on your lips when you are breathless, Shula?" Kyros' voice is low, so low that the vibrating rumble echoes through his chest and into me. My nipples harden as my cheeks flame, remembering what happened the last time he told me that.

"I don't think there is anything you can do about it here... chivalrous one." I tease. I can feel the eyes on us and hear the whispers. Just like his younger brother said, the way Kyros lets me push him is not usual of him. The others seem to take notice, and even though I know too, I do it just to see how far I can. The way he looks at me, I realize, is exhilarating and wakes something that has been long dormant. I tilt my head, waiting for his next move.

"You forget that I can rend a portal right under our feet and take you anywhere I wish." He nearly growls.

"I'm not afraid of you." My voice betrays me, coming out as a whisper, and his eyes darken into black diamonds, reflecting the candles in the sconces on the walls. I may not be afraid of him, but I am terrified of the way my heart flips every time I look at him and he looks back. "Even if I was, wasn't it you who told me not to hide from my nightmares?" He smiles at my question, and it's wicked and beautiful and heats every part of my skin. My lips part as he leans in close.

I am an unwed princess; I shouldn't be anywhere near as close as I am to him, especially in public, but yet I feel myself leaning in. The skin along my arms tickles, and I look down to see his shadows beginning to seep from his dark clothing like an evaporating moisture in the heat that seems to be ever-growing between us. It reaches for me and caresses the skin along my arms that are bent between us. Even though magick such as this is completely new to me, I feel at ease. As though the darkness that it is matches something that lives in my soul and wants to mingle and play with it.

It slides along my chest and the column of my neck. Kyros watches with fervor as he trails the dark tendrils across my skin without a care that so many eyes linger on us. My head tilts back as the shadow curls like a finger, lifting my chin.

"Your heart is telling me otherwise, Shula." His breath puffs out over my lips, and the scent of whiskey tickles my nose.

"My heart is a fickle beast." I smile, dropping my eyes to his lips.

"Oh? I think your heart knows precisely what it wants." He whispers the words into my lips. I close my eyes because at this moment, I know that he is right. Every time I am near him, my eyes track his movements. My heart races in anticipation of his touch. My insides are warm, and my skin comes alive. He evokes a sense of power and strength I forgot I even had. Everything that he said to me as we watched the sun paint the sky floods me, and I realize that it's the power he holds over me that I fear the most.

All my life I have been under the control of a man who wanted nothing more than to break everything about me. I've been locked away and only ever been taught what it was he was willing to let me learn. All those years that my father ruled over my life and the lives of everyone in Eathian, he unknowingly taught me more than he could have imagined. I've learned what it is I never want to be. I learned that pushing violence and fear is not how I would ever want to lead people, and I've learned that just because someone shares blood with you doesn't mean that they share the same values. He taught me what it is to have everything, yet feel as though you have nothing, but it's through all of this, he taught me to love.

Not in the conventional way, but in everything that he didn't do. He taught me to see a person, not for the words they speak, but for their actions; for how they treat those around them; for how they treat me.

Kyros has been unkind, rude, and downright annoying, but one thing has stayed consistent through it all. He has pushed me out of my comforts. He has built up strength, resilience, and fight within me, which I thought my father had beaten out. He has shown me that he can love.

"Kiss me." The words barely slip from my lips before he takes them. His tongue dives into my mouth, and mine meets his in a clashing dance of dominance. I don't notice anything that is happening around us. I feel nothing but the searing line that his touch makes as his hand slides up my spine and he pulls me impossibly closer. When the kiss finally breaks, I slowly become aware of my surroundings. Colette's shocked face is the first I see as her eyes bulge wide. Mavros grins from ear to ear, and Zinya has a look of worry pinching her features.

"I think it's time we call it a night." Zinya says. I feel like I am a child who was just caught doing something she shouldn't have been, and I guess in a way it's true. "It's a big day tomorrow." Zinya continues pinning that glare at Kyros.

Tomorrow.

The day I was supposed to marry.

The day that celebrates the death of my mother.

The day that celebrates my birth and the downfall of a kingdom that was once loved.

"She's right. You need to get some sleep. One of the things that we discussed in our meeting was that you are not to be left alone. Zinya will be staying with you and Colette tonight. I know we talked about only letting go of our responsibilities until we are on the way to Diemos, but I won't leave you unprotected while you are sleeping—not after everything." Kyros says, stepping into me. I know he senses a fight coming back about this, but for once I agree. I don't want to be left alone and feel much better about having Zinya and Colette there. I pull my lip between my teeth and nod. Tomorrow is going to be an emotional day, and I would rather spend the night gathering my strength rather than trying to pick up the pieces of the aftermath.

"You're right." I say, pulling a surprised look across Kyros' face. Kyros takes my hand, squeezes, then nods to the others before guiding me from the dining room. I just hope that the nightmare stays at bay, that tomorrow is better than it's ever been, and that I can get through every one of these new emotions.

Chapter Fifty-Two

Astraea

I lay awake, my eyes trained on a small crack in the ceiling above me for what feels like hours. Kyros walked me to the room that I now share with Cole and Zinya and then left us to speak with his brother. Cole snores lightly just inches from me, but Zinya has yet to sleep. She sits in a chair angled so she can see from the window overlooking the town. We stayed in the house the feast was held in. Kyros said he would be sleeping just next door. None of this has brought me peace of mind. When we were busy and surrounded by others, it was easy to forget for a while what I am about to face. What I have already been facing...

"You are supposed to be sleeping." The chair creaks as Zinya leans forward, whispering in my direction.

"So are you," I say, pushing myself up to sit.

"I'm acting guard dog, remember?" She smiles, but it's quick and falls just as fast as it came. She stands then, walking to the window and dropping her brows. I wouldn't be able to see her at all if it weren't for the moonlight filtering through the window. The full moon casts the sky in silver, lighting her face and hair in an aura of pale light.

"I can't sleep. Not with my mind running away with me." Something about Zinya has always made me feel at ease, and now, in the dark, I feel like I can let my walls down.

"Are you afraid of the nightmare coming back?" She asks without turning to face me. I think about her question for a moment before I shuffle, sitting up fully.

"No, to be honest, he does scare me. I feel more curious than I do afraid." I swallow hard as I try to muster up the real reason I feel so weary.

"Curious... I can understand that. Kyros would hate to hear it." She finally looks over her shoulder at me and continues, "Don't worry, your secret is safe with me. He has plenty of his own." *Don't I know it.* Swinging my legs from the bed, I look down at Colette sleeping peacefully in the bed we were sharing. It's so different from how our lives were just weeks ago. She's safer here, and even with all of the unknown, I'm beginning to think I am too.

"Is the energy the same for the feast as it is for the bonfire?" I ask, coming to stand at Zinya's side. The trees at the border of town reach into the sky like serrated teeth in the mouth of a monster—pitch black and dangerous. Or maybe it's just my thoughts about the danger of the journey through their darkness that causes them to seem so ominous.

"No, but I'm sure it's nothing like you are used to in the palace." Zinya says, looking at me with a sad smile.

"I know you have no reason to believe me, but I don't condone anything my father has done with Eathian. I lost just as much during that war as many others did. Even though the people see that I gained a crown, it has felt more like a noose." I don't look to see how she regards me after that statement. I keep my eyes trained on the vicious skyline. I can't take whatever judgement is surely in her eyes.

"I don't think there is anything you could say to prove to me that you are anything like your father, Astraea. I think anyone who has spent *any* time with you at all could tell that." She says, and I chance a look at her. She's not looking at me, though. The look on her face is unreadable as she stares through the window. My mind immediately begins to wander to my mother and the life I lost the day my father destroyed so many. "You really should get some sleep. Morning will be here before you know it, and after the celebrations, we will leave for Diemos." She says dejectedly.

We both stand there silently for a long moment before I finally let out a heavy sigh.

"You're right." I nod before crossing the room and returning to my side of the bed. Cole grumbles in her sleep, tossing the blankets as she flips to face the other side. Zinya stands stoically still, looking out the window. I'm curious about what she is thinking, but I choose not to ask. She is likely thinking about all she has lost, too. Instead, I let my head rest on the pillow, and I find the same crack in the ceiling and try to force my eyes to lose focus and fall asleep.

It doesn't work. I lay there for what feels like hours. Once Zinya sat back down in the chair, I think she must have fallen asleep because the room is eerily silent with no movement at all. Clouds linger thick in the sky and cover the moon's glow, making the night darker than usual with a full moon. It's probably not good that there is so much cloud cover with the journey we have ahead of us. Clouds mean rain, and rain means more issues with travel. I just hope that we can find shelter under the tree's canopies. There's one thing that we can at least be thankful for, I suppose. We are not going to be in the harsh desert for this journey. It doesn't mean it will be easier.

The door creaks as it opens, and I hold my breath as my heart jumps into my throat. I know who it is as soon as his silhouette is outlined by the low light from the hall. I keep my eyes open and on him as he crosses the room. He first walks over to Zinya, gently lifting a blanket from the end of our bed and laying it over her sleeping form. It's such a stark difference from the way he usually is—all sharp edges and hard lines. The softness he's showing is clearly something he doesn't much allow to be seen. He looks around the room for a moment, takes a deep breath, and I feel rather than see the tension leave him. He blows the breath out in a heavy sigh before silently coming toward the bed. Like a coward, I close my eyes to hide that I'm awake. He gets closer, and his scent clouds around me. Whiskey and charred oak, summer sun and the darkest night. Sin and fire.

"I know you are awake, Shula." He whispers, and I feel his breath puff out over my cheek. I open my eyes, and he smiles just inches from my face. I roll my lips between my teeth to try to hide my returning smile and trap the laugh from coming out.

"What are you doing in here?" I whisper, trying to get my eyes to focus on his darkened face.

"Well, I came in to check on all of you, but it looks like I needed to relieve Zinya, seeing as she has uncharacteristically fallen asleep on duty." He stands to his full height and offers his hand to me. I look at it for a moment before I let my hand slip into his, and he pulls me to sit. My bare legs fall from the side of the bed, and his eyes immediately drop to them. His tongue juts out, wetting his bottom lip before his eyes meet mine again.

"What are we doing?" I ask, fighting the urge to pull the blanket to cover my skin.

"I have something for you." He says, and my brows dip in confusion.

"So you come to get me out of my bed in the middle of the night so you can give me something?" I half laugh as I place my bare feet on the ground. Kyros watches every movement I make, slowly trailing his eyes from my toes to my eyes.

"Yes, I suppose. I didn't plan to. I really was just coming to check on you."

"On us?" I ask as a correction.

"On you." He answers simply, then again offers me his hand. I don't hesitate this time and let him pull me fully from the bed. He guides me toward the door, and I stop suddenly as he begins to pull it open.

"Kyros, I can't go out there like this! I won't have another embarrassing situation again, barely dressed." I hiss quietly through my teeth.

"No one will see you. We are going one door over. Come on, Shula. I promise, I'm sure I care more about other people not seeing you like this than you do." He opens the door wide and pulls me into the hall before I can argue again. I can nearly feel the smug satisfaction radiating from him as he opens the next door down the hall and pushes inside. I look both ways down the empty hallway before I, too, step into the room. Unlike the light grays in the room I was in, this one is swathed in darkness. Deep umber, amber, and bronze accents coat the room in luxury, and the scent is immediately familiar. A lantern on the dark wood desk is the only thing lighting the space, as the windows are covered with thick fabric that doesn't allow any light to seep through.

"This is your room?" I ask, even though it's obvious. Heat rises up my neck as I look at his bed, like I am some innocent virgin. I grind my teeth as I turn away from the center of the room and let my eyes roam the walls instead. Walls that are floor-to-ceiling shelves filled with endless leather-bound books. Kyros lights a narrow candle from the lantern and walks the walls, lighting multiple sconces, and my lips part as I truly take in the beauty of the room.

My fingers automatically come up and trail across the spines of the alluring tomes.

"It is." I jump slightly at how close he is. He wraps his arms around me from behind, and I melt a little into his warmth. We are still forgetting our responsibilities, I remind myself when I start to try to pull away. We haven't been this alone without the looming possibility of all hell breaking loose ever, and while I guess there is still a way that could happen, it brings my heart to pound in my chest.

"Kyros," I move to turn around, but one of his hands drops and then comes back to my stomach, and he presses something hard there.

"Happy birthday, Shula." My heart skips several beats as my hands come up to cover his and whatever he holds wrapped in a swath of fabric. He lets me take what's placed in my hands and steps back when he finally allows me to turn around. I look down at what I hold, which is surprisingly heavy, and then up to him with my brows pinched.

"You—got me a gift?" I ask, blinking away my confusion.

"It's your birthday. Is it not accustomed to give someone a gift on their birthday?" He asks, tightening his hand into a fist, and he cracks the knuckles before he rubs at the back of his neck. "It's just something I saw in the market. It reminded me of you." He pauses. I think this is the most uncomfortable I have ever seen him. Clearly out of his element, my brows dip further, and my lips twitch into a small smile.

"Thank you, I—it's just unexpected." I say as I begin pulling the fabric away. My eyes widen when the first glimmering blade reveals itself, followed by its twin. The body of the blade is Tsalalerian Steel, glittering black like the sands we just came from. I run my finger across the flat edge toward the handle, where at the pommel of the hilt holds a resin circle encapsulating a dainty, yet ethereal blue flower. They are stunning and light, and the sharp edge so undeniably deadly. The steel itself seems to radiate power, humming under my touch.

"How do they feel?" Kyros asks as I walk over to a small table by the settee and place the fabric and holster down. I grip the handles, one in each hand. The weight is balanced perfectly in my palm. Mavros and Zinya have taught me some basics with knives of similar size, and I hold these just the same. One in a hammer grip and the other reversed, ready for both offense and defense. Kyros' eyes brighten as he steps back again, fully assessing me, and I suddenly feel very exposed.

"They are a perfect fit." I say, meeting his eyes. "Thank you."

"Good. I hope you won't need them, but I want you to be as prepared as you can be in the short amount of time we have." He answers. Thick silence lingers between us. Questions that I've asked, and answers he's left unsaid. I turn away and place the knives back in the fabric on the tabletop. "Why haven't you slept?" He asks, and I turn to face him.

"No matter how much I tell myself I can wait to worry until after we leave here, I can't. There is just so much to worry about. When I decided to run away from the life I was a prisoner to, I never imagined that I would be running into anything like I have. It's all so unexpected—it's all so much bigger than I imagined. I thought I was running away, but now? Now I feel like my life before is just chasing me into the next. What difference can one person really make? What kind of change can one person bring?" I chew the skin on my lip as worry eats at me. Kyros remains silent as he lets his stare burrow into me. He takes a slow, deliberate step toward me, and I swallow; heat fills my chest and pools lower with the same ferocity I see blazing in his eyes.

"Well..." He says, his voice gravelly as he takes another step, closing the distance between us. "You've changed everything for me." My breath halts as he slowly slides his hand over my hip and around my waist, lying it flat on the small of my back. Right in that curve that seems to have been made for his hand. My heart takes up a rhythm so quick, I feel as though it has grown wings and flutters every time he is around, and currently, it's trying to escape its confines to take flight right between us.

"Surely, that can't be true." I say, and it tastes bitter on my tongue. I feel the changes he has brought in me; perhaps it's time I accept that I too have changed more than I realize for him too.

"I see it. You are not what I expected. As I told you before, yet here I am again, like a moth to a flame come to burn." He says as he rubs his fingertips in small circles on my spine.

"What do you see?" I say in a hushed tone.

"Everything, Shula. I see all of you. Your ability to stay strong through everything you have endured. Even if I know but a fraction of it, I know enough to know you are worth every challenge that lies ahead." His hand pushes into my hair at the nape of my neck, and he tilts my head up as he leans in close. His breath is warm as it caresses my face. His lips hover, barely touching mine, and they tremble as he closes the small space between us. "You are everything I see now."

Chapter Fifty-Three

Kyros

I've fallen for the enemy's daughter. I hold her gaze and watch her lips part in that delicious way I've come to crave. She trembles slightly in my hold, but I can see in her eyes it's not fear of me or this embrace we find ourselves in. It's anticipation for what could come. I let my thumb score a path across the line of her jaw and tenderly bring my lips to hers. The first brush of them is a question; the second, a promise. She pushes forward, accepting everything I am giving her.

My grip on her tightens as I pull her to me. Giving in to every urge I have been resisting. I pull her from the floor, and her legs swiftly wrap around my waist. I can feel the heat from her barely covered core already, and the sudden influx of breath she pulls in tells me that she can feel just how hard I am pressing against my breeches. Her hands come up, fingers tangling into my hair as the once gentle kiss becomes fevered. We are both breathing hard, and she yelps when I slam her back against the shelf on the wall. A few tomes fall from above and crash to the floor. She laughs, and I devour the sound of it with a ravenous growl. I palm her ass in a bruising grip, fingers digging into flesh, and I nip at her lips.

"Kyros," My name is a plea breathed between ragged breaths; her head falls back against the shelves, and I make my way down her neck, sucking, biting, kissing, tasting. Then we are kissing again. Her hands come to the ties at the neck of my tunic, and she pulls them apart. The fabric splitting with a loud rip. She freezes, then looks at me in shock at what she did, and I can't help the wide smile that splits my face.

"Careful, Shula. You are inviting your demons out to play." I barely recognize my own voice. The deep aching need coating it is entirely new.

"I have run from demons my entire life. You are one I *want* to be caught by." Her voice is husky. Thick with both emotion and lust. Her eyes are heavy as they flick back and forth between mine, churning like a storm I want to get lost in. I shift her weight in my arms, and hands clasp around my neck as I turn toward the bed. A sliver of moonlight shines through the barely parted thick drapes, cutting through the dark bedding like a sharp blade. I lay her down gently, easing my body over hers. The moonlight barely reaches her face, lighting across her eyes, but there in that moment,

I'm reminded once more of the tiny blue flower. The deadly beauty lying before me, just as the scorpion grass in the dark recesses of the forest. She has no clue the hold she has on me.

She has no idea the lengths I would go to protect what is mine. Whether she knows it or not, she is mine. The divine have cursed her to that fate, and there is no getting out of it for either of us.

Her hand trails down my neck, the other one still tangled into my hair at the nape of my neck. She pauses over my exposed chest; my shadows writhe with each caress she gives. I shudder, causing her to lift her eyes to mine. The way my magick responds is like it's reaching for her. It wants to embrace her just as much as I do.

"Touch me," she says as her eyes fall back to my chest, where her fingers run through the patch of hair over my sternum. They trace the small scars that litter my skin and slow to a halt over my pounding heart. I sit up, looking down at her body beneath me, and pull my tunic over my head, tossing it to the floor. She's wearing a thin slip, undergarments that barely cover anything, and her nipples peak as she squirms and arches her back. The hard tips press against the silky material, and a groan slips past my lips as I look at her, fists clenched. She doesn't have to tell me to touch her. I will learn every inch of her skin with my hands. I will taste every part of her, but right now my eyes are starving and devouring everything she is offering.

"Was the princess not taught patience?" I ask teasingly, and she squirms more. I lean forward over her, my leg pressing firmly between her thighs. I drag my finger over her plump lips, letting them fall apart as I do. She tilts her chin up, urging my touches to make a path down her neck and to the valley between her breasts. My finger gets caught on the pendant she always wears, and my shadows pulse with the contact. Similar to the feeling of the Tsalalerian Steel or the sand I've kept close to me since leaving the Dead Sea. I eye it speculatively, but my attention is snared by the goddess beneath me when she arches her back with a moan. Her core grinds on my leg for friction, and I smile.

"So needy." I playfully chide. "Tell me, Shula, should I return the favor of you destroying my tunic?" She gasps as I don't give her time to answer and rip the delicate fabric down the center. A growl builds low in my throat as I look down at her nearly bare to me.

"Are you trying to scare me again?" She asks, breathless and panting. "I told you, you don't scare me." I chuckle darkly, licking my lips, and letting my hand trail down her exposed skin, slipping the tip of my finger beneath the hem of her undergarment. Her breaths shake as she watches me tease the skin in the hollows of her hips with a feather-light touch.

"Your heart beats to the same rhythm either way, Shula." I say, and her brows drop just slightly, but I distract her. Covering her pert nipple with my lips, I suck it into my mouth. Another beautiful gasp fills the silence of the night around us, and I smile with the pink bud between my teeth.

"Great divine, Kyros!" She groans, digging one hand into my hair and the other into the bedding.

"Mmm, I like the sound of that. You want to worship me, Shula?" I let my mouth explore both of her breasts, tugging with my teeth on one and rolling the bud of the other between my fingers. When I finally claim her mouth again, she's nearly begging for me to give her attention elsewhere. Reaching down, I pull at the ties on my breeches, shuffling out of them while I claim her mouth amorously.

Part of me knows I should stop this. That same part knows that when she realizes the truth of all of this, it will only hurt her, but the other part... The part of me that is selfish wants nothing more than to claim her and ask for forgiveness later. She is mine whether she knows it yet or not. There would be no world where she could be taken from me. Not now.

She reaches between us, and this time I let her find what she is reaching for. She rubs her palm along my length, and I grind my teeth together and let my eyes roll back as I close them. Her hand glides up my shaft and circles the sensitive tip, creating a quake to rack my body with a jolt of pleasure. Her hand feels perfect wrapped around me. Pumping slowly in soft strokes.

"If we do this... There is no going back, Shula." I warn her between urgent kisses. She pulls me back down, crushing my lips to hers again before she hisses her response into my mouth.

"I don't want to go back."

"Will you accept my claim on you?" I ask seriously, pulling back so I can look into her eyes.

"You would claim me?" The moonlight flickers as clouds pass over its glow and casts her face in a moving shadow. Her cheeks are flushed and her hair pools out around her like a spilled inkwell. She is devastatingly beautiful and oblivious to the fact that she is already mine. Of course I would claim her. Since the moment I laid eyes on her, I knew, though I didn't want to accept it. It wasn't in the plan. *She* was never the plan, but even as I fought it—*I knew.* I would always choose her. This would always be our future because there would never be anything that stood in the way of me claiming the person who is the other part of my soul.

My twin flame.

"I would claim you in every life—*Always*, Shula." A question shadows her eyes, but she doesn't speak on it. Instead, tears gather along her lashes. I cup her face, hoping the truth in what I'm about to tell her is clear in my eyes. "No matter what happens next, you are mine, Shula. I will never let you go." She nods, accepting my proclamation. "I want to hear you," I say, as I move fully between her legs. Each of her knees rests at my hips, and I rub my hand up her bare thigh and back down again as she takes her time drinking me in. Her lips part, and her tongue juts out before she swallows and finds my eyes.

"I will accept your claim." She says, and my brow twitches just the slightest in question, wondering what she knows about claiming with the Neer people... What it means to be claimed or to accept a claim.

We stare into each other's eyes for a long moment, both of us acknowledging what we are doing, but I am the one who breaks our stare. I drop my mouth to her throat, licking, sucking, and nipping my way along it. Reaching between us, I let my fingers slide between her legs and groan at the wetness I find. She pulls at my shoulder, digging her nails into me, wanting me to give her more with my hand. I circle her clit with a slow, even pressure, before slowly sinking two fingers into her opening. She moans into my mouth, and I can't help the animalistic growl I release as I trap her clit with my thumb.

She rocks against my hand, helping me pump my fingers in and out, and as her breathing gets shorter and quicker, I up the rhythm. Using my thumb to keep the friction right on her clit. She tightens around my fingers, her whole body tensing. I know she is close... I remove my thumb, slowly pulling my fingers out of her, and she slumps, letting out a long breath. I grin at her, though she keeps her eyes closed.

I return to using my fingers to circle her clit when her eyes finally open and she is once again looking at me. A few slow, tight circles and she writhes. Her lips part as I continue to build the friction the way I have learned she enjoys; her chest rises and falls with heavy breaths. A moan builds low at first, then I plunge my two middle fingers into her roughly, keeping pressure on her clit with my thumb. Her eyes fly open as her moan is forced from her. I curl my fingers, pumping, using the heel of my hand now as she rides my fingers. Her fingernails dig into my skin, leaving crescent grooves with how tightly she grips me.

When she begins closing her eyes again, I slow. A wicked smile spreads across my face. I can see the frustration on hers, but when she finally opens her eyes again, I continue my torture. I want her to watch me make her come. I want her to know who controls her pleasure. When I do the same again, she catches me smirking.

"You are a monster!" She grinds out through a smile.

"You are stunning when you are flustered, Shula." My grin spreads as her eyes narrow on me. "I want your attention on me. Watch me bring you over that edge." I say and her hooded gaze once again glazes over with pure need. She drops her legs open, and I sit up fully, taking in her spread out and bared for me, my cock just inches from her entrance.

I sweep my fingers through her parted lips, gathering her wetness, and I stroke myself with it. The tip of my cock is already glistening with its own moisture, and I roll my thumb over it with a growl before returning my attention to her. She palms her breasts as I enter her again with my fingers. This time she meets each thrust with a roll of her hips that makes me ache. *You are playing with fire, Shula.* I work her clit, pumping my hand, fucking her with my fingers while she keeps constant eye contact with me. When she begins tensing and I know her orgasm is near, I up the pace. She keeps her gaze held with mine this time. Her mouth falls open, and a moan unlike the others tumbles from her lips as she squeezes me with her inner walls. I let her have her pleasure. Wringing it from her with a curl of my fingers and pumping harder and faster.

"Fuck," I say, as she squeezes me with her thighs, and with my other hand, I grip my cock. I can't hold off any longer. Leaning over her body, I remove my fingers and line myself up with her entrance. Searching her eyes, I wait there for a moment. My loose hair is falling into my face, and she reaches up, tucking it behind my ear and running her fingertips along the stubble on my jaw.

"Claim me." She says with finality. I clench my teeth as I press the head of my dick against her warmth. She braces herself with a deep breath, all the while keeping her eyes pinned to mine. Achingly slow, I push into her. She sucks in a sharp breath when I am about halfway, so I let her adjust, pumping in and out a few times slowly. She feels so fucking good. I feel her walls relax, inviting me in deeper, and I push in further with each thrust.

"Fuck, you're perfect." I say when I'm fully seated within her. She rolls her hips in response, and I pull her into my lap as I lean back onto my heels. She is now straddling my lap, and the new position makes her cry out. I devour the sound with my mouth, sinking my tongue into her mouth and wrapping my arms around her waist. She begins riding me. Rolling her hips and bouncing on my cock. I hold her, steadying for a few hard upward thrusts, and she cries out, arching her back and sending me even deeper.

"Divine! Kyros!" She calls out, and I sink my fingers into her open mouth, making her suck on her own juices while she rides my cock.

"Fuck, Shula. Tell me you're mine. Tell me now while we're connected that you accept my claim on you." I growl into the skin on her neck and nip at her ear.

"Claim me. I'm yours. I accept. Fuck, I'm—ARGH—YOURS!" She screams as I rock with her. Pushing myself as deep as I can get in this position. I snake my hand up her spine and dig it into her hair at the nape, wrenching her head back and exposing her throat. Her body arches again even more than before. She cries out, her body quivers, and my own release tightens my balls, sending a vibrating pleasure up my spine. We both are ripped from the edge at the same time, and I sink my teeth into her shoulder with a deep-bellied growl. Astraea screams my name, her pussy clenching and squeezing every drop of come from me as she comes for a second time. This time all over my cock as I fill her. Her body slumps as I release the hold on her with my teeth. The metallic taste of blood coats my tongue, and the red stains run down her chest from the jagged marks at the crook of her neck. I run my tongue through it before kissing her again.

We stay there for a while. I kiss her gently, and her lips are stained red with blood when we finally look at each other. She remains sitting on my cock while I am ensnared by the ocean in her eyes. I am a man possessed. Completely ravenous for the woman I just claimed. *Fuck.* She's mine, and when I tell her the truth, it's going to ruin her.

Chapter Fifty-Four

Astraea

The sound of metal scraping on metal startles me awake. The loud screech is slow and menacing, sending a chill over my overheated flesh. I lay on my back, with my heart hammering in my chest. A ray of sunshine cuts through the room from the small crack in the curtains, and Kyros' body is plastered to mine. Both of us are covered only from the waist down with an overly thick blanket for the heat of summer trying to sneak into the manor. A sheen of sweat makes our skin stick together where we touch, and my hair is stuck to my face just the same.

I need a bath.

As I lay there contemplating the night, I again hear the same scraping sound that woke me from my dream. The sound that pulled my attention from the night that Kyros and I shared. Our bodies still languidly in each other's embrace, but I gently push at him so I can sit up and see what that awful sound is. As soon as I do, I scream.

Kyros sits straight up within a second of my scream. He reaches for me at the same time that his shadows uncoil like a striking snake. The monster that has haunted my nightmares stands now just in the shadows. His razor-like claws are outstretched as they reach for me. Scraping together like a blade on a sharpening stone. Kyros' shadows aim for his throat, his chest, and his feet. He dissolves in and out of vision with every attack, like smoke.

"Seeeeennnnnkaaaa," the monster hisses, and that same shock of chills rolls over my skin.

"Leave! You're not welcome here!" I scream out, having heard some chambermaid's rumor that if a demon were to visit you, you could cast them out by telling them they were not wanted. It didn't work. This demon stepped forward.

"*Fuck,*" Kryros grunts, still tangled in the sheet. I reach for the twin blades on the nightstand and hold them in each hand. "Good girl, be ready just in case. He was expecting my attack this time. Something's changed."

"What do I do?" My voice trembles; I'm barely covered by a thin sheet, Kyros too. We have no armor, no backup, and it seems like Kyros' magick is futile against whoever or whatever this creature is now. Kyros throws out both hands, shrouding us in a thick dome of black shadows, and barks an order at me to get his pants from the end of the bed. He tugs them on quickly, leaving the strings loose in the front, and I wrap the sheet around me fully. Kyros grinds his teeth, and sweat builds on his brow. I don't think he can hold back whatever he is keeping away from us.

"I'm going to drop the veil; get behind me. If I have to, I will portal us out of here." Kyros demands, and I do as he says. I move behind him on the bed. My back presses into the wall, and I wait for the sunlight to return to the room. When it does, I am not prepared for what I see.

Horns jut out of the side of a huge creature that now takes up most of the room. Its skull-like head is so similar to a deer, but the gap between the viciously sharp antlers is wider than the length of my arms. It tilts its bony head; hollow sockets unseeing turn toward us, seemingly peering into our souls nonetheless. The stench of death permeates through the air and makes me choke with every breath. Torn and rotted flesh hangs loosely from its skeleton-like body and dangles like scraps of meat left in the smokehouse to dry. It's man-like, but with long hanging claws for hands. So similar to the nightmare creature, but *this*—this is more grotesque—less human and more animal. Entirely monster. A deep clicking growl echoes through the room, and the monster's chest vibrates with it.

I've never heard something so sinister in my life.

Kyros drops the veil, and the creature hones in on us. The nightmare is nowhere to be seen, but this thing seems to know what it is hunting for.

"A Cerkin! *Fuck*—" Kyros' magick is thrown out like a whip, crackling fire lighting the circle immediately as he renders a portal. "Stay with me. No matter what!" He shouts, not giving me a choice when he takes my hand and hurls us through. We land on two feet, but the momentum as we arrive has us running. Kyros pushes me in front of him, and I do everything I can to stay upright. My sheet drags and catches on everything in our wake. He's portaled us into the forest. The trees canopy is thick, and daylight barely makes it through the boughs. I can tell that we aren't far from the village we were just in, though. I can hear the townspeople as they wake for the morning and begin preparing for another night of celebration. As soon as the creature is through the portal that Kyros rendered, it snaps shut.

"What the fuck is that!?" I growl, looking back as it begins to take chase.

"It's a Cerkin. Do not let it touch you. Let me see your knife. Keep the other one ready." He barks out the orders like I am one of his men going into battle. I grind my teeth together. Determined to be strong through this.

"What are you going to do?" I call back. He looks back and forth, then glances up.

"Get behind this tree. Don't come out, Astraea. For anything." The use of my name and not his nickname for me causes the wrinkle between my eyes to deepen as I do what he tells me to. "Have your knife ready just in case!" He repeats, and I clench the grip of the knife in my hand as tight as I can. *Will I be ready to stab a living being with a blade if I have to?*

The bark is rough on my bare back, rubbing painfully against the scars, but I ignore it. The creature roars, and so does Kyros. I press harder into the tree, my knife ready at the center of my chest, where I clutch it and the sheet I am still wrapped in. There is a struggle, but I can't see anything.

Darkness encroaches on my vision, and liquid fire burns through my veins; that same lasso of fire seems to ignite around my middle and up my back. My breathing becomes ragged, and my skin scorches. It has to be panic. This happens in my nightmares. *What happens next? How do I stop it?* My teeth ache with how hard I clench my jaw, and before I know it, I'm ripping myself away from the tree. I can't stay hidden here. I can't—

As I come out from behind the tree, I'm sprayed with a putrid black liquid across my face and chest. Kyros stands, his bare chest heaving, dripping with the same substance. Blood. The Cerkin drops to its knobby knees in the dirt, giving one last strangled clicking growl as it reaches for him with outstretched claws. The black blood oozes from the horizontal slash through its rotted fleshy neck. Kyros takes a measured step back as the beast falls forward to its face with a heavy thud. Dust plumes up around it as it bleeds out, and within moments it's melting into the ground in a black puddle of death.

The forest seems to hold its breath as I stare at the scene before me. Kyros is covered in gore, his shadows a mass of clouds swirling along his skin and mingling with the blood he is coated with. His arms hang to his sides, with my knife held firmly in his grip that delivered the killing blow. His breath comes out in strong, short puffs, and when he looks at me over his shoulder, his eyes are the darkest I've ever seen. Terrifyingly so. The look on his face is pure malice. Everything stops as I stare into the endless chasm of darkness of his gaze. However, I don't recoil. I don't shudder in fear; if anything, I feel myself drawn closer.

Heat pools low in my stomach, and my own breath quickens as I step closer. He stays where he is without turning. His gaze remains focused on me as I approach, but he still doesn't move. Only as I stop inches from him does he tilt his head down to keep his eyes on mine. Something about the moment feels important, like a decision was made, and I can't help but feel grateful that it was him I was with. I lift my hand, not worried about the creature's blood coating our skin. I let my fingers dance along the stubble on his jaw, and he leans into the touch just slightly.

"You killed for me again." I say, and his eyes flick over every inch of my face and linger on my lips.

"I told you before, there will be death dealt by my hand." I can see in his eyes he thinks that I am upset for him killing once again, but in this moment... It's the farthest from the truth. If he had not killed that creature, I'm sure it would be me who was dead.

"Thank you," I say, reaching up on my tiptoes, one hand still holding the sheet in place around my body, and I pull him toward me as I kiss him. At first, it's chaste. Nothing more than a brush of my lips against his, but then he snakes his arm around my waist, pulling me toward him. He forces my back to arch, pressing my body against his. His tongue dips into my mouth, and I open for him, pulling his kiss deeper. What was once silent and still now comes rushing in all at once during this kiss. The sounds of the forest, of people screaming and getting closer with crashing footfalls through the sticks and debris on the forest floor.

"We have a lot to talk about, Shula." He whispers into my lips, holding my face steady with his hand. The other pressing into my back with the still bloody blade in his grip. I nod, but the sadness in his eyes makes me worry that some of the answers I wish to have will hurt me more than they will help me. I also see the truth that he will give them to me regardless.

"I know," I say.

"This is bigger than us."

"We will face it together. We have to." I say, swallowing any fear I have over that statement and trying to appear stronger than I feel.

"I hope it's enough." He finally says after a long pause. His fingers thread through my hair, and he pulls me into his chest. The steady rhythm of his heart matches the feet thundering on the ground as our friends and family approach us at a furious pace. They are too late, though. The monster I hold in my gaze is more vicious than any beast that comes for my body. I see the silent promise in his eyes. He will raze realms to protect me. The most terrifying part? I would watch him do it if it meant that he would stay the nightmare that lives in my heart.

"Are you sure you're ok?" Colette says again. I give her a sidelong look, and she shrugs with her face scrunching up. "Don't look at me like that. You nearly just got killed by a monster that I thought was just legend. There is no way that you are just 'fine' like you say." Her eyebrow jumps, and I release a heavy sigh.

"I will be fine. Right now, I just want to get this over with and get to Diemos. Are you sure there is nothing we can do to skip this?" I ask Zinya, who is standing with her arms crossed over her chest in the room with us. It's the only way that Kyros would let me out of his sight. He instructed Zinya that she was *to stay on two fucking feet with her eyes fucking open and on me at all times.* Zinya's lips have been pursed, and she's been extra broody since we returned. She wanted to talk to Kyros, but he shut her down, saying only *"later,"* before storming off with Mavros, Viltarin, and Rowan.

"I think the princess is stronger than we all think." Zinya looks at me with that same expression that she's been looking at me with since we got here. Something between anger and sadness.

"I know that she is strong. I've witnessed just how much so, plenty of times." Cole pins Zinya with a scalding look, and I take another deep breath, closing my eyes and then continuing to dress for the bonfire. Kyros insisted that after I bathed, I rest. He said he personally would make sure that I got to sleep. He sat on the bed until I finally closed my eyes and slept just as he told me to. His voice was the last I heard, and no nightmares haunted that sleep.

"Has he returned yet?" I ask no one in particular as I look at my body and secure my blades. The one Kyros killed the Cerkin with is now cleaned and returned to me.

"I don't know, but he won't miss the—*bonfire.*" Zinya says, and Cole gives her the same skeptical look I have been wanting to give her.

"What's your deal?" My best friend asks, likely sensing the question I won't ask, and very slowly Zinya turns her gaze to Colette.

"My deal?" She asks coldly. Colette just fights fire with fire and quirks an eyebrow, giving her a bemused look. "My deal is that I'm a warrior and have been stuck on babysitting duty, while the *real* men go out and get their hands dirty. Excuse me if I'm a little pissed off."

"I think we could all use a little fresh air. I'm sorry you've been stuck here with us." I say, and Cole grumbles something that sounds a lot like *'You could just fuck off'* under her breath. Zinya pins her with daggers. She shakes her head with an eye roll and turns to the window. Her arms cross over her chest as she props herself on its edge, pointedly ignoring us in the way she has been lately.

As much as I want to leave right away, I do need sleep after the night and morning I've had, and it would be asinine to leave after dark. Especially now that we know those monsters are not only real but can just show up out of nowhere. Another thing Kyros said he would tell me about later. The secrets he's holding onto just keep growing, but even with them I can't help but feel the wings fluttering in my stomach every time I think of him. Of his mouth on me. Of the words he whispered in my ear. His claim. The spot on my shoulder burns like a burst of fire at the thought.

"Well, it's time to go anyway. The sun is setting, and we have a little bit of a journey to get where we are going. Kyros has just returned." She says coldly, pushing from the wall and grabbing a scabbard that holds a sword she slings over her back. "It looks a little cooler tonight, and we will be in the dunes. You may want to bring a cloak." She doesn't wait for our response before swinging the door open. Mavros stands on the other side, smiling wide when it's fully ajar. He looks at the sour look on Zinya's face, and his smile widens impossibly.

"Why so glum, Zinny?" He looks past her to me and winks before catching a fist in his stomach with a loud *oof.*

"I should do us all a favor and kill you in your sleep." Zinya remarks and just looks at Kyros as he approaches. They don't say anything, but I see the silent conversation they have with their eyes. The same conversation they seem to have every time they see each other these days. Mavros smirks at the exchange before shouldering past his brother and laughing as he runs down the hall and starts messing with Zinya again.

"Get the horses ready. No one rides alone. Doubles only for our group. It will be the same when we leave for Diemos in the morning. I was informed that Khol and Eidola were brought back to the stables. Make sure that they are not the horses we take tonight. They will rest until morning." Kyros says in a low voice to Viltarin, who just nods, looking at me and then at Cole. I see the slight twitch on his lips when he looks at her a little longer than necessary, and I can't help but look away with a smile.

"I'll come with you," Cole interjects, and there is no way that my face hides anything of my surprise. "If that's ok, I mean..." She continues, her freckled face turning muddled with blush. Viltarin clears his throat with a smile.

"Of course." He offers Cole his arm, and she puts a hand on my elbow with a squeeze. Her eyes are saying everything she's already expressed to me during our alone time today. *Talk to him. Tell him how you feel.* Viltarin leads her away, and as they shrink in the distance and then turn toward the stairs, I become very aware that I am once again alone with Kyros.

"Where did you go?"

"Did you get good rest?" We both begin speaking at the same time. He clears his throat, his hand coming up to grip the back of his neck. I smile at him, and if I don't know any better, I think I see a hue of pink rising into his cheeks.

"I slept better than I have in a while." I answer his question, and he offers me his arm. I take it, and he guides me through the house. We walk in silence for a while. As he releases my arm, he threads his fingers through mine. The gesture feels intimate and loud at once.

"When this celebration first started, it wasn't what it is today. It started out sorrowful. The kingdom was no longer what it was. Our loved ones were slaughtered for the mere fact that we had magick or supported those who practiced in the way of the Neer." He says, his hand tightening around mine.

"I was young. The first one was a year after your father took the throne. I was angry. I didn't want anything to do with the celebration. That year it was less of a celebration and more so a day of remembrance. It all seemed to be a waste of time; I remembered every day what had happened to my parents. I saw it happen with my own eyes." His eyes go distant for a brief second, as though he's now remembering that very moment. "I sat there and watched the flames that were supposed to burn away the grief and bring peace to those souls who enter the fire and cross over to Runerth, and only thought about how the fire that once burned inside of me was only smoke and shadows now."

"I'm sorry. It's not enough, I know, but it's all I have." I tell him, pulling on his hand as I come to a stop. "I'm not my father. I never wanted any of this." I tell him honestly.

"I know, Shula." He takes my other hand, threading our fingers together there too. "It's ironic how life has brought us together." He continues. His eyes flick over my face. I notice his gaze flickering from my forehead, eyes, lips, and slowly, I see the subtle flattening of his lips. *Regret*. Does he regret what this—whatever this is—has become? Does he regret me because of who my father is?

"Come on, you two! You will have plenty of time to talk on the back of the horse. Daylight is waning!" Mavros calls out, his usual grin plastered to his face as though he is only one sentence away from mischief.

"He's right. Let's go, Shula. One more night of forgetting. Right?" My lips force a practiced smile, but the way his brows twitch down, I sense he knows it is fake, but I say the lie anyway.

"Of course. One more night of forgetting.

CHAPTER FIFTY-FIVE

Astraea

THE DUNES SPREAD OUT as far as the eye can see, their golden color blanched like fossilized bones. The waning sun lights the sky in a blade of fire along the horizon, and above that, the dark night is already settling in. Kyros' hand rests lightly at my hip, and when the horse stops near all the others, he leans in. His breath on the back of my neck sends a series of shivers through my body.

"You're sure you're ok?" He whispers, and I nod. The ride to the dunes was mostly silent for both of us. I suppose I'm thinking about what is to come and what we have lost. The story Kyros told me of his loss brings up the pain of my own. Though it seems like he remembers everything, I have a different sort of pain with my lack of memories. This is the first year since my father took the kingdom that I have not been in the palace for my birthday. I always dreaded the celebrations my father threw in my name. Even as a child, I knew that what he did was wrong. I could see that his celebrations were nothing more than a reminder of what he was capable of, rather than a celebration of *new beginnings,* as he often called it.

"I'm ok. Are you sure it's alright for me to be here?" I still feel like this is a celebration that I should not be welcome to. He hesitates just long enough that the question settles in my stomach. *He doesn't think I should be here.*

"You are meant to be at my side." His arms wrap around me in a backward hug, and I close my eyes as I allow his warmth to strengthen me, even if his words cause more questions to surface. Zinya wasn't wrong about wearing a cloak; the sun is barely down and the cool summer air is already beginning to threaten a chill. "It's about time we make it down to the pyre. Let's go." Kyros hops from the horse's back and then reaches up to help me down next.

Even though it's been only days since we were last here, my legs seem to have forgotten how to walk in the soft sand. Kyros helps me through it as we make our way to the top of one of the dunes. The sound of people gathering, whispers mostly, carries from the other side like a breeze. When we finally crest the hill, just as the last rays of sun disappear along the horizon, multiple cloaked figures can be seen standing in a circle. They surround a wooden structure in the center of a large body of people. It appears we are some of the last to arrive.

As we walk forward, heads turn toward us and nod to Kyros and me as we pass. Each one reverent, parting ways and giving us an easy path to the inner ring, where the others are already sitting. They sit on throws and tapestries of all colors, which, though muted by the rising silver moon, are still beautiful.

"Who are they?" I ask, looking up at Kyros, who keeps his gaze held on the cloaked figure in the center.

"These are leaders of the Neer people, those thought to have the most powerful magick, besides that of the king." Kyros says, and my brows stitch together in confusion.

"My father doesn't have magick..." I say, looking back to the dark cloaks that are waving in the slight wind.

"Not your father. The *true* king." He says, and any questions I had about that died on my tongue when the drums begin, stealing away my attention. The slow, but powerful rhythm is mesmerizing, and when the pounding becomes strongest, a sudden flash of light—magick bursting into flame—becomes blinding. The torches in each of the Neer leaders' hands blaze, lighting their hooded figures in copper and gold and casting moving shadows of the deepest black across the opening where their faces are hidden. The fire keepers and their mocking display in the braziers back at the palace hold no semblance to the wonder of actually seeing true magick ignite.

"It's amazing, isn't it?" Cole says as we join the group. It really is amazing and everything I have seen only brings up more questions as to why my father is so against the use of magick... She tangles her arm through mine and squeezes me slightly, pulling me from my thoughts. She looks up at Kyros, and so do I as I feel him tense at my side, looking forward. Taking a step away, he drops my hand, then his gaze sweeps back over his shoulder. He looks at me with pursed lips. The nostalgic man who was telling me of his childhood just moments ago is now long gone, and in his place is the broody man I have come to expect.

"I'll be right back. Stay with Mavros." He says gruffly, with no room for argument, before leaving me staring at his back. He walks up to one of the cloaked men in front of us with a torch and clasps arms with him in greeting. Murmurs start up all around us as heads turn to face Kyros. I notice now that he too is wearing a cloak similar to the other leaders. Mavros slings an arm around my shoulders and teases Cole with his fingers at her chin. Rearing back, she swats at his hand.

"Are you always a nuisance?" She asks, but with the gleam in her eye, I know she is just teasing back. A natural smile from undeniable happiness comes to my face seeing her at such ease. It's almost enough to make me finally accept that we have—I have—made the right choice in being here with all of them. With Kyros.

"Today!" A voice echoes around us, calling attention to the center of the pyre. The pyre itself is intricately woven together like a basket and is taller than two men. Baubles and parchment hang from braided branches like gifts on a yule tree. "We gather in these sands that hold the ashes of our lost ones to celebrate their sacrifice and give guidance to those who have joined them. Those who have been felled by the cruel ways of a usurper, an illegitimate king who stole everything from our kingdom!" I feel myself shrinking under

Mavros' arm, and he does too. He rubs my shoulder, smiling down at me with closed lips.

"It's ok, princess. He took from you too. Don't think you don't belong right here." Mavros whispers for only me to hear. He pulls me to where the sand has been cut from the ground in steps, with stone laid on the surface, making tiered seating around the pyre. Mavros gestures for me and Cole to sit, and he, Zinya, and Viltarin take up the space behind us.

When I look back toward the pyre, it's Kyros' stare that slams into me. If I didn't know any better, I'd say he looks worried. His eyes flick over my shoulder, and I follow them to see Mavros with his usual grin gone and only a flat line in its place. Gone is the joking twin, and back is the warrior brother. It doesn't give me confidence that whatever is happening is going to be good. The man standing next to Kyros continues on with his speech about guiding the light of the flame to Runerth and picking apart everything my father has done during his reign.

My eyes stay on Kyros, though. His shoulders remain rigid as he stands next to the Neer leader, as though every word is pulling an invisible thread that is ever tightening his posture, the scowl in his face deepening with every tug.

"Since the night the false king stormed our lands, there has been one thing keeping us all hopeful for the future. The true heir will light the pyre, and he will rise with the flames, just as the Shula Morana. He will be our death flame, and when it is all burned away, a new era will remain!" The word sounds like a gong in my head; loud, echoing, and absolute. My eyes flutter as I try to make sense of what I am hearing and what I am seeing. The Neer leader hands Kyros the torch. With the firelight closer to his face, I can see the jump in the muscle of his jaw. He stares into the flames, then his brows furrow further as he looks up to me. Our eyes clash like swords in battle. Questions, answers, hurt, and betrayal—it all swirls through the air, sinking into me with every breath. *Shula Morana: Death Flame. She will be the death of you. She will be the death of us all.*

Colette reaches over, grabbing my hand, and I can hear her hushed tone as she says my name, but I can't rip my eyes away from the man lighting the pyre. The prince of Eathian. The true heir of the kingdom my father stole. *The true King?* Bile rises in my throat and tears well in my eyes, but more than that, the heat in my chest burns with my rising anger—and something else. I attempt to stand, but a large hand claps down on my shoulder, keeping me in place. I draw my gaze from Kyros, turning to see who is holding me down. Mavros leans in, his hand firmly keeping me seated, but not painfully.

"For what it's worth, we told him to tell you." Mavros says with remorse, and I can't help it; the first tear escapes beyond my lashes. My lip trembles, as do my hands, but I steel my spine. I turn back toward the *rightful* heir: the King. His back is to me as he makes his way around the base, lighting the woven branches into a grate of roaring flames.

"I can't be here." I didn't mean to speak the words aloud; they snuck out just like the tears that now steadily stream down my face. I turn my head and look at Cole. Deep-rooted sadness is filling her eyes. Eyes that likely mirror my own. I was just beginning to feel as though I was somewhere I belonged. I was just starting to feel that perhaps—I could trust. Now everything burns. *Shula Morana; Death Flame.*

"We have nowhere else to go." Colette's voice is so small, smaller than I have heard it in a very long time. Her chin wobbles, and I shake my head, denying that she is right. Snatching my hand out of hers, I stand abruptly. Mavros goes to stop me, but Zinya grabs his arm.

"Let her go. She can't go far. She needs a minute to come to terms." She hisses at him, and even as he looks at me warily, he nods before I turn and run. My feet dig into the sand darkened by the night above. The stars seem to have hidden the moment that realization hit. I was never running. I was a *prisoner*, led to believe my captors cared for me. My mind is now playing so many things on repeat: conversations I overheard and conversations I was a part of. How could I not see what was right in front of me? I am a fool. Always used. I am a pawn. Betrayal burns my eyes and eats at my heart. *It was all a lie.*

I get far enough away that the pyre is just a beam of flame in the distance through my tear-streaked vision. I drop to my knees in the sand. My head falls backward as I bare my soul to the nonexistent stars. *Why? What did I do to deserve this life?*

The sand around my knees begins to vibrate and pulse. Each second it continues, it seems to intensify with ferocity. Then I recognize the feeling, the rhythm. My eyes snap forward and blink rapidly to clear the blurry tears from my vision. Not far in the distance are horses carrying soldiers who wield sharp blades. The deadly curved blades I would recognize anywhere glint in the moonlight.

My father's men.

They found me.

I'm at an impasse. Do I run back to the evil I know, no matter how much I despise him? Or turn back to the man who has lied to me since the moment I met him? Just the thought of going back to my father makes my already aching heart break. My soul is pulling me back to the others, to Kyros. My mind is at war with emotion.

I clench my fists at my sides before pushing up from the ground. This isn't a question about who to trust or who to run to. It's a choice I was never able to make on my own, and now that I can, I realize that someone I've almost never chosen is *me*. When I decided to leave Eathian, I chose myself at that moment, and tonight I will make the same choice again. I chose me, and I chose the people who can't choose for themselves, like I haven't been able to my whole life.

Shula Morana; Death Flame.

I turn back the way I came. I need to—

Screams.

Awful, bloodcurdling, and terrified screams fill the space between me and the pyre. Smoke plumes from the pyre and obscures the star-streaked sky with bleary darkness. I'm running through the sand before I even think to make the decision. Toward the screams and the cloud of what appears to be smoke. As soon as I get close enough to see the people running frantically, I realize that it's not smoke at all but rather a dark, powerful magick. Magick that I've seen before. It caresses my skin like a shaken lover. Raw elation floods me as the shadows blanket over me in a protective second skin. The magick trembles, as if the energy itself could exhale a sigh of relief. Relief that intertwines with my own.

A loud clicking growl breaks my momentary lapse of attention; I swallow as I force myself to keep moving. Quickly, I unsheathe the blades that were a gift from Kyros. They hum in my grip with the same anticipation I feel in my gut. A Cerkin steps forward and tilts its monster-like head at me. *Don't let them touch you.* Kyros' warning from the last time I faced one of these creatures echoes through my mind. Easier said than done I'm sure... *He's not here this time. You have to protect yourself.* I grit my teeth and settle my path toward the beast who stands in my way, ready to face the fight it will undoubtedly give.

A sudden shrieking cry sounds close above me, and my head snaps back just in time to see a Thunderbird dip into the darkness. It dives right into the Cerkin that has its sights set on me. Though the Cerkin is a giant, the Thunderbird is no small creature. Its deadly clawed feet pierce through the barrel of the Cerkin's chest with enough speed to spear it all the way through. Powerful downthrusts of its wings a moment later leaves black blood raining from the sky as one monster carries away the other.

Another shriek, another thunderbird, another Cerkin, and another dead—dozens come into view. The Thunderbirds are not attacking the Neer people, but their savage beaks pierce through the deadly herd of Cerkins that have been let loose to ravage the gathering. My head whips from side to side as I spin in circles, watching as the Thunderbirds seem to come to my aid.

"Kyros and Mavros of Diemos! Release my daughter or pay the ultimate price!" I hear a familiar voice bellow from behind me. My heart beats at a thunderous rhythm as my attention shifts from the carnage unfolding before me and now towards my approaching father. Dread coils around my spine at the sound of his voice. I scan the surrounding area desperately for a way to escape. But an odd wave of relief floods me as I see someone I recognize coming from the direction of the pyre. *Mavros.* Even though seeing him makes the hurt caused by their lies surface. Seeing him charging forward on his horse, alive and well, makes me realize I'm still relieved that he is ok. Zinya sits backward on the saddle behind him, arrows flying and meeting the flesh of men and beast alike. Trailing behind them is another horse in a streak of gray, mounted by two more riders, Viltarin with Colette behind him. Her hair whips out behind her like a crimson flag of warning, as she too wields a bow and arrow. Pride fills me to see my friend look so rightfully placed. She's always been a warrior in my eyes, and now she finally is able to wield the weapons that will strike down anyone who aims her harm. Although my heart aches with betrayal, I still find myself hoping that Kyros too is okay.

I'm afraid to call out. The last thing I need right now is to bring attention to myself. I am in the center of two powerful forces and frozen with fear. My feet are leaden with doubt, though, as I see my father swing a blade through the air. Blood rains over him from the Thunderbird he just slain, and bile rises in my throat.

The remaining Cerkins left standing are halted at once. The Thunderbirds fly higher in the dark sky and cry out in a chorus of panic as a shuttering, forced movement takes over all of the Cerkin, making all of their unseeing eyes turn toward me in unison. It's beyond eerie and sends a coldness to slither down my spine. A vortex of dark matter begins to swirl in the center of the dunes of ruin. A crackle of fire ignites the churning smoke as it now spreads into a portal, just as when Kyros renders one. The Cerkins that have stopped turn their flesh and bone bodies fully to me now. Each one letting out a horrendous echoing howl. I imagine this is what it would feel like to have your soul brought to the demons that guard the entrance of the damned. As the vortex continues to open, the creature that has haunted my nightmares steps from its center. Chaos, blood, and death emanate from him, and he is even more terrifying in this moment than any of the other times I have seen his bone-covered face.

I notice movement and see Cadoc as he rides up to my left, just beyond where my father sits with his fancy armor better suited for books than actual battle. His slack-jawed expression would be priceless, though, if not for the dire nature of the situation we are all now in. Both of their eyes finally see me, where the monster has set his sights. Their gazes drop down to the blades in my hands, the leather wrapping around my body, fitting me like a glove. Cadoc says something to my father that I cannot decipher, and then he points back at the nightmare creature.

Quickly, I spin back to face the creature of my nightmares, but what I see instead causes more confusion. The portal does not close; the vortex continues to be active, and another figure now steps through it. My heart pounds in my chest, and I have to forcibly stop the tears from falling from my eyes. I have had plenty of experience in having to do so; it's not nearly as hard to do as it used to be. Although, with all the emotions that have been storming through me recently, it is notably harder. My father is screaming demands, and the Thunderbirds are screeching in the sky. The fighting continues on, and the wind feels unnatural. It's even harder to keep myself strong staring at the scene before me, but I must.

"Stop all of this." I bite out under my breath as tears breach the barrier of my lashes and streak my face and wet my lips. My tongue comes out involuntarily, causing me to taste the salty weakness. The bitter tang of them causes anger to thrum in me once again. The figure who was coming through the portal is now visible. When the rendered portal snaps shut, it's like we are thrust into a bubble of calm, though the scene around us is anything but.

A woman. She saunters toward me like she is taking a stroll through a garden on an average summer night, ignoring all the death and chaos that consumes the desert around her. Her eyes lock on mine as she strides into the direct path of moonlight. It's like a spotlight shining down on her. Bodies of creatures and men create dark stains that sink into the sand. Steaming puddles oozing black blood with pieces of Cerkin antlers still sticking out from them litter the ground and paint the scene around her in horror.

The bright firelight to her right dances, reflecting on her long, golden brown hair and illuminating the deep red sheer fabric that flows around her like an aura of fire. My breath stalls in my lungs when she speaks.

"Now that I see your beauty in person, I see how you have him so entangled in your vicious web, little spider..." The woman says, though her voice is sickly sweet, the words themselves carry enough hatred to kill. The dress she wears does nothing to cover her scarred skin. What seems to have once been a pale alabaster is twisted and turned pink and deep red in some areas. Half of her face is unblemished and smooth, while the other has the same twisted scars like tree roots branching out under her skin. It's jarring, yet the way she carries herself makes everything about her dangerously beautiful.

"Who are you?" I question with a demand in my tone; the grip on my blades grows tighter with each passing moment. Both of which surprise me, though I hope it's not noticeable. The turmoil around us seems to have slowed, and time itself stands still as her split smile twists and curls up at the corners.

"You look just like her—your mother." Her words stop my heart completely, and a heaviness weighs down my chest as I try to suck in air. *What is happening? Who is this? What does she know of my mother?* She hasn't moved. Though her words have shifted everything within me. "You have her eyes." She continues, her own narrowing as she assesses me. "Don't you think so, Connard?" She addresses my father, and I swiftly look over my shoulder to see him dismounting his horse. He's yelling orders, pointing men in every direction, but their voices don't carry to me anymore. *Can they see me?*

"Who are you?" I ask again, trying to calculate how fast I can get away and get to where Cole and the others seem snared by magick beyond the dome of horrendous tranquility. *Where is Kyros?* Her eyes burrow into me. Taking time on my every feature. Memorizing or recalling? Something about her seems familiar but off...

"I wouldn't think you would remember me. It was so very long ago, and well, I look a bit different than when you were just a child." Her words send chills wrapping around my spine, and I take a slow step backward. Feeling as though the distance between us is not enough and too much all at once. The conflicting thoughts cause a war in my heart.

"I don't know what you're talking about," I say defiantly as she looks at my feet and how I am pedaling backward.

"I suppose you are right. Your father, the vile man that he is, he didn't wish to tell you the truth. The shadows around your fire tell me that he has gone to great lengths to try to hide you away. Stupid man," She pauses, her gaze flicking to my father once again.. A dimidiate smile pulls at her lips as she narrows her eyes thoughtfully as I too look at the man who sired me. "You tried to evade the promise you made, and that was a wild mistake, *King* Connard. Perhaps you forget what the deal was?" She doesn't get a response; I can't hear anything beyond us, and I doubt he can hear anything being said either. Her gaze languidly turns back to me.

"You have heard his call, but still you refuse to come where you now belong, beautiful Astraea?" I feel the blood drain from my face. I know she is talking about the nightmare. My gaze turns to the endless prison that are the eyes that have watched me in my sleep. The nightmare that has caused even hours awake to be riddled with fear. Countless nights waking in a sweat-soaked, choked fear. To where he tilts his head to the side, surveying, waiting... *I shudder.*

Blinking away, I look at the woman closer now. Try to see beyond the scars she wears like beautiful abstract art. The air around her seems to ripple the harder I focus on her.

The silence of the desert; the stillness that surrounds me.

Like the words within my head have created a fissure in the realm, a sound like the crack of a whip makes my eyes fly wide, but a new voice breaks into my mind like a strike of lightning.

"Concede to the shadows, only when you are ready to let your fire burn—" My mother's eyes, pale blue just as mine, burrow into me in the memory. A wrinkle of pain creases her brow as she takes my tiny hand in hers. "You are everything they wish they could harness. Don't let them. Burn as bright as the fires that guide us to Runerth, and when it's time, let them feel the flames." I blink out of the memory as lightning strikes between us, throwing sand out like shards of glass. Instinctively, I shield my face with my arm, and as the sand settles, the cloud of darkness remains.

The crescendo of chaos slams back in on me. Screams of pain. My name being shouted. Gurgling death and clashing of blades. It's deafening.

Kyros emerges from the shadows on horseback, his magick wisps from his body like dark clouds of poison. The heat inside me swells as our eyes make contact, and he snarls as he pushes the horse he rides into a gallop. The dark Tsalalerian Steel blade in his hand glimmers as his shadows writhe around it like an extension of his power.

He is charging forward at the same moment that the nightmare begins lifting his mask. The shadows, so similar to Kyros, whirling around him in a frenzy. The cryptic woman reaches out for me, her scarred hand throwing some sort of gray magick toward where I stand, followed by my father screaming an order at Cadoc who also pushes toward me...Everything happens at once, as if I am in the center of a tornado that is breaking apart. I close my eyes and think of my mother's voice.

"Concede to the shadows, only when you are ready to let your fire burn—"

It's strange how I don't recall much of my childhood. Sometimes I wonder if it was just so bad that I have blocked it all out, or if there was just nothing good worth remembering.

It's a crushing feeling, not knowing how you became who you are because you simply don't remember. Was I always so calloused? Are they there from the scars of a past I don't recall? Or did they develop as an adult to protect me through everything else I would later endure?

One thing stays the same regardless, through memories or none: the pain. The lack of air in my lungs. The feeling of just skimming the surface and then being violently yanked back under just before you can get a full breath. When will my life be my own again? Was it ever? Do I choose to swim, fight the current, and walk out with my sharp chin held high, or do I allow the ocean to thrash me until it eventually spits me out on the beach, all the sharp edges worn down so there is nothing left to fight with?

The heat blazes within my chest. I feel that lasso of fire igniting within me, and from it I know the answer. My eyes fly wide, and white-hot flame fills my vision just as Kyros reaches me. He's no longer on horseback but moves faster than should be possible for being just a man. One hand is outstretched in my direction, the other ready with the dark blade to ward off anyone who comes toward us.

His eyes, dark as night, burrow into mine, and the fire that burns within me flares. More flames whip at the scars on my back, and they feel as though they are splitting open all over again. I think I'm screaming, or maybe it's screams from those around us. I don't know anymore. As fire, bright and hot, bursts from my back like wings, a roar fills my ears. Familiar and distant. Kyros renders a portal, and the last thing I see as I fall is the bright blue of the manticore's stare.

He lands at the brim of a distant dune, and though I know he is too far to hear me, I try to tell him anyway.

"Protect them." I whisper, just as I am pulled through the portal. Kyros' arm wraps tightly around my middle, and I concede to the shadows and let the elusive umbra swallow me whole.

To be continued...

MORE BY BLAKE
THE MOON RAVEN TRILOGY
COMPLETE SERIES

"BUT WITH THE HEARTBREAK, MY RESOLVE STRENGTHENS.
ESE TEARS WILL BE THE LAST I SHED."

EVROSE BAY

A paranormal series of standalones

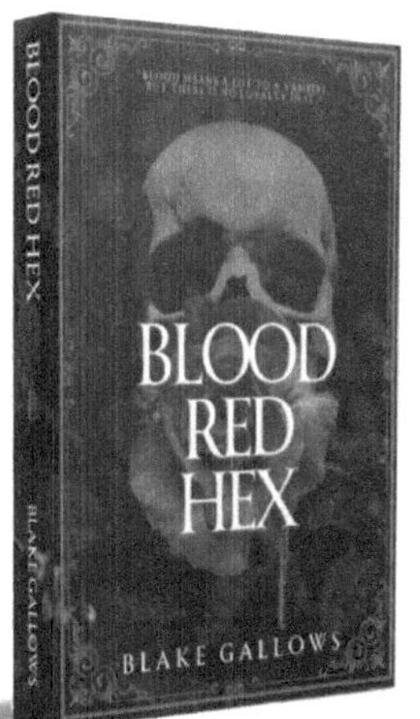

AUDIO COMING

SOON

SECOND

BOOK

TO BE

ANNOUNCED

"A CITY THAT KNOWS NO DIFFERENCE IN BLOOD."

Acknowledgements

Every time I finish a book I feel like this is the hardest part. There are so many people to thank for so many different things along this journey. I would be nowhere without my readers, so first and foremost, I would like to thank you. You are at the core of everything.

The team I have surrounded myself with through this has only grown and evolved, and it's true what they say about it taking a village. From my alphas, betas, street team, ARC teams, editor, and artists I've worked with, I am forever grateful for your contributions throughout.

Gabby and Alex, you two are my soundboard on everything and nothing, and damn, you guys take it so well. Gabby, thank you for everything you do as my PA. I fucking love you. And Alex, you are always willing to help right alongside her. You both are quick to run and jump into the alpha reads, and I am so lucky to have you guys and can truly call you a couple of my best friends.

My beta team: Violet, Megan, Ivette, Jamie, Leslee, and Tiffany. Thank you so much for reading and giving your initial and raw feedback. For most of you, this wasn't your first time beta reading for me, and it makes me so happy to know that you guys are continuing to stick around and deal with my chaos. I love the friendships we have created, and I cannot wait to meet some of you in person in the coming years!

Justin, you are the real MVP. You're always ready to jump into my projects and make them smooth and polished, and I cannot thank you enough. I literally would not be able to get all of this done without your input. Thank you so much!

My amazing husband, Scott, thank you for forever supporting all of my endeavors and at times just smiling and nodding because we both know I am feeling crazy. It will be worth it all in the long run. Thank you for seeing that, for seeing me. I love you.

I am so grateful for everything this year has brought, and I am so looking forward to what is to come! Thank you all so much!

Please consider leaving a rating or review anywhere you can! Thank you!

About the Author

Blake lives in the Pacific Northwest and while she's not writing or reading she's typically living the lavish life of a domestic goddess. Caring for her energy leeches aka her three children, husband, and two Rottweilers. Blake loves nature, camping, riding dirt bikes with the family, and all forms of art. She dabbles in photography, watercolor painting, and loves music.